The Black Orchestra

JJ TONER

Copyright © JJ Toner 2014, 2105, 2016

The right of JJ Toner to be identified as the author of this Work has been asserted by him in accordance with the Copyright, Designs and Patents Act 1988

First published as an eBook 15 January, 2013
First published in paperback 2 April, 2014
JJ Toner Publishing PO Box 25, Greystones, Co Wicklow, Ireland

This revised edition published 10 March, 2016

ISBN: 978-1-908519-54-2

All rights reserved. No part of the publication may be reproduced, stored in a retrieval system, or transmitted in any form or by any means, electronic, mechanical, photocopying or otherwise, without the prior permission of the copyright owner.

This is a work of fiction. Names, characters, places and incidents are either the product of the author's imagination or are used fictitiously, and any resemblance to actual persons, business establishments, events or locales are entirely coincidental.

Other Books by JJ Toner

The Wings of the Eagle, the sequel to *The Black Orchestra*

A Postcard from Hamburg, the third in the Black Orchestra series

Houdini's Handcuffs, a thriller featuring DI Ben Jordan

Find Emily, the second DI Jordan thriller

JJ Toner writes short stories and novels. His background is in mathematics. He lives in Ireland with his wife and youngest son.

www.JJToner.com

DEDICATION

For Pam

ACKNOWLEDGEMENTS

Sincere thanks are due to lots of people for their help in putting this story together, especially my wife, Pam, and my siblings, Dave and Judy, who beta-read early versions, and a certain young lady from Berlin who wishes to remain nameless. The manuscript attracted quite a lot of attention from literary agents, and one in particular prompted a number of significant rewrites. The lion's share of the credit for the final content goes to Lucille Redmond, whose patience knows no limit. Thanks to Anya Kelleye for a marvelous cover and to LionheART Publishing House for formatting all of the paperback editions.

The Black Orchestra

Norddeutsche Ausgabe / Ausgabe A
31. Ausg. * 46. Jahrg. * Einzelpreis 20 Pf.

Ausgabe A / Norddeutsche Ausgabe
Berlin, Mittwoch, 18. Oktober 1939

VÖLKISCHER BEOBACHTER
Herausgeber Adolf Hitler

Kampfblatt der national-sozialistischen Bewegung Großdeutschlands

U47 Sinks British Battleship at Anchor

In the early hours of October 14, 1939, the "impregnable" defences at the British naval base at Scapa Flow in the Orkney Islands were breached by U47, a U-boat of the Third Reich. Commanded by Korvettenkapitän Gunther Prien, U47 successfully completed a difficult and daring manoeuvre to slip past the blockade ships on the Eastern approaches and into the vast harbour. There, they found the battleship Royal Oak at anchor, and completely unaware of the approaching danger! With stealth and precision, the crew of U47 loaded their torpedo tubes and the Kapitän gave the order to fire. Three minutes later, the crew heard a series of monumental explosions and they knew that their mission was a success. The giant battleship HMS Royal Oak was sinking, and behind it, the battle cruiser Repulse was also fatally damaged.

U47 made its escape successfully, and returned to base, at Wilhelmshaven. Today, October 18, the whole crew of the submarine was flown to Berlin to be welcomed home by the Führer himself!

At 11 am Korvettenkapitän Gunther Prien and his crew arrived at Tempelhof airport in three aircraft. Wearing his Iron Cross and his newly awarded Knight's Cross, Kapitän Prien was carried in an open car through the streets of the city to the Reich's Chancellery. There, he dismounted. Accompanied by U-bootwaffe Commander-in-Chief Admiral Karl Dönitz, he paused on the Chancellery steps to acknowledge the cheering crowds, before entering the building . . .

PART 1

1

March 1940

When the war started I was living in Berlin, working as a signalman in the headquarters of the Abwehr. I lived alone. My father had died five years earlier, and my mother moved abroad three years after that.

With the advent of hostilities, all normal life ceased, and I lost contact with my mother. The daily tedium of office hours was replaced by the unrelenting pressure of shift work with nothing to occupy my thoughts but the continuous merry-go-round of work and sleep – until the Friday evening when I discovered Tristan Kleister's body.

#

Kriminalinspektor Glasser of the Berlin KRIPO was the thinnest man I had ever seen. Cheekbones as sharp as blades underlined his sunken eyes. His fingers rested on the table in front of him – two bundles of knuckle and bone barely held together with skin.

"You are Kurt Müller?"

"I am."

"You discovered the body?"

I was still shaking from shock. I tried to compose myself. "Yes. This evening when I came on shift. I signed in at seven forty. Allowing ten minutes to climb four flights of stairs…"

Sitting to Glasser's right, my supervisor, Drobol the cripple chipped in, "Müller's shift started at eight."

The room was small and bare – a table, three chairs, a barred window. On the table, nothing but a black telephone.

The fingers of Glasser's right hand began to drum on the edge of the table, like a piano player running up and down the scales. "Tell me what you saw."

"Kleister was lying on the bench in front of the radio transmitter at station five. There was a small hole in his head, here," – I pointed – "just behind his headphones." I had seen black brain matter on the desk, but very little blood. My stomach heaved at the memory.

"And the gun?" The fingers paused.

"In his hand." There had been a stench of cordite.

"Did you touch anything? The body? The gun, perhaps?"

Glasser was dressed in a dark blue gabardine overcoat and still wore his hat, a homburg. He looked like a man with an urgent appointment elsewhere. He pushed his hat-brim back and leaned forward, placing the points of his elbows carefully on the table. "How well did you know this man?"

I writhed under the intense glare of the two men facing me. Surely they couldn't suspect that I had something to do with Kleister's death?

"Not well. We had a nodding acquaintance."

Kleister and I both worked in the Communications Unit. In truth, I barely knew him, but we spent a few of our short breaks together.

Drobol piped in again, "We work a strict eight-day rota. Around the clock eight-hour shifts with twenty-four hours between. The rota ensures that there are always four men on duty."

What our harsh and pitiless supervisor had failed to mention was the double shift – sixteen hours of intense concentration, with four short breaks – that each man had to work every ten periods. The work was tough, the hours brutal.

Glasser turned to Drobol. "Ah! were there four men on duty during Kleister's shift?"

"There was very little incoming traffic, today," Drobol said. "I sent three of the men home early."

That was a first!

"So Kleister was alone?"

"Yes."

Glasser turned back to me. "You spent some of these in Kleister's company?"

"Yes, up until last week, when our shifts diverged."

The signalmen were a miserable lot, mostly. Many were men who had won their postings in Berlin by political influence. They came and went on the clock, and I imagined them at home in their spare time, kicking their dogs or beating their wives. At work, hardly a kind word was exchanged.

Kleister was one of the few colleagues that I managed to become acquainted with when our shifts coincided for one whole eight-day rota.

"What did you talk about?"

"Nothing, really. He was from Saxony. I think he said his father worked in aircraft maintenance with the Luftwaffe."

Kleister and I did exchange personal histories. I'm sure he said his mother died recently, and he mentioned a sister.

"Is there anything else? Did he seem depressed – unhappy about anything?"

"I couldn't say."

"So, you've no idea why he might have killed himself?"

#

When I resumed my duties, everything had returned to normal in the communications unit. Kleister's body had been removed and the desktop at station five scrubbed clean. I resumed my duties.

Concentration proved elusive, and I made more mistakes than usual that night. My mind kept returning to Kleister as I tried to imagine the depths of despair that would lead a young man to suicide. From what little I could recall of my conversations with Kleister, there had been no hint of the turmoil in his mind.

As I signed out at the end of my shift, Siegfried the night watchman said, "Have you heard?" I liked Siegfried. He was ancient, arthritic and diminutive, with skin like an elephant's and a chest covered in Old War decorations. He always had the latest gossip and loved to share.

"No. Tell me."

"There was another suicide. Another signalman. In the Leipzig office, about thirty-six hours ago. His name was Barnard. They say he was a Gestapo informer."

#

The funeral was held on the following Monday evening. Kleister's father and sister were there. Drobol and I attended. The coffin was conveyed up a cobbled slope to the graveyard on a dilapidated horse-drawn cart. The horse was old, stumbling, suffering its burden. It raised its great head and stared at me for a moment. That large, lugubrious black eye seemed to blame me for the whole miserable affair.

The burial plot had been dug outside the walls of the graveyard, in an area reserved for those guilty of taking their own lives – the most heinous crime in the eyes of the Roman Church. When the interment was over, Kleister's father shook my hand with a questioning look. "Thomas Kleister."

"Kurt Müller. I'm sorry for your loss, sir."

Kleister's sister, Frau Tania Schaefer wore a veil that obscured her face. When I approached her she lifted the veil to reveal dark, intense eyes. I expected tears, but her face was set in a grim expression which I read as anger.

"You knew my brother, Herr Müller." Her voice was husky from tears. "Did you think him suicidal?"

#

The next morning at the end of my shift I spoke to the night watchman again.

"Did you hear the shot, Siegfried?"

"No, sir."

"And who was in the building at the time?"

Siegfried – together with his daytime counterpart, Sigmund the doorman – was responsible for ensuring that every person entering and leaving the building signed the daily log.

"Only Drobol the cripple. Here, see for yourself, sir." He thrust the log book under my nose. I checked it for Thursday evening. As Siegfried had said, everyone that had checked in to the building that morning had checked out again by 7:30 pm – everyone, that is, except our supervisor, Drobol the troll.

I examined the log more carefully. Oberst Krause, the Head of Section III — the domestic intelligence unit — had signed in at midday. When I pointed this out to Siegfried he peered at the page.

"He returned from Leipzig that day," he said, flexing his fingers.

"And where was Oberst Schiller? I don't see his name anywhere." Oberst Bernhardt Schiller was Head of my Section, Section I – Technical & Signals.

Siegfried's head bobbed up and down. "Both Obersts were in Leipzig. Oberst Schiller returned on Friday."

"You told all this to the KRIPO man?"

"He didn't ask."

"And did he look at these records?"

"Not any time that I was on duty, sir, but you'd need to check with Sigmund."

2

March 1940

A couple of days after Kleister's funeral, I met my one friend, Alex Clausen, for lunch at an open-air café on Unter den Linden. Alex worked in the Air Ministry in a role similar to mine. He was a year younger than me, somewhat portly, with a bulbous nose and a God-given talent for making people laugh. We shared an interest in Wagnerian opera.

While we waited for our food, I told Alex about Kleister. His first reaction was a string of profanities.

Finally, he said, "The gun was in his right hand?"

"Yes."

"And was he right-handed?"

"That's not the point."

"The wound was in the back of his skull, you say?"

"Yes, back about here, behind his headphones." I pointed to Alex's skull, high above and behind his right ear.

"You think he couldn't have shot himself?"

"I suppose it's possible. Maybe with his thumb on the trigger. But why reach all the way round there? And why would he have left his headphones on?"

He pondered the problem for a minute or two. To me, then, Berlin was the most vibrant city in the world, and Unter den Linden its jewel. The street was packed with pedestrians, many in uniform, everyone in high good humour. The sparrows were everywhere, picking up crumbs from the tables, several bloated woodpigeons amongst them, trying to blend in.

"So you think someone shot him?" Alex said, rubbing the back of his neck.

"I'm certain of it."

"Your supervisor, this... Drobol?"

"There was no one else in the building."

He gave a low whistle. "If you had arrived a few minutes earlier, you might have seen it happen. Or it could have been you. Fucking hell, Kurt, I bet you crapped in your pants."

"Not quite." I grimaced. "But I lost my breakfast."

"Why would anyone want to shoot this Kleister?"

I looked around. We were surrounded on all sides by office workers and Wehrmacht soldiers having their lunch; no one seemed interested in us.

I lowered my voice. "I don't know."

These were perilous times. People disappeared or turned up dead every day. Alex knew this as well as I did.

The food arrived, served by a middle-aged woman in a grubby apron. The conversation died while we ate. For Alex, eating was a no-holds-barred occupation of unbounded pleasure. He seemed to try to involve as many of his senses as he could. He leaned over his plate, shovelling sauerkraut and sausage into his mouth with little grunts of pleasure.

"It could all be over in a month," he said, wiping his mouth.

The war was progressing well. Austria, Poland and Czechoslovakia had been annexed and a non-aggression treaty signed with the Soviet Union.

"Or two at the most," I replied. "I may be able to go back to Ireland, after all."

We'd spoken before about my ambition to go back to Trinity College in Dublin to resume my studies – an ambition frustrated by the advent of the war.

"Why did you have to go to Ireland to study? Aren't there any good universities in the Fatherland?" he said.

A tram rattled by. I had to wait for it to pass before replying, "I told you. My mother's Irish."

"Ah yes, I remember." He tilted his head, closed one eye and stuck his tongue out. This was his Hunchback of Notre Dame, one of his favourite comic poses. "Your parents met at a youth rally in Munich."

"They met in a youth *hostel* in Munich." I laughed. "There were no youth rallies in those days."

Alex was never forthcoming about his own family. Like me, his father had died young. His mother lived in the north, near Hamburg. He had told me in an unguarded moment that he had a younger brother called Eugen.

"What's your interest in this Kleister?" he said. As always, there was a small portion left on his plate – a pleasure postponed.

"I believe the police have closed the case. They've come to the wrong conclusion." And poor Kleister's been buried on the wrong side of the graveyard wall. "There could be a killer on the loose."

"You mean some maniac who wandered in off the street?"

"No. The night watchman stands guard at the door. I mean someone in the Abwehr."

"Your supervisor? The cripple?"

"He's certainly vicious enough," I said, half joking. "He'd shoot his own grandmother if there was profit in it."

He waited until my plate was empty before polishing off the last of his sauerkraut and sausage, washed down with the final mouthful of beer.

We walked back a short distance together. Before we parted Alex said, "Have you spoken to anybody else about your suspicions?"

"Not yet."

"Well don't. Take my advice and drop the whole thing."

#

Signing in for a day shift a week later, I asked Sigmund if the KRIPO man had asked to see his daily log for the day when Kleister died. Sigmund the doorman was just as old as his counterpart, Siegfried. Like the night watchman, he had served with distinction in the previous war with a row of medals on his chest to prove it.

He shook his head. "I must say, I was surprised. I mean, what's the fucking point of keeping these fucking records if they're never consulted?"

#

I decided to go over Drobol's head and take my concerns to the head of my section, Oberst Bernhardt Schiller. I thought it unlikely that the Oberst would grant an audience to a lowly signalman, but much to my surprise, I was summoned to his office.

Behind his desk stood two swastika standards. The impression was one of busy clutter, accentuated by the presence of several bronze objects littering the desk – an eagle in flight, a miniature Brandenburg Gate on a marble stand, and another eagle peering down at a nest of broken eggs. This piece I recognised, for my late father had had one just like it.

The Oberst was dressed in a plain blue suit. He was a large man in his fifties, very pale, smoking a long Russian cigarette.

I outlined my concerns about Kleister's death. When I stopped to draw breath, the Oberst said, "What are you suggesting?"

"I believe Kleister was murdered, Herr Oberst."

"This is preposterous," he snapped. "The police have investigated these matters, have they not? You and I are not qualified for police work. We must leave these matters to the experts. If you wish to continue to work in the Abwehr, please just attend to your duties, concentrate your energies on the signals. D'you hear?"

"Herr Oberst," I said. "I only ask that you examine the evidence yourself. I'm sure you'll be convinced as I am—"

"Forget this nonsense, Müller. That's an order. Do your duty. Nothing more is required of you."

So there it was. Everybody seemed satisfied that Kleister blew his own brains out. The Oberst was right. It was useless my speculating on Kleister's death. I needed to get back to work and devote all my attention to my duties as a signalman. There was a war to be fought.

3

April 1940

On a warm Sunday in April, I was summoned to a garden party at my uncle's home, on the northern outskirts of Berlin. His staff addressed him as SS-Gruppenführer Heydrich; to me he was Uncle Reinhard.

The occasion marked Uncle Reinhard's recent appointment as Head of the newly constituted Reich Security Headquarters, the RSHA. After years of inter-departmental strife, he had succeeded in uniting under his command all four of the Reich's security organisations: ORPO, the uniformed police, KRIPO, the criminal police, Gestapo, the secret state police, and Sicherheitsdienst (SD), the elite Security Service of the SS.

Placing a glass of schnapps in my hand, he steered me to a secluded corner of the garden. He was much as I remembered him: A tall, thin man in a dark suit, with an egg-shaped head and small eyes.

"I hear you've been causing a storm in the Abwehr," he said.

Instantly, there was an uncomfortable feeling in the pit of my stomach, accompanied by a mental image of men in senior positions in government and the military sitting around gossiping like housewives. Before joining the Abwehr it had been made plain to me that the lines between the Abwehr and the RSHA must never be breached, and besides, my instinct told me that any information given to my uncle would be used against the Abwehr.

"It was nothing," I replied.

"The suicide of a colleague is hardly nothing, Kurt. How well did you know him?"

I felt a sharp pain, as if something had twisted in my stomach. The subject was dynamite; I could say nothing. "Not well."

Uncle Reinhard nodded. "How do you like the work?"

I was relieved – he'd moved on. It seemed he'd been fully briefed on my meeting with Oberst Schiller and needed no more from me on the subject.

I drew myself up. "I intend to enlist at the earliest opportunity."

"You feel that you could do more for your country as a soldier?"

"I thought the Kriegsmarine..."

The glamour of the navy had never been far from my mind since the start of the war. There were so few Berliners of my age not in uniform that I often attracted second glances from people in the street. The feeling of guilt was ever-present, like a festering sore. Besides, I felt that my recent confrontation with the Oberst might have soured my career prospects. Uncle Reinhard's knowledge about that did nothing to assuage my concern.

He gave a thin smile. "Nonsense, Kurt. You are serving your country with distinction, I'm sure. Your language skills must be a great asset to the Abwehr."

"I have English, only. And everything I do is with Morse code, transmitting or recording."

His pencil eyebrows seemed to register mild surprise. In matters of personal grooming, Uncle Reinhard was a paragon: his chin was shaved like porcelain, his eyebrows plucked thin and streamlined as blades; and there was no vestige of nasal hair to be seen in his long, narrow nose.

He continued, "This war with the British will be a short-lived affair. Our non-aggression pact with the Soviets will ensure a quick and decisive victory. Germany is awake again after its long slumber. Germany – the new Fatherland – will put behind it the injustices of the last war, and rise from the ashes."

"Yes, Uncle."

"You should be proud, Kurt. Be proud of your achievements. I never had the opportunity to go to university. You were fortunate. You, and millions like you, will form the backbone of the new Germany – intelligent, educated visionaries."

I murmured something.

"How long since we've spoken?" he asked.

"At my father's funeral. Five years ago."

The hearse was gleaming black, with large wheels and glass panels on either side; drawn by two high-stepping black geldings, and driven by a tall man wearing a morning suit and top hat. At the graveside three more strangers appeared, and the four men lifted the coffin from the hearse. It was a beautiful July day. Mother, leaning heavily on my arm, wore a full length black coat, her face obscured by a veil. The pastor read from his prayer book. Some Lutheran mumbo jumbo. His words may have been a comfort to my mother, but they meant nothing to me. I could make no sense of what had happened. I was angry; and I wanted to strike back at the world for the senseless way that my father had been taken from us —

"Kurt?"

"I'm sorry, Uncle. What did you say?"

"I said I was saddened at his tragic passing. Your father and I were good friends. He was a man of substance, and a true patriot."

"Yes, Uncle."

Bizarrely, he changed subject in mid stream. "What of the IRA? Did you come into contact with them while you were in Ireland?"

"No. I never met anyone from the IRA."

"And what of the Irish people, Kurt? Of course they hate the British. The Irish have been under the British jackboot for centuries. You must have seen their hatred of the British."

I shook my head.

His upper lip curled in a vestige of scorn. "You must have led a sheltered life in Ireland. It seems your head was buried in your books and you failed to see what was going on around you."

The university had been a sheltered environment, but I had spent two of my four undergraduate years living in digs in the city. I had never seen any signs of strong anti-British feelings, nor heard any mention of the IRA. I had seen crushing unemployment and extreme poverty in Ireland; I had seen workhouses and prisons overflowing and hungry children. Perhaps what I had seen in people's faces was hatred, but it seemed more like anger and despair to me. And I had seen all of these things in Germany, too – lives destroyed by the depression that followed the Great War.

The Black Orchestra

#

Uncle Reinhard was seized upon and carried away by his people, murmuring in his ears.

As I stood alone wondering which of my uncle's devious plans I had been sucked into, a tall girl approached. She had dark, shoulder-length hair. Her face was shaded by a wide-brimmed hat. A light blue summer dress cut fashionably short accentuated her full breasts, wide hips.

I thought she would float past me, but she presented me with the back of her hand and said, "Gudrun von Sommerfeld. You look as bored as I feel."

I grasped her hand and clicked my heels. "Kurt Müller. Enchanted, Fräulein."

She laughed and withdrew her hand. "You're related to Reinhard, I believe?"

"He's my uncle," I replied. "Well, he's not actually my uncle." I was babbling.

"So he is your uncle, but he isn't your uncle. I'm glad we cleared that up."

"Herr Heydrich's sister, Edeltraud, is married to my father's brother."

My first impression was that she was older than me, although I thought she had probably picked me out of the crowd because I was the only person in the garden anywhere close to her own age. I stood with my arms crossed, clutching my empty schnapps glass to my chest. I was wearing my only suit – the one I used for work – an ill-fitting, threadbare garment of light wool in navy blue, well past its best. There was a small stain on my lapel. She held no glass, and I was debating whether or not to suggest remedying this situation, when she produced a cigarette from her purse, and lit it with a match.

"You work with your uncle?" She squinted in the early evening sun, her large earrings, shaped like crescent moons, flashing reflected sunlight in my eyes.

"No, Fräulein. I'm with the Abwehr."

"Ah! Admiral Canaris. A distinguished man – but short, and thin."

"I've never actually met him." This was true, although I had seen him on a few occasions. He was indeed a distinguished looking man, not tall – certainly – but I thought he was not as thin as I was.

"Reinhard tells me you are an only child. And your mother lives in Ireland."

So she knew something of me from discussions with Uncle Reinhard.

I said, "And what's your connection to my uncle, Fräulein?"

She replied only with a fleeting smile.

I was uncomfortable with this. It told me nothing, while suggesting some secret close relationship – professional or personal. So what if it was a secret? She could just as easily have given me a vague answer or told me a lie. Her answer was like a slap in the face.

After that encounter, I replayed our conversation in my mind many times. In the re-runs my responses were wittier, my smile more assured, and she melted into my arms every time.

4

April 1940

Days later, Drobol called me into his office – a converted walk-in closet at the end of the corridor – to take a telephone call.

Oberst Schiller, our section head, was on the line. "We have a vacancy in the Translations Unit that we'd like you to fill."

The Translations Unit was where incoming signals sent down from the Communications Unit were decoded and translated. It was a significant promotion.

"You start tomorrow," he said, and the line went dead.

With a move 'downstairs' the everyday tedium of Morse code would be replaced by real world issues and problems. The prospect was exciting, although I suspected that the change would bring with it serious pressures and responsibilities.

The next morning, I presented myself at Oberst Schiller's office on the second floor. He was dressed as before, smoking one of his long cigarettes.

"I understand you have no experience with Enigma or TypeX."

"None, Herr Oberst." The hairs on my spine were tingling. Enigma was the Third Reich's most secret coding system. Used only for the most sensitive military signals, it was unbreakable. TypeX was the British equivalent, similar in concept to Enigma, but of course far less sophisticated.

"Speddig will show you round." He waved his cigarette in the direction of the door and turned his attention to the papers on his desk in front of him. The conversation was at an end. I got up to leave, relieved that he'd made no mention of our previous meeting.

I said, "May I ask why I was selected for this work?"

"Your uncle recommended you," he replied without looking up.

#

"My father is Quartermaster General for the Seventh Army," was how Speddig introduced himself.

Gunther Bartholomäus von Speddig was an Austrian national in his early twenties. He had a full head of dark hair and rimless spectacles that magnified his eyes, giving him the look of an owl. Before my arrival he had sole responsibility for all English traffic; from that day, we would share the work.

My new colleagues were all language specialists. Speddig introduced me to the four others in the room, each man fluent in one other language: French, Italian, Russian and Polish.

He brought me to the third floor where I met Oberst von Neumann, the Head of Section II, the most mysterious, the most glamorous section that ran all agents in foreign territories. The Oberst was a genial type, somewhat rotund. I judged him fond of his food and his beer.

His handshake was firm, and his face lit up with a smile. "Welcome to the madhouse, Herr Leutnant Müller."

Speddig took me to the archive across the corridor from von Neumann's office, filled with boxes of files on ranks of metal shelving, floor to ceiling. The archivist, Manfred Limburg, wore an eyeglass. He stood up, clicked his heels and saluted in the old style. I returned the salute.

"Oberst Schiller told me to expect you," Limburg said. "If you need access to the files, don't forget your F17."

Back in the corridor, Speddig said, "He's a non-commissioned officer from the last war. Retired. Everyone calls him *Oberfeldwebel*."

"And F17?"

"It's a requisition form for access to the archive. You sign it and it must be countersigned by an Oberst or higher. I warn you, nothing gets past the Oberfeldwebel."

Our last stop was the post room, situated in the basement with the boilers. The attendant was an enormous man with huge muscles, dressed in baggy shorts and a filthy floral sleeveless shirt. His build, his incongruous clothing and the dark vault that he lived in, made me think immediately of Wagner's giant, Faffner. He strode across the room and towered over us.

"Bernhardt Drobol, at your service," the giant boomed.

"Is it always this hot in here?" I asked, running a finger under my collar.

The giant grinned, exposing two rows of black, rotting teeth. "Oh, this is nothing. It's much hotter in the summer, and in the winter we have the boilers. There's no ventilation down here."

"If you need any stationery supplies, Drobol's your man," Speddig said, pointing to a row of five large cabinets.

Back on the second floor, I asked Speddig if the postal giant was related to Drobol the cripple.

"Yes, they're father and son," he replied.

It didn't seem credible that an old bent cripple like Drobol could have produced such huge offspring.

Speddig and I had lunch together in the staff canteen on the first floor. During the meal, a music programme on the radio was interrupted by news of the invasion of Norway. Everyone cheered. Someone shouted, "Next stop, Paris," and we all cheered again.

#

Two encryption methods were used by the enemy: British Naval Cypher3 and TypeX. Cypher3 signals had been completely broken by our own Kriegsmarine code breakers, but TypeX signals could only be decoded after we had received the daily keys from the diplomatic bag. This bag came from the Spanish Legation in London, and was routed through Madrid, so it was mid-afternoon before we received them.

All incoming signals handled by the Abwehr were subject to strict controls. This was achieved by the use of special pre-numbered yellow pads. In addition, the Oberfeldwebel created an index entry for each signal. By this means, each signal received, decoded and translated, was uniquely identified, and signals could never be overlooked or lost.

As signals from the battles in Belgium came in, we were the first to hear of every advance. Soon, the British Expeditionary Force was surrounded, their backs to the Belgian coast with nowhere to go. On May 17, the Belgians capitulated, and the German noose began to tighten around the British army in retreat at Dunkirk.

Toward the end of April, I decoded and translated a TypeX signal from the Admiralty in London. It was clear from the contents of the signal that both Hamburg and Bremen were soon to be bombed by the British RAF. In view of the serious and imminent nature of the threat, I took the signal straight to Oberst Schiller, my section head. Upon reading it, he warned me not to discuss its contents with anyone. Then he hurried upstairs to the fourth floor. An hour later, I was summoned to his office.

"Who else is aware of the contents of this signal?" He was ashen-faced.

"No one, Herr Oberst."

"Very well. It must remain so. The signal has been destroyed. In the wrong hands, the contents of this signal would be very destructive to the Reich."

"I understand, Herr Oberst, but the people of these cities will be warned?"

He drew a hand across his face. "We have decided not to give them any warning, for to do so would alert the British to the fact that we have broken their most secret encryption system."

"But Herr Oberst—"

He held up his hand to silence my objections. "As long as we have the means to decode TypeX signals, we have a supreme advantage over the British – an advantage that could shorten the war. But if the British discover that we can decode TypeX – even if they suspect that we can…"

"I understand, Herr Oberst."

When I returned to my desk, Speddig was waiting for me.

"Is there a problem?" he said. "A flap on? Something I should know about?"

"No, nothing."

His colour deepened, his eyes seemed to expand and bulge behind his glasses. He began pacing around my desk, deep in thought. Every few steps he gave a little skip which I found comical.

"I need to be informed if there's anything important going on," he whined.

For close to an hour Speddig tried to bully or wheedle the information from me, but of course I could tell him nothing. By the end of the hour Speddig was red in the face. His skipping made me laugh, which made matters worse, of course. Then his skips progressed to foot stamping and swearing.

"Rumpelstilzchen!" I shouted.

Soon I was weeping with laughter, and everyone in the Translations Unit joined in. The episode ended when Oberst Schiller emerged from his office to see what the noise was and ordered everyone back to work.

#

Signing out that evening, I came across Drobol, the cripple.

He shuffled after me. "I hear you've been asking questions about the night of Kleister's suicide. You interrogated Sigmund and Siegfried."

"I asked them some questions," I said. "It was hardly the third degree."

Drobol scratched the side of his nose. "Don't you think you should leave that to the professionals?"

"The KRIPO, you mean?" I raised an eyebrow.

"I can't understand your interest," He squinted at me.

"Well, I can't understand your *lack* of interest," I snapped. "Kleister was one of your men. Don't you care what happened to him?"

He hesitated. Then he said, "If I were you, I'd just drop it," and hobbled off.

After that encounter, I was convinced that Drobol had killed Kleister and I resolved to bring him to justice.

5

May 1940

I visited the Oberfeldwebel in his archive.

"Müller," I said. "Section I."

He was bald – his head was like a billiard ball – but he made up for this deficiency with a copious moustache of the old style that merged with bushy sideburns to cover most of his face. His complexion was ruddy; his bearing military.

He peered at me through his monocle. "Where's your F17?"

"I don't have one," I replied with a smile. "I just dropped by to have a chat."

"What about?"

"I'm interested in your record keeping."

"Checking up on me, are you?"

"Not at all. I was impressed by the way you operate. If everyone in the building was as precise as you, we wouldn't be in such a mess."

"We are in a mess? I wasn't aware of any difficulties. I'm sorry to hear that." The worry lines that inhabited his forehead were showing signs of colonising his bald head. "How can I help?"

"I wondered about the Signals Index," I said. "I understand you keep an index record for every signal."

"I do."

"Could I take a quick look at one?" He pondered my request. I thought he was about to turn me down, so I added, "Just the Index, not the signals themselves."

"Which Index?"

"How about the German Signals Index for this year - early?"

He handed me the German Language signals index for January-March, each entry in the book a masterpiece of calligraphy, in the

Oberfeldwebel's shaky copperplate. Running my eye down the index entries for the days leading up to Kleister's death, I found what I was looking for. Signal 40/D/1774 received from Leipzig the day before. The Index entry read 'person-to-person'.

I thanked the old man for his help.

A quick check of the records in Section I confirmed that the signal had never passed through the Translations Unit. I knew then that the signal had been in plain text. Kleister would have been able to read its contents.

#

Tiergarten must be one of the most beautiful city parks in Europe with its vast woodland, majestic boulevards flanked by rows of mature trees, and hectares of manicured lawn. One Friday evening at the start of May, I took a detour through the park. The Berlin Philharmonic Orchestra was holding an outdoor performance of music by Richard Strauss, and it was rumoured that something of Mahler's would be included. Tiergarten was crowded. Seeking a quiet corner, I settled at an outside table of a restaurant within earshot of the music, and ordered a beer.

Gudrun von Sommerfeld passed by, dressed in navy blue with a small white bucket hat and white gloves. She looked like a million Marks. I leaped to my feet, hurried after her and touched her on the shoulder. She stopped, turned and said, "Kurt. Kurt Müller, isn't it?"

"Fräulein von Sommerfeld," I responded. "Would you care to join me?"

She hesitated, then accompanied me to my table.

"I only have a few minutes," she said.

To me, her features seemed heavy, as if she had been sketched by an artist's apprentice: her nose was a little too broad; her mouth a little too wide; her chin a little too square; her teeth slightly prominent. But the overall effect was shattering. She was no classical beauty, but she was a beauty nonetheless – a vision of German maidenhood.

She told me she worked in the Air Ministry.

"I have a friend in the Air Ministry," I said. "Alex Clausen. Do you know him?"

She laughed. "There are well over five thousand people in the building."

I asked about her family, and she told me something of her background. Her parents lived in Elmshorn in Schleswig-Holstein. Then rather abruptly she looked at her watch. "Sorry, Kurt, I have to go. I have an appointment later this evening."

I said, "Perhaps we could meet another night. We could go for a meal somewhere."

We agreed to meet the next week at Kindl Stube. And then she was gone. That meeting lasted ten minutes – no more – but it changed my life.

#

The Kindl Stube restaurant is situated right in the heart of the old city. We ordered fish. Our conversation was like a car with a loose clutch – it never got going and kept stalling. Gudrun seemed distant, preoccupied. I asked various questions about her family. Her answers were short and delivered in a monotone, providing the requested information, but without feeling or reciprocation. Several times during the evening I asked if there was something troubling her. Each time she responded with a smile and a shake of her head. The meal was completed in silence. I paid the bill and offered to walk her home to her apartment. She declined, and hailed a taxi.

"Can we meet again?" I said, expecting a refusal.

She agreed, although I had the impression that whether we met again or not was a matter of complete indifference to her.

#

For our second date we had a light meal at an outdoor bar on Unter den Linden. All along the boulevard, the Linden trees were in full bloom, a light dusting of yellow petals underfoot. One or two sparrows flitted around, less lively now, and one lone pigeon ambled about, fattened close to bursting by the excess of the summer trade. Afterwards I took Gudrun for a walk through the city centre. We followed the route of the river Spree. I hoped she thought it charming, romantic, and it was, but in reality it was all that I could afford.

Gudrun was wearing a red dress and another of her bucket hats, this one with feathers attached and what looked like a bunch of grapes. She was like a different person, attentive, interesting, full of the joy of life.

She told me more about her childhood in Elsmhorn. Her father had spent almost the whole of 1935 in prison under some trumped-up charge.

"It was ridiculous. Some idiot accused him of anti-German activities. That was a bad year for us. We had to live off our savings."

"The charges were unfounded?" I cursed myself for the awkward question when I saw her reaction.

"Of course they were. Complete fabrications. My father was never interested in politics. He is a good German. He doesn't support any political party."

I could see the illogic in her last two statements, but I let it slide.

"Did he serve in the last war?"

"No. He has a reserved occupation. He's a dentist."

I laughed. "Dentists were exempt from military service?"

I asked her about her taste in music. This was a more fruitful area, for we soon discovered that we enjoyed many of the same composers, although she knew little of Wagner, which surprised me. Another surprise was her interest in American jazz so detested by the Party. I described my modest collection of three records. "I'd love to play them for you, sometime," I said.

"Perhaps sometime," she replied.

We kissed for the first time that night, our embrace interrupted by a sudden shower of rain that fell from a cloudless sky.

On the night of May 19, the British RAF dropped their bombs on Hamburg and Bremen. Terrible damage was done to both cities, and hundreds of civilians were killed.

I slept badly. I knew that Alex Clausen's mother and brother lived somewhere near Hamburg, but I had been unable to give him any warning of the bombing raid. Torn between my duty and my friendship and burdened by guilt, I was sure that Alex would have managed to warn me somehow, if our situations had been reversed.

The next day I rang Alex and asked about his mother.

"She's fine," he replied. "She lives some distance from the city."

The institution where his brother was living had been hit by a bomb, and he had been found wandering the streets of Hamburg, dazed and disoriented, but otherwise unhurt. The word 'institution' hung in the air like a bad smell.

His last words to me, as the call ended, were, "Thank you for your concern, Leutnant Müller."

On that same day, our army reached the French coast, the British Expeditionary Force was completely encircled, and the British Navy began an emergency evacuation of the troops. The Luftwaffe was dispatched to attack the British ships at anchor off the Belgian coast, and several were sunk. On May 26, a flotilla of small craft began to arrive from the British coast, and many British soldiers were rescued in that way.

The newspaper reports were jubilant. To complete the task, the Wehrmacht had only to close the noose and wipe out the British army. Victory would be ours; the war would be over!

6

May 1940

On our third date, Gudrun was wearing an adventurous combination of a pink dress and a green hat. We went to the cinema. The main feature, called *Journey into Life* was an amusing film about three navy recruits. The accompanying documentary, *The Eternal Jew*, I had seen before. This was a piece of dull Party propaganda. Gudrun found it as distasteful as I did, but we sat through it rather than draw attention to ourselves by leaving.

There were people everywhere that night, happy people, riding in buses, trams and cars, talking, laughing in the streets. The tram bells mingled with car horns and bicycle bells, and music blared from many of the cafés. There were hundreds of bicycles – many without lights. Everywhere, there were men in uniform, hurrying home or perhaps to some illicit rendezvous, moustachioed men, men smoking pipes or cigarettes, some in overalls, men with long beards, in three-piece suits, wearing flat caps or trilbies; there were women in long skirts or short, brightly-coloured summer dresses, all wearing hats or headscarves, women with prams or small children, young girls in ponytails, boys with hoops – and beggars on every corner. It was as if the whole world had come out onto the streets to celebrate my good fortune.

It was a magical evening. We had a long, slow meal under the stars on the forecourt of a famous restaurant. The Bauerhaus, located close to the Brandenburg Gate in the heart of the city, specialised in traditional German food. The warm evening breeze was exquisite accompaniment to the food and wine. A flock of house sparrows occupied the trees on the opposite side of the street and, throughout the meal, individual birds paid fleeting visits to the tables in search of crumbs. This made Gudrun laugh; she seemed to delight in the attention of the birds.

I loved her laughter and I found it easy to amuse her. My description of the "Rumpelstilzchen" episode with Speddig made her laugh so much she had to go to the ladies' room to reapply her make-up.

Later, over coffee, I found myself talking about my father. I told Gudrun about the 1927 Nuremberg rally which I attended with my father. Reaching out, I took her hand in mine. I swear I could feel the whorls of her fingertips in the palm of my hand.

"He gave me so much – my love of the Fatherland, pride in our German heritage," I told her. My father was everything to me. His strong ethical sense was a driving force in my own life. He had often spoken of democratic values and freedoms, and I always tried to live up to his principles.

"He filled my world. I remember standing beside him in a vast crowd at Nuremberg, listening to the Führer. It seemed impossible to be that close to one human being amongst so many." I shook my head. "I haven't explained that very well."

She squeezed my hand. "You felt close to him, closer than to anyone else in that throng. That's natural. The love of a boy for his father. You were what? Thirteen?"

"Fourteen. Some of my happiest moments as a child were spent with my father in the woods and fields near our home, watching the wildlife, or catching rabbits in a snare."

"That's cruel," she frowned and tried to pull her hand away. I gripped her fingers and she relaxed.

"My father considered it a vital survival skill," I said. "And anyway, we hardly ever caught anything."

"And what of the Führer's words?" she asked.

"The Führer's words were inspiring, of course, but I felt they left so much unsaid – so much half said – that each man there could place his own interpretation on the words. All that was left was a sense of his thundering passion, his tireless, indignant patriotism.

"When did your father die?"

"He was killed on my twenty-first birthday — the first of July, 1934."

There were tears in my eyes. Somehow Gudrun's presence seemed to intensify my every emotion.

The Black Orchestra

"The Night of the Long Knives. He was a member of the SA?"

"No, no." I frowned at her, but it was clear that Gudrun didn't realise how offensive her suggestion was. "He supported von Papen. He fought in the last war, at the Somme. He wanted to see Germany rebuilt."

"So why did he die?"

"He was killed by a stray bullet." That was the official explanation, although it made little sense.

She finished her cigarette. I paid the bill and invited her back to my apartment. There was something in the way she looked at me then. She hesitated before saying, "All right, just for a while."

We strolled back to the apartment. As we walked along I reached out and took her hand. Berlin was alive. Away from the bright lights, in the backstreets, the people bustled about on their bicycles or on foot, and dark figures lingered in every furtive shadow.

As we neared my building, she hooked her arm round mine, and I believe my love affair started right there in the moonlight among the crowds in Horst Wessel Platz.

My apartment was a mess. I hadn't realised how slovenly I'd become until Gudrun began to tidy up, that first evening. We spent an hour cleaning the apartment. Gudrun rolled up her sleeves and washed the dishes, while I gathered up all the rubbish and disposed of it. She cleaned the carpet on her hands and knees with a small hand-brush.

I protested. "This is really not necessary. Please leave it, and I'll clean it all tomorrow."

But she would have none of it, and we set to like a couple of demented *hausmeisters*. Soon, the whole apartment was sparkling, everything in its place. She was like a force of nature – an autumn breeze, I like a leaf following in her wake. I made coffee. She smoked a cigarette. When she'd finished the cigarette, she went into the bathroom to freshen up.

I went into the bedroom. When I returned to the living area, Gudrun was in the bathroom, and the bathroom door was open. She had slipped her red dress off her shoulders and folded it down to her waist; her breasts were bare. She turned a soapy face toward me, and said, "Close your mouth, Kurt. Anyone would think you'd never seen a naked girl before."

Dumbfounded, I said, "Fräulein?"

"I don't want to hear any more Fräuleins," she snapped. "Please call me by my given name."

"Gudrun," I said, for the first time, and the sound was sweet to my ears.

She said, "You get into the bed and I'll join you in a while."

I broke the world record for undressing, got into the bed, and turned out the light. A short time later she appeared, silhouetted in the bedroom doorway, naked. She walked across the room, swinging her hips, and slipped into the bed beside me. I was trembling. It was a single bed, no more than a metre wide. We lay face to face for a few moments, breathing in unison. I kissed her. She returned my kiss, then took my hand and placed it between her legs. Her body was warm, her skin soft. Reaching down, I ran my hand up her thigh, starting close to her knee. Up, then down, then up again, inching closer with each stroke. She groaned.

At the end of the last stroke, my fingers brushed her. She groaned again. Then she sneezed.

"*Gesundheit!*"

She sniffed. " Forgive me. My sinuses are blocked."

"I don't think I'm going to be able to unblock your sinuses." I laughed.

She wrapped her fingers around my shaft. "Oh, I don't know," she said, her eyes twinkling. Then, "You're not Jewish, are you?"

Our love-making that night lasted until dawn. I felt as if I had come home from a long, long journey.

As dawn broke, she made breakfast.

I asked her, "Have you had many lovers, Gudrun?"

"Many," she answered solemnly. "But none as good as you."

"Now you're making fun of me."

"No. Not at all."

"You really think I'm better than all your previous lovers?"

"More energetic, certainly."

I tickled her ribs and she laughed. "Leave me be, Kurt. I need to tend to the eggs."

I could have made love to her again at that moment, but for the smell of breakfast.

We spent the weekend together. We walked, we talked; she played Wagner and my three American jazz records over and over on my father's gramophone; and we made love. On Monday morning, as I set off for the Abwehr, she kissed me at the door, like a wife.

That day in the office, I found it almost impossible to concentrate on my work, and when the end of the day finally came, I ran all the way back to the apartment.

The apartment was empty. I sat heavily on the bed and thought, "That was too good to last."

Within an hour, Gudrun arrived at the door in a taxi with two large suitcases and a bag of groceries. One of her suitcases was full of books.

"Couldn't you move some of these?" she said, running her eye over my books. "John Buchan, Albert Camus, Franz Kafka – I thought he was banned – Ernest Hemingway, *Thermodynamics for Beginners*, How often do you read that? And this one — *Einstein's Theories: Space, Time and Relativity* — could get you into trouble."

On Wednesday and Thursday, I met Gudrun for lunch. I bought her a charm bracelet with two charms on it – a dolphin and a flower. On Friday, we bought a double bed with a good mattress. We made love several times that night.

I was elated. After three years of living alone, Gudrun's laughter filled my world. My life was complete.

7

June 1940

I arrived at work on June 3, to find everyone clustered around a radio listening to news of the British retreat from Dunkirk — they were running like rabbits, almost 400,000 of them escaping, though 40,000 had been captured.

On Saturday June 8 I arranged to meet Alex at a mass rally in front of the Dom Cathedral in the Lustgarten. Gudrun agreed to meet us later in Steffi's famous beer cellar on Nauener Strasse.

At this time, Alex shared rooms with a friend, Johann van Horne, and he brought him along. Johann came from an aristocratic family with significant industrial interests. He was younger than Alex, slight, slim and fragile-looking. His clothing was expensive and extravagant, in the Bohemian style – short waistcoats, frilly shirts, tight-fitting slacks and riding boots.

Alex and Johann were wearing Party armbands. The weather was sultry, the sky overcast, with occasional flashes of lightning to the west. There was a huge turnout; every Brownshirt left in Berlin must have been there. A stiff wind from the south stirred the hundreds of flags and banners held aloft by loyal Party followers. A boy in Hitler Youth costume wandered through the crowd, selling paper armbands and small flags. Johann bought an armband and handed it to me. I put it in my pocket. Joseph Goebbels, Minister for Propaganda was the main speaker. The wind made it difficult to hear what he had to say, but it seemed to me that his speech was no more than a rambling rant, denouncing the "enemies of the Reich" and vowing vengeance on all. Almost to a man, the Party faithful howled their approval and a great chant of *"Sieg Heil!"* arose and echoed around the throng.

An old man standing beside me waved his arms about in excitement. At one point, as the crowd roared, he turned to me and shouted, "They'll all be wiped out soon, every one, you'll see." There were tears in his eyes that might have been caused by the wind.

Everybody knew of the government's policy of stripping undesirables of their citizenship and exiling them. Jewish shops had been vandalised on Kristallnacht, and there had been rumours – which I discounted – of a more radical purge of the Jews. The old man's words left me with an uncomfortable feeling in my gut.

Near the end of the rally, the heavens opened; the meeting broke up in chaos with lightning flashing all around and the sound of thunder claps overhead.

We ran for the shelter of Steffi's. The place was heaving. Gudrun had taken a table and was holding stools for Alex and me. Alex foraged for a stool for Johann and we all ordered food and beer.

Johann was the life of the party, usurping the role usually played by Alex. Gudrun found him amusing and I must admit that his remarks – what I could hear of them above the deafening roar all round us – seemed witty. As the evening progressed, Alex flirted with Gudrun. She laughed at his jokes, but it was plain that she had no romantic interest in anyone but me.

I noticed that Alex laughed at all of Johann's jokes, and there were many secret exchanges between them that I could not interpret. When Johann was away from the table, Alex seemed unsettled, smoking almost continuously.

At one point in the evening, while Gudrun and Alex were talking together, I asked Johann what he thought of Wiener schnitzel.

"I'm vegetarian," he replied.

"With occasional lapses," Alex and Johann said, in chorus.

This surprised me as I had thought Alex was deep in conversation with Gudrun. There were similar occurrences throughout the evening. It seemed Alex kept one ear tuned to his friend's voice at all times.

Many of the bars provided free drink, that night; everybody got drunk. Well after midnight, the streets were still choked with thousands of revellers, dancing and singing. The song most heard was Wessel's masterpiece, *Die Fahne Hoch* 'Raise High the Flag.'

Gudrun and I knew only the first couple of verses; Johann and Alex knew several more. The Brownshirts were everywhere. Their behaviour, brash and triumphalist, seemed to say "We did this. See how our Germany has overcome adversity." And wherever groups of people sat or stood, they muscled in with exaggerated camaraderie.

The night ended badly. Fuelled by drink, the conversation turned to politics. Johann made some throwaway jocular remark about the Jews that I found offensive. I came back with, "How many Jews do you know that chose their birth race?"

He retorted, "I don't know any Jews – none that are still in Germany, anyway. Why? How many do you know?"

Alex tried to calm the situation with his Quasimodo face and an ill-judged joke. "We're all Jews under the skin." This time the comic pose reminded me of one of the well-known anti-Jewish posters that adorned the Litfass columns, and it occurred to me that anyone capable of such a facial distortion might well have some measure of Jewish blood. Judging by the look of disgust that he gave his friend I'd say the same thought occurred to Johann.

I admit my next remark was close to sedition, but Johann had angered me. I said, "I'd be willing to bet that many of the Party leaders have a measure of Jewish blood."

Johann had just lifted his stein to his lips. His explosive reaction sprayed us all with beer.

Alex said, "That's crazy talk."

Gudrun stood up, wiping the beer from her blouse. "Can't we talk about something else?" she said, heading for the ladies' room.

"How can you be sure there's no Jewish blood in your family?" I said to Johann.

The disgust on his face turned to contempt. "If there was, I would have left the country years ago."

It took me a while to come up with my next attack. I asked him, "Why aren't you in uniform, Johann?"

"Wouldn't you like to know," was his reply, and the conversation died right there.

When I pressed him to answer the question, Alex caught my eye and signalled for me to drop the subject.

The Black Orchestra

#

On Friday, June 14, our armies marched into Paris. Many of the Reich offices were closed for the afternoon, in celebration.

On June 17, the Cunard cruiser *Lancastria* was sunk by a Junkers 88 off the French coast, with the loss of all hands; people said it was carrying British forces evacuated from France and Belgium. I listened to the BBC that night but there was no mention of the ship or its loss.

Speddig was relentless. He kept reminding me that he was my senior, throwing unnecessary instructions at me. The volume of incoming signals doubled, then doubled again. Even working ten to twelve hours a day we couldn't keep abreast of the work. I rose early each morning to get to work before eight. At night, I would arrive home, exhausted, after nine o'clock, my mouth dry, my eyes running, my mind spinning with signals and codes, Speddig's bleating voice ringing in my ears. Gudrun found me irritable and we argued about nothing.

#

It was not until the third week of June that I had an opportunity to seek out Kleister's last signal. I filled in two F17 forms, and presented them to Oberst von Neumann to be countersigned. Looking up briefly from his papers, he asked what my interest in German signals was.

"I'm just tying up some old work from the communications unit," I said.

The Oberst countersigned both forms and handed them back.

The Oberfeldwebel, guardian of the archive, polished his eyeglass and examined my first F17 form in minute detail before handing me the 40/D box file for March.

I searched for signal 40/D/1774 — the last signal that Kleister had received before his death — but it was missing.

The second F17 was a request for the Hamburg/Bremen signal that had been received in May and suppressed by Generalmajor Oster and the Obersts. I was curious to see if there was any record of the signal in the files. Once again the old man polished his eyeglass before scrutinising the form. When he was satisfied with it, he consulted his English Language Signals Index.

"That signal has been removed from the files." He showed me the index entry. It read "Ref.: GM H. Oster".

"Even so," I said. "I'd still like to see the box file."

He led me to an area of shelving and handed me a box file.

The Hamburg/Bremen signal was indeed missing, but another signal in the box caught my eye. This form was odd. Normally, the top half of the signal – the raw signal – would have been recorded in the Communications Unit by one operator, the two lower sections of the form – the deciphered message and the translation – by a member of the Translations Unit. But it appeared that this entire signal had been written by the same hand.

The signal was a British TypeX that I remembered translating a month earlier. It originated in the War Office in London, and stated that, at full capacity, the British could produce an estimated 2,000 air defence aircraft per month. My recollection of this signal was different — it had said that the estimated production capacity was 1,000 aircraft per month. I examined the handwriting. The letters sloped back throughout. The capital "B" struck me as comical, suggesting a pregnant woman, leaning backward under the strain.

Back at my desk, my heart began to pound. Who had the opportunity to interfere with an intelligence signal? Who would want to, and why? The word "sabotage" rattled around in my mind. Who could I take my findings to? Certainly not my Section Head, Oberst Schiller; not if I wanted to remain in the Abwehr.

8

June 1940

I met Alex for lunch. He seemed unusually subdued.

"Who spat in your strudel?"

"I have a problem. You remember I told you about my brother?"

"In Hamburg."

Alex nodded. "His name's Eugen. He has a minor mental handicap. He has a strange condition. It's difficult to describe. He loves boats."

I laughed. "That doesn't sound like a handicap to me."

Alex remained serious. "He has hundreds of books about boats. He cuts pictures and articles from the newspapers about them, and he draws and paints pictures of ships."

"Sounds more like a hobby than a handicap to me."

"Ah, but it's much more than that. His head is full of useless information about boats. They're his obsession. The pocket battleship *Graf Spee*, is his favourite. Ask him any question – the size of the ship, the size of its guns, the crew complement, its engines – and he'll give you the answer."

"What about U-boats?" I asked.

"U-boats too. U47's his favourite."

"Still sounds like a passionate hobby," I said. "How old is he?"

"He's eighteen."

"And the problem?" I said.

"He has been listed for sterilisation." Alex's eyes looked haunted, like the look that I had seen in the eyes of people on Kristallnacht.

"Sterilisation? Because of an obsession?" It seemed improbable.

He gave me a look that said, *don't be stupid, Kurt.* "My mother has lodged an appeal with the Eugenics Court. His case will be heard next month."

After a minute's thought I said, "I have a contact in the office of the State Secretary for Health. I could ask him if he could do anything to help."

"That would be fantastic," Alex said, his smile returning like a flower opening at sunrise.

"It must remain our secret," I said. "Any attempt to pervert state policy could land us both in serious trouble."

"Our secret," Alex said.

As we ate, I told Alex what I had found on the files.

He was bent over his plate, both hands fully occupied with a generous bratwurst. He turned his head toward me, closing one eye.

When he surfaced, he said, "Are you sure of your facts? Your memory may be playing tricks on you."

"Yes, I'm sure. One thing I am good at, is remembering figures."

"Even so, you could be mistaken." He turned back to his food and it was several minutes before we could resume the conversation. "How many signals have crossed your desk since you joined the Translations Unit?" he asked, before gulping down half his stein of beer.

"I don't know. Hundreds, I suppose."

"Well there you are, then. You're probably confusing one signal with another."

"So, how do you explain the handwriting?"

"You say all parts of this signal are in the same hand?"

"Yes."

He gave this some thought. Then, "I thought you said the signals were all pre-numbered."

"They are. The yellow forms come on pads, pre-numbered."

"So what're you suggesting?"

I said, "Someone must have a duplicate set of pads." It was the only explanation I could think of.

"That's crazy, even for you," Alex said, adopting a quick Quasimodo face.

It did sound crazy.

"Let's just say I'm right, for the moment," I said. "Why would these figures have been altered?"

Alex shrugged. "I suppose if someone was working against the Reich …"

"An enemy spy, you mean!"

"Keep your voice down, Kurt." Alex whispered. He paused to scan the faces around us. Then in a low voice he continued, "An enemy might alter the figures on incoming signals to spread disinformation."

I drew a diagram on a beer mat and showed it to Alex. "All the signals sent out from the Communications Unit are decoded and translated by the Translations Unit before being sent to the OKW (Wehrmacht Central Command). The original is indexed and filed in the archive. Any signals involving air intelligence are copied in the OKW for the Air Ministry."

"So the signal must have been altered by someone located in the Abwehr." Alex said, tapping the beer mat.

I said, "It's difficult to imagine how it could have been altered anywhere else. They would have had to get into the Abwehr archive to change the original copy."

"Always assuming …"

I nodded. "Assuming that the figures really have been altered."

"You'd need to check the contents of the signal that the OKW received. That might confirm the tampering." He finished his bratwurst and his beer and stood up. "I have to get back. I have work to do."

We walked back part of the way together.

I said, "You could check the files at the Air Ministry just to prove that I'm not imagining all this."

"Fine. Let me have the date and reference of the signal, and I'll check it for you."

I wrote the information on a page of my notebook, tore it out and handed it to him. "The signal should say that the British have an estimated defence aircraft production capacity of 1,000 per month."

I thought about this conversation afterwards. It seemed barely credible that someone would keep a duplicate set of forms. But if it was true, how many other signals might have been tampered with? Could this be the work of a British spy?

#

I met Alex briefly the next day. He confirmed that the signal version at the Air Ministry was the same as the one in the Abwehr archive.

I would have to check the version sent to the OKW, the Wehrmacht High Command.

Alex said, "I wouldn't act too hastily, if I were you, Kurt. If you poke a stick into a hornet's nest, you're liable to get stung."

Before we parted Alex said, "I wondered whether Kleister left a suicide note. I've heard it said that very few suicides fail to leave some sort of note."

Why had no one mentioned that before? Suicide victims generally left notes. I had read that somewhere. Surely this was another indication that Kleister was murdered.

When I got home, I told Gudrun about the altered signal. She asked if it could be a simple mistake.

I said, "That's not possible. The original signal specified the number one thousand. The tampered signal had the number two thousand."

"That's just one digit. Sounds like a clerical error," she said.

I explained. "There are no numerical digits in these coding systems, only the letters. The original signal read O-N-E-T-H-O-U-S-A-N-D, the altered signal reads T-W-O-T-H-O-U-S-A-N-D. The three letters O-N-E have been replaced with the three letters T-W-O."

"So you're saying it must have been a deliberate act of sabotage?"

"Beyond question."

I told her that Alex had already checked the Air Ministry files and that we needed to check the office where the signals were first received by the OKW.

"That's the Central office," she said. "Do you know anyone in there?"

"No."

"I do," she said.

#

In the month of June, 350,000 tons of Allied shipping was sunk, most of it in the Atlantic Ocean. Of this tonnage, Gunther Prien and his magnificent crew accounted for 35,000 tons, in his famous U-boat, U47.

On Sunday, June 30 the island of Guernsey fell to the might of our military machine. Again, there was jubilation in the streets. The headlines in all the newspapers announced the imminent invasion of Britain. It was the anniversary of my father's accidental death on the Night of the Long Knives. It was also my twenty-seventh birthday.

9

July 1940

One evening early in July, I remained at my desk until I was sure that everyone else had left the second floor. It was close to eight o'clock. Slipping past Siegfried the night watchman, who was listening to music on his radio, I made my way to the basement.

Four of the five stationery cabinets were unlocked, and I searched them quickly. There were bundles of pads, wrapped in brown paper, each one labelled with the form number ranges on the outside. I found no duplicates. The fifth cabinet was locked.

The following day I went back to the basement and paid a visit to Drobol the giant. I asked him about his work, and he described his daily postal routine. When I asked him about his duties in relation to stationery supplies he looked puzzled.

He scratched his stomach under the revolting floral shirt. "Why do you want to know about that? It's just paper and pencils."

"There seems to be an awful lot of it," I said. "What's in this cabinet here, for instance?" I pointed to the fifth cabinet.

"There's nothing in there." Pulling a bunch of keys from his pocket, he opened the cabinet.

It was full of cheap trophies. Stupid tin cups won by the Abwehr in Wehrmacht football tournaments, chess matches and so on.

My officious colleague Speddig was waiting for me back in my office.

"I took a telephone call for you," he said accusingly. "A woman. She said her name was Tania Schaefer."

Kleister's sister.

"The telephones are not for private calls. I'm willing to overlook it this time, but I must warn you that any recurrence will be reported." His beady eyes shone like beacons through his glasses. He dropped a piece of paper on my desk with a telephone number written on it.

"Yes, thanks, Speddig," I said.

I rang Tania Schaefer that evening from home.

"Today would have been Tristan's birthday," she said. "I wanted to do something to remember him. I needed to talk to someone, someone from his workplace who knew him. I know he didn't kill himself. I just know it. And no one believes me."

"I believe you," I said.

There was a short pause. Then she said, "Do you have any proof?"

"No."

"Don't you have anything that we could take to the KRIPO to get them to reopen the case?" The anguish in her voice was palpable.

"I'm sorry, Tania," I said. The case would never be reopened.

#

On July 16 a Directive issued from the office of the Führer and circulated to all Wehrmacht offices and operational units in Germany. Directive 16 was a command to make preparations for the invasion of England. A number of preconditions for the invasion were listed in the Directive. Principal among these were the neutralisation of the British Navy and the elimination of the threat to the invasion posed by the RAF. The Wehrmacht high command began to lay secret plans for the operation. Scheduled for mid-September, it was codenamed 'Operation Sealion'.

The battle for air superiority over the English Channel was codenamed 'Operation Eagle Attack'. Once it started Alex was unreachable at work in the Air Ministry. Gudrun became withdrawn, and frequently snapped at me over minor irritations.

I bought a newspaper each day, and we listened to the news on the radio every night. I kept a running total of the number of British aircraft shot down by our brave Luftwaffe pilots. But the numbers made no sense. Within three weeks, the reports claimed over 1,700

British aircraft destroyed, while the Luftwaffe's losses were just 207. I knew the figures were likely to be inaccurate, but these looked like blatant distortions created by the Propaganda Ministry.

Alex and I managed to meet briefly one day, and he confirmed my fears. "The Spitfires are running rings around us, and they always seem to know where to find us."

"They have an electronic system," I said. "I read about it somewhere. They bounce radio signals off the 'planes and it tells them where they are."

"Yes, that's the killer. It's called RADAR. Reich engineers are working on copying it, but we're years behind the British."

I told him about my searches for duplicate signals pads, and about the five stationery cabinets in the basement post room.

#

Oberst Schiller sent for me.

When I entered his office, his counterpart, Oberst von Neumann, the spymaster, Head of the mysterious Section II, was sitting facing Schiller's desk. It was difficult to imagine this man at the centre of a web of spies all over the world. He had on a green woollen jumper that he wore all the time: the sort of jumper worn by submariners. The garment was frayed at the cuffs, had brown leather patches on the elbows and clung to his portly frame. A bright yellow file sat perched on von Neumann's knee.

"I understand you lived for four years in Ireland," von Neumann said.

Schiller produced a long cigarette from a desk drawer, and lit it. "You are aware of the work that Hauptmann von Pfaffel does?"

I knew of the Hauptmann: he ran field agents overseas, in Britain and Ireland.

Von Neumann said, "The Hauptmann is under some pressure. You may have been aware of this, Müller."

Actually, I was; everyone knew the pressure that von Pfaffel was under.

"The Hauptmann currently has ten active agents in Great Britain—" from Schiller.

"Twelve," von Neumann corrected him.

Schiller nodded. "And three in Ireland."

"That's fifteen in total," von Neumann said.

It was like a tennis match; first one Oberst spoke, then the other. It occurred to me that I might be the ball.

"A ridiculous number for any one man to handle," Schiller said.

Von Neumann turned to face Schiller. "He's not completely alone, Bernhardt. He does have staff."

"Nevertheless—" Schiller began.

"Nevertheless, the Hauptmann is under pressure. Undeniably," von Neumann conceded.

"I understand, Herr Oberst." I began to suspect where the conversation was heading. All the small hairs on my spine were rising.

"We've been watching your progress with interest, Kurt," von Neumann said.

Schiller added, "Yes, and I have to say, Müller, that I'm very pleased with your work, so far."

Von Neumann handed me the file. It was marked '375'. "I'd like you to examine the contents of this file. See what you can make of it and get back to me."

"What am I to look for?"

"You must look at the file with fresh eyes and see what emerges. You may be able to see things in the record that have escaped the notice of others."

"How long should I take to complete this task?"

"Take as long as you need – say two days," said Schiller.

10

July 1940

From the moment he saw me working on a special assignment, Speddig became my constant companion. In this new situation, he had lost his self-appointed hold over me, and he hovered around my desk like a gnat, doing his little skip and trying everything he could to find out what I was doing. I thwarted him at every turn. Anxious to devote my full attention to the file, it wasn't long before I told him bluntly to fuck off back to his own desk. I was surprised when he did.

The reason why I had been handed this particular file soon became plain. It was the file of Agent 375, codename Ornithologist, stationed in Ireland, who had disappeared without trace.

The first document in the file was a report from another agent – codename 'Stallion' – describing his efforts to locate the missing agent.

Ornithologist had been placed on the east coast of Ireland by parachute jump six months earlier, and had set up an operating base in a village called Ballyruane. From there, he had been able to observe a good portion of the Irish Sea, sending back many reports of ship and aircraft movements, as well as daily weather reports from the area.

Transmissions from Agent Ornithologist ceased abruptly on July 2, and Agent Stallion had been dispatched from his base in Cork to investigate. Stallion discovered very little: only that the people of Ballyruane were welcoming toward Ornithologist, and he was well-liked in the village.

Agent Stallion had failed to locate agent Ornithologist's missing transmitter. What was much more disturbing was that his Enigma cipher machine was also missing. I knew how important it was to prevent this machine from falling into British hands. I had seen the standing orders issued to U-boat commanders: in the event of capture by the British, any and all steps must be taken to prevent seizure of the Enigma machine on board – up to and including scuttling the vessel.

Agent Stallion had done a thorough job. Many of the villagers were listed by name and he had completed short profiles on a number of them.

Rudolf Clancy: Blacksmith. Possibly of German extraction.

William Ryan: Bar owner. A good source of local information/gossip.

Mrs Muldowney: A widow. Runs a café.

And so on. A surprising number of the entries were single women.

I read through the rest of the file. The missing agent Ornithologist, real name Pavel Zapochek, was a tall man – close to two metres. His photograph attested to his Aryan looks, protruding ears and military bearing. There was no mention of any military service prior to his training with the Abwehr, but his appearance seemed inappropriate for an espionage mission. His cover name was Rupert Kinski.

I went through his training records. His performance in the physical disciplines was exceptional, but it was clear that his English was poor. Upon completion of his training, his language tutor, one Herr Haffner, had noted: "Vocabulary – fair. Grasp of syntax – poor. Accent – appalling."

Next, I checked the signals archive.

Most of his transmissions were weather reports. There was just one strange incoming signal. Dated June 20, it read:

BULLFROG MEETING CONFIRMED

I checked the archive of outgoing signals and found the partner to this signal. Sent two days earlier, it read:

MEET BULLFROG NINE THREE THREE TCD JULY FOURTH

Thinking about it, it was difficult to understand how a large man, built like a fortress, and with exceptional combative skills could vanish from a small Irish village. No body had been found, no signs of struggle. It seemed the agent had got out of bed one morning and simply disappeared.

I asked to see Oberst von Neumann and he agreed to meet me immediately.

It was close to the end of the working day. Outside, heavy black clouds hung over the city. A thunderstorm was gathering.

"I've read through that file, Herr Oberst." I said. "Agent Ornithologist seems to be a man with strengths in some areas."

"But not in others?"

"His grasp of the English language was less than ideal."

"His cover story is that he is Polish — which he is. We hoped this would account for his poor English." The Oberst sat back in his chair. He retrieved his pipe from an ashtray and puffed at it. It glowed in the gloom of his office, belching smoke.

I said, "Maybe he should have been posted to Poland?"

The Oberst's laugh was a pulmonary explosion. "Yes, young man, you're right. But we've so few candidates for postings to English-speaking countries, we have to make do with what we can find. And yet, he went undetected for over four months, from March until July." von Neumann chuckled. Thunder grumbled outside.

"He was certainly aided in this by the locals," I said.

"You have personal knowledge of this village? What was it called?"

"Ballyruane. And no, I'm not familiar with it, but it seems likely that the agent had lodgings somewhere in the locality. Agent Stallion identifies a number of single women in the village."

"And you have concluded what? That agent Ornithologist may have taken lodgings with one of these women? This is your main finding?" He paused to shake spittle from the stem of his pipe onto the floor. "On the Richter scale of earth-shattering deductions, this is a pretty minor tremor, wouldn't you say?" He looked pleased with his metaphor.

I pressed on. "I have noted a reference to a meeting with a contact, codename Bullfrog. Who is this contact?"

"An agent, no longer active."

I waited for some further information about Bullfrog, but none was forthcoming.

"Is this agent contactable?"

"No. As I said, he is no longer active."

After the meeting, I felt deflated. It seemed the Oberst was unimpressed by my powers of deduction, and I wouldn't be asked for any further contributions to the work of Section II. The phrase 'no longer active' rattled around in my head. What did it mean? Retired? Captured? Dead?

The following day the threatened storm broke over the city. Thunder crashed and lightning rippled along the western horizon all day. In section II, it was rumoured that one of Hauptmann von Pfaffel's agents had been recalled from Britain, and by evening the rumour had been confirmed. The dismay on von Pfaffel's face was plain for all to see. Agent 92, codename 'Sandbar', was one of his brightest agents. According to the grapevine, the agent had fallen victim to some unspecified illness, and the gossip machine was soon at work. He operated from the village of Bletchley in Buckinghamshire using the cover name Arthur John Stanley.

Placing this event alongside the disappearance in Ireland of agent Ornithologist, it seemed the overseas operations of the Abwehr were in crisis.

11

August 1940

€arly in August on my way home from work, a stocky man in a full-length black leather coat stepped out in front of me. He asked me for a light. I replied that I didn't smoke, and moved to step past him. He blocked my way.

"Let me pass," I said.

A black car drew up at the curb. A second man, similarly dressed, jumped out of the car and took up a position behind me, cutting off my only escape route.

The first man said, "Get in."

My heart began to race.

I was bundled into the back of the car. One of the men sat beside me; the other drove the car. Gestapo headquarters, the notorious 8 Prinz-Albrecht-Strasse, was less than a kilometre to the west. To my relief, the car turned south, heading away from the city centre. After twenty minutes we stopped outside a house somewhere in the suburbs. I calculated that we were in either Marienfelde or Lichtenrade. I climbed out of the car and waited with one of the men while the other one opened the front door of the house.

I was ushered inside and taken to a room at the back of the building.

One of the men said, "Strip."

I said, "You can't be serious!"

No reaction.

"My uncle is Head of the RSHA," I said, folding my arms. "SS-Gruppenführer Reinhard Heydrich is my uncle."

The second man said, "Remove your clothing."

The first man said, "Or we can do it for you."

I took off my clothes, handing each item to the men. I stopped when I got as far as my underwear.

The Black Orchestra

"All of them," said one of the men.

I handed him my underpants.

They left the room, taking my clothes with them.

The room was lit by a single electric lamp in the ceiling. The floorboards were bare. There was no furniture in the room, apart from three sturdy wooden chairs arranged in a circle under the light. The walls were painted a light yellow. There was a bare window, but it was too dark to see anything outside. The fireplace had been bricked up and plastered over, and there was a dado rail running all around the walls; otherwise, the room was featureless. The three chairs, lit from above, were the only centre of focus.

I sat on one of the chairs, my heart pounding. Then I noticed a dark stain on the floor under my feet, splatter marks on the floor to the left and right. I shuddered. I was sure it was dried blood. I had heard stories of how prisoners in Prinz-Albrecht-Strasse were tortured, and how being stripped was the first step. I could think of nothing that I had done to warrant such treatment. Surely the whole thing was a huge misunderstanding. Sitting naked in that strange and hostile environment, it was difficult to believe I'd make it out of there unscathed. Cold shivers ran across my skin.

I conjured an image of Gudrun's smiling face; Gudrun in her blue dress dancing with Alex. They both looked happy.

Nothing happened for an hour. I shivered as the hairs on my body detected every tiny movement of air in the room. Then the door opened and a third man entered. He sat in one of the chairs facing me. He was short in stature, wearing a light grey suit and matching collarless shirt buttoned to the neck. No tie. Perhaps it was because I knew he was Gestapo, but this man looked to me like Mephistopheles incarnate. His eyes were like tiny pins, set in a face that could have been carved from rock. His expression was blank.

"This is an outrage!" I must have sounded like a character in a French farce; I certainly looked like one.

"I have some questions."

"I am with the Abwehr," I said, my voice a little unsteady. My knees were shaking.

"I know who you are. I need to know what you've been doing."

I said, "I don't understand." There was a neat row of three pens clipped to his breast pocket. It was difficult to imagine this man sitting at a desk, writing.

"You've been observed interfering with the archives at the Abwehr." His tone was casual, conversational.

"That's nonsense—"

"Tell me who you're working for."

"I have no idea what you mean." I tried a sardonic laugh which came out as a pathetic squeak.

"You have been seen interfering with intelligence signals," he said again.

I thought I recognised something in his accent, an echo from my childhood in Ulm. Certain vowels were elongated; a trace of a southern accent. I opened my mouth, but no words came out.

"Tell me," he said.

"I have been checking the signals."

"You suspected that the signals had been altered."

"Just one."

"And what did your check reveal?"

"I was mistaken." I was working hard on my poker face, but his pin-eyes were tearing down my defences.

"You found an altered signal."

"I thought I did, yes."

"You checked it out."

"Yes. I was mistaken."

To anyone watching, the scene would have appeared surreal, even comical: two grown men in conversation, one fully dressed, the other naked as a newborn. But to me, my nakedness was anything but comical. Its effect was profound. First, I felt inferior, like a lower form of life, and second there was the feeling that not only my body, but my soul had been exposed to view; how could I conceal anything from this man?

"Tell me about the altered signal."

"What do you want to know?"

"Date, signal reference."

"I can't remember those details." I thought this a plausible lie. I had no intention of cooperating with this man any more than I had to.

He stood up abruptly and left the room. Gudrun's face drifted back into my mind.

The two leather coats came in. One of the men stepped behind me and held my arms; the other man struck me across the face with his open hand. Before my brain could register surprise, he hit me again, a backhanded slap, on the other side of my face. The chair wobbled, nearly toppling backwards.

"Answer the Sturmbannführer's questions."

I tasted blood. Gudrun's face was gone, replaced by the leather coat of the man in front of me, reflecting the light from the lamp overhead.

"Stand!" the man in front of me said.

I struggled to my feet, my eyes closed, my arms still restrained by the man behind.

"Look at me!" the man in front said. I opened my eyes and lifted my head, and he drove a fist into my stomach. Hard. The man stepped aside just in time to avoid the explosion of vomit that sprayed across the floor.

The two men left the room, leaving me gasping for breath, the acrid taste of vomit in my mouth. I sat. The pain in my gut spread up to my chest. A few minutes passed; the pain began to ease, but nothing I tried would quell the constant tremor in my knees.

Rock-face returned and resumed his seat. "That was a small sample of what we can do."

I wiped blood from my mouth. "Does my uncle know where I am?"

"Your uncle."

"Yes," I said, my voice rising. "My uncle SS-Gruppenführer Reinhard Heydrich."

His facial expression changed into something resembling one of the gargoyles on the cathedral at Ulm.

"That has been tried before," he said. "We are not fools, as you will soon discover."

"I strongly suggest that you check it. He really is my uncle."

"Tell me, have you ever been to Hamburg or Bremen?"

"No."

"Two of Germany's most beautiful Hanseatic cities."

I said nothing. They couldn't blame me for the British bombing, could they?

"And you were happy to let them burn."

"I never—"

"You received intelligence that those two most beautiful cities were to be bombed by the British, and what did you do about it? Nothing. Did you send a warning to those cities?"

Shame engulfed me. I shook my head.

"Do you know how many people were killed by your negligence?"

"No—"

"No. You could have saved hundreds of lives and you did nothing."

"I was following orders," I said, and it felt good to tell the truth.

"Your father was in local government housing," he said.

"Yes." Now where was he going?

"You attended college in Dublin. You studied Mathematics."

These were not questions. He was reciting information from my file.

"Correct."

"It would be a pity if the Reich were to lose a well-educated resource like you."

We agree on something, I thought.

"You are not a Party member, I think."

"No."

"But you attend Party rallies."

"Yes, when I can."

"You love the Führer."

"Of course."

He blinked. Then he said, "You know your duty to the Reich."

He stood up and left the room. I waited for the other two to return and beat me again. The tremor in my limbs and the pounding in my chest increased with each minute that went by.

After perhaps ten minutes, Rock-face came back into the room. He was wearing glasses, now – thick rimmed with light lenses – and they transformed him, giving him a studious, almost kindly look. He could have been a school teacher or a university professor. The pens in his pocket made sense now. He picked up his chair, moved it a half-metre closer, and sat down. We were now very close. I could smell garlic on his breath. I was acutely aware of my nakedness.

He said, "Just answer my questions and you'll have nothing to fear from me."

I said nothing.

"Do you believe that you have nothing to fear from me?"

"I do." *And I believe in Father Christmas, too.*

"Answer my questions and you may go home to your young lady."

I shook my head. "I've done nothing wrong."

He ran his eyes over my body. I knew what was coming next. He pulled one of the pens from his pocket and used it to lift my penis.

Not a pleasant sensation.

He peered at it, examining it as a doctor might. "You're Jewish?"

"No."

"And yet—"

"A medical problem, when I was a child."

"You don't look Jewish."

"I'm not. I'm Lutheran," I said.

"Müller's not a Jewish name, is it?"

"I'm not Jewish."

"And yet, you have the Semitic mutilation."

"I told you, it was a medical problem."

He released my organ and it flopped back onto my thigh. Replacing the pen in his pocket with the others, he reached into another pocket of his jacket, pulled something out and dropped it on my bare knee. It was the beer mat, the one with the diagram on it.

"What do you call this?" he said.

"It's a diagram. It means nothing."

"I can see what it is, and I know what it means," he said, pushing his glasses up the bridge of his nose. "It's high treason. That's what it is. The information on here is enough to hang you."

That was when fear turned to terror. I was sure he was right; that beer mat could seal my fate. The tremor in my knees spread to my whole legs, my torso, my jaw.

"That signal?" he said.

I gave him the signal reference number and date.

"What was in it?"

"The British capacity for the production of aircraft."

"Spitfires?"

I nodded.

"And had it been altered?"

I shook my head violently. One last lie. I had to hold the line there. Admitting that there had been sabotage would open floodgates of further questions.

"Were there other altered signals?"

"No." My voice shook.

"Don't you feel better, now, after telling the truth?"

I tried my only escape route one more time. "—Uncle Reinhard."

"SS-Gruppenführer Heydrich?"

"Uncle Reinhard."

Rock-face left the room. There was silence. I stood up. I stumbled, unsteady on my feet, my teeth chattering. The smell of my own vomit filled my mouth and nose. Listening at the door, I could hear nothing. The night was very dark; the window a mirror, reflecting my bloodied face, my nakedness, the desolate scene in the room.

12

August 1940

One of the leather-clad thugs came back. He handed me my clothes, neatly folded, and I put them on. My hands were still shaking. He led me upstairs to a bathroom. Using the gas-fired water heater over the wash basin, I rinsed my mouth and washed my face and hands. My lip oozed blood. When I emerged from the bathroom, Rock-face was waiting, leaning on the banister at the top of the stairs.

He removed his spectacles. "I'm going to give you more time. The Abwehr is a hotbed of subversive elements, and we *will* have the names of all those guilty of treason against the Reich."

I said nothing. I knew they were going to release me.

"From now on, you work for me, and anything you uncover you must pass on. Do you understand?" he said, raising his voice.

"I understand."

"The penalties for non-compliance will be severe. If I find out that you've been holding out on me, I'll have your eyes. Do I make myself clear?"

"Yes."

They took me to the car. We drove north for forty-five or fifty minutes through the centre of the city and out to Uncle Reinhard's estate.

Uncle Reinhard was waiting for us on the steps of Schloss Gruenwald, wearing a dressing-gown and soft slippers. I fell out of the car; my legs still felt like rubber. The two Gestapo men put their arms under mine, one on each side, frogmarched me into the house, and dumped me in a chair in Reinhard's study. The men left.

Uncle Reinhard said, "You have a cut lip, Kurt. What happened?"

"Three men," I said. "Gestapo. They beat me."

"Did you get any of their names?"

"There was an Sturmbannführer. He didn't give his name."

"Von Kemp. How long were you held?"

"I'm not sure," I said. "I left work at seven o'clock. The journey here took about an hour. What time is it now?"

"Ten thirty. They held you for about two and a half hours."

"It felt longer."

"You should have mentioned my name sooner, Kurt. Well, you'll know the next time."

The next time?

He put a small glass of schnapps in my hands and some fresh logs on the fire. I took a sip and winced as the spirit came in contact with my lip.

"Von Kemp was a little heavy-handed, I think. He is a bit … direct. I will speak with him about his methods."

He let me finish my schnapps and poured me another, before picking up the conversation.

I said, "He asked me if I was a member of an orchestra."

"The Black Orchestra?"

I nodded.

"What did you tell him?"

"I know nothing of this orchestra, and I told him so."

Uncle Reinhard poured a measure of schnapps into his own glass and took a sip. "The Black Orchestra is a very dangerous organisation of subversives and enemy agents, dedicated to undermining the organs of the state. They may even be planning the complete destruction of the Reich."

"By what means?" This was all news to me.

"Their methods are underhand and secret. We have reason to believe that they have infiltrated the security service, itself."

"The RSHA?"

"Possibly. It's more likely that they operate from within the Wehrmacht."

"And their methods?"

"I think you've identified some of their work already, yourself. You found some signals that have been tampered with."

My mind was racing at this point. I decided to stick to my story.

"I suspected that a signal had been tampered with, but I was mistaken."

"But what if you were not mistaken? What if signals from our agents abroad really are being tampered with?" Reinhard offered to top up my glass.

Had I stumbled on the work of subversives? If so, how many other signals might have been tampered with? Had they killed Kleister? Was Schiller in league with Drobol? And how long should I remain silent?

"You must be vigilant, Kurt."

"Yes, Uncle."

"You must remember your duty. Be alert at all times, and if you see anything suspicious, you must report it at once."

Uncle Reinhard's driver was roused from his bed.

Waiting at the door for the driver, my uncle shook my hand in an exaggerated manner. He said, "You must give my regards to Professor Hirsch when you see him."

#

During the journey home, my eyelids drooped. The tremor had subsided to a mere full-body shiver. I had never felt so exhausted. A stray thought kept me awake: What did Uncle Reinhard know of Professor Hirsch, my old mathematics professor in Dublin?

The driver completed the journey in less than fifteen minutes. I had barely closed the car door when he accelerated away with a squeal of burning rubber.

Gudrun opened the door of the apartment as I struggled to put my key in the lock.

"My God, Kurt! Where have you been? I was frantic with worry."

"I was with Uncle Reinhard in Schloss Gruenwald."

She saw my lip. "What happened to you? Have you been in a fight?"

"It's nothing. I'm fine." I stumbled through the door.

"But what happened? Where were you? Do you know what time it is? I was worried."

I selected one of her questions. "I told you. I was with my uncle."

"You should have called to say where you were."

"Sorry, I didn't think."

"Did Reinhard hit you?"

"No. Put the kettle on." I collapsed onto the settee.

"Who then?"

"His men."

"Oh my God, Kurt, you could have been killed."

Gudrun threw a quick meal together, and while I ate I related the events of the night – an abbreviated, expurgated version.

When I had finished, she said, "Why didn't you mention Reinhard's name right at the beginning?"

I woke in the middle of the night, shivering, covered in sweat, but with ice in my veins. Gudrun was not in the bed. I was too hot under the covers. I lay awake, replaying the events of the evening in my mind, trying to shake the vision of von Kemp peering at my cock, the feeling of his pen underneath.

Von Kemp knew a lot about me. Was it possible that he was unaware of my family connection to Reinhard? My head was full of the harrowing stories I'd heard about extreme torture methods used in Prinz-Albrecht-Strasse, but they had handled me with kid gloves. I concluded that they knew about my connection to Heydrich and that was why I was taken to that house in the suburbs instead of Gestapo Headquarters and treated in such a restrained manner.

Gudrun came into the room.

"What time is it?" I said.

"It's late. You were talking in your sleep," Gudrun slid back into the bed.

"What was I saying?"

"I've no idea. It was nothing but gibberish."

She pulled the covers up under her chin. I closed my eyes and the scene of Kleister's death came into my mind. Like a still photograph taken from above, I saw myself looking at the body and Drobol at the door. Kleister was slumped in front of his radio, the bullet hole behind his ear. I realised then that Kleister's death had been an execution – cold and clinical – and I could have suffered the same fate in that empty house in the southern suburbs if it hadn't been for my connection to Uncle Reinhard.

I had suffered a severe shock at the hands of the Gestapo, but, for all his reassuring words, Uncle Reinhard scared me even more. He was the one in charge of the police. I decided it was entirely possible that my uncle had orchestrated the whole episode.

PART 2

13

August, September 1940

The next time that I saw Alex was two weeks after my encounter with the Gestapo, at a Luftschutz Civil Defence operation to evacuate Berlin children to the countryside. It had been at an early Luftschutz recruitment rally that Alex and I first met. As section leaders our job was to ensure that three hundred and seventeen giddy children were labelled and loaded onto their correct trains.

The Blitz had begun a few days earlier. Night after night, our bombers crossed the narrow English Channel, their mission: the total destruction of London. It seemed to me dishonourable to bomb civilian targets, and I said so.

"They started it, at Hamburg and Bremen." Alex replied with some satisfaction. "Now they're getting a taste of their own medicine."

I told Alex about my interrogation by the Gestapo, watching his face. "They knew about the altered signal. They accused me of altering it."

"My God, Kurt, how did they know about that?" he said.

I said nothing, but the look I gave him would have curdled butter.

He stared at me in amazement, or feigned amazement. "We're friends, aren't we?"

Two girls came up to me. I checked their labels. One was for the north, the other for the north west. The girls asked if they could stay together and I took a moment to explain why that wasn't possible. They embraced and joined their lines.

Alex said, "You think I'd rat on a friend? I swear to you, Kurt, I never told them anything. Someone in the tavern must have been listening."

"I don't think so."

When all the children were on board I played my trump card.

"They had the fucking diagram."

"Christ! How the hell did they get that?" Alex was all wide-eyed and innocent-looking. "Anyway, the diagram was nothing."

"Tell that to the Gestapo," I said.

"I swear to you, Kurt, I never gave it to them."

I walked away. I knew he was lying.

Alex and I avoided each other for a while after that. I knew I couldn't trust him with any sensitive information, but it seemed best to continue the appearance of friendship. I said nothing to Gudrun about his betrayal.

#

Gudrun shook me awake at 5 am. I had suffered a nightmare, but my memory of it quickly evaporated. I was left bathed in sweat, with a pounding heart and a splitting headache. Gudrun put the kettle on. There was something on my mind, some half-thought or memory in my subconscious. I had no idea what it was, but I knew it was important. After about thirty minutes, the submerged memory broke the surface.

I know who altered that signal.

I arrived at work that morning before 8 am. Siegfried the night watchman was still on duty. Scanning the signatures in the doorman's security log, the backward-sloping handwriting with the comical capital "B" was not difficult to find. My suspicion was confirmed; it was the hand of the Head of Section I, Technical & Signals, Oberst Bernhardt Schiller!

The implications of this discovery were shattering. It seemed Schiller was a subversive, altering intelligence signals and doing who knew what other damage to the war effort. Was this why he had reacted so violently to my revelations about Kleister's death? I considered taking my discovery to someone in Abwehr senior management. But who could I trust?

After several days of thought, I wrote a short anonymous note, addressed to Admiral Canaris, the supreme commander of the Abwehr, head of all military intelligence. I specified the number and date of the altered signal, and named Oberst Schiller as the perpetrator. I sent the note through the internal post.

The shivering in my bones subsided, but my sleep continued to be erratic.

Toward the end of the month, our largest battleship, *Bismarck*, was launched. Newspaper and radio reports about the ship continued for three days. I took no pleasure in the announcements.

On the night of August 25, the British RAF dropped several bombs on the outskirts of Berlin. Lying in bed, Gudrun and I could hear the drone of the aeroplanes, the thump thump of anti-aircraft batteries and the dull thud of distant explosions. Gudrun was frightened. I was a little apprehensive myself, but I assured her that the bombs were nowhere near us. In the morning, the newspapers dismissed the raid as ineffectual, but it was clear that a new chapter had been started in the war.

There was no reaction to my note. September arrived, and the tremor in my hands persisted. It was barely visible, but I could feel it. Nightmares plagued my sleep, and during the day I was constantly on the lookout for the State Police. Every sharp tone, every raised voice, startled me. Even a furtive glance from a stranger was enough to trigger my paranoia. The simplest of tasks became an ordeal. Using a ration card to buy a loaf of bread from my local baker meant a tension-filled journey across Horst Wessel Platz followed by a dash for the safety of the apartment; a trip to the barber was like the Odyssey. I felt safest in crowded places, and yet found the U-bahn unbearable, trams and buses less so. The city became like a vast desert, the apartment and the office my two principal oases.

Early in the month, Gudrun handed me a note from her contact in the OKW. It read: 'Signal 40/En/733. Date received: 11 April, 1940. RAF estimate a production rate of 2,000 air defence aircraft per month at full capacity. Source War Office, London.'

The British aircraft production figure had been altered on this version of the signal, too.

At this point I must admit that, thanks to the brutality of the Gestapo and a lack of reaction to my anonymous note, I had lost all interest in altered signals.

The Abwehr resembled an ants' nest; everyone had a job to do, and everything revolved around Admiral Canaris – the "queen" of our colony. Although seldom seen, we always knew – as if by some special sense – whether or not he was in the building.

For three days in September, the Admiral was missing. Rumour was that he had been called away by the Supreme Command of the OKW for a review of our performance. For those three days, the Abwehr was like an ant colony under attack. Orders were given and revoked or countermanded soon after; tempers flared; petty squabbles arose on every floor.

#

Almost exactly a month after my meeting with von Neumann, I was summoned by Oberst Schiller.

"I've spoken with Neumann," he said. "He's told me of the excellent work you did on the case of that missing agent. He's requested that you be re-assigned to his Section for a trial period, effective immediately."

He obviously wanted to get rid of me. I was chilled, thinking of Kleister's body, the wound behind his headphones glistening with blood.

"Thank you, Herr Oberst," I said. His smile was warm, but I wasn't fooled. I knew I was talking to a subversive, a suspected member of the evil Black Orchestra, and a traitor to the Third Reich. As he spoke I searched his eyes for signs of treachery. I saw none.

"You'll continue to work for me on a part-time basis, until such time as I can find a replacement."

I emptied my desk into a cardboard box and moved upstairs to the third floor, where I presented myself to Oberst von Neumann the spymaster in his submariner's jumper, the pipe clamped between his teeth.

"Come in, Herr Müller. Welcome to the madhouse," said the Oberst. "I think I mentioned at our meeting in Schiller's office that Hauptmann von Pfaffel is overburdened with work. I'd like you to take over some of the Hauptmann's workload."

"I am to operate agents in enemy territory?"

He grinned. The expression on my face must have been comical. "Not enemy territory, Kurt. You have an intimate knowledge of the Irish Republic. You will take over the day-to-day operation of the three agents currently working there. Ireland is a neutral country, after all, hardly enemy territory."

There was that spine-tingling sensation again.

"I am honoured, Herr Oberst."

"Yes, well, don't let me down. If all goes well I'll expect you to assume total command of all field operations in the Republic of Ireland, and you may be considered for a promotion to the rank of Oberleutnant."

I was elated by this news. Leutnant was a fine rank for someone of my age, considering I had nothing but basic military training; Oberleutnant was a serious promotion.

The Oberst took me to my new office. The room was tiny. It had been created by means of a hollow plaster wall that bisected one of the windows. There was just one desk.

Squeezing between the wall and the desk I sat down. The chair welcomed me with a squeak.

As he was leaving, the Oberst said: "Agent Ornithologist is your first priority. See if you can come up with a plan to find him, and his equipment."

Apart from the clamour of my own heartbeat in my ears and the squeaky chair, there was no sound. I knew I was facing a difficult future, and it filled me with apprehension; there were so many unknown factors. I knew nothing about field espionage operations, and even less about military intelligence. I had no knowledge of the British war machine. What did I know of Irish attitudes to the British? To the war? Toward Germany? I suspected from something

Uncle Reinhard had said, that the Wehrmacht were hopeful they could tap into the traditional Irish hatred of the British through contact with the IRA, but I had no knowledge of the IRA, and no idea how to contact them. And finally, I wondered whether my illustrious uncle had engineered this, my latest promotion, as he had my last.

14

September 1940

Gudrun did a small dance around the kitchen table; then she hugged me. The gramophone was playing *The Ride of the Valkyries*, which seemed appropriate. "An Oberleutnant, at your age!" She turned the volume up. "We must go out and celebrate."

Immediately, our neighbour began hammering on the wall.

I crossed to the gramophone and turned the volume down. "I'm still a Leutnant, Gudrun. My promotion hasn't happened yet, and will depend on how well I do. I might make a complete strudel of it."

"You'll have to get yourself some new clothes." She hugged me again.

"What's wrong with the clothes I have?"

"How can you expect to make anything of yourself, dressed like an undesirable?"

She rang Alex and Johann and we arranged to meet.

"Herr Oberleutnant Müller," Alex greeted me, "many congratulations."

A month had passed since our last meeting but I was still furious with him for what he did.

I said, "Not yet. Still just plain old Leutnant."

Alex slapped me on the back. "This could be the start of a meteoric career."

"That hurt," I said.

Johann said, "Smile, Kurt. We're celebrating your good fortune."

"This has fuck all to do with good fortune," Alex said. "This man has talent, right down to his fingertips."

"Don't be stupid, Alex," I said, throwing him a glance that told him exactly where he stood.

We walked south to the market at Kreuzberg. Even at this late hour, the stalls were still open, the scene alive with throngs of people. We mingled with the crowd, strolling between the stalls, picking through racks of clothing. I bought a draught excluder in the shape of a long, thin Dachshund and Johann bought an identical one for their apartment.

At a stall selling charms I bought two new charms for Gudrun's bracelet – an eagle and an iron cross. She was delighted.

Alex was in great form, acting his part. He beamed at every passer by.

Playing along, I said, "You look like the cat that got the cream."

"I am," he said. "I heard from my mother last night. The Eugenics Court has heard my brother's case. The decision's been reversed. The court ruled Eugen's condition 'non-malignant' whatever that means. His name has been removed from their sterilisation list."

"That's wonderful news," I said, and I meant it.

Johann said, "Don't forget to thank your man in the Ministry of Health for his help."

I glared at Alex again, raising an eyebrow that said, *I thought that was supposed to be our secret.*

Alex gave me a sheepish grin. "There are no secrets between Johann and me."

It occurred to me then that Alex might have told Johann about the altered signal; what if Alex had taken the beer mat home and Johann had found it? Maybe Alex was innocent, after all; perhaps Johann was the one who sold me out to the Gestapo.

Before we left the market, I used some of my clothing coupons to buy a dark blue overcoat. Then Gudrun and Johann found me a black leather briefcase, "to complete the disguise," as Johann put it.

Gudrun stood back and looked me up and down. "Now you look like someone important."

Alex laughed. "Why do I keep wanting to hand you my papers for inspection?"

We had a meal at an outside table. The old Kaiser summer was dying; autumn, the young pretender, was impatient for the throne. It was still warm, but the breeze was a little strong; Gudrun kept her shoulders covered.

Later, we found a bar. The beer was expensive, the music loud. Johann and Gudrun danced, and then Gudrun and I. It was fun, but I could tell from the expression on Gudrun's face that my performance on the dance floor didn't match my performance in the bedroom.

"How can someone with such small hands have such big feet?" she shouted above the music. Not my proudest moment.

Alex took a turn with Gudrun. I tried talking to Johann, but we couldn't hear one another above the music. I watched him for a while. He seemed to be enjoying himself like everyone else, but I wondered what dark machinations were simmering behind those doe eyes. Then Alex sat down and Gudrun and Johann danced together again. A surge of emotion washed over me. As I watched her, I wanted to sing, to sweep her in my arms, to declare my love out loud.

Alex handed me his empty glass, pointed to the bar, and the spell was broken.

When the bar closed, at 2 am we wandered the streets like four homeless vagabonds. I marvelled at how many people – couples for the most part – were still up and about in the city at that late hour. We passed through Leopold Platz with its elaborate wrought iron lampposts. Near the bottom of Leopold Strasse we came upon a late-night bar and Johann suggested we go inside.

"We are celebrating the promotion of my best friend," Alex called out to some strangers passing by in the street, adopting his Quasimodo pose – shoulder raised, head to one side, eyes half closed, tongue sticking out.

To avoid any further embarrassment, we entered the bar and the drinking started again. We had a couple of rounds of beer. Then we moved to a table under a canopy in the open. Gudrun said she wanted no more beer. I think she meant to say that she wanted no more alcohol, but Johann ordered a round of schnapps. After those, it was my turn to order, and before we'd finished that round, Alex ordered another. And so it went for another two hours or so.

#

Gudrun was the first to notice that something was wrong. A group of seven men in uniform was advancing up the street toward us, shouting and jeering. As they came closer I could see that their attention was focused on a man in civilian clothes, clutching a leather briefcase. There was nothing remarkable about this man. He was middle-aged, balding, wearing spectacles. His suit was dark, and he had on a red tie. Apart from his clothing there was nothing to distinguish the one man from the other seven. The mob – for that's what they were – half-pushed, half-carried the man before them. My first thought was that he might have been a Jew, but I couldn't see the six-pointed star anywhere on his clothing. As they drew level with us, I could see the expression of terror on his face. It was the worst thing I had ever seen – worse even than the sight of Kleister's dead body. I stood up, clenching my fists; the impulse to intervene was intense.

Alex pulled me back into my seat.

"Sit still," he hissed. "Don't interfere. You can do nothing."

The feeling of helplessness was overpowering; like a powerful narcotic, it drew the strength from my legs, the blood from my face. I looked at the others. Alex was staring fixedly into the café, away from the scene; Gudrun was sobbing, her face buried in her hands; Johann was smirking, laughing.

The procession passed by, heading toward Leopold Platz. I turned to Johann and said, "You found that amusing?"

"A Special Unit tidying-up operation," he said. "Obviously a criminal of some kind."

We all knew of the Special Operation Units, the *Einsatzgruppen*, but I had never seen them in action. These units were the brutal cutting edge of Heydrich's RSHA, armed groups of policemen, Waffen-SS and volunteer vigilantes, with a free hand to dispense justice on the streets.

Johann continued to extol the work of the Special Units. He spoke with passion about "natural justice" and "people power."

When Alex joined in with, "We will cleanse the streets of all undesirables!" I burst out,

"What right does any citizen have to judge another? Isn't that why we have judges and advocates and courts? Isn't every man innocent until proven guilty in a court of law?"

Johann grinned. He said nothing. Alex gave me a pitying look and said, "The courts are too slow, the outcome too uncertain. This way justice can be swift and sure." I opened my mouth to object, but he continued, "I'm sure the courts will be re-established once the Reich has triumphed, once the Fatherland has been rebuilt."

This was a side of Alex that I hadn't seen before. I considered reminding him of his own brother's narrow escape at the hands of a similar court, but I said nothing.

Gudrun's eyes were red and swollen. "Where were they taking him?" No one answered her.

At last, at the end of the long night, we split up. Gudrun and I headed north, Johann and Alex west. In Leopold Platz, we found the man's briefcase, its contents scattered and blowing about in the wind. I picked up one piece of paper. It was an invoice headed "Hoffmann's Drapery".

We found the man hanging from one of the elaborate wrought iron lampposts. The square was deserted.

Uncle Reinhard was on my mind for the rest of the evening. The Special Operations Units acted under his authority. I thought I knew the man, his wife, his three young children. How was it possible for such a devoted family man to preside over such brutal operations?

That was the night when I finally rejected my uncle, his Nazi Party and everything they stood for. The brutality, the twisted propaganda, the persecution of the Communists and the Jews. As long as the country was at war I would continue with my work, but I wanted no part of Adolf Hitler's vision for Germany.

And from that night something new was added to my nightmares – the image of a small man, missing one shoe, hanging from a lamppost, his feet swaying gently in the breeze.

15

September 1940

When I awoke, my head was throbbing, the bitter memory of Uncle Reinhard's lynch-mob weighing on my mind. The tremor had returned to my hands, a pain like sharp needles behind my eyes. I was now convinced that it must have been Johann who told the Gestapo about the altered signal. Alex's declaration that "there are no secrets between Johann and me" left little room for doubt.

Gudrun lay on the bed on her back fully clothed, clutching her handbag, snoring. I drank a half-litre of water before leaving the apartment and another half-litre at my desk. The squeak from my chair seemed louder, more irritating than usual. I groaned and vowed never to get drunk again.

Hauptmann Edwin von Pfaffel, deputy to spymaster Oberst von Neumann and the man who ran all the spies in Britain and Ireland, was about thirty-five years old, prematurely grey, his face a map of worry-lines. His office looked as if it had been hit by a tornado, the desk, the floor and every available surface covered in bundles of files and papers.

He glanced at me, said nothing, ran a hand through his hair, lit a cigarette, and threw the spent match in the general direction of his overflowing ashtray.

"Oberst von Neumann asked me to give you these." He slammed a small bundle of yellow files on the desk.

"Thank you." I picked them up. There were three files.

"Don't thank me, Leutnant," he snapped. "This was not my idea."

I couldn't understand his attitude. I would have thought he'd be grateful for some help, given his workload.

I left the Hauptmann fuming in his office, closed the door of my tiny office, squeezed around behind my desk and read the agents' files one by one.

Agent 223, codename Stallion, located in Cork since December 20, 1939. He worked in the Cork steel factory and most of his intelligence concerned the logistics of steel production. There were strong connections between the Irish steel operation and British Steel, and he had been able to provide various titbits of information which shed light on the British capacity to produce war materials. He was also the agent who had investigated Ornithologist's disappearance.

Agent 257, Slingshot, deployed February 10, 1940 by U-boat off the north west coast of Donegal. Reported by Agent Ornithologist to have been captured February 11, 1940 and interned. Report confirmed: Irish Foreign Office, March 1940.

Agent 316, Nightingale. This file contained just one page. There was no indication of the agent's name or address, and no record to show where he worked apart from the single word: 'Dublin'. There were no training records, and his photograph was grainy and out of focus. I wouldn't have been able to recognise the man from this picture, even if he were standing right in front of me.

I went in search of Oberst von Neumann, and asked him why there was so little information in the file about Agent Nightingale. He replied that the agent was so successful that his personal details and photograph had been expunged from the records.

He said, "You could check his Blue file."

I looked questioningly at the Oberst and he explained, "Blue files are highly classified. Generalmajor Oster has custody of those."

Admiral Canaris was the titular Head of the Abwehr, and Generalmajor Oster was his second-in-command. The three Section Heads – the Obersts – reported to Oster, while the Generalmajor, and he alone, reported to the Admiral. In effect, Oster ran the organisation, deferring to Admiral Canaris only on matters of policy.

The Oberst said, "For now, the first order of business is to introduce you to Heinz Franzelberg."

I'd never heard the name before. "Heinz is one of your men?" My head was pounding, my eyes burning. I made a silent vow never to drink alcohol again. Not for any reason. Not ever.

"No, not exactly. Heinz is a sort of free agent. He provides all sorts of services to the three sections of the Abwehr."

It seemed improbable for one man to provide services to three sections as diverse in their operations as Technical & Signals, Overseas Operations and Domestic Intelligence.

"Heinz can do almost anything. If you need something found, Heinz will find it. If you need to lose something, Heinz can make it disappear. If you need information, Heinz will know where to go and who to ask. Heinz is a genius."

Heinz Franzelberg arrived at my desk that afternoon. He was a small man in his sixties, with hooded eyes and a full set of very white, even teeth which I thought must be false. His large flat nose looked as if it had been broken several times, and seemed to occupy more than its share of his face, as if it had been sewn on badly, by Baron von Frankenstein himself. He had a strong head of black hair – almost certainly dyed.

"Von Neumann said you wanted to see me." He spoke with a slight lisp.

I told him I'd been put in charge of the agents in Ireland. He waited for more information, but I said nothing further. I was uncomfortable with the situation; I wasn't sure how much this man – who was a civilian, after all – knew about the current operations of the Abwehr.

He said, "First, you should find out what each of your agents' objectives are. Second, how do they operate? Agents can have many functions, sabotage, intelligence gathering and so on. In Ireland, spreading unrest, perhaps. Some agents work outdoors, with binoculars and such-like, others get their information by insinuating themselves into industry or the organs of the state. If you're really lucky, you may have some with positions of responsibility in government or the armed services."

"You mean the *British* armed services."

"Yes, ideally, but the Irish armed services probably share a lot of information with the British. They are close neighbours, after all."

I said, "I'm familiar with short wave radio transmissions, encryption and so on. I'm assuming that the diplomatic bags are used for low level stuff, like weather reports."

"Oh no." He treated me to a buck-toothed smile. "Weather reports are critically important and have a short useful life. What use is information that there was a gale blowing over the Atlantic yesterday?"

"I've heard the agents are trained in commando warfare. Is that true?"

"It's pretty thorough. They cover armed and unarmed combat, use of the transmitter, Morse code, language training and local customs – that sort of thing – map reading, parachute jumping, sabotage and so on. All of the training is carried out at Brandenburg an der Havel."

"What do you know of Agent 375, Ornithologist?"

"I heard he disappeared. Nothing more."

"Have you worked overseas on Abwehr business yourself?" I asked.

"Yes, I've worked in Cambridge and Hertfordshire." He switched into English. "But never in Ireland. My English is pretty good."

His English was indeed excellent, his accent almost perfect.

When Heinz had gone, Oberst von Neumann came by my office again. "I forgot to tell you that Heinz has a criminal record for bribery, extortion, dealing in stolen goods, among other things. But don't be too alarmed. Since he started working for the Abwehr, his criminal activities have all been sanctioned by the Reich."

16

September 1940

The very next day, I was recalled to the Translations Unit in Section I to help with a sudden influx of signals. Word had come through from military headquarters that the date of Operation Sealion had been put back and a new secret plan for the Eastern Front was under discussion. The increased workload was the result. For three whole weeks I was occupied with Wehrmacht signals dealing with this new, secret Operation 'Barbarossa'.

Throughout this period, whenever I had occasion to visit the archive, I kept an eye out for any other signals in Oberst Schiller's hand. I was convinced that there must be others, but I found none. Tight-lipped and wide-eyed, Speddig the owl watched my every move. He continued to lord it over me even though I clearly outranked him since my promotion to the spymasters' section.

A month had gone by since I had sent the anonymous note to Admiral Canaris and Oberst Schiller hadn't been arrested. As far as I could tell, he hadn't even been questioned. I was perplexed, but determined to continue my investigation alone.

Remaining in the office one evening until everyone else had gone home, I tried Oberst Schiller's door and found it unlocked. My heart in my mouth, I slipped inside. His room was tidy, with just a few papers in his in- and out-trays. I checked these and found nothing of interest. The desk drawers were locked, as were his filing cabinets, but there was a cupboard standing against one wall which was not locked. The doors moaned as they swung open. I listened for a moment. There was no reaction from Siegfried at his desk down just one flight of stairs.

It was a stationery cupboard, and I searched it eagerly, hoping – expecting – to find bundles of duplicate pre-numbered three-part signal pads. There were none.

#

On September 17 Operation Sealion was put on indefinite hold, and the volume of signals traffic began to return to normal.

A few days later, I presented my proposal for the recovery of Agent Ornithologist, his transmitter and his priceless Enigma machine. My plan was to send the shadowy agent Nightingale from Dublin to investigate.

Oberst von Neumann read the document, his face turning red. When he had finished, his head resembled a beetroot with hair. He glared at me.

"This will not do, Müller!" he roared. "Nightingale may not be used for a mission like this. Our best agent in Ireland must never be put at risk."

"Not even for the recovery of a missing Enigma machine, Herr Oberst?"

"Not for anything. Not even if the life of the Führer himself were at stake. Do you understand?" He threw my document at me across the desk. "You'll have to come up with something better than that. Think about it and give me something by this afternoon. No need to re-type it, just give me a verbal report by three o'clock."

I came away from that meeting deflated once again. In hindsight, the use of Nightingale must surely have been considered – and rejected – by von Pfaffel and Oberst von Neumann before I came up with the idea. It was not the brilliant scheme that I thought it was. I felt stupid. I had no idea what other course of action I could suggest. I closed my office door to eliminate distractions, and thought about it for an hour. Nothing came to me. Not a spark, not a glimmer of an idea. I felt like a drowning man.

I spoke with Hauptmann von Pfaffel in his office.

"My proposal was rejected."

"Were you given a reason why?" He seemed to accept me as an equal now, and I suspected he was glad of my help. I took his sheepish smile as an unspoken apology.

"No reason. The only effective agent we have in Ireland—"

"Nightingale."

"Apparently Nightingale is too precious to risk on this operation."

"He is an exceptional agent." Was that the hint of a smirk on the Hauptmann's face?

"Yes, so this mission should be quite simple for him." I spread my hands, still clinging to my sinking life raft.

"I can understand the reluctance to use him. If we lost Nightingale, field operations in Ireland would be at an end."

"Could we send in one of your agents, Hauptmann? You must have someone who could travel to Ireland undetected. Someone in Northern Ireland, perhaps?"

Von Pfaffel frowned. "Out of the question. I can't afford to risk any of my agents. We're under pressure to perform in Britain, as it is. Imagine what would happen if I risked one of my agents and he didn't return. We'd both end up in a labour camp."

I rang Heinz Franzelberg at his home and he agreed to meet me in the office. As soon as he arrived I explained my problem. "I thought we could send one of our other agents to investigate."

"Sounds like a good plan." He flashed his perfect teeth at me.

"I thought so, but when I proposed it, the idea was rejected."

I must have looked crestfallen at this point, for Heinz assumed a sorrowful demeanour in sympathy. "Did they say why?"

"Not really. I gather it's too risky."

"So, you know what you must propose."

Now I really was feeling stupid. Heinz was telling me that the solution to the problem was right under my nose.

"You don't mean…?"

He threw his head back and laughed.

17

September 1940

"How can you be a field agent?" Gudrun was making pastry. She had flour in her hair and on her nose. She looked comical – lovely, but comical. She put down her rolling pin. "What do know about spying?"

"I won't be a field agent. I just need to go back to Ireland to sort out a few problems."

"Couldn't they send someone else?"

"I have to go myself."

She wiped her hands on a damp cloth and blew her nose loudly. "Will it be dangerous?"

"I know the country well. There should be no danger."

The first part of this statement was true. The second was no more than a fervent hope.

"When are you going?"

"The trip hasn't been approved yet, but if it is…I'm not sure. Some time in the next few months, I expect." Another imponderable.

Our love-making that night was fiery. Our passions were aroused by the thought of being apart, and she kept me waiting longer than usual. When, at last, we coupled, I took her with the ferocity of a wild beast. It was all over in a matter of seconds.

Afterwards, I lay panting by her side. She wrapped her arm around my chest and clung to me like a drowning sailor in a vast ocean.

"You're worried about this trip to Ireland, aren't you?" she said.

"No, I'm just a little tired."

I was tired, but I was also quite apprehensive about the trip. I had never even seen a U-boat, and the prospect of travelling in one filled me with anxiety, tinged, I suppose, with a boyish excitement.

"Well you should be. You realise that if the authorities catch you, they'll lock you up until the war's over."

"They won't catch me."

"And what if you're captured by the British? The British shoot spies."

"I'm not going to get shot."

"You might. The Gestapo might shoot you."

"In Ireland?"

"Where better? You won't have Reinhard's protection over there."

That's true, I thought. I said, "I don't think there are many Gestapo in Ireland."

"It takes only one."

"Ah, but they say the Gestapo always work in pairs." I laughed.

"The Irish might shoot you," she said, quietly.

"The Irish police don't carry weapons."

"It's not the police I'm worried about. What about the Irish Republicans? From what I've read about them, they have plenty of weapons, and they seem a trigger-happy bunch."

"They're harmless." In reality, I knew nothing about Irish subversives.

"What would I do if I lost you?" she whispered.

"You won't lose me."

Of course I knew that she might. I had a small inkling of the perils that I was facing. And I was sure there were many others beyond my imagination.

"You might not come back. U-boats are dangerous. The British hunt them and send them to the bottom of the sea."

"You *won't* lose me." I said again, with emphasis.

After that we lay together in silence.

#

The following day, Speddig appeared at my office door. "There's someone at the reception desk asking for you."

It was Kleister's sister, Tania Schaefer. Unencumbered by veil and sombre clothing she was a delight. Small and dark, with large eyes and a smile as broad as the Moser valley.

I found her chatting with Sigmund the doorman, clearly smitten, his usual gruff expression replaced by a simpering grin. I signed out and took her to the nearest beer cellar. We ordered coffee.

While we waited to be served Tania told me that she was studying music at the Dresden conservatoire.

"What instrument?" I had noticed that her hands were long and slim.

"I play the cello."

"And what of Herr Schaefer?"

"He was killed in action in Norway." A fleeting shadow passed over her eyes.

When the coffee arrived, Tania asked me if I had any further information about her brother's death. I told her the police were satisfied that he had taken his own life; the case was closed.

"And what about you? What do you think?" she asked.

"I think he was murdered, but I don't know why or by whom."

"I've learnt that another Abwehr Signalman died the day before Tristan, in the Leipzig office."

"Where did you get that information?" I glanced around nervously; the conversation was sliding into political quicksand.

"I'm from Saxony. I have contacts in Leipzig. The information wasn't difficult to come by."

"Then you'll know this man's name?"

"Gustav Barnard. I believe he left a suicide note."

So it was suicide. I had wondered.

"What about Tristan, did he leave a note?" she said.

"No. That was one of the reasons why I don't believe your brother took his own life."

"And the other reasons?"

"I'd rather not get into that," I said.

"Don't give me that shit!" she hissed. "I've had nothing but obstruction and evasion from every government agency from Berlin to Leipzig and back again."

"I'm sorry—"

"Sorry's no good to me, you...*pissenlit!*" She raised her voice. Heads were turning; people were watching. "I need to know what really happened to my brother. Can't you understand that? Why can't anybody understand?"

She paused for breath and I said, "I *was* disappointed with the KRIPO investigation. It seemed to me they settled on suicide far too easily. It was almost as if—"

"As if they didn't want to find the truth." Her eyes lit up in the gloom.

I sipped my coffee, my silence intended as an affirmation of her last suggestion. Her temper cooled as quickly as it had flared, and just as quickly, those at the bar lost interest in us.

We spent a few minutes swapping stories about Tristan. At the door of the beer cellar, we shook hands.

"I'll not rest until I've uncovered Tristan's killer," she said, a grim expression on her face.

"Be careful, Tania. If he was murdered and you get too close, you could be placing yourself in mortal danger."

"I realise that, but I have to know. I won't rest until I find out what really happened to my baby brother."

That conversation left a bad taste in my mouth. Desperate to find someone to blame for her brother's death, it seemed Tania considered everybody in the Abwehr culpable. And in truth I felt a measure of guilt, as my silence had contributed to the cover-up.

18

September 1940

The next morning there were minor floods on many of the streets of Berlin. For the first time in living memory the trams ceased operating. I walked to work.

"Can you tell me what are the operational objectives for agents in Ireland?" I asked von Pfaffel.

"Sounds like you've been taking to Franzelberg," he said. "Well, let me see. In the first place, the Irish have a long tradition of hostility toward the British. The British have been a force in occupation in Ireland for many centuries. Second, it may be possible to arm the IRA and, with a little intelligent organisation, they could form a fighting unit to distract the British and divert British military resources from their war effort.

"The Republic of Ireland shares a land border with the British which could be useful for sabotage activities. And as you know, the Irish are stupid. We may expect them to do whatever we ask of them without question. In any event, the Irish will do anything for money."

I thought these last two points were well wide of the mark. I had met some stupid Irishmen – certainly – but to paint the whole race with such a broad brush was nonsense. And as for the last point, I saw this as blatant arrogance.

That evening, I sent a request to Generalmajor Oster's office for sight of the Blue files for Agents Nightingale and Ornithologist. And the day after that I paid a visit to the shops and bought myself a new suit. It had to be altered – I was nothing but skin and bone – and it was a week before I received it. Gudrun was pleased with my choices of material and style, although she said she felt the epaulettes on the shoulders were a little outmoded.

Next, I requested the operational files of agents in training who were earmarked for possible placement in Ireland. There were just three of these.

The first was a circus strongman – Martin Gertz – who had spent some time in Ireland before the war. His English was better than average. The file noted that he could neither read nor write. He was 62 years of age.

The second was a retired diplomat who served in German West Africa and various other African territories. His name was Ebenezer Diehl. His English was passable, but at 77 I thought he was too old to be much use as an active field agent.

The third looked to me a likely candidate for the work. He was 24 years old, and had served three years in the British Merchant Navy. His name was Fritz Dieter Blesset.

19

October 1940

One Monday morning in early October, I found a note on my desk ordering me to report to the spymaster, Oberst von Neumann.

"With regard to the recovery of Agent Ornithologist and his equipment, your request to travel to Ireland has been rejected." Before I could react, he continued, "You must realise by now, that Abwehr operations in Ireland have been sadly lacking. We have placed four agents in the field, and they're a sorry bunch."

"There's Nightingale," I said, probing. I had failed to find out any more about the agent than what was on the single sheet in his file, and my request for sight of his blue file had disappeared into the blue yonder.

"Ah yes, there is Nightingale, of course. Would that we had more agents like him in the field."

"And Stallion, in the steel works in Cork."

"Stallion is a poor fool. He thinks he's a wonderful agent, but in reality, his information is next to worthless."

I said nothing. I had understood that Stallion's figures on the steel production from both the Cork factory and British Steel were vitally useful.

"Field operations in Ireland are your responsibility now, Kurt. And you must see what a disaster they've been in the past." I opened my mouth to respond, but he rushed on, "We have lost agents and equipment. Some agents have been captured before they could send back any intelligence. Large amounts of money have been spent without any return. Little or no information is coming back, and when transmissions are received, the quality of the information is poor. I mean, it would be funny if it were not so laughable."

I nodded obediently like a good little Leutnant. He was not to be stopped in his flow.

The Black Orchestra

"You've heard about 'Radio Free Ireland', I suppose."

I shook my head.

"It was last year. The IRA requested a powerful transmitter, and we sent one over." He waved a hand in the air, as if swatting an invisible fly. "The Irish used it to set up an illegal radio station. They sent out daily anti-British propaganda for about three weeks, until they were caught."

"Three weeks?" I tried not to laugh. "And the transmitter…?"

"Confiscated. The whole miserable episode was an unmitigated disaster. And nothing would please the SS more than to be able to demonstrate serious fault in our organisation. That might provide Himmler with a pretext for a takeover."

He slapped the table. "And we're making it easy for them. The Propaganda Ministry has a similar agenda. I'm sure you realise there's no love lost between Joseph Goebbels and Admiral Canaris. And there's great rivalry between Reichsmarschall Göring and Generalfeldmarschall Keitel. How Göring would love his Air Ministry to take over a significant part of the Field Marshal's empire. We are at the front line, here, Müller. It's up to us to keep these wolves from the door."

"It seems to me," I said diffidently, "that many of our problems – perhaps all of them – arise from the training. We recruit civilians and quickly train them as agents. Agents are placed in situations beyond their competence. Also, I have questions about the quality of the recruits – some of those on file appear ready for a geriatric home."

"An old man may still be heroic." He smoothed his grey hair indignantly. He ordered me to go to Brandenburg and conduct a review of the training there. "Not a formal review; report back to me in confidence."

"Very well, Herr Oberst." I got up to leave.

"Before you go…" he said, and I sat down again. "The Propaganda Ministry has been in contact. They have started a search for a war hero, someone that they can present as a model to the German people. They'll be sending a man round to find a suitable candidate."

"But surely the Abwehr is the last place they should be looking. Our agents can't be identified publicly."

"Yes, yes. I agree with you, Kurt, but Propaganda are not to be dissuaded. You will co-operate fully with their man when he arrives, but make sure that he finds out nothing important."

My cup of misery was overflowing. The Oberst seemed to be asking me to turn straw into gold; my trip to Ireland had been rejected, and I was to be lumbered with a visitor from the hated Ministry of Propaganda and Public Enlightenment.

#

Toward the end of the month I received a letter in the office, postmarked Leipzig. The handwriting was big, sweeping, full of energy.

Dear Kurt,

Just a quick note to say that I've been busy. I obtained a copy of Gustav Barnard's suicide note from the Medical Examiner's Office in Leipzig. I've managed to trace Barnard's parents. They have a farm near Lunzenau in Mittelsachsen. I'm going out there tomorrow to see them. I'll write again if I learn anything useful.

Your friend,
Tania Schaefer

There was no return address on the letter or the envelope.

I was simultaneously amazed and apprehensive, amazed at what she had done and apprehensive about how the authorities might react if they found out.

20

November 1940

Alex rang. He said he had something he needed to discuss, urgently. We agreed to meet in a beer cellar.

Alex wolfed his food down. I had never seen him eat like this before. Gone was his slow sensual enjoyment of the experience, his careful hoarding of that final morsel; this meal was devoured heedlessly and in haste. He finished his food before I did, and then sat in silence, watching the waitresses rush about clutching bundles of frothing beer steins.

"Were you really that hungry?" I asked him.

There was no response.

"You said you had something to discuss."

"Not important," he muttered, shaking his head.

If this was some kind of joke, it was not up to his usual standard.

I finished my food. We settled the bill and Alex set off at a brisk pace with me in tow. We kept to the main streets. As we walked he kept looking over his shoulder, like a man with a guilty secret.

"What's the matter, Alex?"

"I think they're watching me."

"Who?"

"Who do you think?"

"Why?" I sounded like a broken gramophone record. Alex was making no sense. In peacetime, I would have been laughing out loud at his performance.

His voice dropped. "Have you ever heard of 'Boniface'?"

I shook my head. "What is it? A code word for something?"

"Yes. It's British and it's top secret. What about Bletchley?"

After a moment's thought, I remembered where I'd heard that word. That was where the recalled agent, Agent 92, had operated from. I said, "That's an English village in Berkshire."

"Buckinghamshire. I believe Boniface is a deciphering operation, and Bletchley is where it's all happening." At this point his face contorted with inner turmoil. It was obvious that possession of this secret had been an intolerable burden.

"What are you suggesting? That the British have broken Lorenz SZ38?"

Many among the rank and file in the Abwehr suspected that the SZ38 cipher had been broken, but I thought it unlikely that Alex would be privy to this conjecture.

"It may be much worse than that. They may have broken Enigma."

"You can't be serious." I laughed. This was foolish nonsense. Nobody could break such a complex system. You know that." Enigma was more complex than Lorenz SZ38, by several orders of magnitude. Everyone knew it was safe.

"We've broken the British Cypher3 code, haven't we?"

"Yes, but Enigma is far superior to Cypher3."

"And how did we break Cypher3?"

"An agent in the British military."

He nodded, and my laughter died on my lips.

"Think about it," Alex said. "All it would take is a single British agent in one of our security organisations."

His argument was irrefutable. Schiller's pasty face swam into my mind.

Alex quickened his pace and I lengthened my stride to keep up. We completed a figure of eight, starting and finishing at the statue of Frederick the Great. I asked Alex where he got his information from, and he shook his head.

"I can't tell you that. I'd be putting two friends in jeopardy."

"What about Johann? Does he know?"

"No." There was a look of horror on his face. "How stupid do you think I am? The knowledge could place him in harm's way."

You don't mind putting me in harm's way, I thought.

On the way back to the office, I mulled over what Alex had said. Had he really discovered something, or could his story be an elaborate plot designed to entrap me? I resolved to watch out for the codename Boniface in the Abwehr files, but without taking any undue risks.

#

The bombing raids on London, which had started on September 7, continued for fifty-seven consecutive nights, finally ending on November 3. Meanwhile U-boat losses in the Atlantic were mounting.

November 9 was a public holiday – the "Day of the Movement" – a celebration of the Beer Hall Putsch of 1923.

Gudrun suggested a walk into the city centre. The weather was dry, but cold, with temperatures three or four degrees below freezing. We wore our warmest winter clothing, I my dark blue coat and matching civil defence hat; Gudrun her full-length coat in cream-coloured wool and a headscarf. She clung to my arm as we walked. The streets were sparsely populated. Any people that we did see were hurrying with purpose toward warm destinations, pushing plumes of breath before them. Attracted by the welcoming smell of newly-baked bread, we ventured down a side street. Here, we passed a number of small, boarded-up shops with the words *Achtung Juden* and the six-pointed star painted on them. One of them – a music shop that I had frequented before the war – had been burnt out, with gaping blackened holes for doors and windows. It seemed to me that these were modest, honest businesses.

Gudrun's grip tightened on my arm.

I said, "This must be the Zionist threat that everyone is so concerned about."

#

On the night of November 14, Luftwaffe bombers carried out a dawn raid on Coventry, with heavy loss of civilian life.

I rang Alex in the morning.

"Coventry was hit last night." He said it before I did.

"Yes, I know."

"They say the city was levelled."

"It's one of their most important industrial centres," I said.

"There were heavy casualties."

"Over one thousand, I believe."

Nothing more was said on the subject: the telephones were not safe. But I knew what Alex was thinking: If the British had broken our ciphers, surely they would have evacuated Coventry before the raid, and saved many civilian lives. But of course we had suffered civilian casualties in Bremen and Hamburg rather than reveal our code-breaking successes to the British.

21

November 1940

A couple of evenings later I found myself at my desk, alone with my squeaky chair. I strolled around the building which, apart from Siegfried the night watchman, was deserted. Now was my chance to search the offices of the three Obersts: von Neumann, the spymaster, Krause, the head of domestic intelligence and Schiller of Technical & Signals, whom I knew had altered at least one signal. I was hoping to uncover something about Alex's codename Boniface, and a supposed British deciphering operation.

Oberst von Neumann's office on the third floor was locked. Hauptmann von Pfaffel's was not. As usual, his desk was covered in papers. I went through them quickly, but there were so many papers that the task was hopeless. I found nothing of interest. I hurried down to the second floor and tried Oberst Schiller's office. It was unlocked, and I slipped inside. A search of the papers on his desk revealed nothing incriminating and no mention of Boniface. I tried his desk drawers, and found one of them open with three colour photographs inside. They showed the body of a man slumped over a table, a gun in his hand, a hole in his head. Blood and red and grey brain matter covered the table. I suppressed a strong urge to retch. The photographs were date-stamped with the KRIPO crest and the name of the Leipzig police district. The back of the photographs all bore the caption 'Gustav Barnard'.

Signing out that night, I noticed that Speddig's signature was missing from the outward log. Siegfried confirmed that Speddig was still somewhere in the building. I thought it strange that I hadn't seen him, nor had I seen any lights on the second floor. Had Speddig been skulking owl-like in the dark, watching me?

The next day, I told Alex that my searches for Boniface had come up dry.

"Mine too," he said. "I've tapped every source I have and came up with absolutely nothing."

#

An external call was routed through to my desk.

"Herr Müller? This is Thomas Kleister, Tristan's father."

"How may I help you, Herr Kleister?"

"Tania's been arrested by the police. Last night. I can't even find out where she has been taken. I'm sorry to trouble you, but I couldn't think who else to call."

A dozen thoughts flashed through my mind. It was as I'd feared. Tania's snooping had come to the attention of the police.

After the call, I went in search of Heinz.

"Can you find out what happened to this girl?" I handed him a piece of paper. "She was arrested last night."

"Tania Schaefer," he read. "Who is she?"

"A friend."

"Leave it with me," said Heinz.

#

November continued in sombre vein. My work settled into a routine of providing what support I could to my two active agents in Ireland, Stallion and Nightingale.

Stallion's intelligence reports were irregular and threadbare. His main contribution consisted of detailed quality reports from the steel plant in Cork. These showed a steady deterioration in the quality of materials being imported, from Britain mainly. The implication was that British steel quality was dropping, but I suspected that the British were keeping more and more of their best materials for their own industries. Given the war, I thought it surprising that they could spare any steel for Ireland at all.

Transmissions from the mysterious Nightingale continued in a steady stream. He had access to information of the highest quality from a staggering variety of sources. Reports received from Nightingale in November alone included the following:

A mass movement of infantry regiments from Yorkshire to the Home Counties

Repositioning of artillery weapons along the south coast.

Winston Churchill's annual consumption of cigars.

Detailed listings of RAF aerodromes and squadrons.

National projections of British munitions production for 1941-42.

This information was eagerly received by the military headquarters and by the various ministries. I found myself continually on the telephone, talking with officials from this or that ministry, hoping for further information from my agent. Occasionally, I was asked if specific information might be requested from Nightingale. Many of the callers asked where my agent was located; was he operating in an Irish government ministry, or from the British Embassy in Dublin, perhaps? To all of these questions, I answered that I couldn't say. Of course I didn't have the answers.

Even Gudrun had heard about my agent through the grapevine in the Air Ministry. Lying in bed, her head resting on my chest, she said, "I hear he's two metres tall, and has dark wavy hair. They say he's a bass-baritone, and that he foreswore a career in the opera to enter the diplomatic corps."

I laughed. "That's complete nonsense, Gudrun."

"One of my friends has seen an old photograph of him, dressed in the uniform of a Leutnant General. She says it was taken in Dresden in 1939, and he looked about twenty-five." She began twisting my chest hairs into whorls. "Imagine! A general at twenty-five!"

I said, "I've seen only one photograph of the man, and he was not in uniform. He looked perfectly average."

"He can't look average. Honestly, Kurt, you have no soul. Could I see the photograph?"

"No, you couldn't. It's top secret. Ouch! That hurt."

22

December 1940

On the night of December 12, and again on December 15, Sheffield was bombed heavily. Again there was no mass evacuation reported, nothing to indicate that the British had foreknowledge of these raids.

On December 16, the British began a large scale military operation in North Africa aimed at driving the Italians back from an encampment at Sidi Barani. Our job was to decode the British signals and re-encode the information in them for transmission to our allies, the Italians. Some of our earlier signals never reached their destination, and the British were able to take the Italian armoured units by surprise.

When the extent of the intelligence debacle became clear, Speddig took the brunt of the initial criticism, as the self-appointed senior member of our English language group. He declared that the fault lay with the Italian team, and a shouting match ensued. I refused to take part, to Speddig's disgust.

An internal Abwehr investigation was conducted by Drobol the cripple, under the leadership of Oberst Schiller, to determine the reasons for the failure. The results of the investigation were never made known to anyone below the rank of Oberst. Nobody was ever officially blamed or reprimanded, and the incident was quietly forgotten. I began to wonder if there was anybody at the helm of the good ship Abwehr, or if the fate of everyone in the country was in the hands of incompetents or madmen – or British spies. The last war frequently came to mind, the disastrous campaigns plotted by incompetent generals on both sides that caused the slaughter of millions.

#

On December 22, Gudrun took a train to her parents' home in Schleswig-Holstein. Before she boarded her train, we visited the shops, where Gudrun bought a large Swiss doll.

"It's for my niece," she said. "Her name's Anna. She's seven."

I thought it strange that Gudrun had never before mentioned having a niece.

On December 29 a heavy bombing raid on London caused a firestorm. The newspapers called it the second Great Fire of London. In the streets of Berlin the Brownshirts celebrated, but I felt nothing but revulsion at the carnage. It seemed to me the conduct of the war – on both sides – had sunk to a new low.

At midday on New Year's Eve, Admiral Canaris, Generalmajor Oster and the three Obersts all left the building together in three grey-green Kriegsmarine cars. The Generalmajor and the Admiral were in uniform. I asked Sigmund what it was all about.

"They've gone to Kriegsmarine Headquarters. That's all I know."

I asked Hauptmann von Pfaffel what was happening. He shook his head and disappeared into his office without a word.

Heinz was more forthcoming. "They're attending a high level meeting to discuss increasing U-boat losses."

#

When Gudrun returned early in the new year I took her to the opera. We met Alex and Johann there, and the four of us attended a performance of Wagner's Gotterdammerung by the Berlin National Opera Company. Gudrun dressed up for the occasion in a coral coloured two piece suit with wide cream lapels, and matching cream belt and shoes. Her crescent-shaped earrings and a tiny cream-and-gold hat completed the outfit. She looked like ten million marks.

When the opera was over, we hurried to a large beer cellar where we joined in the New Year celebrations. We ordered a meal.

The opera was magnificent. Alex and I had seen it performed before, of course, but the other two were new to Wagner. We had to explain the storyline to them.

"Siegfried loves Brunnhilde," I said.

"So why did he go off with that other one?" said Gudrun.

"That was Gutrune of the Gibichungs," Alex said, arriving with a bunch of foaming steins in his hands and handing them around. "She tricked him."

"She drugged him with a magic love potion," I added.

"They all say that," Johann said, and we laughed.

23

January 1941

Heinz slouched into my office in early January, wearing a bright yellow waistcoat and spats. His extravagant clothing together with his flattened nose reminded me of Kenneth Grahame's Toad of Toad Hall.

"I have news of your friend, Frau Schaefer. She's in the labour camp at Ravensbrück."

I was horrified. "On what charge?"

Mister Toad shrugged. "She may be suspected of anti-German activities, or maybe she just looked sideways at somebody important. Who knows?"

"Is that all it takes?"

"It's the price we pay for strong leadership. Would you like to visit this person?"

"No, but her father would."

"Sorry, Kurt, I can arrange for you to visit the camp, no one else."

The following Tuesday, I met Heinz at Bahnhof Lichtenberg. Our travel and identity papers were scrutinized by a member of the ORPO, the national uniformed police, before we were permitted to board our train. The journey to Furstenberg took two hours. Kilometre after kilometre of rural countryside rolled by, cloaked in a thin layer of snow. I thought: this is the real Germany. The trees, the cattle tranquil in the fields, small towns glimpsed in mountain cleavages, all bearing witness to the stability, the eternal continuity, of things familiar, things mundane and good, things German.

Heinz had made reservations at a small lodging house in Furstenberg. We checked in, and enjoyed a leisurely meal. After the meal, we sat by a roaring fire with the remains of our second bottle of Liebfraumilch. I asked Heinz how easy it had been to arrange our visit to the camp.

"The Admiral's name will open most doors in the Reich, although that was not enough. I had to play our trump card."

"Uncle Reinhard?"

"Precisely. The camps all operate under Heydrich's direct authority. You should have no difficulty accessing any of them."

We retired for the night. I was apprehensive about what we would discover the next day, but delighted to find myself in the countryside again. Before getting into bed, I stood by the open window in my pyjamas, and inhaled the thick country air. It was nearly dark. Outside, I could see a large oak tree in silhouette. The light from my window caught the occasional flash of passing bats squeaking to one another.

My room was on the second floor, at the back of the building, but I could hear the sound of traditional music from the tavern across the street at the front: the accordion vibrato, the piping recorder, a rasping trumpet, a trombone glissando, and a tuba's oompah, oompah, pounding out the beat. I closed the window with a sigh and climbed into my bed.

I awoke refreshed after a sound night's sleep – with no nightmares – on a wooden bed with a thin mattress. Heinz was waiting for me in the breakfast room, rubbing his back. I smiled at him. "Did you sleep well?"

"No," the old toad replied. "The bed was like a rock."

We had boiled eggs and cheese for breakfast. After the meal, we found a driver waiting for us in the reception area who drove us the short distance to the labour camp. Stepping out of the car at the entrance to the camp, we were welcomed by a playful flurry of snow.

"Leave the talking to me," Heinz said.

The camp was a miserable looking place, a large compound filled with long wooden huts and surrounded by an electrified fence of barbed wire. Guard towers manned by armed soldiers in greatcoats were placed every fifty metres or so along the perimeter. The whole camp was draped in a dusting of snow which did nothing to improve its sombre appearance.

We were shown into a waiting area, and offered coffee by a young woman in uniform. After the customary fifteen-minute wait we were led into the camp commandant's office, where we found two SS officers, in full uniform, waiting to receive us. One man stood by the door, an SS-Obersturmführer by his uniform. The camp commandant was seated behind a desk. He looked about 40 years of age, greying at the temples.

"You found the accommodations satisfactory?" he asked, his falsetto voice a strange accompaniment to his black uniform.

"It was adequate, thank you, Commandant," Heinz replied.

"You are here to visit one of our guests?" This was addressed to me.

"Frau Tania Schaefer, Herr Commandant," I replied.

"And your interest in this undesirable, Leutnant Müller?"

Heinz responded, "Purely personal, I assure you."

"Your letter of introduction is signed by Generalmajor Oster, I see." He glanced down at the paper on his desk. Then he looked directly at me. "I have a passing acquaintance with the Generalmajor, and with the Admiral of course. However, you should understand that this facility is run and operated by the Schutzstaffel. We have the clearest mandate from the Führer himself, and I will expect you to respect that mandate. As a member of the Wehrmacht, you have no jurisdiction here. You may speak with this… Frau Schaefer, but your conversation will be monitored at all times."

"I have a small food parcel," I opened my briefcase, "and a letter from Frau Schaefer's father."

The SS-Obersturmführer stepped forward and held out his hands. I handed him the parcel and the letter, and he left the room with them.

"These items will be examined for contraband," the Commandant said. "If they pass inspection, then they may be conveyed to the prisoner."

We spent fifteen minutes with the Commandant's 'guest' in a small room at the rear of the main building. The room was equipped with a rough wooden table and four chairs. The only light came from a row of small windows high up on one wall. A female camp guard, stood by the door.

Tania was dressed in prison clothing, a blue smock over striped trousers. She looked tired and hungry. She sat on the edge of her chair, hunched forward, like a woman carrying an anvil on her shoulders. There were dark rings around her eyes, and her hair was unkempt and dirty. She looked like a woman in her fifties, although I knew she was no older than twenty-five. Her hands were cupped together, palms up, the left hand cradling the right.

Heinz introduced us. "My name is Heinz Franzelberg. Leutnant Kurt Müller of the Abwehr, you know."

She stared at Heinz in total bemusement.

"We met at your brother's funeral, and again in September," I reminded her.

There was no reaction. The guard at the door shifted her feet.

I asked her if she knew why she had been incarcerated. I knew the answer, of course, but I needed to get some reaction from her.

Her head came up slowly. "I never believed it."

"You're speaking about Tristan, your brother?"

She uncurled her hands. The skin was blistered and broken, the nails ragged. "The light. The light hurts my eyes."

I glanced at Heinz. The room was dark, the light barely adequate. Heinz shook his head, and I pressed on.

"Tania," I said. No reaction. "Tania, look at me."

She raised her eyes to mine.

"I got your letter."

"It wasn't his handwriting," she said, her eyes sliding sideways to the guard.

"The suicide note? You're sure?" I glanced at the guard, but she seemed not to have heard.

"I showed it to Barnard's parents. It wasn't his handwriting. He was murdered, just like Tristan, but I don't know why."

Heinz threw me a questioning look. I ignored him.

Tania slipped back into her dreamlike state for a few minutes. I asked what conditions were like in the camp. She appeared not to have heard me. She moved her head slowly from side to side, as if she were having trouble focusing on our faces. I tried the same question again.

"I was foolish." Smiling, she began to move her head backward and forward and then round in a circle. I glanced at Heinz.

The Black Orchestra

Then Tania said, "What was your question?" Her head steady now, eyes focused on mine, she seemed alert.

"I asked what conditions are like in the camp," I replied.

"There's a quarry. We work there. They blast huge boulders from the quarry walls. Then we break them up into smaller rocks. Others break the rocks into stones."

The SS-Obersturmführer entered the room and handed the parcel and the letter to Heinz. Both had been opened. Heinz placed them on the table in front of Tania. She reached over, took the items, and examined the writing on the parcel. She asked us to wait while she read the letter. She had some difficulty extracting it from the envelope; her hands were trembling, and her fingers — once the lovely fingers of a cellist — were like thick sausages, refusing to do her bidding.

When she had read the letter she stuffed the food into her mouth like a feral animal, shoulders hunched, her eyes on the guard.

On the way back to the car, I asked our guide, the SS-Obersturmführer, when our friend was likely to be released. The snow flurry had died, mysteriously.

He replied, "Let me put it this way, Herr Leutnant, I've been here eleven months, and in that time only three people have been released, to the best of my knowledge."

"How many have been admitted?" asked Heinz

"About ten thousand," the SS-Obersturmführer replied.

On the long journey back to Berlin, Heinz asked me to explain what Tania had said about the forged suicide note.

"It's nothing," I said. "A private matter."

After that, there was little conversation between Heinz and me. The interview with Tania ran over and over in my mind like a film in a loop. I felt vaguely nauseous, although I had never suffered from motion sickness. Mile after mile of rural countryside rolled past. I thought: is this how Germany – the real Germany – is now? The trees, the cattle in the fields, quiet mountain villages, all bore witness to a great lie – an ancient Germany that was gone. Something huge and ugly had entered our lives. Germany had changed. Nothing about this new Germany could be mundane, now; and things familiar would never be the same again.

It seemed Tania had proved that Barnard, the Leipzig signalman, was murdered. I thought that maybe both Barnard and Kleister had been killed because of the same signal, Barnard for sending it, Kleister because he was the one to receive it.

After a long silence, I said, "Is this what the war has done to us?"

#

After that, the fear and revulsion that had been my constant companions were seasoned with anger.

I gave Gudrun a short account of my trip, avoiding as much of the unpleasantness as I could. Before I had finished she was weeping silently. It was as if she could see the true horror of the camp in my eyes. She busied herself in the kitchen. I put the radio on.

When she returned, she seemed composed. Avoiding my eyes, she said, "You could write to Reinhard. Ask him to release Tania. Tell him she's a friend. Point out how trivial her offence was"

This thought had occurred to me on the train. I knew that Reinhard had supreme control of the labour camps.

That night, I imagined Reinhard Heydrich as a lion tamer in a circus sharing a cage with huge, man-eating creatures, keeping them all in check with an upturned chair and a crack of his whip. Then the cage was a large compound, surrounded by an electric fence with armed watchtowers. Like a veil lifting, I became aware of the extent of Reinhard's power, and the depth of evil at his command. Memories of burnt-out shops and some of the Führer's anti-Jewish ranting flooded my mind. Was the mass eviction of the Jews Heydrich's work as well? And what if the rumoured purges were real?

I wrote to my uncle the next day, addressing the letter to his home, and two days after that, I rang Thomas Kleister.

"I met with Tania," I said. "I gave her your letter and the parcel."

I couldn't think what more I could say.

24

February 1941

The weather continued overcast and cold, and the snow began to fall in earnest. The temperature plummeted. It wasn't long before most of the minor roads became impassable; only horses and drays could venture into them. The main roads were like snow-covered ice rinks, almost impossible for cars and buses, and lethal for bicycles. The trams were the only way to get about, and every tram that passed was overflowing with passengers. Berlin without its bicycles was a strange place; it took on an unfamiliar aspect, as if it had shed an outer layer of clothing. The few pedestrians that ventured out could be seen placing their feet with care, in strange, exaggerated ways, like puzzled ducklings on a frozen lake.

One Monday morning in February, I arrived at the office a little late.

"Good morning, Sigmund," I said, stamping the snow from my boots.

Sigmund smiled and winked at me. "And good morning to you, young sir."

When I arrived on the third floor, it seemed everyone had been eating cake; wherever I looked, people were smiling. When I entered my office everything became clear. There was a young woman perched on a chair in front of my desk.

"Liesel Martens," she said. "Reich Ministry of Public Enlightenment and Propaganda."

I was shocked into silence. I knew someone from the ministry was coming, but foolishly, I had expected a man.

Liesel was petite, almost like a doll, her hair blonde, her nose neat and turned up in a way that made her nostrils seem permanently flared; her lips were full and painted bright red. She wore a dress with a plunging neckline and a red floral motif that matched her lipstick.

I struggled past my desk to my chair. As was usual for a Monday morning, there was a small mountain of messages and incoming transmissions to be dealt with.

"I would like to start by interviewing you about everything," she said. She wore a strong, musk-laden perfume, like blossoms in autumn.

"Everything?" My chair squeaked in protest.

"Yes. The Wehrmacht, the OKW, the Abwehr, your job, the spies, the war."

"I have rather a lot of work to do, Fräulein, as you can see. Perhaps we could do the interview later."

"Fine." She sniffed. "Give me some files to read and I shan't disturb you any further."

"Files?"

"You must have files – dossiers on each of your spies."

"Yes, Fräulein. Forgive me."

I gave her agent Slingshot's file. Slingshot had been interned days after arriving in Ireland.

It took her ten minutes to read the file. "That one was no good. He's been captured. Can I have some more files, please?"

"I'm sorry, Fräulein. I need the rest of them for my work."

"What, all of them?"

"There are very few agents in Ireland at the moment."

"In Ireland? You run spies in Ireland?"

"Yes, Fräulein."

"Who runs the spies in England?"

"You will need to talk to Oberst von Neumann about that."

She wriggled her way out of my office and went in search of the Oberst.

Fräulein Martens had lunch with Oberst von Neumann. It was close to 3:30 by the time the Oberst returned from lunch that day, flushed and a little unsteady on his feet — and alone.

"I expect she's pretty." Gudrun stood over me, legs apart, hands on hips.

"Not really."

"I thought so. Tell me what she looks like."

"She's small. She has an upturned nose."

"Like this?" She pushed the tip of her own nose back. "Go on. What else?"

"Her eyes are blue."

"You've been looking into her eyes! I thought as much. Tell me, what colour are my eyes?" She turned her head away.

"Green."

"Lucky guess. What shape is she?"

I drew a pear shape in the air. She threw a cushion at me.

Liesel was waiting for me in my office the next day.

"We could do that interview now," she said.

"What did Oberst von Neumann say?"

"He said I should work with you."

I took a minute to rearrange the papers on my desk. "Did you point out how few agents I have?"

"Yes. I thought I'd do a composite."

"A composite?"

"Yes, you know, take the best features from all of your spies and build one super spy for the newspapers."

"But that would be fiction," I said.

"Yes."

The interview started. I told her a little about my background, saying nothing about Uncle Reinhard. I told her how our agents operate in the field. She asked about their training.

When I mentioned the Brandenburg unit she clapped her hands. "I've heard of the Brandenburg Regiment. They're famous. I'd love to visit them."

Following the interview, I escorted Liesel to the main door of the building. Sigmund the doorman saluted as we passed.

On the pavement outside, she said, "Well, goodbye, Kurt. I expect you'll be glad to get back to work."

"Not at all, Fräulein, I have enjoyed your company, and I hope we meet again soon."

I moved toward her, intending a kiss on her cheek, but she stepped away down the steps, and was gone, leaving me feeling foolish.

I got very little work done for the remainder of that day. Liesel's perfume hung in my office, and the memory of her lingered in my mind, the way she tossed her plaits over her shoulder, the way she rubbed the tip of her nose...

#

Hauptmann von Pfaffel made the arrangements for my training trip to Brandenburg. The day before I was due to travel I met Oberst von Neumann in the corridor.

"Oberst Schmidt is expecting you," he said. "Take what you need from the training on offer. Skip whatever you think is unnecessary. And report to me any deficiencies. I've agreed that Fräulein Martens can travel with you." I raised a questioning eyebrow at this, and he continued, "The Fräulein expressed an interest. I couldn't see any harm in it."

Gudrun was livid. She accused me of being unfaithful. I assured her that it was nothing but a short business trip; I planned for it to last no more than a single day, and if it took longer, Liesel and I would return to Berlin each night. Gudrun flounced into the bedroom, and locked the door. I had to spend the night on the settee.

In the morning we had a fresh row.

"You kept me awake all night, you know," she waved her arms about.

"How did I manage that?" I said.

I was the one on the settee.

She shouted at me, "You're stubborn and inconsiderate."

"Are you saying you don't trust me?"

"Why should I? I've seen you eyeing other girls."

"What other girls?"

"Plenty of them. There's that Sophie from across the square, for one."

I had no idea who she was talking about. I said, "She's a good looking girl, that Sophie."

"There you are," she shouted. "I knew it."

When I returned home from work that evening, Gudrun was gone. I checked the bedroom. All of her clothes were missing and her suitcase was gone. The kitchen had been tidied as if in preparation for a new tenant; her toothbrush and toiletries were gone from the bathroom; and the bookcase showed gaps where her books had been. The only thing of Gudrun's that was left was the dachshund draught excluder that I had bought for her in the flea market.

There was a note, but not from Gudrun. It was typewritten in block capitals on official Gestapo notepaper. It read:

WARNING! KEEP YOUR NOSE OUT OF MATTERS THAT DON'T CONCERN YOU OR YOU WILL END UP LIKE THESE TWO.

I found a brown paper parcel, half-opened on the floor. Placing it on the table, I peered inside to find two dead rats, lying side by side.

Gingerly, I closed the parcel, took it outside and disposed of it in a dustbin. It occurred to me then that I was living on borrowed time. The Gestapo were still interested in me. I considered ringing my uncle; he could call his henchmen off. But Uncle Reinhard was my trump card. I wanted to save that for a more serious occasion. Besides, I was pretty sure that, if he issued a reprimand von Kemp would find some even nastier way of paying me back.

There was no answer from Gudrun's parents' telephone number in Elmshorn.

25

February 1941

Liesel found an empty compartment on the train. She was wearing a short woollen overcoat in a strong black and white herringbone pattern and a smart black hat. I hadn't seen her for nearly a month, and yet I felt a strange intimate continuity in our relationship; it was as if no time at all had passed since our last meeting.

She pulled a long cigarette holder from her bag, added a cigarette, and lit it. She crossed her legs and smoked in an exaggerated manner, blowing smoke around the compartment.

From the moment the train began to move, she talked. She told me her life story. She was born half-way up a mountain in Bavaria, the eldest of five children. Her father was twelve years older than her mother. They were sheep farmers. Liesel grew up to the sounds of cowbells and Alpenhorns, cut off by snow in the winter. Her early education was intermittent and erratic: she had to take time off school to help out on the farm. Later, her elderly father suffered an aneurism and became a permanent invalid. From that day onward, Liesel's mother and siblings had to run the farm without him.

Liesel hated her father, not only for his political views – he supported von Papen and his Catholic Centre Party – but also because, as long as she knew him, he was an old man. He died in 1937, aged 72.

"That was his final betrayal," she said.

Liesel's mother had a cousin who worked for a small provincial newspaper, and through this connection, Liesel began a career in journalism. That was in 1930. Her big break came a year later when she covered the suicide of the Führer's niece, Geli. In 1933, Liesel joined the NSDAP newspaper *Völkischer Beobachter*; and in 1935, she landed a plumb job in the Ministry of Propaganda.

When she ran dry of personal recollections, she said, "Tell me about Tristan Kleister."

Taken aback by her question, I stammered, "T...Tristan who?"

"Kleister. I heard he was a Gestapo agent in the Abwehr who committed suicide." She watched my face closely as I collected my thoughts.

"Where did you hear about that?"

She lifted a shoulder. "My people are always interested in that sort of thing."

"Your people?"

"At the ministry. We keep a watching brief on the other government agencies."

"Including the Wehrmacht?" I couldn't disguise my astonishment.

"Especially the military. So what can you tell me about Kleister? I hear you discovered his body."

"I'd rather not talk about it." Now my surprise was replaced by alarm. Where was she getting her information from?

"I heard he shot himself," she pressed on. "Was suicide confirmed by the Medical Examiner?"

"I haven't seen the report."

My opinion of her journalistic talents rose several notches. Her question about the work of the Medical Examiner cut to the heart of the matter, but of course I knew I would never see his report.

She asked about me. I began by telling her about my father and our close relationship. I said nothing about Uncle Reinhard. I told her about my father's untimely death on the Night of the Long Knives.

"He was SA?"

"No. He was a local government official."

Eventually her eyelids closed, and she nodded off. In repose, her flared nostrils, and gentle snores gave her a slightly porcine look that I found irresistible.

I went in search of the toilet. Stepping into the corridor, I noticed a small man wearing a light raincoat and carrying a black umbrella. The umbrella seemed too big for one of his stature. He had a pleasant demeanour, with a rosy complexion and the hint of a smile. I thought he looked familiar, but I couldn't remember where I might have seen him before.

#

The supreme commander of the Brandenburg training unit, Oberst Nikolaus Schmidt, was a military man from the old guard, a decorated hero from the last war, in his mid to late sixties. He wore half-moon glasses and a Wehrmacht uniform, but no medals or decorations.

He was expecting us. He nodded briefly to me, and turned his attention to Liesel. "My dear Fräulein, Welcome to the Brandenburg Unit."

Liesel flashed her eyelashes at the old man. "Thank you, Herr Schmidt."

"I have organised a tour of the training facility. Afterwards, I will be happy to answer any questions you may have."

There was a knock on the door and a stocky man appeared. He had the physique of a prize-fighter; his hair was close-shaved.

"This is Hauptmann von Beuhl. The Hauptmann has offered to be your guide for the duration of your stay."

Liesel left with von Beuhl and the Oberst turned his attention to me. "Welcome, Herr Leutnant. And how may we help you?"

"I would like to sample some of your training programmes and to meet the three candidates for field operations in Ireland."

"Diehl, Blesset and Gertz?"

"Yes. Perhaps you could outline the programme for me."

The Oberst listed the main areas, counting them off on his fingers: "Weapons, explosives, sabotage, radio set-up, coding and transmission, airborne techniques, field survival, unarmed combat, language and orientation, and of course, physical fitness."

"I'd like to start with the English language and orientation class, Herr Oberst." I tried to sound casual, as if my choice had been plucked from the air at random.

He glared at me. I was sure that he had divined my true purpose. "That is Herr Haffner's area."

"His qualification?"

"You may observe Haffner's methods." Schmidt continued as if I had not spoken. "But you will say or do nothing to disrupt the normal functioning of his class. Do you understand?" He peered at me over the tops of his glasses.

"Yes, Herr Oberst."

"I am allowing this intrusion as a personal favour to Oberst von Neumann, but I will not tolerate any interference with our work. We have a lot of ground to cover in a short time, and interruptions or interference cannot be tolerated. Is that clear?"

"Crystal clear. What other class would you recommend?"

"You should sample our locks and safes module, part of the sabotage course. There is some fresh material in there that you might find interesting."

Schmidt took me to a classroom and introduced me to Herr Haffner, English language and orientation Instructor. I sat at the rear.

The lesson for the day was concerned with domestic matters.

Water was obtained from a "faucet"; a large saucepan was called a "cauldron"; all people in big houses had butlers and footmen; dogs were "hounds"; most hounds were poodles; and all meat dishes seemed to consist of veal.

Throughout the session, Herr Haffner constantly deferred to me, making eye-contact and raising a questioning eyebrow. Each time, I felt obliged to nod encouragement, although I had to bite my lip to stop from shouting out my objections or bursting into laughter.

English dialogue instruction was equally excruciating.

"May I take your arm, Madam?"

"Is this a school for mixed children?"

"Where can I buy beans and apple pie?"

"May I have veal with my potatoes?"

Knowing that I was interested in Irish conditions, the instructor presented the class with a typical Irish scene. We were asked to imagine that we needed to spend the night at a small farm in the Irish countryside, in County Tipperary.

"Where is the nearest town?"

"That will be Ballynewcastle, in the County of Kilkenny."

"Is it far?"

"Twenty kilometres, as the crow flies."

"It is nearly dark."

"Where are you from, tell me?"

"We are from the mainland." The instructor seemed to regard the Republic of Ireland as an off-shore island run from Westminster.

"You are a long way from home, so."

"That we are. We strayed from our chosen course."

"You must be travelling people, so."

"We are, to be sure."

It was like a bad production of one of J. M. Synge's plays.

"Well, sit yourselves down by the fire and my wife will make you a veal sandwich. It is a bitter night for anyone to be out."

"Is it all right if we spend the night here?"

"Yes, of course you must spend the night here."

"What time do you rise in the morning?"

"At cockcrow."

"I prefer eggs for breakfast."

At this last exchange, I erupted with laughter, and had to feign a coughing fit to disguise my reaction.

Herr Haffner explained that the Irish people had their own special version of football, called Gaelic. It involved hitting a ball with a stick. Everyone in the countryside followed these games, and it was essential for anyone travelling the Irish countryside to keep abreast of the latest results.

By the end of the session, I was transfixed with a steely grin. I'm sure my face was red as a radish from the effort of restraining my mirth.

26

February, March 1941

Over lunch I met several trainee agents who were intended for deployment in Britain. It was immediately clear to me that those selected for service in Ireland had all been rejected as unsuitable for service in England. Obviously, Ireland merited nothing but the dregs. In the afternoon, I was provided with a room in which to interview the candidate Irish agents.

First in was Martin Gertz, 62 years old, short, with a chest like a barrel. I remembered from his file that he was illiterate. I asked him a few simple questions in English. His responses were grammatically weak; his accent heavy. I handed him my planned schedule of training activities for the following day, and asked what activities he would be engaged in.

He handed it straight back. "I don't have my reading glasses with me."

The 77-year-old, Ebenezer Diehl was a pleasant enough fellow, thin as a ferret and with a similar disposition. His grasp of the English language was first class – probably better than mine – although I thought his choice of words a little archaic. At his age, his career as an agent was likely to be a short one.

Last in was Fritz Dieter Blesset, tall, with broad shoulders and a striking mass of blond hair. He seemed mature for his age; his English language skills were strong; he could read and write; and he seemed intelligent. My spirits rose. I began to wonder what was wrong with Blesset that von Pfaffel had rejected him.

It was late in the day before I discovered the answer. I attended a sabotage training session dealing with lock picking and safe cracking. Participating in the lesson, I learned to pick a couple of simple locks.

Blesset had been selected to demonstrate his skills with the lock pick to the class. Quite suddenly, and for no apparent reason, he shouted "Hey!" At the same time, his hand shot upward and he struck himself on the side of the head. Not one of those present made any remark on the incident.

Later, as we were leaving the class, there was a similar episode. His arm shot upward in a sort of grotesque Party salute, accompanied by a shout of "Heil!"

"Are you all right?" I asked, my heart sinking.

"Yes, yes, I'm fine, thank you," he replied.

I spoke to Oberst Schmidt about Blesset.

"He is a fine young fellow, isn't he? A pity about his Tourette's."

"His what?"

"Tourette's Syndrome. You must have noticed."

"I noticed some unusual arm movements and a shout."

Schmidt nodded. "That's Tourette's Syndrome. Named after the physician who discovered it. It's a harmless condition."

"This is a medical condition?" I had never seen anything like it before.

"Yes. Many famous people have had the condition. Mozart, for one."

"Is it curable?"

"No, I believe there is no cure." When he saw the expression on my face, he continued, "I realise it may be a drawback in the field."

I groaned. What an understatement!

Soon afterwards, I managed to speak to Blesset again in private. "You have a condition," I began.

"Yes," he replied happily. "It's called Tourette's Syndrome. It's named after the physician who discovered it. Mozart—"

"Yes, yes. What I need to know is: can you control it?"

"I have medication that helps."

"Does it work?"

"Most of the time."

Most of the time! This young man was going to be useless in overseas espionage operations.

At the end of the day, I asked Oberst Schmidt about Agent Nightingale.

"Ah yes, Nightingale. A superb athlete, and his English was excellent. He spoke like a native."

"I thought he *was* a native. Could I take a look at his training records?"

"Of course."

He showed me into the room I had used before, and gave me the file to examine. Unlike the yellow file on my desk in Berlin, this one contained a good photograph of Nightingale. He looked young, fit, intelligent, with that indefinable look of self-confidence that is the mark of a leader. Was there something familiar about him? I removed the photograph from the file and slipped it into my briefcase.

The file was full of superlatives. He could run like a cheetah, swim like a dolphin, and fight like a lion; he could open any lock or safe; he was expert with explosives, and an accomplished marksman.

Before leaving, von Beuhl presented me with a set of lock-picks and a small cardboard box. Inside the box was a single purple capsule.

"What's this?" I asked von Beuhl.

"Cyanide capsule," he said.

#

The train back to Berlin was crowded. The man with the oversized black umbrella was there again, standing in the corridor. Was he watching us? He bore a pleasant smile; seemed lost in his own thoughts. I decided I was just being paranoid, suspecting every innocent stranger of watching me.

Liesel was in expansive form. She spoke in a loud voice, and at length, about some of her past journalistic triumphs. I listened patiently, as did everyone else in the compartment. Apparently, she'd won the Journalists' Club Award for Best Travel Writer – Culinary Section for 1935 as well as two silver medals for her coverage of local politics for her first newspaper – the one in Frankfurt.

Shortly before arriving in Berlin, Liesel asked me to tell her again the story of my father's death on the Night of the Long Knives.

"A stray bullet, you say. That was unfortunate."

There was something about her tone…

"You don't suppose there was anything more to it?" she asked. "I mean, that was the night of the hummingbird."

"The hummingbird?" I looked at her questioningly.

"Never mind, Kurt." She turned her eyes away.

"What's this hummingbird?" I persisted.

"It's nothing. Please forget that I spoke."

From that moment, the word lodged in my head like a thorn, popping into my thoughts constantly. I thought about the phrase "a stray bullet". It seemed obvious to me now that the actions of that night in 1934 were conducted by *Einsatzgruppen* Special Operation Units. There must have been a lot of stray bullets flying around that night. And Uncle Reinhard was in command; in my eyes that made him at least partly responsible for my father's death.

#

Even before I opened the door of the apartment, I knew that Gudrun hadn't returned. I sat on the settee with the draught excluder on my knee and tried to gather my thoughts. I couldn't believe that she had really left me, and yet the evidence was everywhere. Descending into gloom, I sat for a long time, our last conversation running through my mind. When I emerged from my contemplation, it was dark, and hunger was gnawing at my innards.

I picked up the telephone and rang Gudrun's parents' number in Elmshorn.

"Is Gudrun there?"

"She's not available to come to the telephone."

"Please put her on."

I could hear a child's voice, "Who's talking, Grandmamma?"

Gudrun's niece.

The connection was severed abruptly.

My main feeling was one of relief. I was having difficulty coming to terms with the thought that I might never see her again, but at least her safety was assured.

The paperwork had accumulated during my absence. Agent Nightingale had transmitted a dozen intelligence reports that had to be cross-referenced, filed and sent onward. Agent Stallion had requested additional funds, and he had obtained copies of a series of official police transfer forms concerning the arrest and detention of agent Slingshot. He had sent in copies of these forms in the diplomatic bags. They showed how the agent was passed from Garda custody in Galway to Garda Headquarters in Dublin, and from there to the prison service at Mountjoy for transfer to the internment camp at The Curragh, Co Kildare.

The transfer forms showed that he left Galway with £1,700; and arrived at Dublin HQ with £1,400. At the time of his transfer to the prison service he had £1,000, and he was interned at The Curragh with £800 in his possession. Perhaps von Pfaffel's analysis of the Irishman's love of money was not so far from the truth, after all.

27

March 1941

Days turned into weeks, February became March and Gudrun didn't return. The only explanation for her absence that I could come up with was the Gestapo message and the contents of that parcel.

During that period I had lunch with Alex almost every day.

"Still no sign of Gudrun?" he asked.

"She's visiting her mother."

"And she hasn't been in contact? Have you tried to contact her?"

I threw a look at him that told him to change the subject. He got the message.

"You look miserable. When did you last shave?"

"I thought I might grow a beard."

"Don't. It wouldn't suit you. You're too thin."

I shrugged. "Have you heard of 'Hummingbird'?"

"No. Is it a code word? Where did you hear it?"

"Never mind, Alex." Telling him about Liesel would have been too complicated.

#

I succumbed to sloth, spending my rations in cheap cafés, most nights. My nightmares turned to lurid erotic dreams, all revolving around Liesel. My work began to suffer. Weeks after my trip to Brandenburg I still hadn't completed the report on my findings there. Oberst von Neumann asked Heinz Franzelberg to spend some time with me, to see if he could find out what was troubling me.

Heinz soon divined the root of the problem.

"It's girl trouble, isn't it?"

In truth, I couldn't say what was wrong with me.

"It's that girl from the Propaganda Ministry, isn't it?" he said, reading my mind.

"She mentioned the codeword, Hummingbird. Do you know what it means?"

"No, but leave it with me. I'll make some enquiries."

#

I completed my report on the Brandenburg Unit and submitted it to Oberst von Neumann.

He got back to me within the hour.

"This is a pretty damning report, Kurt. Is there really nothing good you can say about this training?"

"Nothing. Given its shortcomings our agents have little or no chance to infiltrate English-speaking countries."

The Oberst put his pipe in his mouth, unlit, clamping the stem between his teeth. "I can't release this, you realise. I have no idea how Generalmajor Oster would react." He dropped my report into his wastepaper basket.

I blinked. The pitch of my voice rose a semitone. "Don't you think the Brandenburg Unit should be told how poor their training is?" I thought there might be steam rising from the top of my head. It took all the self-control at my disposal to raise no further objection.

The Oberst said, "Your proposal for the recovery of agent Ornithologist's equipment has been reconsidered." My heart skipped a beat. "It has now been approved."

My immediate reaction to this news was something close to panic. The prospect of leaving my comfortable office and venturing out into the real world – the real war – was frightening. I maintained a calm exterior. "Thank you, Herr Oberst."

"What of Blesset? Is he ready to travel?"

My apprehension turned to horror. "You want him to travel with me?"

"Yes. I thought that was agreed."

"We had not discussed it."

"What of the other two?"

I groaned. "Herr Oberst, I believe neither Gertz nor Diehl is fit for this work. They are both too old."

"They were selected by von Pfaffel."

"They were *rejected* by von Pfaffel. Gertz is sixty-two. Diehl is seventy-seven."

"Diehl may be a bit old for the work, I grant you, but I've seen Gertz. He's fit as a flea."

At this point I thought that the whole organisation was living in a dream world where muscle-bound illiterates made good agents.

I took a deep breath. "The man can't read or write. He would be unable to encode or decode messages, or even read them, if somebody else decoded them."

"That could be a handicap." Oberst von Neumann agreed. "Very well, contact Oberst Schmidt. Find out when Blesset's training will be complete. I have made enquiries on your behalf, and the U-Bootwaffe has agreed to the mission in principle, if and when other priorities permit, but only under certain conditions.

"In the first place, there must be no advance notification given to anybody in Ireland of the details of the landing – not even the expected date of the drop. Second, the U-boat commander – and he alone – will decide when the mission will start, and third, he will decide where the drop will be made. Fourth, it must be understood that the U-boat commander may cancel the mission at any time, before or during the voyage. The U-Bootwaffe was most insistent on this point. Completion or cancellation of the mission will be entirely at his discretion."

"I understand."

"And finally, the mission will be one way only. There is no possibility of taking you on the return journey."

I blinked. "So how am I to return?"

"You should have no difficulty taking a normal commercial flight through Madrid or Lisbon."

I considered this reply for a moment or two before asking, "How long will it take to arrange the trip?"

"Months, usually. You should expect to travel in the summer. But you must make your preparations early, and be ready to travel at a moment's notice."

"Very well, Herr Oberst."

After that meeting, I was despondent. Nothing was going to change. The time spent gathering information about the Brandenburg Unit had been wasted. It seemed Abwehr senior management was content to bury their heads in the sand and let things slide. It occurred to me that I might be more useful if I enlisted in the Kriegsmarine after all.

28

March 1941

On Friday, March 7, U-boat U47 was sunk with all hands off the west coast of Ireland. Alex heard about it from his contacts in the Kriegsmarine. He rang me at home with the news. There was no mention of U47 on the German news that night, but the kill was broadcast on the BBC.

On Monday March 10, Nightingale's report confirmed everything that the BBC had said. U47 had been surrounded by three British destroyers near Rockall, and sunk with all hands. The Monday newspapers were full of the story of the sinking, and the tragic loss of her brave commander. I bought a copy of *Völkischer Beobachter*, and took it back to the office. There was a large photograph of the U-boat commander, Gunther Prien, on the front page. I laid it on the desk. Then I opened my briefcase, and took out the photograph that I had liberated from Agent Nightingale's Brandenburg file. The man in the file photograph was younger, and he was dressed in civilian clothes, but there was no doubt about it: The two photographs were of the same man.

Of course it was impossible that the commander of a U-boat could be an agent sending back daily intelligence reports from Ireland. Clearly, someone had placed a picture of Gunther Prien in Nightingale's file. I still had no picture of the agent.

On Tuesday I bought a bicycle. I needed a convenient way of getting about and so many of the city's people used bicycles I thought I might as well join them. It was an old machine with a tendency to creak and groan. Once I discovered its preferred leisurely pace, we got on fine.

#

A week later, Heinz arrived in my office early, carrying a large camera and a tripod. He suggested that we use the canteen on the first floor. The place was deserted. Heinz set up the tripod, and took my picture several times. When he was satisfied with the shots, I found a pot of coffee on a warm stand, left over from the night before. I poured out two cups of coffee and we sat at one of the tables.

I gave Heinz the details of my cover story. I would pose as an Irish national, a post-graduate maths student, based in Trinity College, Dublin.

"Name?" Heinz asked.

"Kevin O'Reilly." I knew my mother had reverted to her maiden name.

"Sounds authentic enough. What are you doing in the south of the country?"

"Where in the south?"

He shrugged. "Wherever the U-boat drops you. Could be the coast of Kerry, Cork or Waterford."

"A walking holiday?"

"What about Blesset?"

I frowned. "Better make him my poor lunatic brother, Rory."

Heinz nodded. "What about clothes?"

"What did you have in mind?"

"You'll need clothes with Irish labels."

"I have some slacks, some underwear, a jumper, an old pair of shoes. I'll need some shirts."

"Right," Heinz said, "and Blesset will need a complete outfit."

After this meeting my trip to Ireland, which had assumed a dreamlike, unreal quality for a long time, became an immediate and real prospect.

#

Near the end of the month, I spoke to Alex.

"Any more news about Boniface?" I asked him.

We were in the open, walking by the canal. Alex immediately

began to look all around as if someone might be listening. "Keep your voice down. And don't say that word."

"As you wish." I thought he might be feigning paranoia as a joke.

"I have found nothing further about... that word," he said. "You?"

"Nothing."

"Have you searched the Abwehr archive?"

I laughed. "And how easy do you think that would be? There's a dragon at the gate of our archive. In the first place, you have to specify precisely which file you want to see and second, you need a cast iron excuse to view it."

"You could come up with some plausible story."

"Maybe, but all requests must be countersigned by an Oberst."

"You obviously don't take...that code word...seriously." He sounded irritated.

"You'll have to narrow it down a bit. Give me some dates to work with."

"Try June 1940."

"I'll need a day," I said.

"I don't know. Early June. Say June 7."

"Fine. I'll see what I can do."

Back at the office, I filled in an F17 form and asked Oberst von Neumann to countersign it.

"What's it for?" he asked.

"I want to dig out any reports of recent sabotage activities in Britain carried out by subversives from Ireland."

The Oberst signed the form and handed it back to me without further comment.

I approached the Oberfeldwebel with care. I smiled and handed him my F17 form.

He examined the form with his eyeglass. "The English signals?"

"Yes, for June of last year."

"Right," he said, handing me the English Language Signals Index book for 1940. "Follow me."

He led me to the relevant section of shelving. "Try not to disturb anything too much. I like order and tidiness," he said, and went back to his desk.

I spent close to two hours searching through the files, but found no mention of the code word Boniface.

#

I buried myself in my work and became very busy, often remaining in the office after normal hours. Most of this extra work was generated by the large volume of signals received from Nightingale. His intelligence continued at the highest levels, and it was important to relay this information to the other agencies without delay.

One evening, after everyone else had left the building, I took the stairs up to the fourth floor with Boniface and Hummingbird in mind. It was dark. There was nobody about. I listened for a few moments for any sounds that might indicate others on the floor. Apart from the tap-tap of Morse and the squeal of radios from the transmissions stations, all was silent. Standing in shadow at the end of the corridor, was a large imposing door with a nameplate that read Canaris, Reichsadmiral. Next came the office of Generalmajor Oster. Tentatively, I tried the handle and was surprised when the door swung open. I slipped inside.

Oster's office was large, with a vast desk of antique walnut. Four large red-and-black Reich swastika standards stood limp behind the desk, two on either side. A number of decorative pieces littered the desk: a miniature marble Matterhorn, a bust of the Führer in pewter, and a small bronze eagle crouched over a nest of broken eggs – identical to my father's and the one on Oberst Schiller's desk.

The walls were covered in maps and photographs. A glass-fronted bookcase stood in one corner, a man-sized safe against another. The desk drawers were all locked. A battery of filing cabinets standing against one wall were also locked.

I ran my eye over the books in the bookcase. There was nothing of interest there. I looked at the maps. One of the photographs on the walls caught my eye. I froze in disbelief. It was an old framed photograph, captioned Munich, 1909. It showed a group of seven young men smiling in sunshine. The photograph was not remarkable in any way. What made my heart stop was that I recognised it. There was an identical photograph amongst my father's things in a cardboard box in my mother's apartment in Dublin. The thin, tall man in the centre was unmistakeable. It was Generalmajor Oster; on the far right, wearing a jumper, and with a full head of hair, Oberst von Neumann; the second young man from the left was my father; and between my father and Oster, stood Professor Stephan Hirsch, my mathematics professor. I continued to peer at the photograph in the gloom, but I couldn't identify any of the other three men.

As I came out I saw two ghostly eyes staring from the top of the darkened staircase, the street lamps outside reflecting from Speddig's glasses. He must have seen me emerging from Generalmajor Oster's office. I greeted him as I passed, but he made no response, tracking my progress down the stairs in silence.

29

April 1941

On April 20 – the Führer's birthday – I was summoned to Generalmajor Oster's office. Oster's secretary showed me into a small bare room – the same room where I had been questioned about Kleister's death by Glasser, the KRIPO man. The room was equipped as before: a table, a telephone, three plain chairs, the window barred.

She handed me two thin blue files, marked Most Secret.

"You may read these files, but they must not leave this room."

"May I make notes?"

"That is strictly forbidden," she said. "Ring me when you're finished."

I sat down on the unwelcoming wooden chair. The telephone had no dial on it. Curious, I picked it up.

"Yes?" It was Oster's secretary.

"Could I have a cup of coffee?" I said.

I opened the first file. Nightingale's name was Henry John Lightfoot. He carried a legitimate Irish passport. He was born in 1901 in County Tipperary. His father was a postmaster. He had seven sisters and no brothers. He spent three years in college in Cork, graduating in 1923 with a degree in history and economics, followed by another three years in the University of Dresden as a postgraduate. In 1926, he was awarded a Masters degree in Political History. His thesis was entitled: *The Rise of Zionism in Europe: The Politicism of Economic Power*.

His current position was Undersecretary in the Irish Department of External Affairs, in Dublin.

The agent's photograph in his blue file was the same useless grainy picture as the one in the yellow file in my desk.

The second file was that of Pavel Zapochek, codename Ornithologist. He had an impressive background in communications. According to his file, he had sufficient knowledge and skills to repair a broken radio transmitter or receiver in the field. The objective of his mission was to report back on the movement of British ships and aircraft in the Irish Sea. His cover name was Rupert Kinski.

The requested cup of coffee never materialised.

As soon as I got back to my office, I jotted down the main points from both files.

#

It was a few days later that I finally met Oberst Egbert Krause, the head of Section III. I had little or no contact with the people of his section on the first floor. They were concerned with German domestic intelligence matters, whereas my focus was on operations overseas.

Oberst von Neumann had arranged a meeting to review my work, and I had arrived early that day, intending to clear my desk and spend a few minutes in preparation for the meeting. Before heading for my small desk and squeaky chair, I grabbed a cup of coffee from the canteen.

Oberst Krause was there, sitting alone at one of the tables, reading a newspaper. He called out to me. "Müller! Leutnant Müller, a moment of your time."

I had no idea who he was, but I could tell from his age and bearing that he was not someone I should ignore.

He closed his newspaper, folded it away, and introduced himself. Then he said, "I hear good things about you."

"Who's been speaking about me behind my back?"

"Oberst von Neumann speaks very highly of you, Generalmajor Oster, too. And you've come to the attention of the Old Man. He has been watching your career with interest."

"I'm sure the Admiral has much more important things to think about," I said, dismissing the Oberst's obvious flummery.

Oberst Krause was a big man, with a pleasant, disarming smile and the earnest, unblinking stare of an eagle.

"I've heard that you've been working late. You were seen on the fourth floor well after dark."

Speddig.

I decided to ignore the implied criticism. If the Oberst had a complaint about my behaviour, let him make it directly. The Oberst and I both knew that for us to discuss anything concerning overseas intelligence would be a serious breach of Abwehr rules; his jurisdiction extended only as far as the German borders.

I said, "My new job keeps me very busy."

He smiled toothily. "I believe you have a friend in the Air Ministry."

Gudrun?

"He works in the signals section."

"Alex Clausen, Herr Oberst."

"I wondered how you met Herr Clausen."

"We met at the Luftschutz civil defence programme – We joined on the same day."

"Ah yes, of course. You didn't know him before that?"

I was unsure where the conversation was leading. I threw him a frown. "No, Herr Oberst. Is this important?"

"No, no, not at all. We like to see our people engaging with others outside of their working circle. It encourages teamwork, builds morale, strengthens inter-departmental ties – that sort of thing. You understand."

"I think so, Herr Oberst." I didn't, but you have to be polite.

After that meeting, I thought hard about what the Oberst had said. It seemed Speddig was spying for the Oberst within the building. I was depressed by the realisation that, even within the confines of the Abwehr, Germans were spying on Germans. That the Oberst knew about Alex was unsettling, that he thought it important even more so. It seemed my every move was being observed by someone or other.

It occurred to me later how alike the three Obersts were. Like three jacks from the same deck of cards, they were all big men of similar ages, all three exuded charm, and all carried themselves with the gravitas that comes with serious responsibility.

#

That same evening SS-Sturmbannführer von Kemp was waiting for me at the door of the building. Instantly, the tremor returned to my hands. It was like a programmed response. My interrogator looked comical, perched atop an old ladies' bicycle. He wobbled in beside me as I pedalled toward Horst Wessel Platz.

I said, "Did you send that parcel?"

"A small piece of police humour." He showed no vestige of a smile. "I hope you liked it."

"My girlfriend didn't think it was funny when she opened it."

He was silent for a few minutes. We rode on, side by side, like old friends.

"You have been observed checking the British archives again. What were you looking for?"

"I was searching for evidence of Irish Republican activity in Britain."

"Did you find any?"

"No."

"Why not? There's been plenty of IRA activity in England."

"Not since the start of hostilities."

Again, he lapsed into silence, concentrating on keeping his front wheels aligned with mine.

Within sight of Horst Wessel Platz, he said, "You do remember what I said at our last meeting?"

"Specifically?"

"You work for me. When you find anything suspicious in the files, you will report back to me without delay."

"Of course."

He held out a hand, grabbed my handlebars and brought us both to a halt. It was a clumsy act that nearly brought us both crashing to the ground.

"This is not a game, Müller. Make no mistake, if you cross me, your uncle will not be able to save you again. Do I make myself clear?"

"Perfectly."

Bluster, I thought. Oh, von Kemp was every bit as dangerous as he wanted me to believe, but I knew that his hands were tied. He lacked the authority to rough me up again, and these intimidating tactics were all that he had – for the present.

For all that I could reason away the threat, the tremor in my hands persisted that evening, accompanied by a disturbance in my gut. The conversation with von Kemp went round and round in my head. Unwilling to face my empty apartment, I ate in a café close by. My ration book and wallet were both sorely depleted, and I had to settle for a vegetable risotto with dry bread and tap water. When I re-entered the apartment after dark, I found the bedroom door closed, light showing under it. My heart thudded in my chest. Had von Kemp sent someone to search the apartment? I turned on the living room light to find Gudrun's books back on the bookshelves. The apartment had been tidied; all of my half-eaten pizzas, empty beer bottles, and old newspapers were gone.

Gudrun was sitting up in bed, reading *The 39 Steps*. She looked up at me as I entered. My heart soared.

"You're late," she said, as if she had never been away.

I stood and stared at her.

"Aren't you surprised to see me?" She grinned.

"Of course. I thought I'd lost you."

"You know I love you," she said. "You must have known that I'd come back."

"I love you too, but I wasn't so sure that I *would* see you again."

"Silly boy!" She beamed at me, and returned to John Buchan.

And that was that. I washed and shaved and slipped into bed beside Gudrun and our life together resumed as if nothing had happened between us.

I described my trip to Brandenburg. She laughed when I told her about Blesset's unfortunate affliction.

"It really is nothing to laugh about," I said. "It seems to me that someone is working to ensure that all efforts by our agents in Ireland fail."

30

May 1941

On May 8 and 9, the British dropped their bombs on Hamburg. Once again, thanks to our ability to decode British TypeX signals, we had foreknowledge of the horrifying raids, and once again, no warning was given to the people of Hamburg.

I asked Alex if he had news of his mother and brother.

"No," he said. "But Eugen has moved to a more rural institution."

Alex predicted a retaliatory bombing raid on London.

"You have seen the orders?"

"No, not at all, but it doesn't take a genius to work it out."

That night, the Luftwaffe unleashed a torrent of bombs over London. The following day, Operation Sealion, the planned invasion of Britain, was abandoned. The order to stand down the operation was received and relayed to all ministries on May 11.

I began to appreciate the significance of the altered signal. That signal exaggerated the capacity of the British to replace lost aircraft. Obviously, it would have had little effect on its own, but if there were a number of similar altered signals, the cumulative effect might be to discourage the invasion.

On Sunday May 18, Gudrun, Johann, Alex and I went to the zoological gardens. It was a typical, warm summer day. Birds were singing their hearts out in every tree. As soon as we entered the zoo, it occurred to me that the native birds living within the confines of the zoo were special. Unlike normal sparrows, starlings and so on, these birds had chosen to share their lives with exotic creatures from all round the world. It seemed to me a perfect analogy for the German occupation of other countries: Poland, Denmark, Norway, France, Czechoslovakia… Surely, German troops living in these occupied countries must be like these native birds living an uneasy life among strangers.

I tried to explain my idea to the others.

"You mean like those birds that live on the backs of wild buffalo, in Africa?" Johann suggested.

"Or the tiny fish that clean the basking sharks' teeth?" Gudrun said.

"Wrasse." I said.

"What are you twittering on about now, Kurt?" said Alex. "You do come up with the strangest notions."

In the big cats' house, we stood for a while, observing a full-grown lioness paced back and forth behind the bars

Johann said, "It's cruel."

Gudrun agreed.

"What d'you expect?" said Alex. "It's a zoo."

"They could be given a bit more room to walk around," I said.

"They should take them back to their own countries and let them go," Johann countered.

"Isn't this an analogy for something, Kurt?" Alex gave us his Quasimodo look.

My mind was full of the labour camp at Ravensbrück, but I smiled and said nothing.

On the tram back to the apartment, I noticed a tall, sad-looking man wearing a dark three-piece suit, a light raincoat and a flat cap. His clothing suggested an office worker, but his cap was the garb of a labourer. I thought he might have been a domestic servant – a footman, perhaps – or an undertaker's apprentice.

The next day, Monday May 19, our magnificent battleship, *Bismarck*, sailed out from Gotenhafen in northern Poland. The Abwehr was awash with the news, but we were warned to keep the information to ourselves until the Propaganda Ministry released it to the press.

I couldn't contain my excitement; I told Gudrun about it that night.

"This is a big battleship?" she asked.

"The biggest ever launched. Its guns are huge. So big that other ships won't be able to get anywhere near it."

On May 21, the newspapers announced the launching of 'the world's greatest battleship'.

On Monday, May 26, the newspaper headlines were full of the news that the *Bismarck* had sunk the British Battle Cruiser *HMS Hood* near Greenland. This was the second big German naval victory of the war, after the sinking, by U47, of the *Royal Oak* in Scapa Flow in October of '39. According to the newspaper articles, *HMS Hood's* magazine suffered a direct hit, and the ship was blown to oblivion with the loss of all hands.

Gudrun asked me that night how many men had lost their lives.

"Who knows? Perhaps twelve or thirteen hundred."

"That's horrible," she said. "Think of all those poor mothers."

"The fortunes of war," I replied.

#

Liesel Martens dropped into the office on May 27, her snub-nosed face as cute as ever. She was wearing a short black skirt and a white blouse. She looked like a waitress or a nurse from the hospital. It felt as if we had never been apart, although it had been three months since our last goodbye on the train from Brandenburg.

She dropped two typewritten pages on my desk. "It's finished. I hope you like it."

"When will it be published?"

She turned her head to one side. She said nothing. The look on her face suggested an unspoken question.

"You mean it might never be published?"

"It's possible." She shrugged.

"But I thought the ministry wanted a story about an Abwehr hero?"

"They did – two months ago. Priorities change. And during a war, priorities change very quickly."

I picked up the document and looked at it. The front page carried a head and shoulders picture of a figure in silhouette and the headline: Ernst Huber – Reich Superspy.

"Ernst Huber? Who's he?"

"He's my composite. Read it. Let me know what you think. If you don't like it, tell me. Be as brutal as you must. I'd much rather you were honest than kind."

"When do you want it back?"

"You can keep it. Throw it away if you don't want it."

I took Liesel's piece home and showed it to Gudrun.

She laughed when she read it. "It's like treacle," she said. "Surely no one will publish this!"

ERNST HUBER – SUPERSPY

This is Ernst Huber - the man who could win the war for Germany. Unknown to his countrymen, unremarked by the enemy, Ernst Huber toils away alone and in secret behind enemy lines. The information that he gathers is vital to the war effort. To know what the enemy is thinking – that is the Art of Modern Warfare.

Ernst Huber lives far from his native land, in enemy territory. He listens, he watches, he notes what he hears and sees, and each day he sends what he knows back to Berlin. His stock-in-trade is a code book and a powerful radio transmitter. He is a spy, and he spies for the Fatherland.

Not that he is the only one, for there is a legion of patriotic men and women like Ernst, working silently, diligently for the greater glory of the Third Reich. What makes Ernst Huber unique is the quality of the intelligence that he gathers. For none is better, none more skilful, and none more invisible than Ernst the Superspy.

Born in the last century, and with a distinguished 1914-1918 war record behind him, Ernst Huber is no intellectual. Not for him the ivory towers of academia, the rewards of commerce, or the glories of the race track. His training was second to none. A crack shot, a master of all forms of armed and unarmed combat, of safe-cracking, lock-picking and sabotage, and at the peak of physical fitness, Ernst is an opponent to be feared by any enemy.

Huber is his own man. He lives a simple existence, seeking nothing for himself but his daily bread and the chance to serve his country. Quietly, stealthily, surreptitiously, he goes about his business, and the Reich is the richer for it.

And when the war is over, when the Fatherland has triumphed over its enemies, as it surely will, when that day comes, there will be no accolades for Ernst. Not for him, medals or awards, bands or parades. Ernst will quietly disappear back into obscurity from whence he came. Unsung, unknown, this, perhaps our greatest hero, will look for no recognition, nor will he receive any.

And when, at last, he lies down for his final rest, Ernst Huber will know what he has achieved for his country. Only he will know, for he will die in obscurity, surrounded by his loved ones, venerated as an old and humble man.

Perhaps some day, in that fair future of the Thousand Year Reich, the name of Ernst Huber will be honoured for his gargantuan contribution to the New World Order, to the ending of the war, to the final victory, to the Greater Germany.

That same night, the newspapers had further, dreadful news of the *Bismarck*. The great battleship had been hunted down and destroyed by the British, near Brest, in Northern France.

"How many deaths this time?" Gudrun asked.

"Two thousand, estimated." I replied gloomily.

"The fortunes of war," said Gudrun.

I thought: What a stupid expression! There was nothing fortunate about the deaths of our brave sailors who died on the *Bismarck*, or about the British who died on the *Hood*.

Toward the end of the month, I was given a tentative date of November for my U-boat trip to Ireland.

31

June 1941

On June 1 the British surrendered the island of Crete, just two days after the landing of a massive Wehrmacht force on the island. Alex reckoned we now had control over the Mediterranean.

On June 2, Oberst von Neumann appeared in my office. "Come with me," he said.

I followed him out the door and into his office. He stood by the door, closing it firmly as I sat down.

"Is there something wrong, Herr Oberst?"

"Yes," he said, lowering his large frame into his chair. "It's agent Nightingale. He will have to be silenced at once."

I was stunned by this statement. I stammered, "But, but, Herr Oberst... Nightingale is our best agent in Ireland. Without him, we have nothing."

He pulled his pipe from a drawer in his desk and began to fill it. "We have Stallion."

"Stallion is worthless. You've said so yourself. Nightingale gives us troop movements, air intelligence, marine intelligence, valuable information about British Cabinet meetings – all sorts of first class information."

"And don't you think we could obtain this information from other sources?"

I pondered the Oberst's question for a couple of seconds.

"From intercepted TypeX signals?"

"Precisely," he said, striking a match and applying it to his pipe.

"Are you saying that we could have obtained some of the information that Nightingale has sent us by decoding enemy signals?"

"No." He blew a cloud of smoke toward the ceiling. "I am saying that we *have* obtained *all* of the information supplied to us by agent

Nightingale by decoding intercepted British TypeX transmissions."

All of it?

"You mean to say that Agent Nightingale is of no value to us at all?"

"Is that what I said, Kurt? I am saying nothing of the sort. What I said was that Nightingale's information – all of it – has been received, verified and confirmed thanks to our ability to intercept and decode British TypeX transmissions."

I shook my head in bewilderment.

"All right," he said, pointing the stem of his pipe at me. "What cipher does Nightingale use?"

"Lorenz SZ38."

"Which the British have broken months ago." He clamped his pipe between his teeth. "We can presume that they don't know where Nightingale is located. Oh, they know he is in Ireland, they may even know that he is in Dublin, but they can hardly ferret him out and arrest him. Ireland is a neutral country, after all, and Agent Nightingale is a native Irishman."

He released a huge cloud of smoke. "Let's try another question. What is the one thing that the British don't know about the Abwehr?" He returned the pipe to his mouth.

"That we have broken their TypeX cipher?"

"Precisely. And that is the one piece of information that we must protect at all costs. The British believe that their TypeX system is far superior to Enigma. They have failed to break Enigma, so they must be confident that TypeX is also unbreakable."

"And Nightingale…"

"When the British read Nightingale's signals, they are convinced that we are receiving all of this great information from our super-spy, based in Ireland."

"And not from intercepted TypeX signals."

"Exactly. So you see how valuable Nightingale's transmissions are to us? They act as a shield to cover our deciphering success."

"Does this mean that Nightingale is not actually gathering all of this intelligence?" I asked.

"Some of it is his own work, low level stuff, mostly. That report about U47, for example, was taken straight from the British newspapers. The really good stuff we send him through the diplomatic bags. He simply encodes it all and sends it straight back, using the Lorenz SZ38 cipher." He leaned forward and grinned. "The British intercept, decode and read the signals and say, 'Damn, that German agent in Ireland is good.'"

"So why does he need to be silenced?"

"He is in danger of being discovered by the British."

"But you said the British can't touch him in Ireland."

"Not if they play by the rules. But we have reason to believe that they're planning to move against him."

"We will need someone else to take his place."

"Eventually, yes."

Immediately after that meeting, I sent a signal for encoding and transmission using my codename, Roberts:

To Nightingale, From Roberts
Cease all operations
Radio silence imperative until further notice

#

In the third week of June, began the largest military operation in human history. Operation Barbarossa was launched with the invasion of the Soviet Union across a 2,500 kilometre front. Signal traffic volumes in all languages exploded, and once again I was asked to lend a hand in the Translations Unit of Section I. The only way I could keep abreast of my normal work was by expanding my working day to nine, ten, and then eleven hours.

The early news from the Eastern Front was good. The Soviets put up little or no resistance, and wherever they took a stand, their forces proved inferior, wilting under the irresistible strength of Blitzkrieg.

On June 30, my birthday came round again. Gudrun cooked a special meal to celebrate. But like all of my birthdays, it was a bittersweet occasion, being also the anniversary of my father's death.

32

July 1941

June had been hot; July was sweltering. The air seemed heavy and humid. Everyone said that an electric storm was threatened and that the oppressive weather would improve as soon as it arrived. Throughout the summer, the man with the flat cap followed me everywhere I went and I became quite used to his presence. He never approached or said anything to me, but he was there whenever I ventured outside.

On Bastille Day, July 14, an ambulance arrived at the front door of the building. Hauptmann von Pfaffel was carried down the stairs on a stretcher and taken away to hospital.

In the office, speculation was rife. Some said he had had a heart seizure, others that his mind was gone. There was general agreement that the cause of the Hauptmann's health problems could be traced to a signal received that morning from England. It was rumoured that one of his agents had been apprehended by the British.

I waited a couple of days for the furore to die down. Then I sought out the signal in the archive. It was from one of von Pfaffel's agents in Britain. It reported that another agent –Agent 38 – had been arrested by the British police and charged with a series of burglaries.

It soon became clear that the loss of Agent 38 was a serious blow, not only to the Abwehr, but to the conduct of the war. The decryption information that we had been receiving daily through the Spanish diplomatic mail dried up. Without this information we were blind to TypeX signals traffic.

The one good thing that came from this – or so I thought – was Speddig's mood. He took the loss of TypeX signals traffic – and the kudos that went with decoding and translating British signals – as an affront. I'm sure he was convinced that the British had singled him out and were conspiring against him personally.

The Hauptmann was released from hospital and returned to his desk after a week. He looked older and more care-worn than ever.

Not long after that, the Abwehr ant hill was under attack again; Admiral Canaris was absent for several days, and a strong rumour circulated around the office that he had been relieved of his command. When he returned, informed opinion had it that he had travelled to the Führer's private residence in the Berchtesgaden, and that the Führer had been persuaded to reinstate him.

#

Gudrun wore her lightest clothes, but she found little relief from the heat. Her sleep was disturbed most nights. When she did sleep, she snored, and her snoring often woke me.

She changed. Our lovemaking stopped. We quarrelled about trivial matters: the laundry, whose turn it was to clean the dishes. I made attempts to build bridges, but to no avail. It seemed the heat was too much for Gudrun, and she became less and less approachable. Separation never occurred to me; I loved her too much for that, and I was sure that we would become friends and lovers again as soon as the weather abated.

I took to working later and later. Every day I bought the Party newspaper, *Völkischer Beobachter*, and read it from cover to cover.

The newspaper was full of invective and nationalistic superlatives, printed on poor quality newsprint with ink that came off on my hands. It seemed to me that this organ of the State was attempting to drive a wedge between the Right and the Left, to polarise the whole of German society. The newspaper displayed an uncompromising attitude to 'un-German' activities. The Communist Party was singled out as a nest of evil enemies of the German people. According to the newspaper, Bolshevism was a bankrupt political philosophy that should be stamped out at all costs. Waste and greed were the two great evils of the soul that were working to destroy Germany from within. Greed was seen as the great sin of the "Zionist State" that had preceded the Third Reich; waste was an intolerable crime that must be eliminated from German life if the New Germany were to break the unjust shackles of the Treaty of Versailles, and rise from the ashes.

It was sickly stuff, but I read it all, absorbed it, analysed it, and then washed it from my hands. I felt as though I was listening to the Führer delivering one of his famous Nuremburg speeches, and indeed, much of the copy in the newspapers had its origins there.

The more I read, the more I felt out of tune with popular opinion. I could not accept that the ills of the depression and run-away inflation of the early Thirties were entirely the result of the unrestrained greed of a few Zionist bankers, or that the KPD was plotting a proletarian revolution that would destroy us all. I believed that the country needed to be rebuilt, and that strong leadership was needed to restore German pride, but I balked at the idea that strong leadership must mean the dictatorship of one man or the imposition of law and order by jackboot and cudgel.

And then one day, I found a snippet on an inside page and my heart did a small somersault. The piece concerned the fashions worn by the elite of German society at the premier of one of Leni Riefenstahl's films. Actresses were described as being adorned with exotic jewellery, feathers and silks, snake skin and furs. The article was published under the by-line Liesel Martens.

After the initial thrill of discovery, I was assailed by two contrasting emotions: first I felt let down, like post-coital deflation; then I felt foolish that Liesel was still there in the back of my mind. The discovery provided its own clarity, however; like a butterfly emerging from its chrysalis, Liesel burst from my subconscious, invaded my conscious thoughts and flooded my bloodstream.

In the afternoon of that same day, Heinz arrived in my office.

"That code word you asked me about," he said. "I found it – eventually."

"And?"

"I was looking in all the wrong places. I naturally assumed it had something to do with overseas operations. But it's quite old. It's from 1934."

"And?" My heart was in my throat with anticipation.

"Hummingbird was the codeword used to initiate action on the Night of the Long Knives."

33

August 1941

On the fourth day of August Liesel's article "Ernst Huber – Superspy" was published simultaneously in several popular magazines. On the fifth, Oberst von Neumann called me into his office. I could see that he was upset about something, sitting behind his desk, his face red, his eyes ablaze. His whole body was rigid.

"Shut the door."

When I did he threw a magazine at me. "Now tell me, what is this?"

It was a copy of *Signal*. He had folded it open at an inside page, where Liesel's article appeared, along with the head and shoulders silhouette picture.

I said, "This is Fräulein Liesel Martens's article."

"And what do you think of it?" The Oberst clutched his unlit pipe in his left hand.

"I thought the writing was good."

"You couldn't see anything wrong with it?"

"Perhaps a little overdramatic," I said.

"And what impression do you think the public will get from reading it?"

"I'm sorry," I said. "I can see you're upset, Herr Oberst—"

"Upset? I think you could say that! Why wouldn't I be upset, when this... this... article tells the whole fucking world how badly we treat our men? No honours, no medals, no recognition. All they can look forward to is death in obscurity and poverty."

"I don't think it says—"

"And where's the Abwehr mentioned in there? Or the Wehrmacht? Anyone reading that would think that Joseph Goebbels was personally operating all overseas agents."

His voice was rising. Now it dropped to a hiss. "And where did she get that name? Don't you know we have two agents called Huber operating in the field? Two! And one of them is called Ernst."

"We have an Ernst Huber? I had no idea, Herr Oberst."

"You should have checked before you sanctioned the article."

"Sanctioned? I read it before it was published, Herr Oberst, but I didn't think it was my job to sanction it."

His voice rose to a squeak. "This was your responsibility."

"I'm sorry, Herr Oberst. It looked innocent enough to me."

"This is not your finest piece of work, Leutnant. At the very least you should have shown the article to me before giving it the go-ahead. Now get out of my sight."

#

At eleven o'clock in the morning of the nineteenth, Alex rang.

"She rang me here – at the office," he said. This was obviously one of Alex's pranks.

"Who did?" I said, playing along. "The queen of Sheba?"

"Meet me in ten minutes."

"Lunchtime, Alex. It's only eleven."

"I'll come round there," he said. "Meet me outside."

He hung up before I could protest.

I waited fifteen minutes before going down to the first floor. Alex was waiting for me on the steps outside. He looked dishevelled, ashen. He looked ill. I had never seen Alex like this.

He was almost weeping. "My mother rang."

"Your mother."

"She rang me at the office."

"Your mother rang you at the office." He wasn't making any sense.

"She never rings me at the office," he said. Then, "You've heard about this new law?"

"What new law?"

"The Prevention of Genetically Deformed Offspring."

"Oh, that law. Yes, I've read about it, but it's not new."

"They've started a new programme." His hands were in motion, smoothing his hair, scratching the back of his neck, rubbing his face.

"Wasn't that the law behind the sterilisation programme? I haven't heard about any new programme."

"They've started killing people – people who are a drain on society." He stared into my eyes, willing me to tell him it was not so.

"You mean people who don't work? I read about re-education camps. But not killing, surely not killing—"

"My mother's received an official notification ..." His voice failed him.

"Your brother has been put back on a list ...?"

He shook his head. Then in a strangled voice he said, "She never rings me in the office, you see." He looked as though he might fall down. I gripped his arm.

"You can fight it in the appeal courts, again. What are they called? Eugenics Courts?"

"This letter," he said in a broken voice, "speaks about his 'sudden death.'" I stared at him in disbelief. His face was distorted. He looked as though he were crying, and yet there were no tears. "The thing is, she never rings me at work."

Alex seemed to crumple, like a piece of paper. I released his arm and he collapsed onto the steps. He sat with his arms folded across his shins, head on his knees. I sat down beside him and put an arm around his shoulders. A few people glanced at us, then hurried on by. After a while, he recovered a little of his composure.

"If she wants his remains she must collect them in the next seven days. Otherwise they will be disposed of."

"Remains?"

"Ashes. They have cremated my brother," he moaned.

I gripped his shoulders and said nothing. I couldn't think of anything to say.

"She keeps asking if she should send him a food parcel. I need to explain it to her. She keeps asking. She doesn't seem to understand."

"You should go," I said. "She needs you. Go. Go now. Do you have money for the train?"

He looked at me, the eternal torment of hell and all its demons in his eyes. "How do I tell her? *What* do I tell her?"

"Leave now," I said. "You'll know what to say when you get there."

He shook his head again. Then he stood up and hurried away. I watched him go, crouched, pushing himself forward, like an old man climbing a hill. I watched until he had been swallowed up in the crowd and I could see him no more.

#

I never had a brother, and I always felt that my life was the poorer for it. Certainly, my childhood was. Most of my friends at school had siblings, and although sisters were sometimes considered more of a curse than a gift, even sisters were better than nothing. Brothers were cherished, like trophies. Older brothers provided all sorts of benefits, and younger brothers were a source of pride in the playground.

I tried to imagine how Alex was feeling, and what emerged angered me. How was it possible that something as abhorrent as this – such a devastating personal loss – could be good for the Fatherland?

I could see how certain members of society might be seen as unproductive, but it seemed unthinkable that the authorities could put their social theories into practice in such a brutal way. My thoughts turned, once again, to the people in the labour camps. Were these miserable people really "undesirables", as the SS would have us believe, or were they merely unfortunate victims of a cruel, uncompromising regime?

And what of the Jews? We all knew that these people were the subject of a relentless nationwide evacuation programme. What if the rumours were true and some of these, too, were being euthanized, possibly hundreds of them?

#

Gudrun was devastated by the news. There was no way I could keep it from her and no way that I could obscure the arbitrariness and brutality of what had happened. She cried a lot and spent long periods locked in the bedroom or the bathroom.

From that day she changed. It was nothing I could have described in words; everything continued as before; we did all the same things; our conversations were as they had been; and our love-making was as frequent as before. But I had the feeling that something had been lost; some modicum of warmth, of passion, of our unique bond was gone forever. It was as if she thought I was partly to blame for what had happened to Eugen.

34

September, October 1941

September was hotter still, the hottest month of the year. In the capital, the grey concrete streets were like vast mirrors reflecting the searing sun; the heat rebounded in waves from the faces of the massive buildings, wrapping us all in its clammy embrace. Cicadas sang incessantly in the trees. The pavements became too hot to walk on. Car radiators steamed; Litfass columns peeled; sticky pedestrians scurried from one shady spot to another, and sweating horses snorted their discomfort.

Indoors, there was no relief from the heat, either. Offices became ovens. Offices with fans were no better, as there was nothing but hot air for the fans to circulate. Everyday office politics engendered bitter disputes; disagreements grew into shouting matches; old grudges, long forgotten, resurfaced; and arguments between colleagues erupted into life-or-death conflicts.

I adjusted my route to and from work to take me past the Propaganda Ministry in Wilhelmstrasse. I could not shake a feeling of unfinished business with Liesel; perhaps I hoped that an accidental encounter might be enough to reignite the embers of our friendship. The heat made it impossible to remain in any one place for more than a few minutes, and my excursions past her place of work never resulted in any encounters, accidental or otherwise.

Even at night it remained stifling. Gudrun cooked very little, preferring to serve cold dishes. I longed for luxuries: salads, a taste of sausage, fruit. She seemed to lose her good humour, and with it much of her poise. Her limbs seemed heavier. Her smile was replaced with a grim tight-lipped scowl, and her flesh sagged.

Both of us too sticky with sweat to bear another's touch, it was impossible to make love. We would lie in the bed, side by side, careful to avoid even the smallest contact. I lay on my back, without cover; Gudrun slept on her side with her back turned toward me.

Near the end of September the weather broke. Dark clouds rolled in from the east and built up like a shroud over the city. The skies opened and the temperature fell. A warning lightning flash to the east was answered by two from the west, the three thunder rolls arriving within seconds of each other. The next flash was very close, accompanied by a sharp, metallic crack that rattled the windows.

Gudrun was petrified. She rushed about the apartment looking for a safe place to hide. Finally, she joined me in the bed. The electric storm continued for thirty minutes or so, before it began to move away. When the danger had passed, we found ourselves bathed in sweat, embracing like newly-weds.

We each had a quick wash, and then we made love. Perhaps it was the thrill of the fear, or because it had been more than two weeks since we last coupled, but that night's love-making was unusually passionate. I felt a deep release that I had not felt since our first night together. Gudrun opened herself to me with abandon and climaxed quickly.

An hour later, we made love again, and this time Liesel came into my mind, unbidden. It was as if she was there, in the room, mocking me. I felt a pang of guilt that killed my passion stone dead.

I lay on my back with my arm across my eyes, trying to erase Liesel's image from my mind.

Gudrun lit a cigarette. "What's the matter, Kurt?"

I shook my head. "It's nothing."

#

Thomas Kleister rang again the next day. This time the call reached my desk without the intervention of Speddig the busybody. I was surprised to hear from him. It had been nine months since my visit to the labour camp

"I hope you're ringing to say that Tania been released," I said.

"No, but I'm still hopeful. I've been sending regular food parcels."

"That should help." Secretly, I wondered if such food parcels would make it past the guards.

"Have you heard anything new about Tristan's death?"

I thought, what a burden for a father to carry – a son killed, a daughter in a labour camp. "I've heard nothing. I think there's not the faintest chance of the case being reopened. And even if it was, I'd be the last person to hear any news."

"There was one thing, since your last call," he said. "Tristan had booked a winter holiday in Austria for last year. I received a refund in the post from his lodgings. I thought it strange that he would plan and pay for a holiday and then kill himself."

#

On October 2, Operation Typhoon – the final drive to Moscow – began. The office was abuzz with excitement, the atmosphere electric. Signals traffic again began to peak, and the staircase was busy with runners.

Reinhard Heydrich's name was on the front page of the newspaper. I bought a copy. The article announced his appointment as Deputy Reich Protector for Bohemia and Moravia. He was to be based in Prague.

#

During October, I spent a lot of time with Alex. His alcohol intake had increased since his trip to Hamburg, and I sensed that he had fallen out with Johann. Of course there was only one thing that he could talk about. His despair had turned to anger. He railed against the government to anyone who would listen. Wherever he went he carried samples of his brother's art. Displaying these in public, he would buttonhole passers-by to ask their opinions. His natural sense of fun was still there, but it had turned into something bitter, something caustic.

"What do you think, Madam? Are these the work of a genius? No? Maybe? You're not sure? That's understandable. After all, they are the work of a deranged, malignant lunatic."

The Black Orchestra

No matter how hard or how often I tried to distract him, the conversation always returned to the same topic. His anger was like a virulent disease; it bubbled and festered in his mind.

While he was talking, inventing new ways of endlessly expressing the same ideas, it occurred to me that perhaps Eugen's death was partly my responsibility. If I had warned Alex prior to that first bombing raid, Eugen might have been moved somewhere safe; then he would not have been discovered wandering the streets of Hamburg, and he might not have come to the attention of the authorities.

Alex needed his companion more than ever since tragedy had entered his life. Gudrun decided to call Johann on the telephone, to see if she could engineer a reconciliation. I heard only Gudrun's side of the conversation.

"You must know how much Alex is hurting just now... What...? Why can't you just speak with him? He needs you... What do you mean...? You're not serious... What...? You *are* serious... The greater good, you say... What about his feelings...? I can't believe you said that... How do you think you'd feel—? ...The Fatherland my backside! Come on Johann, you can't be that unfeeling... Well, you know where you can stuff your Party ideals! Yes, that's what I said, and I meant every word. You're a cold, miserable bastard! You don't deserve Alex!"

She slammed the telephone down. "Did you hear that? I can't believe that anyone could be so heartless, so blind, so stupid. What does he think, that letting one handicapped person live will bring the mighty Reich to its knees?"

35

November 1941

$f$ollowing the extreme high temperatures of September and the cooler storms of October, November started cold, but the roads were still clear of ice and snow. Pushing my breath ahead of me I cycled to work, wrapped up in my dark blue overcoat and one of Gudrun's woollen scarves, my mind full of my impending trip.

Without warning, a black car veered across the street and struck my front wheel. The impact threw me sideways from the bicycle. I cracked my head on the cobblestones, and lay there, winded.

Two men in leather jumped out of the car. I was having difficulty focusing, but I thought I recognised them from my interrogation months ago. They lifted me to my feet and bundled me into the back of the car. Then we were speeding through the streets of Berlin. I was aware of a siren, softer and lower than a normal police siren. My head hurt at every jolt. I reached up and discovered blood; my hair was sticky with it and it trickled down the side of my face.

The driver looked at me in his mirror and said, "Don't get it on the seat."

I had no idea which direction we took, but we drove at speed for about thirty minutes. When we hit the suburbs, they switched off the siren. We continued on into the countryside. The car turned left, then left again onto an uneven surface.

We stopped. The pain in my head had eased, but there was blood in my eyes.

One of the men pulled me out of the car and stuffed an oily rag into my hands. "Clean yourself up with that."

The driver remained behind the wheel.

The car was parked on a dirt track surrounded by pine trees. I

The Black Orchestra

used the rag to clean the blood from my face and hands, then dropped it on the ground. Poking me in the back with something hard, which I assumed was a gun, the man propelled me to the side of the track, over a stile and onto a dirt track.

"Walk," he said.

I began to panic. Stories abounded of bodies found in woodland. What other reason could they have to take me to such a place?

The trees grew thick on both sides, cutting out most of the daylight; the smell of the pines was intense, filling my head with unwanted childhood memories. I followed the track for about a kilometre before coming to a clearing.

"Halt!" the gunman said.

I turned to face him. "SS-Sturmbannführer von Kemp—"

"Will be here shortly to do the honours." He cocked his gun, and a fresh wave of panic washed over me.

Just then, two ramblers appeared on the track. I have no recollection of their age or sex. I remember colourful woollen clothes, strong walkers' boots and walking sticks.

The gunman's eyes swivelled toward them and I hesitated for a second. His was a small calibre weapon but, at two metres distance – or less – he couldn't miss. Certain that my last moments had arrived, I gave a roar, put my head down and charged him.

My head connected with his chest, and he fell on his back, grunting, *"Scheisse!"*

I scrambled to my feet and turned to run, but he grabbed my ankle and I fell. Then he was on top of me. I landed a few blows, and managed to push him off and ran down the track.

I heard shouts behind me, but no shots. Diving off the track into the forest, I crashed into a large tree, hurting my left forearm. Ignoring the pain, I forced my way deeper and deeper into the wood.

My progress was slow; the trees were young, planted close together, their branches intertwined. Underfoot, the ground was uneven and treacherous. I could hear shouts, unintelligible, distant. I barged on through the undergrowth without regard to direction. Sweating, I threw off Gudrun's scarf.

Bursting through the edge of the virgin forest, I came to an area of older, taller trees, spaced further apart, a carpet of pine-needles underfoot. Pressing on, I made good ground for perhaps ten minutes before coming to a halt and slid into a sitting position against a tree, exhausted.

Listening hard, I could hear only bird sounds, nothing of my pursuer. I was safe for the moment, but I had no idea how far I had run, or in which direction. I closed my eyes. The pain in my arm had spread to my shoulder, and blood had seeped down from my head into my shirt.

The sound of the siren started. Moving twenty metres in one direction, then in another, I got a fix on the sound and headed toward it. It was my best hope of finding my way out of those infernal trees.

I found the walkers' track and what might have been the same clearing. I walked on. Then I could see two black cars through the trees. I was too close. I hurried back maybe two hundred metres and ducked in amongst the trees. I wondered about the second car. Perhaps von Kemp had arrived to 'do the honours'.

I waited.

Von Kemp appeared on the track dressed in a full-length woollen coat accompanied by the leathercoat with the gun. They drew level with my position and stopped. I froze and held my breath.

"Take this as your last warning, Müller," von Kemp called out. "I know you can hear me."

They walked back to the cars and drove away. I waited a few minutes before making my way to the stile. Not long after that two ramblers – maybe the same two – happened by. They brought me to the nearest small town where I found a taxi to take me back to the city.

The gunman had had a clear opportunities to shoot me and had failed to fire, I thought as the taxi jounced along. Perhaps he froze. That seemed unlikely. Perhaps von Kemp had left instructions that I was to be kept alive until he arrived to 'do the honours'.

PART 3

36

November 1941

I checked into the hospital. The wound on the crown of my head required a couple of stitches. My left forearm was broken, and my hands and face had suffered minor scratches from the trees. Gudrun said it was lucky I landed on my soft head. My forearm was put in plaster, and they kept me in the hospital for three days to check for signs of concussion.

On the second day I was visited by a tall man with grey hair, wearing the uniform of a general. I knew who he was, of course. This was the charismatic Generalmajor Hans Oster, second in command to Admiral Canaris, and a living legend in the Abwehr. I knew from the photograph in the Generalmajor's office that he and my father were acquainted, but I needed a moment to recover from the shock of meeting the great man.

"I've been meaning to call into your office to meet you," he said. "You know I knew your father? Your mother too, before they married."

"You knew my mother?"

He beamed at me. "She was a good-looking woman. I might have married her myself, if your father hadn't beaten me to it. How is she?"

"She's well," I said. "She lives in Ireland."

"Well, what happened to you? I hear you rammed a car with your bicycle."

I laughed. "The car crossed over to my side of the road, Herr Generalmajor. The police took me to a pine wood somewhere."

"Call me Oster," he said. "The title is too cumbersome. What did they want?"

"I think they meant to shoot me."

"Not very likely," he said. "The Gestapo can be a little over-theatrical at times."

"I escaped and hid in the trees. They've been harassing me for information. I have been interrogated once already."

"When was this interrogation?"

"Last summer."

"You should have told me about it at the time. What questions did they ask?"

My instincts were to trust him, but could I trust my instincts? I decided that I'd have to trust somebody and it might as well be this genial, friendly Generalmajor.

I told him about the altered signal. I explained my theory about the impact of the signal on Operation Eagle Attack – now called the 'Battle for Britain'. He showed no reaction. Even when I revealed the identity of the saboteur, his expression never changed.

"I wrote to the Admiral about it, but he took no action."

"Well that's one mystery solved," he said. I waited for something further, but the Generalmajor remained silent.

"I discovered another signal that had been removed from the archive," I told him. "I believe this signal would have exposed a Gestapo informer working inside the Abwehr."

He considered my words for a moment. Then he said, "You have proof?"

"Of sorts. Signalman Kleister handled the message the day before he died."

"I don't follow. Are you saying that's why he committed suicide?"

"I don't believe it was suicide, Herr Oster. I'm no expert, but it seems obvious to me. The bullet hole was too far back. I don't see how he could have managed it. And why would anyone place the gun in such an awkward position? And besides, I don't believe that the gun would have remained in his hand, and there was very little blood—"

"We really should leave these considerations to the experts, don't you think, Herr Müller?" He smiled.

I shook my head. "The Signalman in Leipzig who died – Gustav Barnard – was murdered too."

"And you know this how?" The expression on his face was one of total incredulity.

"The suicide note was a forgery. His parents will confirm this."

"I see. So you believe that both Signalmen were murdered, and the KRIPO got it wrong?"

"The Berlin KRIPO conducted no proper investigation. I believe they were covering for an informer working for the security services."

He sat, turning his leather gloves in his hands. "I was never happy about those two suicides, occurring as they did so close together. And I wondered why a Gestapo informer would feel the need to kill himself, anyway. What was in the missing signal?"

"I didn't find the actual signal, Herr Oster. Someone removed it from the archive. The Index specified the signal as 'person-to-person.'"

"Let me guess. It originated in the Leipzig office."

"Yes, Herr Oster."

"There may be a record of the message in Leipzig," he said.

From that moment my heart was lifted. I now had a powerful ally.

As he was leaving, the Generalmajor said, "I shall speak to my opposite number in the RSHA. Rest assured you'll have no more 'accidents' like this one."

"Thank you, Herr Oster."

A weight was lifted from my shoulders. The Generalmajor's reaction to my revelations about Schiller was worrying, but I was confident that he would act on my information. I resolved to leave everything in his hands.

I was discharged from the hospital on the same day that the British aircraft carrier *HMS Ark Royal* was torpedoed and sunk by U81, November 13.

My U-boat excursion had to be postponed because of my injuries. This was a disappointment. I had waited so long for it that my apprehension had gone and in its place there was nothing but frustration. When would I ever travel to Ireland?

37

December 1941

For weeks after my ordeal in the pine forest, I slept poorly and only for short periods at a time. That moment in the forest clearing facing a loaded gun remained vivid in my mind, fuelling the continuing tremor in my bones.

Von Kemp never left my thoughts. I couldn't believe that he intended to have me killed. Granted I'd given him no information so far, but what would he gain by my death?

On Saturday December 6, the telephone rang. Gudrun answered it. I was in the bath, attempting to keep my plaster dry. When I emerged from the bathroom, she said, "The Abwehr rang. Someone called von Pfaffel. He said they want you in the office right away."

I cursed under my breath as I struggled to pull on my shorts with one hand.

Promising Gudrun that I'd get away as soon as I could, I hurried into the office.

Section II was almost fully manned by the time I arrived. Oberst von Neumann and Hauptmann von Pfaffel were both at their desks. It looked like a busy weekday; the only indications that it was not were the way people were dressed and Sigmund was not on duty – Siegfried the night watchman had taken his place.

I reported to Oberst von Neumann. He was dressed as always. Obviously, his off-duty clothes and his work clothes were the same. I had a mental image of a wardrobe full of frayed green U-boat jumpers with leather patches.

"The shit's hit the fan," he said, eyeing my broken arm. "Schiller will explain."

I took the stairs down to the second floor. Oberst Schiller was on the telephone. The Translations Unit was packed. There were three

Russian language specialists on duty, where normally there were two. I could tell that the Communications Unit was fully manned, too, as there was a continuous flow of runners carrying signals from the fourth floor.

Oberst Schiller dropped the receiver back in its cradle and turned to me. "Counteroffensive," he said. "The Reds are defending Moscow. Help Gunther Speddig."

Speddig was sweating. His fingers flew over the Enigma on his desk, but it was clear that he had no hope of keeping abreast of the influx; the stack of raw signals in his in-tray was growing. I greeted him with a hearty thump on the back, and sat down at the desk beside him. We worked together for four hours without a break. By the end of that period, there were just three signals in the in-tray and the supply from the fourth floor had dried to a trickle.

"Time for a bite to eat," I said, stretching my bones.

"We still have to translate that lot," Speddig nodded toward the pile of English-language signals that our efforts had produced.

"After lunch," I said. "Come on, get your coat."

I had spent very little time with Gunther Speddig when we worked together in Section I. We had lunch together twice during that three month summer period. I think he felt that I was still a couple of rungs lower than him on the food chain, and besides my social calendar had been full in those days with Gudrun and Alex.

We chose a small café, not far from the office and a window seat where we could watch the world go by. As we ate, he tried to pump me for information about my new job. I could tell by his expression that he was still envious. Neither of us was in any hurry to return to work. I ordered a second round of beers. He looked at his watch.

"The signals can wait a few minutes more," I said.

Walking back to the office, Speddig said, "What do you know about Operation 'Anthropoid'?"

"Nothing. What is it?"

"It's a British codeword for some sort of operation, Army, Navy or Air Force, I'm not sure. Whatever it is, it involves the Czech resistance. They've been sending over supplies – small arms, grenades and explosives."

Translation of the incoming signals took the rest of the day; I arrived home, exhausted and cold, at about eight o'clock. Gudrun warmed some soup and I sat by the fire wrapped in a blanket, like a wounded soldier. I retired to bed early, but sleep eluded me. I lay there, as usual, staring at the ceiling.

The next day, Sunday December 7, the Japanese attacked the American fleet at anchor in Pearl Harbour, Hawaii. Schiller made the call this time.

"The transmitters are hopping. We need you on the fourth floor."

The man with the flat cap was back. He followed me from the apartment to the office.

In the Communications Unit on the fourth floor five operators were on duty. I took station five – the one where Kleister had died – put on Kleister's headphones, and began to record incoming messages. It took a few seconds to reset my mind to Morse. After that, it was as if I had never left the unit.

After the eight-hour shift I returned to the apartment completely drained and went straight to bed. I lay there for hours unable to sleep. When Gudrun came to bed, I told her what had happened in the Pacific.

She said, "The Americans will enter the war, now."

"I don't see how they can avoid it."

"The war is lost, so," she said in a flat monotone; she could have been reading from a train timetable. I knew she was right. The Japanese had woken the slumbering giant. Once more history would judge the German people and find us wanting.

#

Alex and Johann were reconciled in time for Christmas, although it seemed to me that their friendship had taken a battering. Gudrun refused to have anything more to do with Johann.

I told Alex about her telephone conversation with Johann.

Frowning at me, Alex said, "What are you saying?"

"Be careful. Be careful what you say to Johann."

Alex's eyes narrowed. He stared at me as if seeing me for the first time. "You never liked Johann. I knew you were jealous of our friendship, but this is too much. What kind of friend are you?"

I had never seen this side of my friend's personality. Gone was his good humour, his generosity of spirit; in their place contempt and naked hatred.

"I'm looking out for you, Alex," I said. "Just be careful. That's all I'm saying."

"I don't need you to look out for me," he snarled. "Johann and I are friends for life. There's nothing you can do about that and nothing you say will change it."

"D'you believe you can trust him?" I said quietly.

He hesitated before answering. "Can anyone really trust anyone? Can I trust you? How does anybody know who to trust these days?"

Gudrun and I had planned to take a cottage in the Alps for a short holiday, but the workload in the Abwehr made it impossible to get away. As she had the year before, Gudrun spent Christmas with her parents in Elmshorn. I accompanied her to the railway station. As I helped Gudrun lift a bulky doll's house onto the baggage compartment – a Christmas present for her niece – the man with the flat cap watched us from behind a large pillar. He was still there as the train lumbered out of the station, but when I turned to leave the station he was gone.

38

January 1942

Gudrun's absence hit me hard. My body-tremor continued at a reduced level, accompanied by a skin-crawling feeling that I couldn't shake off. I was getting no more than three hours sleep each night, and spent a lot of evenings in the local bar. When the bar was closed, I took to drinking alone in the apartment.

On January 5, the plaster of Paris on my arm was removed. Gudrun rang from Elmshorn to say that her father was unwell.

"It's nothing serious," she said, "but I feel I should stay for a few days more."

In the early evening of the following day, I arrived at Wilhelmstrasse in time to see most of the ten thousand employees of the Propaganda Ministry surge onto the streets and head for home. I recognised no one. I stopped one man and asked if the Ministry had exits on other streets.

He frowned at me. "Yes," he shouted, "there are exits on three sides of the building." I expect he thought I was from the country. Maybe he wondered why I wasn't in uniform. "Are you looking for someone?"

"Liesel Martens. Do you know her?"

"No. Ask at the reception desk." And he was gone.

I hurried back to Horst Wessel Platz, decided not to bother eating, and went round to my local bar. Several of the locals came in, and I was soon caught up in a meaningless argument with two old men about the Treaty of Versailles, war reparations, and their effect on post-1918 German society. The drinks kept coming. By closing time I was incapable of standing unaided; I think I was trying to make a critical point concerning the rise of the Party, but I couldn't get anyone to listen. I'm not sure how I got back to the apartment but I slept for six hours and awoke the next morning still dressed in the clothes I'd been wearing the day before.

After work that day, I went back to the apartment and busied myself making a simple meal. I put two small potatoes in a pot to boil. Why not just ask at reception? What better way to re-establish contact? I washed and prepared a stick of celery. It was such a sensible idea. I could say I wanted to discuss her article. There is a glaring mistake in the second paragraph, Fräulein. I chopped up the celery and put the pieces in the pot with the potatoes. But there wasn't a glaring mistake, was there? I wanted to congratulate you on getting the story published. Thank you very much, she'd say. Goodbye. Or maybe I could say I wanted to meet her again to talk about … about a follow up article, a follow up article about how Ernst Huber got caught? About a really great piece of intelligence that Huber sent back before he was trapped by the British, tortured horribly, and killed. I opened a tin of tuna, and cut four thick slices of bread. Maybe I could just ask her out for a meal.

She'll probably turn me down.

The next day was Friday. I wore my best new suit – the one with the epaulettes – and brought an extra clean shirt with me to work. At 4 pm I changed my shirt, left the office and hurried round to the Propaganda Ministry. Flat Cap was nowhere to be seen.

"Liesel Martens," I said at reception.

"Are you expected?" the doorman enquired. Like Sigmund, he was in his eighties.

"Tell her Ernst Huber is here," I said.

Five minutes later, she appeared at the bottom of the staircase. Her dress was cotton, printed with an elaborate floral pattern of greens and yellows. I was reminded of a tablecloth in my parents' dining room at home, in Ulm, when I was a boy.

She smiled at me. "Ernst Huber, I never thought I'd see you again."

"In person, Fräulein," I said. "I'm here to take you away from all this …" I waved a hand in a wide arc, taking in the entire building and the ancient doorman.

"I'll get my coat."

The paralysing frost of December was gone, but it was still quite cold. We found a tavern with a warm cellar and ordered two steins of beer. Then we had a small schnapps each and ordered more beer.

I said, "Oberst von Neumann was livid when he read your article. He said it reflected badly on the service. We don't give our agents medals, let them die in obscurity, that sort of thing."

"That was just a bit of poetic licence."

"I know. And I liked the article. I thought it encapsulated the life of the foreign agent rather well."

"You liked it? Really?" She blushed. "You're too kind, Ernst."

"My name's Kurt, remember. Kurt Müller?"

We shared a traditional meal at Marni's. I ordered a bottle of Beaujolais and we finished it between us. On the way out of the restaurant, she stumbled and fell against me. "Oops! I think I've had too much to drink."

"Let me take you home," I said. "Where do you live? Is it far?"

She wagged a finger under my nose. "No, no, I don't want you in my apartment, Ernst. Just find me a taxi."

"Kurt. It's Kurt." I hailed a taxi and helped her in.

"Von Bismarck Apartments, Viktoria Strasse," Liesel told the driver.

Her apartment was centrally located, to the north of the Tiergarten. I paid the driver and helped Liesel up the steps to her door. She handed me her keys. I opened the door, and we went inside.

She staggered into the bedroom, and fell on her bed. I took off her shoes and got her under the covers with her head on the pillow. I watched her sleeping for a minute or two. Under her upturned nose, her small mouth was slightly open, her upper teeth and the tip of her tongue peeping out, giving her that familiar porcine look that I so admired.

"Good night, Fräulein," I bent over her to kiss her forehead.

Her eyes snapped open and she threw both arms around my neck. "Get into bed, Ernst."

"You're drunk, Liesel." I was trapped in the bear-hug of her arms.

"Shut up and get into bed."

The Black Orchestra

I removed her arms from around my neck, and placed them by her sides.

"Go to sleep, Liesel, you're tired."

She closed her eyes. I watched her for a while. There lay the object of my wildest desires, the woman that I had dreamed about, trying not to think of her, for six months. How could I leave without touching her? What if I let this moment go and such an opportunity never again presented itself? I would be haunted by my unfulfilled desires. I leaned over, and cupped her two breasts in my hands. Small, round and firm, they fitted my hands perfectly. She awoke with a start.

"Oh Ernst, make love to me." She was wide awake. She pulled me down onto the bed, wrapped her legs around me, and began tearing at my clothes.

We had sex. The whole thing was animalistic. Intellect was absent; instinct took over. She was drunk – much drunker than me – and yet she found the energy from somewhere to take from me everything that I had to give. It was all I could do to get her to wait long enough for me to put on my condom. I felt as though I could have been any man, and afterward I felt as if I had been devoured whole, consumed, sucked dry and discarded.

She slept noisily. I passed the time tracing the cracks in the ceiling. As dawn broke, I got up and went into the bathroom. There were two toothbrushes in a tumbler by the basin. I searched for shaving supplies, but found none. I wandered into the kitchen in search of coffee. When I returned Liesel was in the bathroom. I could hear her brushing her teeth. She reappeared, wearing a full-length dressing gown. She said, "Put your clothes on, Kurt."

I did as she requested.

"Breakfast?" I suggested, with what I thought was a conspiratorial smile. After all, we had been naked together all night long.

She shook her head. "I want you to leave. Please leave now."

"Look, you were drunk – we both were. You shouldn't blame yourself for what happened last night."

"I don't," she said, tight-lipped. "I blame you." Suddenly, she was shouting. "You took advantage of me. I trusted you and you took from me what you wanted. You pig. You animal. How could you treat me like that?"

"You took from me, too," I said.

"Just leave," she screamed.

As I stepped through the door, I turned and said, "I'll ring you at the Ministry."

"Don't bother," she said, slamming the door in my face. A middle-aged couple shuffled by, wide-eyed, like startled rabbits.

#

My ego slightly bruised, I hurried away from the Von Bismarck apartment block, and entered the Tiergarten at a brisk pace. The whole park was bathed in weak, misty sunlight, sapping all the colours. I could see three horse riders cantering among the far trees, otherwise, there was nobody: a few stray dogs rummaging in the overspill from litter bins; a thousand frosted spiders' webs sparkling in the grass. And no sign of Flat Cap.

It was 6:30. I headed east toward the city centre. Behind the cathedral's bulk, the apartment blocks and grey tenements, the sun was rising; its light filtered through the misty remnants of yesterday's frost haze. The city was still asleep, the streets devoid of cars. A few bicycles could be seen rattling over the cobblestones. An empty horse and dray clattered by on its way to collect coal for the day's deliveries; the driver standing on the dray, reins in hand, knees bent like wishbones. A lone tram whined across my path, taking early starters to work.

I looked back. Fifty metres behind, a man with a large black umbrella was keeping pace with me. He was too far away to identify, but I thought it might have been the smiling man from the Brandenburg train.

I strode through the Lustgarten and into the warren of small streets behind the cathedral. After a few blocks, I stopped at an all-night café. The place had no customers, the owner preparing for the day ahead. I sat at a table outside and ordered coffee.

The café owner appeared with a cup of steaming ersatz coffee. I

The Black Orchestra

paid him, and he left. My heart sang. I felt like Siegfried, returning to Brunnhilde after his night of drugged and drunken debauchery with Gutrune of the Gibichungs.

The man with the black umbrella came up the street, striding with a rolling gait, like a sailor on shore leave. When he saw me, he stopped and became interested in the display in the window of a small shop. I knew then for certain that he was following me. It seemed Black Umbrella had taken over from Flat Cap. Either that or von Kemp was now using a two-man team to follow my movements. I was alarmed by the idea.

The café owner reappeared by my side. "Busy night?" he said, leering at me. His accent was coarse, like a Russian or a Pole. I gave him no answer and he scuttled back to his lair in the bowels of the shop. I thought: do I have a 'recently fucked' sign on my forehead?

Liesel's reaction was a little harsh, I thought. My involvement had been largely involuntary, after all. But of course I had to acknowledge, with a strong pang of guilt, that I *had* sought her out and engineered the situation.

A small boy came down the street. He was no more than ten years old, one of those street urchins that roamed everywhere in the city, dirty, dressed in the remnants of a school uniform. I had read an article in the newspaper about them. Many were Romany, their begging organised by criminal gangs; others were Jews, left stranded when their parents were jailed; a small percentage were victims of the war – German children orphaned and made homeless by British bombs. The boy stopped by my table, and held out his hand. The article had said that it was a mistake to encourage these outcasts by giving them anything, but I found it impossible to ignore his pleading brown eyes. I gave him two marks; His tiny fist closed around the coins, and he ran off.

Black Umbrella followed me home. In the morning, he was gone.

#

Listening to the BBC news and reading despatches from the Eastern Front, it was clear that, by mid-January, we had suffered a catastrophic defeat, not at the hands of the enemy, but by the cruellest of Russian winters. Unprepared and ill-equipped for the extreme weather conditions, many hundreds of thousands of men and vast quantities of war machinery had been lost. The military might of the Reich's armies had been rendered worthless; the destiny of the war in the East had been decided.

39

January 1942

On Monday morning, January 12, Oberst von Neumann called me into his office.

"Word has just come through. You're to meet your U-boat at Wilhelmshaven. You sail Saturday morning, first thing."

After so many months waiting, this news struck me like a lightning bolt.

"I've made out a list of the tasks I need you to complete in Ireland." He handed me a list:

Locate Agent Ornithologist
Recover his equipment.
Set Blesset up as replacement for Ornithologist, if necessary.
Otherwise, find another base for Blesset.
Contact Professor Hirsch.

"You want me to talk with Professor Hirsch?"

"Yes. He's a useful contact, sympathetic to Germany's cause. He may have useful intelligence for us."

I had intended speaking with the professor if I had time; that the Oberst had made it official, I found surprising and perhaps a little disturbing.

Hauptmann von Pfaffel was to take back control of my agents for the duration of my trip. He had never fully recovered from the shock of losing Agent 92 and his hands trembled like a puppet dangling on invisible strings.

"This bunch are hardly worth bothering about," he said.

"Agent Nightingale—"

"Used to be a good source. What has he produced in the last six months?"

"Nightingale's been silenced," I said. "The Oberst ordered it. There was a danger that he might be discovered."

Von Pfaffel snorted.

Heinz was waiting for me in the office after lunch. He handed me a set of papers in the name of Kevin O'Reilly. The passport was Irish; it had a green cover with a gold harp in the centre. I flipped through it.

"This is my real date of birth."

"Why complicate matters by changing it?"

"No stamps?"

Heinz shook his head. "You've never been out of the country. You prefer holidays at home."

"In youth hostels, obviously" I opened the Youth Hostel Association card. It had five triangular stamps in it from centres in the south of the country, Cork, Kerry and so on.

"Check the exact order," Heinz said. "You'll need to remember your itinerary in case anybody asks."

He handed me a second passport, ration book, and youth hostel card. These were in the name of Rory O'Reilly. The youth hostel stamps were the same as in mine; the passport unused.

I laughed when I saw Blesset's passport photograph. "He looks like a frightened rabbit."

Heinz shrugged. "Doesn't everybody?"

#

On Wednesday evening I met Gudrun at the railway station. She was wearing a light pink dress and matching hat. I recognised the dress, but I couldn't remember seeing the hat before.

"New hat?" I said as she kissed my cheek.

"Yes, do you like it?" she responded, doing a twirl. It was shaped like a Wehrmacht helmet with feathers on top.

"Very fetching."

We took a taxi back to the apartment. She seemed happy to see me, inspecting my arm, recently released from its plaster-cast. In the taxi I asked about her father.

"It was nothing," she said. "A head-cold, nothing more. Now tell me what mischief you've been up to."

"Oh," I replied. "I read a book." I looked out the window. The streets were crowded again.

"What was it?"

"Just a book. You wouldn't like it." I said, rubbing my left eye with a bent knuckle. I reached over and tapped the glass. The driver half turned his head toward me. "Can't you go any faster?"

Gudrun opened the door of the apartment and stepped inside. I followed with her suitcase. She took off her hat and collapsed onto the settee. I joined her; the horrible pink helmet between us.

"Put the kettle on," she said, searching her bag for a cigarette.

Later, I told her that my U-boat trip had been confirmed and my journey would start on Friday. She looked at me in shock.

"But that's only two days from now!" She leaned across the pink helmet and wrapped her arms around me.

We kissed. Then she stood up and hurried into the bedroom. She closed the door. After a few minutes I followed her. The curtains were drawn; it was quite dark. I reached for the light switch.

"Don't put on the light," she said.

I stepped into the gloom.

She was lying on top of the bed. I could see that she had been crying. I sat on the edge of the bed and took her hand in mine.

"It's not a dangerous mission, Gudrun," I said. "It's really nothing to worry about."

"But there's a war on," she sobbed. "Look what happened to Kapitän Prien in U47."

"That's different. U47 was hunting in the British shipping lanes. Our U-boat won't be shooting at anyone."

"Are you sure?"

"Yes, I'm sure. Their orders are to drop us safely on the coast of Ireland. After that, they can torpedo as many British ships as they like."

"You always do that," she said.

"What?"

"When you tell a lie, you rub your eye with the back of your finger."

I said, "Dry your eyes. I want to take you out for a meal. Remember our first night together? We went to Marni's and then you cleaned the apartment."

"Was it Marni's? I thought it was that other place – what's it called? – near the Brandenburg Gate." She turned away. "I don't think I want to eat out tonight. I look a mess. And our ration cards are low. Anyway, I'm not hungry."

We made love slowly. I think she really thought that this could be our last time; she wanted to savour every moment, every morsel of joy, in case the memories had to last a lifetime. As we made love, I couldn't help thinking about my experience with the drunken Liesel. Gudrun had so much love to give, and enjoyed so much what I had to give in return; Liesel took what she wanted and gave nothing back. Gudrun made love like a woman, and she encouraged me to reciprocate; Liesel had been like a wild animal, giving nothing, and expecting everything in return. When, finally, I entered her body, Gudrun drew me in. She held my hips in her hands, directing and controlling my thrusts.

Afterwards, she lit a cigarette. I lay on my back staring at the cracks in the ceiling. They were barely visible in the gloom, but I knew them all. I was overcome with remorse. I had purged Liesel from my mind; she no longer occupied my thoughts as she had before; but I regretted what had happened between Liesel and me. I resolved never to let Gudrun find out; the knowledge could destroy her love, which I now knew, was more precious to me than my own life.

40

January 1942

On Thursday night, Gudrun refused my advances, and we lay awake, side by side, for hours. She wept silently, and nothing I said seemed to help. It was as if I had died already and she was lying beside my dead body.

On Friday morning, I rose early and dressed in my old Irish clothes – underwear, slacks, jumper and shoes. Only my shirt and socks were German.

Gudrun laughed through her tears. "What are you wearing?"

"From this moment onward, I am an Irishman."

She dried her eyes and clapped her hands, the thrill of the adventure banishing her gloom. "What's your name?"

"Kevin O'Reilly," I said in my best Irish accent.

"Well, may I wish you a very good day, Mister O'Reilly." Her English was excellent.

"Why thank you, kind madam," I said. Then, "No, that should be, 'Thank you kindly, madam.'"

"You're very welcome, sir." Then, in German, "How do the Irish say 'Bon Voyage'?"

I had to think about that for a while before I came up with, "May the road rise up to meet you."

Before leaving the apartment, we embraced. She cried. She told me to be careful. I assured her that I would return safe and well. Finally, there were no more words. She hugged me.

#

I had very little to carry with me: my false papers, a comb, a razor and brush, my lock-picks, and that small cardboard box containing the cyanide capsule that von Beuhl had given me at Brandenburg.

Blesset and Heinz Franzelberg were waiting at the railway station. Alex was there too. He seemed to have locked away inside him the grief of losing his brother, but he was changed. No longer the happy-go-lucky Alex of old, it was as if his free spirit had been smothered in a blanket of despair.

Blesset was dressed in baggy grey trousers held up with string, ramblers' socks and boots, a faded blue and white striped shirt, lacking a collar, and a brown jacket with "US Navy" written across the back in large red letters. The piece de resistance was a flat cap made by sewing several small pieces of tweed together. It sat crookedly on his head, barely restraining his thick blond hair. The overall effect was of a straw-headed scarecrow fitted out with old clothes salvaged from a waste bin. He was carrying a small rucksack.

Heinz handed me a similar rucksack. "There are shirts and shoes in there, as well as some English money."

"No Irish money?" Blesset asked.

"They use English money as well as Irish," I said testily. "Didn't they teach you anything at Brandenburg?"

Blesset glanced at me like a startled antelope. His arm shot up in a Party salute "Heil!" he shouted. I turned away in disgust.

Alex gave me a book entitled *The Life and Times of Richard Strauss*.

And then we were on the train, leaning out of the window. The guard blew his whistle and waved his green flag, the train began to move.

My main feeling was one of exhilaration, tinged with apprehension. My greatest adventure had started.

The journey was in three stages. The first stage – Berlin to Hannover – took one hour and thirty-seven minutes. We had the compartment to ourselves. I pulled down the roller blinds on the windows to the corridor, and spent the time getting to know my travelling companion.

Blesset was a typical product of Nazi Germany. His father had enlisted early in the SA Brownshirts, and raised his son to follow the NSDAP philosophy to the letter. Blesset had distinguished himself as a leader in the Hitler Youth and, as soon as he was old enough, had

The Black Orchestra

applied for entry to the SS. This was denied, so he took a junior position on board a German merchant ship, bound for South Africa. After a couple of years, he missed boarding his ship at Mogadishu and joined the British Merchant Navy, where he was trained as a signals officer. The day that his service with the British Merchant Navy was spotted by an eagle-eyed scout for the Abwehr, Blesset's life changed forever.

Dressed as he was, he looked comical, but his scarecrow disguise seemed to cause him no distress. I believe that he was proud to wear this eccentric outfit; I'm sure that he saw it as a special sort of Reich uniform – one that he, and only he, had been selected to wear.

"Why did the SS turn you down?" I asked.

"Tourette's," he replied.

"And this was not seen as a problem by the Abwehr?"

He shrugged and looked out of the window. He seemed unconcerned by his condition. I wondered if he had given any thought to the difficulties he faced as an agent in a foreign country.

It was close to 6 pm by the time we arrived at Wilhelmshaven, where a driver met us and took us to the U-boat base in a grey Citröen car with Kriegsmarine markings.

Dozens of U-boats were moored at the base, tied side-by-side as in a marina. On shore were rows of large galvanised sheds with pitched roofs covered in camouflage tarpaulins. We could see racks of torpedoes inside some of these, where the doors were open. One or two of the U-boats had plumes of steam rising from them. There were few people about.

"Report to Captain Richter, U84," the driver said. He pointed down the line of U-boats, then got back into his car and drove off.

We walked down the boardwalk until we found U84. Gingerly, we stepped from the boardwalk onto the deck of the U-boat. Blesset started up the conning tower ladder, and I followed. Half way up, he stopped.

"What's the matter, Blesset?" I called out to him.

"It's nothing," he said. "Give me a minute."

After a few seconds, he continued upward, and we both reached the platform at the top of the conning tower. The hatch was open. I peered inside, but could see nothing.

Blesset wore a gloomy expression, and his face was flushed. His right arm shot upward, accompanied by an unintelligible shout.

I said, "Are you all right?"

He nodded.

"Come aboard," a voice called from below.

41

January 1942

Like Alberich descending into the depths of Nibelheim, I followed Blesset down the ladder into the darkness of the U-boat.

It took a short while for my eyes to adjust to the gloom of the interior, after the bright sunlight outside. Captain Richter stood near the bottom of the ladder, beside him, his First Officer. As I became accustomed to the light, I began to make out the crew at their posts, silent, staring, like the enslaved Nibelung dwarves.

Like all submariners, Captain Richter was a small individual. His jacket was short, like an aviator's, worn over a thick woollen jumper that I was sure had leather patches on the elbows like Oberst von Neumann's. I soon discovered that conversations with the Captain were short and intense; time was precious in the highly-charged environment of the submarine, and words were never wasted.

I began by introducing myself. "Kurt Müller."

He nodded. "Müller." Clearly, I had already wasted one word. "And Blesset?" he nodded to my companion.

Blesset's right arm shot up in a Hitler salute. "Heil!" he shouted. I glanced at him. Blesset's face was flushed bright red.

The captain frowned and said dryly, "None of that here."

He led us through the ship to our cabin. It was a small room equipped with two bunks and two small lockers. I took the lower bunk, Blesset the upper.

The captain stood in the doorway, one foot in, one foot out of the cabin.

"The toilet is five metres for'ard. Follow your nose. Stay in the cabin until we're at sea. After that, you may move about, but keep away from the engine room and the forward torpedo room. If we see any action, stay out of the way in your cabin."

"Are we likely to see action?" I asked.

"We won't be looking for any, but if the opportunity presents itself… We sail at first light. Dinner is at twenty hundred hours."

Captain Richter left us, and I turned my attention to Blesset. He was sweating heavily.

"What's the matter?" I asked.

"I'm not happy in confined spaces. I'll be all right in a minute."

At 8 pm we took our places at the captain's table. He introduced us to his First Officer and his Chief Engineer. The crew were all under 1.7m tall, and I couldn't shake the feeling that Blesset and I were from another, taller race, intruding in their world. A galley hand served each of us with a plate of lamb with small potatoes, baby carrots and cabbage.

During the meal the conversation was muted. We spoke about the progress of the Wehrmacht campaigns in Belgium and France. There was no mention of U-boat operations in the Atlantic, although it was common knowledge that they had already contributed as much to the war effort as had General Rommel's campaigns. It was noticeable how much the rhythm and tone of the conversation was dictated by the captain. His mood was constantly changing: jubilant one minute, with talk of recent battle victories; doleful the next: how could anyone predict the final outcome of the war? His officers followed his mood changes with alacrity, like musicians following a complex score. They were like a football team; I imagined that nothing short of death could break the bond of loyalty between these men and their captain.

No mention was made of our mission. The captain had simply extended his hospitality to encompass Blesset and me, and we were now part of his team for the duration of the trip. Blesset said nothing during the meal, and mercifully, his Tourette's remained under control.

To end the meal, the captain ordered schnapps, and the galley hand hurried off to fetch it.

We never received our schnapps. First, we heard the angry clatter of anti-aircraft guns. Then, one of the men appeared at the door of the officers' mess. "Enemy aircraft, Captain" he said, "coming in fast."

The Black Orchestra

The captain and his officers ran to their stations.

Blesset and I hurried back to our cabin just as the first bombs started to fall. We could hear them whistling as they fell and then the crashes as they exploded above us. Blesset lay on his bunk hugging his pillow, his eyes wide in terror. Within minutes, the submarine was moving, the hatch was closed and we began to dive. Now, we could hear the sound of the bombs as dull muffled thuds above us. We continued to dive and to move out to sea, the sounds of the bombs receding all the time.

After forty-five minutes, the captain gave the order, "Periscope depth." And shortly after that, we surfaced. Blesset's eyes were closed. I could tell that he wasn't sleeping, but he seemed to have reached an inner calm.

It was only later, when we were well out to sea, that I began to tremble, struck by the shock of the attack and the horror of what might have happened.

We travelled through the night on the surface without incident. I slept well, Blesset too, and we awoke late. To me, the U-boat felt like a place of refuge, beyond the reach of the Gestapo.

When we emerged from the cabin, the captain said, "You've missed breakfast." He invited us "up top". We climbed the ladder and out onto the conning tower platform. The sea was grey, choppy, with small white wave crests. A low mist clung to the surface at the horizon on all sides.

"It's very rough," Blesset said. His face was green.

The captain laughed. "This is the North Sea," he said. "This is as calm as it gets."

I asked, "Where are we?"

"Off the coast of Holland." The captain pointed to our left, but I could see nothing through the mist.

Lunch consisted of cold meats, cheese and sauerkraut. Afterward I asked to see the communications room. The room was tiny. There was a chair, a bench, a large Telefunken receiver/transmitter taking up one whole wall, and, occupying most of the available space on the bench, an Enigma machine. This was a Kriegsmarine model, with four rotors. As soon as I saw it, my spine began to tingle. I could hear the tinny sound of Morse.

"Are you receiving?" I asked.

The communications officer shook his head. "There is traffic, but it's not for us. But I will be transmitting soon, if you're interested."

I stayed and watched as he used his Enigma to encode a short message. Then he put his headphones on and transmitted his signal. I thanked him and returned to the cabin to sleep.

Blesset was ill. He sat on the lower bunk – my bunk – head between his hands, moaning.

"You'd better take the lower bunk," I said.

He waved his hand at me. I wasn't sure if he was thanking me or if the gesture was a feeble Tourette's spasm. I climbed into the upper bunk and turned out my overhead light. Blesset continued to groan. After a while, I climbed down from the bunk, pulled Alex's book from my rucksack, and handed it to Blesset.

"Here," I said. "Try reading this."

I slept well again, the second night. When I awoke I noticed something different about the U-boat. The motion of the vessel seemed smoother, the drone of the engine louder. I could hear secondary muffled engine noises, like heavy aircraft flying overhead. Blesset was snoring, the book on the floor beside his bunk. I smiled. There's nothing like a good biography to induce sleep.

I dressed and went aft to the operations room. Captain Richter was resting in his cabin. The crew spoke in hushed tones.

"We are submerged," the First Officer murmured. He put a finger to his lips. "Silent running." He showed me the navigation chart. "We're here," he said, pointing to the chart at a point level with Dungeness on the south coast of England. "We're just leaving the Straits of Dover, heading into the English Channel."

"What is that sound?" I said, as a secondary engine droned past.

"Ships overhead on the surface," he said. "You'll be hearing a lot of those. We won't surface again until we're through the English Channel close to Land's End, in about nineteen hours." He trailed his finger along the map and stopped where the tip of Cornwall juts out into the channel.

I began to feel ill. I couldn't shake a sensation that the air in the submarine was running out; I felt that I had to concentrate on the very act of breathing to avoid suffocation. Blesset woke up, washed and went in search of breakfast. He said he felt better. I went back to my bunk where I lay dozing for an hour or so, *The Life and Times of Richard Strauss* on my stomach. When, finally, I opened the book. A small piece of paper fell out. It was in Alex's handwriting. It read:

Sandbar
Helmut Becker
c/o Marianne Dreyfuss
Glienicker Strasse 23
Aldershof

I recognised the codename Sandbar. That was the British agent operating in Buckinghamshire. So Alex knew this agent, and he had left the note for me to find. I was intrigued. I committed the name and address to memory and flushed Alex's note down the toilet.

For most of that day I slipped in and out of consciousness. Sleep brought with it erotic dreams involving Gudrun's body and Liesel's face, mixed in with a horrible nightmare. I was in Ravensbrück, dressed in prisoner's stripes and with a number on my back. The commandant wore a green jumper with leather patches on the elbows. He smoked a pipe. He smiled at me while I was being dragged away between walls of barbed wire. His face was indistinct, but he had Drobol junior's teeth and Uncle Reinhard's small, dark eyes.

During my waking hours I felt like a criminal, incarcerated in a metal cage from which there could be no escape. The constant beating thud of the U-boat engines seemed to mark out and delineate my mortal time. I was roused by the crew to take my place for meals with the officers and Blesset at the captain's table. I was poor company, escaping back to the sanctuary of the cabin as soon as social decency allowed.

After what felt like an aeon, we surfaced again, and turned north on the last leg of our journey.

42

January 1942

At 5 pm on Wednesday January 28, the U-boat came to rest off the south coast of Ireland. Two hours later, darkness fell. Captain Richter shook our hands and wished us good fortune. Blesset gave a crude version of the Hitler salute and a shout of "Heil!" to which the captain responded with a broad smile.

One of the crew rowed us the short distance to the shore and dropped us off on a beach of shale.

The air was thick with drizzle. It was cold and dark. I knew there was a half-moon that night, but it was obscured by a thick layer of cloud.

Setting off across the fields, we came upon a dirt track, and followed this to a small road with high hedges on either side. After fifteen minutes we spotted a light to our left. There was a gate leading up to a small cottage. I knocked on the door.

"Leave the talking to me, Rory," I said to Blesset.

The door opened and an old woman peered out at us. She was tiny, bowed at the shoulders, her head wrapped in a black woollen shawl.

"Come in," she said.

We stepped into the cottage and our host found us two seats by the fire. Everything about the cottage was primitive. It had two rooms, with floors of packed earth. The open fire served as cooker and was the only source of heat in the house. For fuel she had damp turf, supplemented by wood detritus from the beach. The musky smell of the turf was everywhere, the air thick with acrid smoke.

Soon, we were sitting at the table, eating homemade soda bread with salted butter. The tea was strong enough to build a wall with. There was no milk or sugar.

"Where are ye boys from?"

"Dublin."

At this, her face cracked into a broken-toothed smile. "So ye're de Valera's boys." She laughed. She coughed. Then she was possessed by an uncontrollable cascade of coughing, each successive phlegm-hawking rushing after its predecessor, torn from ever deeper recesses of her quaggy lungs.

Blesset poured some water from a jug into a cup from the dresser and held it out to her. She waved it away.

"It's nothing." She dried her eyes on her shawl. "Where are ye headed?"

"Back to Dublin. Our walking trip is over."

"Walking trip, is it?" The tone of her question told me that our cover story was blown, like a horse that had fallen at the first fence. I swore silently.

We slept by the open fire and set out early the next morning. As we were leaving, she asked for a half-crown as payment for the bread and butter. We had no coins. I handed her a crisp new five-pound-note.

"Ah no, I can't change that. Don't ye have anything smaller?"

"That's perfectly all right. I want you to keep it."

She protested. She tried to return the note, but finally, reluctantly, she accepted it. I was glad to hand over the money. Five pounds might pay for her turf supplies for a whole year, or her food for a month. I knew she was no fool, and probably suspected who we really were. The money would ensure her silence.

The drizzle continued. It was still dark, but with a hint of daylight in the sky. We followed the boreen in what I thought was a northerly direction. We came to a single-track paved road, then to a wider road with white markings which straggled at last into the village of Belgooly, little more than a crossroads, with half a dozen small houses, a church and two public houses. A signpost showed Kinsale 3 miles to the left, Cork 12 miles to the right, Kinsale 3 miles straight ahead, and back the way we had come, Kinsale 4 miles. We turned right. One mile further on, we found another signpost. This one stood at a crazy angle, partially absorbed in the hedgerow, pointing to the left. It read "Ballymartle 1" and below this, a small railway symbol.

Ballymartle was another crossroads village. In the drizzle, it looked to me like a miserable place, but it had one thing that lifted my spirits: it had a railway station.

We found a bench in a dilapidated shelter and sat down to wait for a train. Sunlight filtered through the drizzle and flooded the scene. Stretching as far as we could see on all sides were pale birch trees glistening, misshapen and tall, like thin, grey giants frozen in a hundred-year argument. For the first time since we landed on the beach, I began to relax. I closed my eyes.

A voice called out after a while, and I opened my eyes. A man stood in a field beyond the opposite platform.

I waved to him. "When's the next train?"

The man lifted his cap and scratched his head. "You could be in for a bit of a wait. The last one went through here ten years ago."

Blesset leapt to his feet and gave the man an involuntary Hitler salute.

We returned to the main road, and set off toward Cork. There was traffic on the road, now, and it wasn't long before we were picked up by a passing truck, piled high with beets. We squeezed into the cab beside the driver.

He dropped us off at the railway station in Cork.

"Thanks," Blesset said as we stepped down from the cab.

"You're very welcome, Fritz," said the driver.

"How did he know my name?" Blesset asked, when the truck had driven away.

"I expect it was just a lucky guess."

I reasoned that the driver could be relied on not to expose us to the authorities. We could expect ambivalence from the Irish. Few of them would actually help us, but most wouldn't go out of their way to hinder us, either. This 'blind eye' approach was all that the British could reasonably have expected, of course, given the state of Anglo-Irish relations.

#

The Black Orchestra

The train pulled into Kingsbridge station at noon. We joined the throng of Dublin commuters heading down the quays toward the city centre. The mist had lifted and the sun appeared spasmodically between the clouds.

Crossing the river Liffey, we hurried past the gates of Trinity College to Grafton Street and its prosperous shops. Blesset bought a pair of trousers and a leather belt in Switzers. I bought a complete change of clothing. They accepted our clothing rations without demur. We emerged from the shop and into Wicklow Street.

I stopped outside a solid wooden door sandwiched between two shopfronts and rang the bell.

"Who is it?" my mother's voice from behind the door.

"It's Kurt, your son."

She opened the door.

"Kurt? Is it really you?"

"Yes, Mother, it's me." A strange ache invaded my chest.

She threw her arms around me. When she released me, there were tears in our eyes.

She shook Blesset's hand.

"This is my friend, Rory."

We spent some time catching up. I hadn't seen her for over seven years, and there had been no contact since the outbreak of war. At first glance, it seemed that she hadn't changed; but, as she spoke, I began to notice small signs of aging – a wrinkle here, a grey hair there.

She said, "Have you found yourself a girlfriend, yet?"

"Yes, Mother. Her name's Gudrun."

"What's she like? Do you have a photograph?"

I shook my head.

"How long are you staying?"

"I'm not sure. Maybe a week or so. Do you have room for the two of us?"

"We'll manage." She smiled at Blesset. "What's your surname, Rory?"

"His name's O'Reilly," I interjected. "The same as mine."

She frowned. "So this isn't a social visit?"

"We're here on a mission. If anybody asks, Rory's my brother, and we've been living here as long as you have."

"And what do you do for a living, Kurt O'Reilly?"

"I'm a postgraduate student, and my name's Kevin."

"And what about you, Rory? What do you do?"

"I'm not sure—" Blesset began.

"Rory's not quite the full shilling. He's a little eccentric."

"Isn't that always the way." She sighed. "Is there anything else I need to know?"

"We've just arrived back from a walking tour in Cork and Kerry. And we have the youth hostel stamps to prove it."

Mother cooked a meal. "I try to keep abreast of developments in Germany, but the newspapers are full of the war, now, and when they do report on German domestic affairs, the Irish newspapers seem to over-dramatise everything."

"Like what?"

"They speak of running battles in the streets between the Brownshirts and the Communists, and marauding death squads."

"Those reports are probably accurate," said Blesset.

43

January 1942

By ten o'clock, Blesset was asleep in his chair. My mother and I sorted out a makeshift bed for him in the spare room, and he retired for the night. I asked to see my father's things. Mother went into the bedroom and returned a short while later with a large cardboard box.

"Everything of your father's is in this box," she said.

I pulled out the small bronze eagle standing over her nest of broken eggs and asked my mother about it.

She shook her head. "I have no idea where he got it from. It's pretty, though, isn't it?"

I found my father's ceremonial dagger, presented to him in recognition of services to the Centre-Right Party. It had a short blade, engraved with the words: "For Fatherland and Freedom". The handle was black, with a double-headed eagle, the blade blunt as a butter knife. My father had used it as a letter-opener, and I had played with it as a child.

"May I keep this?" I asked.

"Of course. Take anything you want."

I searched the contents of the box until I found the photograph. I showed it to her.

"That's your father at university with his friends."

"Can you identify any of the people in the picture?"

She put on her reading glasses, and held the picture under the light. "That's Hans Oster. He was a handsome devil. The last I heard, he was a colonel – Oberst – in the Wehrmacht."

"He's a Generalmajor in the Abwehr now. What about the others?"

"This one here is your old professor from Trinity. The American, Stephan …"

"Stephan Hirsch."

"What a dreamboat!" She laughed. "And this is Erwin von Neumann. He was a cheerful soul. And that's Isaac Ruben on the left."

"Von Neumann I know. What became of Isaac Ruben?"

"He was Jewish."

We fell silent. When I asked her about the others, she shook her head. "I can't remember. I'm not sure if I knew any of them."

"When I spoke to Hans Oster, he said he had fond memories of you," I said. "Were you and he lovers in those days?"

"No, of course not. We were friends. Why, what did he say?" There was a look of horror on her face.

"He said he might have married you if my father hadn't beaten him to it."

"That's just plámás." She laughed again. "But he did have a fine head of hair in those days."

"He still has."

I turned the photograph over. On the back, in faded handwriting, was the legend: 'The Black Orchestra, Munich 1909'. My heart skipped a beat.

Mother spoke about her concerns for Germany, her fears for my welfare. She mentioned the Führer's appointment as Chancellor on January 30, 1933. "A dark day for Germany," she said through clenched teeth. "May 10 was another dark day," she added.

I shook my head. I had no recollection of anything of significance happening on that day.

"That was the night when the students burned their books. Thank God you went to university in Ireland."

"Thanks to you and Father."

"Your father was a wise man."

"Uncle Reinhard said something like that to me," I said.

I wasn't sure that she heard me, for she had slipped into the world of her private memories. She was silent for a few minutes. Then she said, "And how is your uncle Reinhard?" I detected no warmth in her voice.

"He is well, Mother. He has been appointed Deputy Reich

Protector for Bohemia and Moravia. He lives in Prague, now. He prospers."

"I'm sure he does. You know ... I read about him from time to time, in the newspapers."

Before I closed my eyes that night, I thought about the Black Orchestra. It was something my father was involved in at university, in 1909. And yet Uncle Reinhard had said it was a dangerous subversive organisation working within the security apparatus of the Reich, today. If it was the same organisation, it had survived for over thirty years. Surely this wasn't possible. And yet, the faces in the photograph were all working closely together today.

#

The next morning, Friday January 30, I left Blesset in the apartment and headed into Trinity College on my own. The new term had just started; the college was full of students returning to their studies after their winter holiday.

I entered through the front gate, and took a few minutes to read the notes and notices on the students' notice board. Front Square was alive with students, most of them freshmen, hurrying to lectures. Immediately, I was transported back to my college days. I strolled through Front Square and into New Square, behind the Rubricks. New Square is a neat, Georgian square with three-storey terraces on the east and south sides, the Rubricks to the north, and the Museum Building on the west side. The centre of the square contains a green area with trees and a lawn tennis court. The Mathematics Department is located at number 39, in the centre of the south terrace. I stepped inside, and climbed the stone staircase to the second floor. I stopped at a door bearing the name of Professor Stephan Hirsch, and knocked. There was no answer.

A notice board on the third floor listed Professor Hirsch's lecture schedule for the month. Fridays, 9:30 to 11:30 he was delivering a lecture to the third and fourth year students, in room 39.2.2. I went back down to the second floor, found the room and stepped inside.

Six students, sat among the rows of benches. They all turned their heads briefly as I entered. I sat at the back of the room. The professor was in full flow. Begowned in black and with a light dusting of chalk dust, he looked much as I remembered him: tall, heavy, with a broad face and generous demeanour, his hair long but thinning on top; an occasional strand falling across his face to be swept back in that familiar gesture. His method of delivery had not changed in the years since I had known him. His deep voice and soft New England accent, the way he emphasised his words with his hands, made it impossible not to be carried along by his enthusiasm for his subject.

I recognised some of the symbols on the blackboard. This was tensor calculus, one of my least favourite subjects. The professor turned to face the students. He gave no indication that he was aware of the new face in the audience.

At the end of the lecture, the students filed past. Professor Hirsch spent some time gathering up his notes before placing them inside his leather briefcase. Once the last student had left, I stood up and made my way forward.

"I know you," the professor said. "Müller, class of '36."

I laughed. "What a memory! I expect you always remember the awkward ones."

"Not at all. You were an excellent student. How's your mother?"

"She is well, thank you."

The professor looked at his watch. "I have to dash," he said. "I have a faculty meeting in a few minutes. Meet me here at five-thirty this evening." And he left.

44

January 1942

I whiled away a pleasant day on the college campus. With my slacks and dilapidated shoes, I looked just like a student – although older than the rest. My cover story of postgraduate student made a lot of sense. I recalled the last message sent to Ornithologist,

June 18: 'Meet Bullfrog 933 TCD July 4.' And Ornithologist's reply

June 20: 'Bullfrog meeting confirmed.'

Building 9, in Front Square, was used for student living accommodation and tutorial rooms. I climbed the stairs to the third floor. The label on the door of room 3 read: 'Professor S. Hirsch'. So the codename Bullfrog referred to the professor. There could be no doubt about it.

The professor reappeared at 5:30 pm. He smiled warmly. "I'd like you to see my home. It's not far."

He led me to his car – a green 2-seater Riley Lynx – and we drove south, away from the city centre. There was barely enough room for the two of us; we sat shoulder to shoulder, snug as sardines in an anchovy tin.

"You never went back to America?" I said. "I seem to remember that you were on a temporary posting to Trinity back then."

His shoulders shook with laughter. "Yes, I was on extended sabbatical from the University of Arizona. But I suppose Ireland got under my skin. I never went back."

"Not even for holidays?"

"No. I have no one left in America, now. Whenever I do manage to get away on vacation, I visit the old cities of Europe, Paris, Barcelona, Florence."

"Berlin?"

"Before the war, yes," he said. "What about you? You were a promising student. What have you done since leaving college?"

"Nothing academic, I'm afraid."

There were three years after graduation when I could have taken on postgraduate work, and didn't. After that, the war provided a convenient excuse. Secretly, I suppose I feared failure.

It took no more than fifteen minutes to drive to the professor's home in the countryside, just outside the village of Dundrum. The building was a rambling farmhouse with an open barn attached, in the French style. The barn had a flat tin roof set sloping backwards, like a peaked cap worn back-to-front.

He parked the car in the barn and took me around to the back of the house, where there was a large lake with reeds around the edges, populated with water fowl. A small boat bobbed at the end of its tether. The clouds had dissipated, blown away by the breeze. It was a cold, clear night; a good strong half-moon reflected on the choppy water.

When he saw the expression on my face, he laughed. "Impressive, isn't it? Not many people have a lake in their back yard."

"Does it ever flood?" I asked.

"All the time. I keep a supply of sandbags handy."

"It's beautiful."

"It's nothing but a pond, really."

"It's not deep?"

"Oh, it's deep enough in the centre." He opened the front door of the house, and led me inside.

The hall floor was covered in black-and-white tiles, like a chessboard. The skirting boards on both sides were black with mould. I could see into the kitchen at the end of the hall where a single tap hung, dripping over a large white ceramic sink. Behind the front door was a mahogany hall stand, seven feet tall, holding a number of coats, hats, umbrellas and Wellington boots. A staircase occupied half the available hall space.

"This way," he said, climbing the stairs. He led me to one of the bedrooms at the back of the house. There was no bed, just a couple of chairs. He opened a large wardrobe. Sitting on a shelf inside the wardrobe, was a short wave transmitter/receiver.

I recognised an old friend. "That's an SE 90/40."

"Yes, and it's nearly time for me to contact Berlin."

I was stunned into silence for a moment or two. Then I said, "What's your call-sign, Professor?"

"I don't think I have one of those. When I had one, it was OFR."

"That's *Ochsenfrosch* – Bullfrog. And your code book?"

"I use this." He showed me a code book that was nothing like any I had seen before. It had the single word 'Gruenwald' on the front cover.

"This is not Lorenz. What is 'Gruenwald'?"

"It's what I use," he said.

I pulled up a chair, sat down and watched as the professor encoded his short message, using his strange code book. I checked the frequency setting of his transmitter. It was set at 3137.5 kilohertz. At exactly 6 pm he transmitted his signal.

"How often do you transmit?"

"I listen for incoming signals every night at this time, and I transmit if I have anything to say."

"What did your message say?"

"Only that you have arrived."

"You were expecting me?" Nothing was going to surprise me, now.

"Yes, of course. I know all about you."

"You do?"

"I know that you're a nephew of Reinhard Heydrich's. You started as an Abwehr signalman. You were moved to Section II to work with von Neumann. You run the agents in Ireland."

I opened my mouth to say something, but no words came.

"And I reckon they're a pretty motley crew, if you don't mind my saying so." He laughed throatily.

"Is there anything you don't know?"

"Your current mission. I can guess, but I'm not really sure why you came to Ireland."

"I'm here to visit my mother."

He looked sideways at me with a crooked smile. He said, "In a U-boat? You must have had a better reason to travel than that."

He switched off the transmitter and led me back downstairs. There was a small door under the staircase, secured by a bolt and padlock.

"Follow me," he said, unlocking the padlock and the door and stepping inside.

Behind the door a set of stone steps led down into a cellar. He turned on the light, and I followed him down. The cellar was warm, carpeted throughout, and with pictures and maps on the walls. There was a strong smell of damp, mildew; a legacy of earlier floods. Against one wall stood a large desk, and on the desk, a telephone.

"You may talk freely to me," said the professor. "I'm on your side."

"Which side is that?"

"Germany's. I'm on Germany's side."

I looked down at my shoes. I needed time to gather my thoughts. "Tell me about the Black Orchestra."

"What do you want to know?"

"What is it?"

"It was a chess club."

This was not the answer I had expected.

He stood up, removed a framed photograph from the wall and handed it to me. It was a copy of the same photograph that I had found in Generalmajor Oster's office and among my father's things. "The club was set up in 1908 in Ludwig Maximilian University, in Munich, to celebrate and study the method of Emanuel Lasker. Probably the greatest chess player that ever lived, Lasker was born in Germany and held the world championship title for twenty-seven years – from 1894 to 1921."

"And the name? The Black Orchestra?"

"Ah, Lasker used to say that he could hear the pieces making music, like an orchestra. And he preferred the black pieces."

"Can you identify the people in the photograph?"

"I had more hair in those days." He pointed at the central figure in the picture. "This is Hans Oster. And this is Erwin van Neumann. Your father, I'm sure you recognise." He pointed to the figure on the extreme right. "This is Ruben, on the end, and this is Egbert, standing beside Oster."

"Egbert Krause?"

Could it be the same man?

"Was that his surname? I don't recall."

"So who's the last one? The second from the right."

"Why, that's Schiller, the dummkopf of the group."

I took the picture over to the light. Krause was difficult to identify, as I had met him only once, and the figure in the photograph was partially in shadow. I could see now that the man between him and von Neumann was Oberst Schiller, no question about it. The heavy eyebrows, though darker then, were unmistakeable. And then my mind was in turmoil. Oster and the three Obersts were all at university together, and all four men belonged to the same chess club. And now, thirty years later, they were all in senior positions in the Abwehr!

I handed back the picture. "I presume the club disbanded when you all left college."

"Yes, but you never lose the affiliations made during your college years, do you?"

"So you're still friendly with the members of the club?"

"I have fond memories of them, if that's what you mean." The professor stood up.

"Is that all?"

"Well, you can see that Hans Oster has surrounded himself with old friends – Krause, von Neumann and Schiller." He grinned. "Let's go back upstairs. It's a little damp down here."

I thought this a classic understatement – the whole house was damp. We climbed the stairs out of the cellar, and the professor led the way into a large, icy living area at the rear of the house overlooking the lake. Like the rest of the house, it smelled of mould and it felt damp; there were black patches high up on the walls and on the edges of the carpet. The focal point of the room was a fireplace with a mirror hanging over the mantel, and on the mantel, a small bronze statue of an eagle peering down at three broken eggs.

I picked it up. "I've seen this before. There's one amongst my father's things, Generalmajor Oster has one, and Oberst Schiller too."

Professor Hirsch sat down in an armchair at one side of the fireplace; I took the opposite armchair. He said, "Oster had them made in 1933, when Adolf Hitler came to power. The eagle is Germany, the eggs her broken dreams."

"So there *is* a continuing bond between the members of the Black Orchestra!"

"You could say that."

"And your current role, Professor?"

"You may not be aware that your uncle has been attempting to foment an uprising by the IRA. An action hostile to the British would divert some of their war resources."

"I knew that he had thoughts along those lines."

"More than thoughts. I have been in contact with the IRA, and I can tell you that they plan to conduct an offensive against the British."

"When?"

"That has not been decided. They're not fully prepared or equipped. But soon."

"Here in Ireland, or in Britain?"

"In Britain. They're planning a bombing campaign aimed at several British targets."

My mind was spinning again. How was I supposed to operate our agents in Ireland without any knowledge of this man's activities? He must have been the best agent we had in Ireland – maybe better even than Nightingale – and yet I hadn't been informed about him.

I said, "Who is your IRA contact?"

"His name's Sean Short."

I asked about the IRA plans and the professor gave me the details. Attacks were planned for the House of Commons, Buckingham Palace, the National Gallery, the British Museum, Scotland Yard, the palace at Windsor, Hampton Court, Blenheim Palace, the Docks at Southampton and Chatham in Kent. Logistical supplies required were explosives, detonators, handguns, heavy machine guns and ammunition. In addition, half a million pounds sterling would be required in cash to finance the planned campaign.

"That's quite a list," I said, scribbling everything into my notebook. "Is that everything?"

"No," the professor replied. "The most important item is missing from that list. A transmitter. The last transmitter that we supplied was detected and confiscated by the authorities, and it's of supreme importance that the Irish subversives can communicate directly with Berlin."

"I'd like to meet this Sean Short," I said, expecting a refusal.

"And so you shall." He looked at his watch. "I think we should call it a night. I'll take you back into town."

"I have many more questions," I protested. "You must tell me what became of agent Ornithologist."

"Yes, yes, I will answer all of your questions. But I'm tired and I have college work to do before tomorrow. You should think about what I've told you, write down your questions and I promise I'll answer them all the next time we meet."

"And Sean Short?"

"Here, let me." He took my notebook and pen, and wrote the name SEAN SHORT in block capitals. "I'll contact Sean and arrange a meeting."

"How long will it take to arrange?"

"A few days. A week at the most."

We agreed that he would place a note for me, under the name Kevin O'Reilly, in the students' notice board at the college main entrance as a signal when he had arranged the meeting with the IRA man.

45

January 1942

The next morning, Mother prepared two packed lunches and Blesset and I headed out for the bus terminus where we boarded a bus bound for Wicklow.

Blesset was agitated. Several times on the way to the bus he'd startled passers-by with shouts accompanied by sudden arm movements. Once we had taken our seats he seemed more settled. The journey took a little over an hour. The bus was old, and this, in concert with the poor state of the roads, ensured a bumpy, uncomfortable ride. We alighted at Rathnew, and the bus continued on its way, belching black smoke.

Rathnew to Ballyruane was no more than two miles. We walked it in twenty minutes. Ballyruane was a small village, very neat and tidy, with a post office, a public house, a few shops, a café and a church. We entered the café and sat down.

We waited five minutes before an old woman appeared wearing a colourful apron.

"Good morning, boys, what can I get you?"

Boys?

"Two cups of tea, please," I said.

She wrote down our order. "Can I get you anything else? Biscuits? Cakes? We have some excellent cakes, baked fresh this morning."

I said, "No, thank you." And simultaneously, Blesset said, "Yes please."

"Cake it is, then," the old woman said.

I remembered her name from Stallion's report. When she returned with our order, I said, "I wonder if you can help us, Mrs Muldowney."

"Oh," she was taken aback. "You know my name."

"Yes." I smiled. "You're famous in these parts. We're looking for a friend of ours."

"Well, I shall help if I can," she wiped her hands on her apron.

"His name is Rupert. He's Polish."

"The bird watcher! You're friends of his?"

"Yes. Do you know where we might locate him?"

She shook her head. "He was here for a while, but I'm afraid he's left."

"Where did he go?"

"Nobody knows. He just disappeared. There were rumours – there are always rumours – but really, no one knows what happened to him." She sat on the edge of a chair at one of the other tables. "We had another man here, making enquiries about him," she added.

Agent Stallion.

"I think Rupert lived in the village for some time?"

"That he did."

"Do you happen to know where he stayed while he was here?"

"Well, as a matter of fact, he stayed here. Above." She pointed a finger to the ceiling. "Would you like to see his room?"

She led us upstairs and into a room at the back of the shop. The bed was made up, the room empty.

I said, "He left nothing behind?"

"There were one or two things. Some clothes and a suitcase."

"And where is the suitcase now?" I asked.

"I gave everything to his girlfriend, Jane Jackman."

"And where might we find Miss Jackman?"

"She lives in the cottage at the end of the village, just across the road from the post office."

Before we took our leave, I asked to use the bathroom. She led me toward the back of the café. On my return journey I put my head around the kitchen door, and there I saw an SE 89/90 radio receiver/transmitter, sitting on the kitchen table.

I looked around for Agent Ornithologist's Enigma machine, but there was no sign of it.

At Jane Jackman's cottage, I knocked on the door.

"Who is it?" a tiny voice called from behind the door.

"We are friends of Rupert," I replied.

Jane Jackman opened the door. She was a tall, thin, freckled girl in her late thirties. "Do you have news of Rupert?"

"No, but we need to talk to you, Miss Jackman. May we come in?"

After some confusion on both sides, Jane admitted that she had taken possession of Rupert's 'typewriter'. She handed me the nameplate; it read 'Enigma'. "Is this what you're looking for?"

"Yes. Where's the rest of it?"

Her eyes filled with tears. "Rudolf Clancy the blacksmith smashed it with a hammer. Olive, his wife, tried to use it, but it was broken. Nothing she typed came out right. Rudolf said it was possessed…"

Blesset and I exchanged a glance.

"Clancy's a brute," she added.

"Do you have any idea where we might find Rupert now?" Blesset asked.

She shook her head. "No, but I received this a couple of months ago." She handed me a postcard. It was postmarked Dublin and contained a short personal message signed 'Rupert'.

We found Rudolf Clancy at his forge, working on a horseshoe. He was a massive man, not as tall as Drobol the giant, but from the same mould. We introduced ourselves as friends of Rupert. I asked to see Rupert's 'typewriter'.

"It's broken," he boomed, his voice like the voice of Odin in Valhalla.

"I'd still like to see it."

"It's no good," he roared. "I smashed it."

He led us to a storage area for scrap to the rear of the forge. There, I found Agent Ornithologist's Enigma machine in a thousand pieces.

I thanked the blacksmith and we left the forge.

Strolling out of the village to the south, we came upon a hill and climbed as far as a large boulder close to the summit. The hill overlooked the Irish Sea. A heavy mist hung over the water, but I could imagine this an ideal lookout for an agent of the Reich.

The Black Orchestra

"This is where I want you to stay," I said to Blesset.

"On this hill?"

"In Ballyruane. Mrs Muldowney has room for a lodger and she has a short-wave radio in her kitchen. I'm sure she won't mind if you use it from time to time."

A shadow passed over Fritz Blesset's face.

"This will be your lookout point," I said. "I'd be willing to bet that you could see as far as the coast of Wales from here on a clear day."

We sat on the rock and ate our packed lunches. When we had finished our meal, I handed Blesset one thousand pounds in crisp new five-pound notes. He put the money in his backpack. "That should be enough for a year, at least," I said. I held out my hand and Blesset shook it. His face was a picture of dismay. I pulled him toward me and wrapping my arm around him. "You'll be fine. Now off you go and charm the widow Muldowney."

I watched him hurrying back to the village. Before he disappeared from view I saw him throw a Hitler salute at the watching cattle in the fields.

46

February 1942

I returned to Rathnew and caught the bus back to Dublin. I recalled agent Nightingale's details extracted from his Blue file.

Henry John Lightfoot, graduated: 1923 University College Cork
Position: Undersecretary, Department of External Affairs, Dublin.

The tattered remains of a telephone book in a public telephone box provided a number for the Department of External Affairs. I rang the number, and asked to speak with Henry John Lightfoot.

After a short while, the operator said, "We have nobody of that name. Are you sure he's with this Department?"

"Yes, unless he's moved on."

"Hold a minute," she said. Then, "I've checked my extended list, and he's not there either."

"The extended list, what's that?"

"That's the list of present and past officers, going right back to the foundation of the State."

I went to the National Library in Kildare Street and consulted the alumni of University College, Cork. Checking the list of names of graduates for 1923, there was no entry for a Henry John Lightfoot.

Bemused, I returned to my mother's apartment in Wicklow Street. She was at work. I made a list of all of the questions that I wanted to ask the professor when next we met. It was vital to the success of my trip that I got answers in full to all of them.

Determined to find the missing agent, Ornithologist, I took a taxi to the headquarters of the *Irish Press* newspaper the following day, and placed a notice in the Lost and Found column:

I used his real name. "Pavel Zapochek. Please contact Robert at…" I appended my mother's telephone number.

The Black Orchestra

I checked the student notice board at the university's main entrance each morning, but there was no note posted there from Professor Hirsch. I called in to the newspaper offices each day, too, but there was no response to my Lost and Found notice. After three days, I decided to try a different approach. Setting out early in the morning, I travelled around the city centre to each of the soup kitchens and hostels for the homeless.

It took several hours, but eventually I found him sitting, propped against a wall in an alleyway, nursing a wine bottle. I almost didn't recognise him, for he was sporting a full beard, and wearing a full length dark overcoat with pockets torn. His boots were broken, his trousers barely long enough to reach his ankles. His protruding ears gave him away.

"Rupert," I called out to him. "Rupert Kinski, how are you?"

He ignored me.

"Pavel," I said. "Pavel Zapochek. It is you, isn't it?"

That got his attention. He put down the bottle and struggled to his feet. "What did you call me?"

"It's all right," I said, adding in a low voice, in German, "My name is Robert. I am from Berlin."

His eyes lit up. He shook my hand.

"What happened to you?" I asked.

He spoke in German. "I got word from an agent in Dublin that the British were coming to arrest me. I fled. I had very little money."

"Why didn't you go to the embassy?"

"I did. I told them who I was. They didn't believe me." He shrugged. "They could tell I was from Poland."

I told Zapochek that I would vouch for him if he returned to the embassy. He took a moment to consider. Then he said, "No. Thank you. I'm content as I am."

"On the streets?"

"Yes. I get one good meal a day, and my friends look after my other needs."

"But don't you have a life – family – back home?"

Switching to English, he said, "My old life is gone, now. There's nothing left for me in Germany. I am a homeless Irishman, and that is how I shall end my days."

I spent some time trying to persuade him to come with me to the embassy, but it was hopeless. He had been totally absorbed and assimilated into Irish street life. I gave him some money and walked away.

My feelings after this encounter bordered on envy. There was something seductive about his chosen way of life, following the open road; treating each day as a new beginning, with no responsibilities and no thoughts of the great issues shaking the world. I tried to picture myself dressed in an old smelly greatcoat, begging alms from passers-by. But then hadn't Alex said that a beard wouldn't suit me?

#

On day six, a notice appeared on the college notice board: "Kevin O'Reilly: Meet SH, Number 39, February 13, 18:00."

The professor was waiting for me when I arrived. It was dark and raining – a dull, persistent precipitation, anticipating a heavier torrent. We squeezed into his car. The rain increased in intensity every minute, and by the time we arrived at the professor's house, the windscreen wipers were barely coping. He parked the car in the barn, and we ran through the rain to the front of the house. He led the way into the living room and switched on the lights. I shivered; the room seemed colder and damper than before.

"I will light a fire," he said. "If you have questions, you may ask them while I work." He knelt in front of the fireplace and began to transfer cold ashes from the grate to a galvanised bucket using a small shovel.

"What can you tell me about Agent Nightingale?" I asked.

The professor looked up at me, frowning. "What do you want to know?"

"Why has he been silenced?"

"I was told that the British were close to locating him." He reached for a pile of newspapers, tore off several individual sheets, and twisted and rolled them into balls. Soon, he had a neat pile of rolled-up newspaper in the centre of the grate.

"You know who he is?"

"His name's Lightfoot. He works for the Civil Service."

"I rang the Civil Service. They never heard of him."

The professor made no reply, busying himself preparing the fire.

The Black Orchestra

"Professor?"

He looked up at me and said, "Lightfoot is a cover name. The Abwehr have gone to extraordinary lengths to protect his identity."

"But you know who he is?"

"I can say no more about that. Move on."

"Tell me about agent Ornithologist. Why did you remove him from his station?"

"I didn't remove him. I had orders from Berlin to eliminate him. I thought it better to let him run."

I took a moment to absorb that information.

"I located him," I said. "He's living rough in Dublin."

"Delighted to hear that he's okay," said the professor. "He should have gone to the embassy."

"He did. They turned him away."

The professor added an outer layer of damp turf to his pyramid. Then he struck a match and lit the fire. He stood up. "Excuse me a moment, Kurt, I need to wash my hands. Fix us both a drink - whiskey for me. You'll find everything you need in the sideboard." He left the room.

I was losing my patience. Here was an agent that I knew nothing about operating in my territory, using an unauthorised radio frequency. I needed answers. I stepped over to the sideboard. The farmhouses of Ireland are full of them: massive pieces of furniture fashioned in remote outhouses by self-taught cabinet-makers, veneered in polished walnut or oak and decorated with carved curlicues like brocade. This one stood on four squat splayed legs with clawed talons for feet; not the sort of furniture that you could comfortably turn your back on.

I opened the top drawer. There, nestling among a selection of assorted glass tumblers, I found a Walther PPK. I picked it up, wrapping my fingers around the handle. The pistol fitted my hand perfectly.

A sound from the hall signalled that the professor was returning. I slipped the gun into the belt of my trousers, under my jumper. Then I lifted two glasses from the drawer, and closed it.

47

February 1942

I waited until he had settled into his armchair. "Why wasn't I informed about you? I'm supposed to be in charge of all agent operations in Ireland, but I've been told nothing of your activities."

"I used to operate as an agent for the Abwehr," he replied, "but not any more."

"And your transmitter?"

He shrugged. "Nowadays, I'm a sort of unofficial agent."

"Unofficial?" I was astonished. "Reporting to whom? The frequency setting on your transmitter is not one used by the Abwehr."

He paused, perhaps considering his next answer. Then he said quietly, "My transmissions are picked up in Gruenwald."

"*Schloss* Gruenwald? You have a direct line to Reinhard Heydrich?"

"I have."

What next?

"Is that where the order to eliminate Ornithologist came from?"

He nodded. I could feel the Walther in my belt. I laid my hand across my belly and touched the butt of the gun with my fingertips.

"Why?"

He shrugged. "My best guess would be that the agent was too successful."

"*Too* successful?" I echoed his words, keeping my voice as even as I could.

"Yes. It really wouldn't suit your uncle's plans to have an agent of the Abwehr who actually does work useful to the Reich." I'm sure my jaw must have dropped, because he continued, "Your uncle would like nothing better than to have the Abwehr discredited as an intelligence organisation. That would allow the RSHA to occupy that space."

"But to order the elimination of an active agent in the field, I can't believe that. If it is true, then he is guilty of high treason," I said with feeling.

"Oh, it's nothing but petty office politics to Reinhard," he replied with a dismissive wave of his hand. He rose, went over to the sideboard, and opened the drawer.

He must see that the Walther is missing.

I wrapped my fingers around the butt of the gun and held my breath. He selected a fresh tumbler, holding it up to the light for inspection. "And you can be sure that your uncle will be able to deny everything," he continued, closing the drawer.

Crisis over.

I said, "I don't suppose it has escaped your notice, but our agents operating in Ireland have all been abysmal failures."

"Apart from Nightingale."

So he knew how valuable a source Nightingale had been.

"I've seen our agent-training operation in Brandenburg. Those agents are doomed to failure before they even start."

"It's the same for agents posted to Britain."

I wondered about the extent of his knowledge of the Reich's intelligence operations in Britain.

"What can you tell me about Agent 92?"

"Codename?"

"Sandbar."

"That's Arthur Stanley, operating out of Bletchley." he said. "I heard he had been recalled."

He was well briefed. Where was he getting his information from?

"Yes, but why?"

"I don't know. You'd have to ask von Pfaffel that."

"What about Agent 38? I don't have a codename, but I think he was the source of some highly important intelligence from London."

"That would be the daily TypeX codes," the professor said. "I heard he was arrested for burglary."

Was there anything this man didn't know?

I said, "That was the story circulating in Berlin, but it sounds unlikely. It seems to me that there is evidence of a conspiracy to undermine the operations of the Abwehr in Ireland."

"And Britain," he agreed, nodding vigorously.

"My uncle warned me about an active and dangerous subversive organisation, working for the downfall of the Reich — called the Black Orchestra."

"Did he, indeed?" The professor raised an eyebrow.

"Was he wrong? Am I not right in assuming that the Black Orchestra is still active?"

"Not as a chess club."

"As a subversive organisation?"

"That is correct."

Finally, a frank admission. I took a mouthful of whiskey. Its oily warmth wrapped itself around my tongue and rummaged its way into every secret corner of my mouth. Was the whole story about to unfold?

"So you admit it?"

"The Black Orchestra acts in the best interests of Germany."

"But against the Third Reich."

"That is correct."

"And the members of this organisation are …?"

I expected no direct answer to this question. I was amazed with what came next.

"I may not know all of them, but Hans Oster and his three section heads are all active members, certainly."

"And you?"

"I am proud to be a member." He raised his glass. "We toil for Germany – for the Germany that will emerge after the fall of Hitler's Reich." He closed his eyes, and swallowed a mouthful of whiskey.

"You believe the Reich will fall?"

"Sooner or later it must, for it is built on a foundation of ashes. The Black Orchestra's operations will hasten that day."

So it was all true! "Using what methods?"

"We do what we can in the shadows. You have seen some of our work already."

Uncle Reinhard had been right. It occurred to me then that I could never be permitted to return to Berlin with this information. I had to assume that the professor had planned everything in advance. But how was he going to keep me from reporting back? He could tell the Gardaí and have me interned, or I could be eliminated. The gun in my belt was my only trump card. I wrapped my fingers around it again.

I said, "Why did Kleister die?"

"Kleister?" He shook his head. "Sorry, I never heard of him."

"And Boniface?"

He shook his head again.

"It's a British codeword."

"It means nothing to me."

"My friend believes it might be the codeword for British decryption operations."

"That's Bletchley again. Professor Turing is leading that operation."

"Turing?"

"He's a famous Mathematician. Studied at Cambridge."

"And the Bletchley operation?"

"Who knows? I assume they are trying to break German ciphers."

"Enigma?"

"Yes, I reckon so. You understand how they work?"

I shook my head.

"The first six letters in every signal contain the call signs of the sender and the target. Knowledge of the call signs gives them six letters to start with."

"And after that?"

"The rest is just plain hard work."

He was telling me everything. I grew more and more nervous, but I pressed for information. "I'm not sure I understand how the Black Orchestra hope to achieve their aims. I mean, why not just give Enigma to the British?"

"That's not an option, for three reasons. In the first place, the Wehrmacht would simply switch to a new system. Second, the British *have* been approached. Generalmajor Oster offered his help and they refused."

I was dumbfounded by this news. If it was true, then Oster was guilty of high treason. And how could the British refuse such valuable information? "Why?"

"They seem to think that no German is a good German."

Short-sighted, but understandable.

"And the third reason?"

"Our methods are more subtle. The Abwehr is in a unique

position of trust and influence which must not be compromised. If it was—"

"Uncle Reinhard would take over."

He looked at his watch. "Still no sign of Sean Short. I don't suppose he'll—"

There was a squeak from the floorboards above our heads. We both heard it at the same time. I stood up and looked across at the professor.

"Point it at me," he whispered. "I am your prisoner."

"What?"

"The gun," he said. "Point it at me."

I took the pistol from my belt and pointed it at the professor. He picked up the whiskey decanter.

Heavy footsteps descended the stairs, and Von Kemp stepped into the room. He held a Luger pistol in his right hand, pointing straight at me, his right elbow tucked under his ribs. Advancing into the centre of the room, he swivelled his body around to the right. His gun arm remained in position as he turned, like the turret of a panzer tank. Now, the pistol was pointing at Professor Hirsch. Von Kemp was dressed in a charcoal grey suit, his polished black boots were smeared with mud.

He spoke in German. "Thank you Herr Leutnant Müller. I shall take it from here."

Speaking in perfect German, very calmly, the professor said, "You are SS?"

"Gestapo," von Kemp replied, with the faintest hint of a heel-click.

The professor said, "How long have you been listening?"

"Long enough."

The professor beamed. "So you know that I report directly to SS-Obergruppenführer Reinhard Heydrich."

"Yes, but you are a traitor," von Kemp replied flatly.

"How can you be sure of that?"

"I heard everything."

"But how do you know I was telling the truth? Has it not occurred to you that I was spinning a web to entrap our young friend, here, to test his loyalty to the Führer?"

The Black Orchestra

Von Kemp shook his head. "I heard it all."

"What is your rank?" The professor's voice was the voice of command.

"SS-Sturmbannführer."

"Do you know my rank?"

"You have no rank."

"SS-Obersturmbannführer," said the professor. "The question is do you believe that you have the authority to shoot someone of my rank?"

"You are a traitor to the Reich," von Kemp said again.

"Kurt here is Herr Reinhard Heydrich's nephew."

"I am well aware of that. Oberleutnant Müller and I are old friends."

Friends?

"I am going to pour myself a drink. Please lower your gun," the professor said.

Von Kemp made no move to lower his gun. "Herr Müller has done the Reich a great service today, by exposing you and your nest of vipers," he said.

Moving slowly, the professor tilted the heavy decanter and filled his glass.

"Would you like a drink Sturmbannführer?" the professor said.

Von Kemp shook his head — and the professor threw the decanter. It hit the Gestapo man on the chest, knocking him off balance. The professor leapt forward, and grabbed von Kemp's gun hand. The Luger went off with a loud retort, followed by a popping sound. The ejected cartridge hit the carpet with force and ricocheted across the room.

"Müller," von Kemp shouted. "Shoot him, Müller."

I pointed the Walther and pulled the trigger. There was a click. Then I grabbed the eagle statuette from the mantelpiece with my free hand, and swung it round in a single movement. There was a sickening crack as sharp bronze met brittle bone. They went down together.

48

February 1942

Von Kemp lay on his back, his lifeless eyes staring up at me, a dark pool of blood growing on the carpet behind his head.

My hands were shaking; my knees rubber. Still grasping the eagle statuette and the gun, I staggered to the armchair and fell into it.

The professor picked up the decanter and returned it to the drinks cabinet. "Spilled very little." He peered into my face. "You look a bit green. Are you all right?"

I handed him the Walther. "Give me a minute."

"There's a tap in the kitchen," he said, and when I gave no response, he added, "You need to wash your hands."

I rose, took a deep breath and made for the kitchen, where I cleaned the blood from my hands and splashed my face with cold water.

Back in the living room, the professor poured me a large glass of brandy. "Drink this."

"Your gun failed to go off, Professor."

"It's not loaded."

"Shit, professor! What was I supposed to do with it? Throw it at him?"

He sipped his brandy and said nothing. I took a mouthful of mine. Where the Irish whiskey had been sharp, oily, the brandy was smooth and refined. I felt it slide down my throat like nectar, warming as it went.

"You knew him – the Sturmbannführer?" the professor asked, pointing to the body.

"Yes. Let's just say I'm intimately familiar with his interrogation methods."

The professor replaced the Luger in von Kemp's shoulder holster.

Together we rolled the rug around von Kemp's body. The professor found a ball of twine, and we tied it tightly around the rug. Then we carried the bundle through the kitchen and out to the rear of the house. The professor tucked some rocks into the rug, wedging them against the body, some at von Kemp's feet, more at his head. We lifted the bundle into the boat, I rowed us out to the centre of the lake, and we dropped the bundle over the side. The rain was teeming down, heavier than ever.

As we watched the bundle sink, I thought about what I had done. I had killed an important member of the Gestapo. I had no regrets; von Kemp was a thug. But I had crossed an invisible line. Twenty minutes earlier, I would have considered myself a loyal, if troubled, member of the German war machine; now, I was a fully paid-up member of the resistance. It was a good feeling. There were dissenting voices in my gut, but my mind was convinced that I had done the right thing.

"What was his name?" the professor asked.

"Von Kemp," I said. "How deep is the lake?"

"Deep enough."

Back at the house, I asked how the Gestapo man could have gained entry to the house.

The professor smiled sheepishly. "It's an old house. A four-year-old armed with a bucket and spade could find a way in."

I asked how von Kemp was able to hear our conversation from upstairs.

The professor pointed out a grille in the wall by the fireplace. "That's a ventilation duct. It leads directly to the bedroom. From up there, you can hear a pin drop down here."

"Didn't you take a gamble, telling me the truth?"

"Not really. I remember you from college and I knew your father well. It was Hans Oster's idea to give you the opportunity to join us."

I digested this information in silence for a minute or two. Then I asked, "What do you know of my father's death?"

"The Gestapo shot him on the Night of the Long Knives."

"He was killed by a stray bullet."

"Is that what they told you?" He shook his head. "You know

Heydrich and his cronies made a list of people to eliminate that night. The list was called Hummingbird..."

"My father's name was on a list?" A sudden obstruction in my gullet interfered with my voice.

"I'm sorry, Kurt. I assumed you knew."

My mind was in turmoil. "Why was his name on the list?"

"I believe the Nazis submitted a planning application for a vast outdoor arena in Ulm for their rallies. The plan would have involved the destruction of a number of buildings of significant historical interest—"

"And my father opposed the plan?"

"Along with a number of other city councillors, yes. As a result, the Nazi Party reverted to the Nuremburg site."

I recalled what my uncle had said to me in his garden that day, the day when I first met Gudrun. He said he liked my father. He said I should be proud of him. He said he regretted Father's unfortunate and tragic death.

"And you are in league with these butchers?" I growled at the professor.

"I communicate with Heydrich – yes, but that is not to say that I am in league with him. That's the pearl in the oyster. Your uncle believes that he has an ace up his sleeve. I represent his best hope of overcoming the Abwehr, a flanking movement with which he will outmanoeuvre his enemies." He poured himself another brandy and topped up my glass. "In reality I will be his undoing. From my position of trust I can manipulate, misinform and misdirect. All of his scheming will come to nothing."

The fire had taken hold, spitting bright fibrous sparks across the floor. The professor added another piece of turf, and the furnace at its heart barely paused before devouring it. Acrid smoke lingered and clung in the air. On the walls the dark mould retreated.

It had been quite a day. When I awoke that morning my priorities all revolved around my job, and how to shore up the intelligence operation in Ireland. Now, just a few hours later, my perspective had changed utterly. I knew that Reinhard Heydrich was responsible for my father's death. As the professor had said, the evil that was the

Third Reich must fail, and I yearned to play my part in its downfall.

I had an urge to pee. The professor directed me to a small room at the back of the house. It had a sign saying "Restroom" on the door. When I emerged, the kitchen floor was flooded, and water was streaming in under the door.

I called the professor.

"Try these on for size," he said, shrugging on a coat and throwing me a pair of Wellington boots and an overcoat. The boots fitted me well enough. I put the coat on, we stepped out through the front door and hurried around to the back.

The rain was still teeming down. Rounding the house, we were struck by the full force of the rain and wind pounding our faces. The lake had risen several inches, and was lapping against the wall of the house and barn. Professor Hirsch led me to a pile of sandbags lying against the barn wall. We stacked them at the kitchen door until it was secure from the encroaching lake.

"That should hold it," he shouted in the wind.

We fought our way through the wind and rain to the front door and back inside the house, where we threw off our coats and boots. The water had advanced out of the kitchen and onto the tiled floor of the hallway, half way to the front door.

"You go warm yourself by the fire," he said. "I'll mop up this lot and join you in a while."

I put on my shoes, shook the rain from my head, and stepped into the living room. The lights were dim and welcoming; the fire blazing high in the fireplace, hissing as the occasional drop of rain made it all the way down the chimney. A pair of black shoes, covered in mud, stood steaming by the hearth; and standing against the wall at the fireside, a puddle of water growing at its tip, a half-rolled black umbrella.

49

February 1942

My smiling friend, the black umbrella's owner, was standing by the sideboard in his stocking feet. He gestured with the gun in his hand, indicating that I should sit by the fire. I sat down in my usual armchair.

"Call Hirsch," he said. The look in his eyes suggested that refusal was not one of my better options.

"Professor," I called out. "I need you in here."

Professor Hirsch entered the room and froze, the mop in his hands, dripping on the carpet.

"Step away from the mop," Black Umbrella said, "and take a seat."

"Who the devil are you?" the professor said.

"My name is SS-Untersturmführer Hans Wenther. You may call me Hans."

"Well, Hans," the professor said, sitting down in his armchair, "you are the second gunman to invade my home in one night."

"I am well aware of that," Wenther replied. "The man you killed was called Heinrich von Kemp. He was a good man."

"In what sense?" said the professor.

I frowned at the professor, attempting to catch his eye.

"Your next clever remark may be your epitaph."

The professor said, "You should know that I report directly to SS-Obergruppenführer Heydrich."

"I know that you are a traitor to the Reich."

Hirsch looked indignant. "I had to kill your friend," he said, "because he would not or could not understand my role."

"He understood very well," Wenther replied. "His mistake was misinterpreting Oberleutnant Müller's role. You are a traitor to the Third Reich, and so is Herr Müller, here."

"If that is what you honestly believe, then it is your duty to report your suspicions to your superiors in Berlin," the professor said.

Wenther shook his head. "I know my duty," he said, his eyes unblinking. "Now, please step into the hall."

"I am an American citizen," the professor spoke with authority.

"You are an enemy of the Third Reich. Move."

We both stood up and went slowly toward the door. Wenther followed, keeping the gun trained on us.

"This is neutral Irish soil," the professor said. "Do you think it wise to point a gun at an American citizen on Irish soil? And Kurt here is Reinhard Heydrich's nephew. He is in Ireland on a fact-finding mission for his uncle."

I had to admire the way the professor could think on his feet. The game was up; anyone else would have been pleading for mercy by now, but the professor was no quitter.

"I am aware of these facts. Now, I would like you both to step into the hall."

The professor tried one more gambit. "You realise, Hans that this whole thing was set up by Herr Heydrich as a loyalty test for SS-Sturmbannführer von Kemp – a test that he failed."

"That is ridiculous. Now open the cellar door and climb down."

The professor unlocked and opened the door and we descended the stairs, turning on the lights as we went. At the bottom of the stairs, Wenther said, "Over there, by the desk."

I glanced at the professor. He seemed unconcerned.

"I would suggest that you allow me to contact Herr Heydrich." He leaned across the desk and picked up the telephone receiver. "The Obergruppenführer will resolve this—"

The gun went off with an ear-splitting crack that echoed off the cellar walls. My heart leapt. The professor went down. I dropped to one knee to render assistance. It was only then that I realised the cellar floor was flooded to a depth of five centimetres. Under the professor's jacket, I could see a growing blood stain on his shirt. Wenther pointed his gun at me and pulled the trigger.

The gun jammed.

The gunman swore, "*Scheisse!*" and then ran back up the steps.

He closed and locked the door from the outside. I heard the bolt slide into place and the dull clunk of the padlock, followed by an ominous silence.

I removed the professor's jacket and tore off his shirt. The bullet had entered his chest close to the right nipple. His eyes were glazed over, and there was a trickle of blood from his mouth. He lifted an arm and waved it about. "Go after him."

"Don't speak. I'll get help," I said. I propped him up against the wall and lifted the telephone. It was dead. I clambered to the top of the steps and tried the door, rattling it. And shouted, "Hans, let us out of here. Wenther, this is a mistake. Let us out and I will explain everything."

There was no answer. I hear a sound like a train, far away, moving along the tracks. And then the water came – a torrent of water, rushing under the door, pouring down the staircase. I lost my footing and tumbled down the stairs.

#

I woke, coughing, in water a metre deep. It was icy cold. I waded over to the professor and checked his pulse. He was unconscious but alive, his breathing shallow, gurgling gently. The blood from his mouth had dried. He was safe from the water for the moment, but the torrent rushing down the steps was unrelenting. Several books floated past me; then a wooden chair. I watched the water level for a minute. How quickly was it rising? Too quickly. The light in the ceiling was flickering. I looked up. Water poured from the ceiling in several places. It seemed the lake had flooded the entire ground floor and was seeping through the floorboards from the living room above.

Then the light flickered, fizzled, sparked—and went out.

50

February 1942

Groping in the dark, I found the professor's desk and chair. I anchored the chair against the end of the desk, close to where the professor lay against the wall. Positioning my legs on either side of the professor, I leant down, put my hands under his armpits and half-lifted, half-dragged him into the chair. I recovered his jacket from where I had left it on the desk, and wrapped it around his shoulders. It was wringing wet, but I thought it might give him some protection against the cold. Working by feel, I located the cable running from the back of the dead telephone. I ducked under the water, followed the cable back as far as I could, and cut it with my father's knife. Then I cut the other end at the instrument. I used this cable to tie the professor into his chair, to prevent him from sliding back into the water. Finally, I propped him up against the wall to stop him from falling sideways.

And still the water continued to rise. I did a quick calculation: the room was about two metres high. The water had risen ten centimetres in about ten minutes, and was already up to my lower ribs – about one metre ten deep. Ninety centimetres – maybe one metre – to go, rising at one centimetre per minute. That gave us roughly an hour and a half. Strapped in his chair, the water was nearly up to the professor's shoulders. In that position, with his chin on his chest, he had maybe twenty centimetres – twenty minutes. If I held his head above the water, maybe thirty, leaving aside the question of the icy cold acting on a man already in shock.

I turned my attention back to the door. Clinging to the wall, I edged up the stairs, the rushing water threatening to send me hurtling back to a watery death at every moment.

At the door, a thin beam of light shone through the keyhole.

Pressing my back against one wall, and wedging my feet against the other, I secured my position, reached into my jacket pocket, and pulled out my lock picks.

Picking locks in the training centre hadn't been easy, but here, with cold unresponsive fingers and limited mobility, it was impossible. The picks slipped from my grasp into the torrent. I swore. Reaching down blindly with my left hand, I caught them washing past. I tried again, and managed to get a pick wedged inside the lock mechanism. I closed my eyes and tried to conjure an image of the tumblers. I rotated the pick through a complete circle without encountering anything. I pushed it in further and tried again. Resistance! I applied force, but nothing happened. I rotated the pick the other way until I encountered what might have been the same part of the lock's mechanism. Again, I applied a little force but nothing moved. Desperately, I applied a greater force and the lock yielded, with a loud click. I turned the door handle. The door opened about one centimetre and stopped, held firm by the padlock. Encouraged by the small opening that I had created, the torrent increased in intensity. I nearly fell again.

Hopelessness engulfed me. The whole lake was pouring through the door and the ceiling. There was nothing I could do to stop it. The padlock would seal our fate. The only question was would we freeze to death or drown. Angrily, I seized the door handle and wrenched the door toward me. The gap around the door increased to two centimetres and the flood increased again. I tried brute force on the door handle again, and again.

The third time, the handle broke off in my hand. I gave a cry of despair, forced my fingers around the edge of the door and pulled with all my strength. The bolt held firm.

"Kurt, where are you?" A voice from above.

"Blesset," I yelled. "Is that you?"

"Where are you?"

"We're in the cellar. Get this door open, before we drown."

I heard him wading toward the door and rattling the padlock. "It's locked."

"I know it's locked. Find something to break the padlock from the chain."

The Black Orchestra

"There's nothing here."

"Try the barn, and hurry."

Three minutes later, Blesset was back. "Stand clear," he shouted.

I scarcely had time to jerk my face away before the door crashed open. I came close to death then, for as the door opened I lost my grip. The flood turned to a river and I was washed, tumbling, down into the cellar again.

I came up for air beside the professor. He was conscious, his mouth underwater. I ducked underwater and untied the cable. He fell free of the chair. Now we were floating – and rising – rapidly. I held on to him, as the rising water carried us to the top of the steps, together with two chairs and several books. I climbed out. Blesset reached out a hand to me and between us we pulled the professor to safety.

The kitchen and hall were like a river. We heaved Professor Hirsch onto the stairs above the water level, then Blesset opened the front door, and the river streamed out. Blesset and I waded upstream to the back door and pushed it shut. Together, we replaced the sandbags. When we re-entered the house through the open front door, the stream had died; the water level in the kitchen and hall, was dropping. The cellar was full to the ceiling.

"Stay with him, Blesset." I ran past the professor, up the stairs, pulling off my wet clothes as I went. I found the bathroom, stripped off the rest of my clothes and dried myself quickly with a towel. Then I found the professor's bedroom, flung open the wardrobe and grabbed some dry clothes – underwear, a pair of trousers and a shirt. I tried on a pair of the professor's shoes; they were two sizes too big.

I returned with dry clothes for the professor. He coughed, reached into his trouser pocket, and pulled out his keys. He handed them to me and waved an arm toward the door.

"You need help," I said.

He shook his head. "Follow him," he said; his voice a hoarse whisper, barely audible. "You must catch him, before—"

"I know," I said. "Don't worry, professor, we will catch him."

We carried him upstairs. Blesset found a dry blanket and wrapped it around the professor.

As we were leaving the house, I checked in the living room. The black umbrella was gone. I seized an overcoat from a hook in the hall and we ran to the barn.

I knew that it was imperative to catch Wenther before he reported to his superiors. What he had seen would place the professor in mortal danger from Heydrich and would lead me to the gallows for certain.

51

February 1942

The Riley coughed as if it knew it was in strange hands, then roared. Everything was unfamiliar. The gear stick was on the wrong side; I couldn't find reverse gear, and when I did, the car shot backwards out of the barn, bounced through several potholes, and ran into a hedge. Blesset opened the passenger door and climbed in beside me.

"Where are we going?"

"Nowhere," I replied, "unless I can find first gear."

I pushed to gear stick forward, found what I think must have been third gear, and stuttered up the driveway toward the gate and into the road toward the city centre. I found second gear. Visibility was poor; the windscreen wipers had seen better times, and changing gear was a nightmare. A line of traffic built up behind us.

"Wenther is a British spy," I told Blesset. "He has stolen secret information from the professor and must be stopped before he leaves the country. He will expose all of our operations to the British if he gets away."

"Right," said Blesset, staring ahead through the misted windscreen.

His Tourette's seemed under control, for which small stroke of good fortune I was thankful.

I spotted a telephone box, pulled over and dialled 999.

"Which service?" the operator asked.

"Fire and ambulance," I replied. "There has been a shooting and a serious flood."

I gave the operator directions to the professor's house. When she asked for my name, I hung up and jumped back in the car.

"How did you find me?" I asked Blesset. "And why were you looking?"

"Heinz asked me to keep an eye on you. And your trail was easy enough to follow. Your mother told me where to start."

"You saved both of us from a miserable, damp death." I glanced over at Blesset. His face was set, staring through the smeared glass.

I drove on through the rain to Northumberland Road, an affluent area close to the centre of the city. Two parallel rows of Georgian houses faced each from either side of a wide tree-lined boulevard, the residences of the rich and famous: doctors, solicitors, members of the Dáil. The road also contains several embassies. I parked outside the German Legation at number fifty-eight, and rang the doorbell.

A voice answered on an intercom, "Yes, can I help you?"

"I am a German citizen," I said in German. "Please open the door."

"I'm sorry, sir," the voice replied. "The Legation is closed for the day."

"I was to meet a friend here," I said quickly. "Hans Wenther. Has he been here?"

"We did have another caller about fifteen minutes ago, sir, but as I said, the Legation is closed."

"He's not here," I said to Blesset, as I restarted the car.

I pulled into the traffic, the windscreen wipers barely keeping up with the downpour.

"Watch out for a large black umbrella," I shouted to Blesset.

He snorted. "There are umbrellas everywhere."

We entered Westmoreland Street, which leads directly to the river Liffey and to O'Connell Street, Dublin's main thoroughfare.

#

Wenther's rolling gait gave him away. "There he is," I shouted.

Pulling over to the curb, I switched off the engine. We both jumped out of the car, but by the time we started our pursuit on foot, I had lost sight of him again. I estimated that he was 50 metres ahead of us. On the quays a sea of people moved away to our left, west along the quay, another stream moving north across O'Connell Bridge. Funnelled between the buildings, the wind drove the rain into our faces, making it difficult to stand.

The Black Orchestra

"Which way?" Blesset shouted, water dripping from his blond hair and across his face.

"You go that way," I said, pointing west up the south quay. "I'll check on the other side. Whistle if you find him."

I pushed my way across the bridge; the river a raging, moiling torrent, its surface littered with tree limbs and other debris, rushing headlong downstream. My hair was sodden, the water running down my face. I wiped my eyes and spotted Wenther, his black umbrella lowered into the wind, battling his way up the north quay. I put my fingers into my mouth and gave a loud whistle. Wenther turned his head at the sound and saw me.

I ran forward, turned west and followed Wenther up the river. He was waiting for me at the metal arch of the Ha'penny Bridge, his umbrella in his hand, rolled now and held like a sword. My head was lowered, and I came upon him suddenly. He thrust at me with his umbrella, its spike sharpened to a fine point. I looked down to see my coat ripped from waist to hem. I jumped backward, colliding with a pedestrian who fell, swearing, into a group of others. Wenther advanced, thrusting with his lethal umbrella. I backed away, keeping close to the parapet wall. He had every advantage: his back was to the wind, whereas with the rain driving into my eyes I could barely see; his full length leather coat provided him with shelter from the elements; I was dressed in light, ill-fitting clothes; and he was armed, while I was not. I reached into my pocket and pulled out my father's letter-opener knife.

Again, he jabbed his umbrella at me; I dodged again, and my back hit a lamppost. Sandwiched between the parapet wall and the post, I had nowhere to go. He smiled, and drew his arm back for the final blow. And that was when Blesset appeared by his side.

"Heil!" Blesset shouted, and his arm shot up and forward. He caught Wenther on the side of the head, knocking him off balance. I dodged toward the Gestapo man, swept his feet from under him, and he toppled over the parapet.

Wenther fell with a faint smile on his lips; he made no sound. The crowd of Dubliners cried out collectively as Wenther went over the parapet; as he hit the water, they gasped; and they groaned as he sank below the surface. The rolled umbrella floated for a moment or two before it, too, was dragged under.

One man said, "Jaysus, he's a goner. The river's in flood."

"He's prob'ly drownded already," said another in a lugubrious tone, peering into the roiling waters of the river.

A woman pointed at me and said, "You kilt him. I saw you push him over."

Another woman leapt to my defence. "Don't blame him," she said. "I saw it all. He tried to save him."

"That blonde fella hit him," the first man said.

I looked around for Blesset, but he was gone. I tore myself free of the grasping witnesses and hurried across the Ha'penny bridge, throwing my father's knife into the river as I went. I got back to the car, plunged in, and sat shivering for a few minutes. Across the river I could see a police car arriving, the excited crown pointing into the river.

Ducking down behind the wheel, I started the engine and drove to the university. I took the car in through the rear entrance, and parked it in Professor Hirsch's spot, dropping the keys through his letterbox. Then I skulked out of the university grounds and back to my mother's place.

52

February 1942

The following day, I telephoned each of the hospitals in turn. Professor Hirsch had been admitted to St. James's Hospital. The nurse in charge said that he had had a comfortable night. She was not at liberty to provide any more detailed information about her patient over the telephone.

I put the professor's clothes in a bag and left my mother's apartment. I caught a bus to the hospital. I was surprised to find the professor sitting up in bed in a private room, reading a book.

"Did you catch our friend with the umbrella?" he said.

I replied, "He went for a swim in the Liffey."

"Good. The police have shown some interest. We need to get our stories straight."

I nodded.

"Wenther broke in. He was a stranger looking to rob us. I offered him a drink. He shot me, locked us in the cellar and ran off."

"You look remarkably well," I said, "for a man with a bullet hole in his chest."

The transformation was astonishing. When Blesset and I had left him, he seemed close to death. Now his cheeks were rosy, his good humour almost fully restored.

"The bullet grazed my right lung, but there was no damage to any vital organs." He smiled. "The damage to my jacket is much more serious, and the shirt is beyond repair."

"How is your lung?"

"The doctors say there will be some scarring, and my lung capacity on that side will be reduced, but I'll live. Half an inch to the left and the damage might have been fatal."

"Does it hurt?"

"Only when I laugh."

"The fire brigade must have got to you pretty quickly," I said.

"They were there within a half hour. I was able to walk to the ambulance. The fire service had already begun to pump the water out before I left. They offered to drain the lake, by the way."

"You declined, of course."

"Of course."

"One thing puzzles me," I said, "Where did you first meet Heydrich?"

"I've never met him. I established contact through diplomatic channels in '38. Your uncle was content to have an independent source in Ireland."

"You've been in contact with him all that time?"

"On and off, yes."

"So why not transmit the IRA plans directly to Heydrich? Why give them to me?"

He shrugged, and winced. "Your uncle wanted your involvement. I can only imagine that he doesn't fully trust me."

I asked about the IRA leader, Sean Short. "Is there still a chance I might meet him?"

He shook his head. "They're like rabbits, these subversives. They run and hide at the slightest sign of trouble."

"I could stay a bit longer. A week, maybe."

"No point. I doubt if Short will show his face in public before Christmas. Who came to our rescue?"

"Fritz Dieter Blesset. I brought him over to replace Ornithologist."

As I was preparing to leave the professor grabbed my arm and fixed me with his gaze. "Remember the Black Orchestra's watchwords: hard work, dedication, self-sacrifice, courage and strength of will. For a better Germany and the destruction of the Third Reich."

#

The Black Orchestra

I found two burly gardaí waiting for me when I stepped out of the professor's hospital room. They wheeled me outside and into the back of a squad car.

We drove in silence to the police station in Pearse Street. The desk sergeant asked for my name and address.

"Kevin O'Reilly." I supplied my mother's address.

"Occupation?"

"I'm a student." When he reacted to that, I added, "A postgraduate student."

I was shown into an interview room in the basement. The room was equipped with a table and four chairs. It had no windows. I was given a cup of lukewarm tea.

Two plainclothes policemen entered and sat down opposite me at the table. One of them was carrying two folders. The top one was labelled "Shooting February 13, 1942".

"My name is Inspector MacManus. This is Sergeant Conroy. We would like to ask you a few questions concerning the injury suffered by Professor Hirsch yesterday."

Sergeant Conroy asked the first two questions. "You do know Professor Hirsch?"

"Yes, I am a postgraduate student in his department."

"And were you with him yesterday when the incident occurred?"

I said that I was.

"So tell us what happened," the inspector said, "in your own words."

"The professor and I were at his home, discussing mathematics, when we were surprised by an intruder armed with a pistol."

"What sort of pistol?"

"I have no idea."

The inspector exchanged a glance with the sergeant. "Continue, please."

"He demanded money. The professor said we had none. He offered him a drink. The gunman marched us into the cellar. He shot the professor. He would have shot me too, but his gun jammed."

"His gun jammed," the inspector echoed my words. I wasn't sure if his tone was sarcastic or merely incredulous.

"He locked us in the cellar. Then he removed the sandbags and opened the back door."

"You saw him doing this?"

"No," I answered patiently. "But the cellar began to flood. I forced the door open and escaped."

"Are you saying you didn't know this gunman?"

"Of course not! I had never seen him before."

"Did he speak to you?"

"Just a few words, 'Raise your hands.', 'Give me your money.', 'Open the cellar door.', 'Go down the steps.'"

"And was there anything strange about his accent?"

I scratched my head. "I don't think so."

"He didn't sound foreign?"

"No."

The two policemen looked at each other. Then the inspector said, "You were seen driving a green Riley Lynx through the streets of the city in an erratic manner."

I laughed. "I'm not a very good driver."

"Do you have a licence?"

"No, but it was an emergency."

"Where were you going?"

"To get help for the professor."

"An eyewitness has reported that there were two men in the car." The sergeant said. "Who was the second man?"

"Your eyewitness was mistaken. It was raining heavily and there was a strong wind."

They exchanged another glance.

The inspector opened the second file. "There was a drowning incident in the river shortly after that. We believe that you and your companion were at the scene."

I glued an expression of astonished innocence onto my face. "What happened?"

"A man fell over the parapet into the river and was sucked under. We recovered his body near the mouth of the river."

"Who was he?"

"We were hoping you could tell us that," the sergeant said. "He was carrying no identification."

"His clothing was German," the inspector added.

"How extraordinary."

"We believe that these two incidents are connected. And I believe you know a lot more about this affair than you've told us."

"I've told you everything I know."

They cautioned me for driving without a licence and without due care and attention, and I was released. I left the police station with a broad smile on my face. I couldn't help comparing the interrogation methods of the Irish police with those of the Gestapo.

53

March 1942

I spent the last two weeks of February in Dublin. Uncertainty and danger awaited me in Germany and I was glad of the respite. Finally, when March came, I felt I could delay no longer. I told Mother that I must leave, and we spent our last evening together in quiet conversation. The apartment was barely heated with an electric fire with two parallel bars. That night, both bars were on – the fatted calf for the prodigal son.

She kept smiling throughout the evening, but I sensed her deep sorrow at my impending departure; she couldn't be certain of seeing me ever again. We talked about old times when my father was alive and before I left for college. My memory of when we lived together as a family stretched for just nine short years – 1924 to 1933. During the early years – up to 1924 – I saw little of my father, as he worked long hours; I was asleep most nights when he arrived home from the office.

"He regretted that," she said, in English. "He always regretted missing so much of your childhood."

"*Er war ein guter Vater*," I said: he was a good father.

She replied, "*Er liebte dich.*": he loved you. And then in English, "You're so like him."

My mind flooded with memories of a thousand conversations from the past, both of us constantly switching between the two languages. It would have sounded strange to anyone listening, but to us it seemed the most natural thing in the world. There are some phrases that sound so much better in English, others that require the precision of German.

"You miss him," I said. "*I* miss him."

"His life was cut short," Her hands were busy with her knitting. I couldn't remember a time when her hands were idle.

"A stray bullet," I said. "Do you still believe that story?"

"You should leave Germany," was her reply.

"Where could I go?"

"You could live here," she looked up, and when I laughed she said, "In Ireland, I mean."

"But I'm a Wehrmacht officer. I'd be locked up."

"You're not locked up now."

I thought about it. My future in Germany was precarious. Wenther's body would be repatriated, and it was only a matter of time before the Gestapo found out about von Kemp's death and my role in it. As a fugitive, there would be no hiding place in Germany, and escape to Ireland seemed my only possible option.

"What are you knitting?"

"It's for a neighbour. Her daughter's expecting a baby."

And suddenly I understood my mother's unspoken dream. I was her only child, her only hope for grandchildren.

"You'd like Gudrun," I said.

"You could bring her with you."

I thought it might be possible, with the help of Heinz Franzelberg and his camera.

#

For the first leg of my return journey, I took a commercial flight from Dublin to Lisbon. At Lisbon, I checked in for a connecting flight to Berlin.

There was a two hour delay.

My change of heart was like a religious conversion. I marvelled at it. Try as I might, I couldn't pinpoint the exact moment of decision. The killing of von Kemp had been the point of no return, but I knew my mind was made up long before then. But when? Was it the death of Alex's brother, or earlier than that, the sight of Tania's broken hands in Ravensbrück, or even earlier, the sickening encounter with the lynch mob in Leopold Platz?

And why had I taken this huge, irrevocable step anyway, when so many millions were happily following the Führer, like the pied piper of Hamlin? I knew it wasn't courage, but if not courage, then what? Amongst my fellow countrymen, I was in a fairly unique position; I had seen for myself what life was like for the inmates of a labour camp; I had endured a Gestapo interrogation and lived. Most citizens of Germany knew only what the Propaganda Ministry told them.

I remembered a story my mother told me as a child about a wild goose called Otto who stubbornly refused to migrate with all the other geese for the winter. Perhaps I was like Otto the goose, simply too stubborn to follow the crowd.

Everything had changed. I had killed two representatives of the legitimate German government, and taken sides with a subversive organization. I was now an assassin, a multiple killer, and an enemy of the Reich. If my actions were discovered I would be hunted down to face immediate execution, just like Otto the goose, who enjoyed his freedom for a while before a poor family caught him for their Christmas table.

I felt no fear, no trepidation, only a deep and passionate loathing for the Third Reich and a determination to do whatever I could to further the ends of the Black Orchestra. I tried to recall the professor's last words to me, the watchwords of the organization: courage, hard work, self-sacrifice, all sentiments indistinguishable from those of the Party. Only the end result was different.

I bought a cup of tea from a youth in a kiosk and took it to a small table. From my investigation it seemed likely that Henry John Lightfoot was a total fiction. I thought about this for a while. Von Neumann had explained Nightingale's true function: to transmit highly secret British intelligence reports, using a compromised coding system, to cover for the fact that we had cracked TypeX. But how was this possible without a real agent in the field?

The information I had gathered about the professor was sketchy. Bullfrog, Gruenwald, 3137.5 kilohertz, the pearl in the oyster. I opened my notebook at the page where the professor had written SEAN SHORT in capital letters. There was something odd about the professor's handwriting. I scratched my head. Why had he written the name at all? And why write it in such big letters, taking up the whole page? Short was a common enough surname in Ireland, and Sean was probably the most common Christian name after Patrick and Michael. SEAN SHORT. I peered at the professor's writing. There was nothing unusual about the letters. They were formed quickly, written with a flourish, but nothing... Then I noticed something. There was a gap between the SE and the AN of SEAN, and another gap between the SH and the ORT of SHORT:

SE AN SH ORT

My heart skipped a beat. It was an anagram. Combine AN and SH to get HANS. Then combine SE and ORT. SEAN SHORT was a simple anagram of HANS OSTER.

#

It was after midnight by the time I got home. I turned the key in the lock and opened the door as quietly as I could. The apartment was in darkness. I slipped off my shoes and trousers, and slid into the bed. Gudrun stirred; she half turned toward me and coughed. I held my breath. Then, reaching behind her, she found me.

"Kurt," she murmured. "You're home."

I wrapped my arms around her and we slept. As dawn rose we made love in the half-light. Her body was warm, soft and welcoming, her embrace passionate. I was weary from my travels, but nevertheless we reached heights close to the ecstasy of our first night together.

As Gudrun made breakfast I gave her an account of my trip. I omitted the intrigue surrounding the professor, and made no mention of the two Gestapo gunmen. I told her about my conversations with my mother. Gudrun sat close to me and laughed at everything I told her. She particularly enjoyed my story about the disused railway station at Ballymartle.

PART 4

54

March 1942

During my U-bahn journey to the office, all my old fears and paranoia returned. Had I seen that bearded man on the aeroplane from Lisbon? Was he on the flight from Dublin? Why was that woman with a child staring at me?

The streets of Berlin were a shock. They seemed empty. Where there had been men and women in uniform everywhere, there were almost none now, and there were fewer civilians on the streets. Buses and trams seemed less frequent and while bicycles were to be seen everywhere, there were fewer of them. None of the commercial advertisements on the Litfass columns looked fresh, and the rest were Wehrmacht recruitment notices or government proclamations.

Upon arrival at the office, I opened my briefcase, removed the bronze statuette and placed it on my desk.

Von Pfaffel stuck his head around the door. "Good trip?"

"Very illuminating."

"The Oberst wants to see you."

I entered Oberst von Neumann's office and looked around.

"You're searching for something?"

"A bronze eagle with a nest of broken eggs."

He laughed, opened a drawer in his desk, lifted out the statuette, and placed it on the desk. "Welcome home, Oberleutnant."

The debriefing was quick and thorough. I had achieved all of the official objectives of my mission: Blesset had been placed in position with access to a transmitter; I reported that agent Ornithologist was dead and his Enigma machine had been destroyed.

The Black Orchestra

Generalmajor Oster sent word that he wished to see me. I climbed the stairs to the fourth floor.

"You spoke with the professor's IRA contact?" the Generalmajor said.

"No, but I have his name here." I opened the notebook at the relevant page and handed it across the desk.

The Generalmajor guffawed. "Very good. Is this your idea of a joke?"

"The professor's."

"You collected your father's eagle?" He handed me back the notebook.

"Yes, Herr Oster. It's on my desk downstairs."

"You've earned it."

"You heard what happened in Dublin?"

"Professor Hirsch gave me the short version." My reaction must have showed on my face, for Oster said, "Don't look so concerned. Only I know the story."

"Oberst Krause has an eagle as well?" I asked.

"Yes. With yours, there are now six in the building."

I frowned. I stood up, took the photograph from the wall and handed it to the Generalmajor. "Krause, von Neumann, Schiller, yours and mine," I said. "That makes five."

He beamed. "And who do you think took the photograph?"

"There is another member of the Black Orchestra?"

"Yes. There were eight members in the original chess club."

"And the eighth member?"

"We called him 'The Old Man' even then," Oster said, grinning.

The full weight of this information struck me immediately. Admiral Canaris was Hitler's most trusted intelligence chief. The depth of the Black Orchestra conspiracy was breathtaking. I replaced the photograph on the wall, and resumed my seat.

"You must expect further contact with Merlin," said Oster.

"Merlin?"

"Your uncle. The codename is the one used by the British in their signals. We use it too – informally. It seems to fit him so well."

"Heydrich's been posted to Prague."

"Yes, but he will seek you out. He has a great interest in the professor's IRA contacts."

As I was leaving, Generalmajor Oster touched my arm. "One final word of advice, Kurt. Remember that the Black Orchestra is strictly an underground organisation. In the office, everything you do, everything you say, must be consistent with your Abwehr role. You must act out your part at all times. One wrong move could bring the whole edifice crashing down. And trust no one. In Germany, the walls have eyes."

#

Sitting in my tiny room, I was struck by the strangest feeling. All around were the sights and sounds of a familiar office, and yet everything had changed. I knew that, from now on, nothing about my work would be normal or mundane; everything I did – even the most trivial of tasks – was charged with energy, with danger and with a new, secret agenda.

I found it hard to look my colleagues in the eye. Surely they must know that I had killed, not once, but twice. It seemed impossible that such a great secret would not show on my face for all to see. Everyday conversations required all of my concentration, as I struggled to remember how the old Kurt Müller would have reacted, responded.

The first order of business was to build a plausible story to explain the disappearance of von Kemp. I extracted one of the Garda transfer documents from Agent Lightning's file, and showed it to Heinz. The official Garda insignia was embossed near the top.

"I need a blank copy of this form," I said. "Top priority."

"Right, leave it with me."

Heinz reappeared three days later, wearing a new lime green waistcoat and carrying a small parcel. The parcel contained a bundle of Garda transfer forms. The Irish police insignia embossed at the top of the form was impressive.

"Good job," I said. "How many are here?"

"Two hundred."

"I only needed one."

"Keep the rest," he said, with a toady wave of his hand. "You never know when they might come in handy."

I put one of the forms into a typewriter and filled it out. It was a concise account of how one Heinrich von Kemp, German citizen, had been interned at the Curragh Camp. Once the counterfeit form was complete, I put it through the system, knowing that, by official or unofficial means, it would come to the attention of von Kemp's superiors in the Gestapo.

#

A week after my return to Berlin, I had heard nothing from Alex. I rang his number at the Air Ministry. A stranger answered, "We haven't seen him since last week."

I rang Alex's home number. The telephone rang for two minutes before he picked it up.

"Yes," he barked. "Who is it?"

"It's me."

"What do you want?" His voice sounded rough.

"Are you ill? I rang the Air Ministry. They said you haven't been at work all week."

He hung up.

I went around to his apartment and knocked on the door. There was no answer. I knocked again, louder. Still no one came to the door. I called through the letterbox. No response. Johann appeared, carrying a small bag of groceries, his Bohemian clothing style as flamboyant as ever. He looked older than I remembered him. I was surprised to see him, as I had thought he and Alex were no longer friends.

He opened the door and invited me in.

"What died in here?" I said. The place stank of stale tobacco fumes and ash.

The apartment was in darkness. Johann switched a light on. I found Alex in the living room, asleep on the settee, a half-empty bottle of cheap vodka on the floor beside him. There was another bottle, empty, on a chair nearby.

"Alex," I said. Then I shouted, "Alex, wake up."

I shook his shoulder, and he opened his bleary eyes. He hadn't shaved for a week and his breath was foul.

He swung his legs off the settee and sat with his head down, close to his knees.

"Put the kettle on, Johann," I said, throwing open the windows.

It took two hours to restore Alex to a reasonable level of respectability. He protested and fought us for a while, but by the time I was preparing to leave he'd had a wash and a shave and swallowed a litre of coffee. He was coherent, although still not fully sober, and I think we had convinced him to return to work the next day.

Johann showed me to the door.

"Thanks for coming around, but there was really no need. I would have looked after him."

"I thought you and he had quarrelled."

He hesitated before answering, "We've been friends for a long time, Alex and me."

"How long?" It was an innocent enough question, born of idle curiosity and with no malice. The way Johann reacted to it, took my breath away.

"What concern is that of yours? Who appointed you Alex's guardian angel?"

"Alex and I are friends."

"Well you can fuck off. Alex doesn't need friends like you any more."

He slammed the door in my face before I could say another word.

55

April 1942

Two weeks after that, I was helping Speddig in the Translations Unit of Section I when I decoded a British Cypher3 signal that read as follows:

OPERATION ANTHROPOID TARGET MERLIN CONFIRMED.

The call signs indicated that the signal originated in London and was intended for the Czech resistance movement in Prague. There was only one interpretation that I could place on it: An assassination attempt on Reinhard Heydrich was imminent. I waited until Speddig was out of the room, then I slipped the decoded signal into my pocket.

I knew that Heydrich's death would make my position difficult – perhaps impossible – but I was resolved to do whatever I could to undermine the Nazi regime and hasten its end. If the British and the Czechs planned to eliminate Uncle Reinhard, who was I to stand in their way?

#

I found it impossible to sleep that night. Something was scratching at my brain like a grain of sand in an oyster. I woke with a start at 2 am.

"What's the matter?" Gudrun said.

"The pads are pre-numbered," I said. "Go back to sleep."

Bathed in sweat the next morning, I climbed out of bed and had a quick wash. I hurried into the office. Nerves on edge, I struggled through to the end of the day. As usual, Gunther Speddig was the last to leave the section.

"No home to go to?" he said.

"I've a few more things to do."

"Well, see you switch off the lights before you leave."

Finally, I had the second floor to myself.

I pulled the Cypher3 signal from my pocket, put it on the desk and smoothed the creases to flatten it as best I could. The signal bore the number 42/En/1911.

I made my way to the archive. It was locked. After ten minutes' work with my lock picks, I had made no progress. I tried von Pfaffel's office. His door was not locked. Slipping inside, I searched his desk drawers. The third drawer on the left held a bunch of keys. I took them to the archive door, and moments later, I was inside.

I stood quite still for a moment, listening. I knew there was no one else in the room, but the memory of the gimlet-eyed keeper of the archive made me hesitate. I went to the Oberfeldwebel's shelves and took down the index book for English language signals for 1942. On the last page, I found the following entries:

42/En/1909 London Cabinet Office : Cabinet Meeting

42/En/1910 Agent 221 : Coal Production, Wales

42/En/1911

42/En/1912 Agent 171 : Weather Report East Anglia

And so on.

There it was. The gap between record 42/En/1910 and 42/En/1912, was as wide as the Moselle River Gorge. It was bound to be noticed. I had to do something about it.

The entries were all written by hand in black ink, in a shaky copperplate. I blanched at the prospect of forging the Oberfeldwebel's handwriting, but I could see no other possibility.

Sitting at the Oberfeldwebel's desk, I found his pen and several pieces of blank paper. Then I composed a short entry and began writing it over and over, doing my best to reproduce the Oberfeldwebel's handwriting. After forty minutes, I took a deep breath and wrote a new Index entry at 42/En/1911:

'Ref.: GM H. Oster.'

Under close scrutiny, nobody would believe that the entry had been made by the same hand as all the others on the page, but it was a passable job that would fool a casual observer. I closed the book and returned it to its place on the shelf. Then I closed and locked the archive door, and returned the keys to von Pfaffel's desk drawer. As soon as I got home I burned the signal and my working sheets.

56

April 1942

On Thursday, April 23, I left the office at 4 pm and took a No. 87 tram south east, intending to visit the address that Alex had left in the Richard Strauss biography.

Sandbar
Helmut Becker
c/o Marianne Dreyfuss
Glienicker Strasse 23
Aldershof

Flat Cap boarded the tram behind me. I was seized by panic. Had the Gestapo discovered the truth about the deaths of von Kemp and Wenther? If they had, I could expect the harshest treatment. Flat Cap made no move to approach me, however, and my pounding heart slowed.

I jumped off after a couple of stops, and took the U-bahn back into the centre of town. Flat Cap accompanied me, maintaining a discreet distance between us. I left the U-bahn at Potsdamer Platz and returned home.

Next, I packed a small suitcase and caught the U-bahn toward the centre of town. There was no sign of Flat Cap. I left the U-bahn at Alexanderplatz and took a No. 12 tram westbound. Still, there was no sign of Flat Cap, but I noticed an older man in a dark coat and fedora, who might have been on the U-bahn. I jumped off the tram, and switched back to the U-bahn where I bought a ticket for the airport at Tempelhof. The man in the fedora followed.

Carrying my suitcase, I entered the airport building, and made my way to the departures desk. There, I bought a one-way ticket to Frankfurt.

"The next flight to Frankfurt will be called in forty minutes," the ticket clerk said as she handed me my ticket. "You should proceed immediately to the departures lounge and wait there."

I walked away from the desk toward the departures lounge, found a suitable vantage point behind a structural pillar, and watched. Fedora flashed a badge at the desk clerk. A short conversation ensued, the clerk waving his hand in the direction of the departures lounge. Fedora looked at his watch, and then hurried away to a row of telephone booths.

I walked – then sprinted – to the arrivals area on the ground floor, where I left the airport building. Throwing my suitcase into the back of a taxi, I jumped in.

"Neanderstrasse," I said to the driver.

He started his engine, and headed into the traffic. "Where have you come from?" he asked, smiling into the mirror.

"Paris," I replied, and the conversation died like a beached whale. Paris was a city recently occupied. The only Germans travelling there by air in 1942 were Gestapo or SS.

At Neanderstrasse, close to the centre of the city, I left the taxi, paid the driver, and jumped aboard a No. 87 tram bound south east. There was no sign of pursuit. The tram took me as far as the bridge at Köpenick, close to the lakes, where I dismounted. I strolled down to the Müggelsee and hung about there for three-quarters of an hour, feigning interest in the yachts. When I was satisfied that there was no one following me, I went back to the bridge, crossed into Aldershof and knocked on the door of number 23 Glienicker Strasse.

The door was opened by a fresh-faced girl with pale skin. She can't have been more than twenty years old.

"Fräulein Dreyfuss? Fräulein Marianne Dreyfuss?"

"Yes," she said nervously.

"My name is Kurt. I'm a friend of Helmut's."

"You know where he is?" Her eyes were immediately wide with excitement.

I shook my head. "No, I'm looking for him. I was hoping you might be able to help me find him."

"I don't know where he is." Her eyes filled with tears. "We were to be married. I thought…"

"May I come in?"

She hesitated, then stood to one side. I picked up my suitcase and stepped inside the apartment. It was small and neat. A crucifix hung on the wall over the door. A religious statue occupied one windowsill; I recognised it from my time in Dublin – the Infant of Prague. She made tea. She spoke about Helmut. He was eight years older than her. They had been sweethearts since before she left school. They were wildly in love, and planned to marry. She showed me a boxful of letters from him. Most of the stamps were post-marked Brandenburg. She handed me the last letter. It was dated November 1939. It started with the greeting "My little Toadstool" and ended "Your Loving Caterpillar". Helmut explained that he had been chosen for a special mission for the Reich, and that he wouldn't be able to write again until his mission was over. He asked her to wait for him.

He had come back, quite suddenly, in March – just five weeks previously – and they had started to plan their wedding. Then, just as suddenly, Helmut had vanished, leaving no word.

She began to cry; her slight shoulders shaking. "I'm sorry." she wiped her eyes with her fingers. "I've been really worried about him."

"When did you last hear from him, Marianne?"

"Five days ago, on Friday. He left here in the evening at about ten. We arranged to meet in Dresdener Strasse on Saturday, to pick out flowers for the wedding..."

"He didn't turn up?"

She shook her head. "I waited for over two hours." She covered her face with her hands, and her tears flowed again.

She left the room, her shoulders shaking. When she returned she had recovered her composure.

I said, "Do you know Alex Clausen?"

"No, I never met him, but Helmut spoke about him all the time."

"Alex is a good friend of mine," I said.

"Could you give me his telephone number?" She looked up at me. "Maybe he knows where Helmut has gone."

I shook my head. "Alex is... away, like Helmut. He won't be back for a while."

"Maybe Alex and Helmut are together, on the same secret mission."

"It is possible." I nodded. I felt like a swine.

As I was leaving, we exchanged home telephone numbers. I asked her if Helmut had left any papers behind.

"No. He had his own apartment in Neukölln." She blushed quickly. "I hope you didn't think that we lived together."

"Of course not, Fräulein."

I took a tram back to the city centre and walked to the office. The man with the fedora was on duty at the front of the building on Tirpitzufer.

#

Uninvited, I barged into Hauptmann von Pfaffel's office, slamming the door closed before sitting down. The Hauptmann looked as troubled as he had the first time I met him; his eyes dark-rimmed; his face crossed with worry lines; his grey hair in dire need of a comb. My dramatic entrance had done nothing to help.

Dispensing with preliminary pleasantries, I said, "What have you done with Agent 92?"

His eyes narrowed. He sat back in his chair and reached for a cigarette. "What concern is that of yours, Müller?"

I had anticipated this reaction. "I know that Herr Becker has returned to German soil."

"You do?" he said, blinking rapidly. My use of the agent's name was as effective as a fist delivered to his solar plexus.

I followed this with a couple of quick jabs, "I know he was in Berlin last week, and that he disappeared on Saturday last. I have spoken with his fiancée. She has asked me to help her locate him."

"His fiancée?" he said smoothly. "I had no idea he was betrothed."

"They were planning their wedding. Then her fiancé vanished without a word of explanation. The young lady is distraught."

"Understandably," he said.

"So where is Helmut?" I said; the Christian name another body blow.

The Hauptmann paused to catch his breath. He was on the ropes.

"It is none of your concern," he said. It was a question – a challenge – but I was in no mood to justify myself. I pressed home my advantage.

"Very well," I said, standing up. "I must take this upstairs."

He hesitated, then waved his arms at me. "No need for that, Müller. Please sit."

I sat down again. He stubbed out his cigarette half-finished in his ashtray and lit another.

"Agent 92 was recalled," he began. "You know that. The official story was that he was ill."

"And the truth?"

"He reported that he had discovered some intelligence of the highest import. We had to recall him. He insisted that we would have to bring him home so that he could deliver the information in person. He said it was too dangerous to transmit."

I raised my eyebrows. "And the intelligence?"

He shook his head and said, "He would speak only with Admiral Canaris. He said he could trust no one else with the information."

It was my turn to hesitate.

"And where is the agent now?"

"He was shipped out to Poland" the Hauptmann turned his face away. He looked old and weary – much older than his years. "Oberst von Neumann questioned the Old Man about it, but there was no explanation given."

So Helmut Becker was a casualty of the Black Orchestra – an offering on the altar of an ideology. This organisation, made up of good and honourable men, was not averse to sacrificing one or two German souls for the greater good and in pursuit of its lofty goals. Nietzsche's famous saying came to mind: "Be careful when ye fight monsters, lest ye become one."

It occurred to me then for the first time that the Black Orchestra might have been responsible for Kleister's death. I had no doubt that anyone who might expose the organisation would be killed without a second thought. The stakes were too high.

I rang Marianne Dreyfuss. When I broke the bad news, there was a long silence at other the end of the line.

"Are you still there, Marianne?"

"Yes," a whisper. "He's not coming back, is he?"

"Don't lose hope," I said.

#

Another week went by with no word from Alex. I assumed he'd gone back into drunken hibernation. I mentioned this to Gudrun.

Instantly, her smile disappeared, replaced by a look of anxiety. "I've been ringing the apartment, but getting no answer for three days, now. I have this terrible feeling. I think there may be something horribly wrong."

I picked up the telephone and rang Alex's number. The ring tone sounded odd. There was no answer. I replaced the handset. "His telephone may be disconnected. I'll go round there at lunchtime tomorrow, and see what's happening."

57

April 1942

I left the office at midday and caught a tram to Alex's apartment. No one answered my knock on the door. I peered in through a window, but could see nothing. I found the caretaker of the apartment block and asked him to let me in, explaining that no one had been able to contact Alex for several days.

The caretaker opened the door and I stepped inside. He followed me in. The interior of the apartment had been destroyed. The living room floor was littered with papers, drawers, broken furniture, and empty bottles. The settee had been ripped open, its innards spilled. The bedroom was the same, the mattress sliced open, clothes scattered everywhere. The kitchen had been taken apart: broken crockery crunched underfoot and food lay trampled into the floor. I picked up some pieces of crockery. When I turned to say something to the caretaker, he was gone.

The bathroom door was smashed in, hanging at a strange angle on one hinge. I found Johann's dachshund draught excluder eviscerated on the floor. There was blood in the bath. It seemed this was where they had made their stand. The signs were not good. Someone with a penchant for violence had come into the lives of my friends and taken them away. It occurred to me that I might have found two dead bodies in the apartment. At least they were probably still alive.

The telephone was dead; the cable at the rear of the handset had been cut. Sliding open the drawer in the bottom of the telephone stand, I found Alex's handwritten list of numbers and removed it.

The caretaker had returned to his cubby-hole on the ground floor, where I found him absorbed in the previous day's copy of *Völkischer Beobachter*.

"Have you called the police?" I asked.

He looked up from his newspaper and shook his head. "You go ahead." He placed a telephone on the shelf between us. "It's nothing to do with me."

First, I found the number for Alex's mother on his list. I rang her.

"Frau Clausen," I said. "This is Alex's friend, Kurt Müller."

"Alex!" She sounded, delighted. "When are you coming to visit me again?"

"No, this is Kurt. Is your son there?"

"I told you, Eugen has gone away. I'll ring you when he returns." She hung up.

I rang Johann's family home in Salzburg.

"Hello, this is the van Horne residence," a young woman's voice.

"Is Johann van Horne there?"

"Who's speaking?"

"A friend."

"Master Johann is not here," the young woman said. "Would you like to leave a message?"

"No, thanks." I hung up.

The cubby-hole wall was covered in stickers, cards, notices. Fanny was available for French lessons, Matilde for full body massage. Claus could solve your plumbing problems at reasonable rates. The National Opera Company would be performing 'Die Fledermaus' on dates long past.

Behind the notices and stickers, someone had written some useful telephone numbers: a doctor, a taxi company, an undertaker, the dog and cat warden, a Hitler Youth number, a dance instructor, another undertaker, several baby sitters, the local branch of the BDM – the League of German Maidens – a pregnancy clinic, an ORPO number and a KRIPO number.

I lifted the telephone, and rang the ORPO number.

"I want to report a missing person – two missing persons."

"Your name and address?" a woman's voice; a programmed response.

I gave my name and address. "Look, my friends have been missing for two days—"

"Friends, you say? Not members of your family?"

"Their names are Alex Clausen and Johann –"

"We cannot take a missing person report if the persons missing are not members of your immediate family."

"But they have no family in Berlin."

"I am sorry," the voice said. *"Auf Wiedersehen."*

I rang the Air Ministry, and spoke to Gudrun. I asked her to find out when Alex had last been seen. Then I rang the KRIPO, and asked to speak with Herr Glasser. He was out of the office and wouldn't be back until tomorrow. Did I wish to leave a message?

Later, I told Gudrun only that Alex and Johann were missing. I said nothing about the devastation in their apartment and the blood in the bathroom. Gudrun seemed to read my mind. She cried out and began to tremble.

"They've been taken," she whispered. "We'll never see Alex again." I gathered she wasn't too concerned about Johann. I wrapped my arms around her and held her tight.

#

It was close to lunchtime the next day before I had a chance to call the KRIPO again.

Kriminalinspektor Glasser remembered me. "Abwehr," he said. "The signalman suicide. You have something to report?"

"A crime. Something violent."

"A domestic? A robbery? A murder? Please be more specific."

"My friend's apartment has been destroyed. There is blood in the bathroom."

"Better give me the address."

Oberst von Neumann agreed to let me have the afternoon off, and I took a tram to Alex's apartment.

Glasser was waiting for me outside the building. He looked just the same as before; he wore the same hat, the same gabardine coat, and he was just as gaunt as I remembered him. He flashed his KRIPO badge at the caretaker, and we entered the apartment.

The place was empty. All the debris had been removed, together with all of Alex's and Johann's personal effects. In the kitchen, the flooded floor had been cleared, the fridge emptied, the broken crockery removed. The eviscerated mattress was missing from the bed. The bathroom had been cleaned; all traces of blood were gone. The bathroom door had been re-hung, the damage expertly repaired.

I looked at the caretaker.

"Somebody came yesterday with a truck." He shrugged the way only a caretaker can. "I assumed they were police."

"ORPO, KRIPO or Gestapo?" Glasser asked.

"You all look the same to me," the caretaker said.

I spoke with Glasser on the pavement outside. I asked him if he could make enquiries about my friends.

He shook his head. "I'm sorry. There's nothing I can do."

"I thought there was a level of cooperation between the various arms of the security forces," I said. I had nothing to base this on. It was simply wishful thinking.

"There is – between the ORPO and ourselves, but the others are a law unto themselves." His angular shoulders moved under his uniform like knives.

It seemed my friends were out of reach.

58

May 1942

Leaving work on the second Monday of May, Reinhard Heydrich's car was waiting for me at the entrance.

The driver stepped out. "Your uncle wishes to speak with you."

"My uncle's in Prague," I objected.

"He's back in Berlin for a short visit. Please get in."

I climbed into the back of the car, and was transported to Schloss Gruenwald in Blankenfelde.

The great house, its windows shuttered and boarded, had been empty for six months. During that time, the lawns had reverted to wild meadows; the hedges were overgrown and bulging on all sides. The plasterwork on the walls was chipped here and there, grey patches of stone showing through the cream paint. There were signs that a few of the slates on the roof of the house had slipped. Wood pigeons perched in a row along the apex. Inside the house, in every room, the furniture was covered in white sheets, and there was a fine layer of dust everywhere.

The driver showed me into the library. Heydrich had made this one room habitable, the dustcovers removed from the furniture. The windows remained shuttered; the lights were on.

There had always been a curious absence in his eyes, but on that day he seemed more distant than usual. He greeted me with a lean smile, and gestured to an armchair by the fireplace. I sat down; he sat opposite. A table by his chair held a telephone, a pen, and paper.

He began with a few pleasantries. How was my trip to Ireland? My mother? Had my mission been a success? No mishaps along the way? As we conversed I considered wrapping my hands around his scrawny neck and squeezing the life from him. Of course it was not an option, but I took pleasure from the idea.

He asked me if I had made contact with Professor Hirsch. A trick question. I'd seen the professor sending him notification of my arrival.

"Yes, we met."

"And what did he tell you about Boniface?" He fixed me with his penetrating gaze.

"Boniface?"

"It is a British operation. You must know of it."

"I don't think so."

He paused for a moment, and then he blinked. "Did you discuss the professor's contacts with the IRA?"

"Indeed we did. All seems well on that front. The professor has established contact with the leader of the organisation on the east coast."

"His name?" The question was delivered just a fraction too quickly; his eagerness transparent.

"Short, Sean Short."

He picked up the paper and pen and wrote the name down.

"And their plans?"

"Did you receive my letter?" I asked.

He raised a thin eyebrow. "Remind me."

"I have a friend in Ravensbrück. I asked if you could have her released."

"I have no recollection of the letter. Your friend's name?"

"Frau Tania Schaefer."

He wrote the name down.

"Since then two more close friends have been taken. Their names are Alex Clausen and Johann van Horne."

"Alex Clausen," he wrote as he spoke. "And...?"

"Johann van Horne. I'd like them released. I'm sure they've done nothing wrong."

"I'll see what I can do," he said.

He and I both knew that he could make anything happen – the impossible, the unthinkable.

I ran through the professor's fiction: planned locations for IRA attacks, their logistical needs – guns, ammunition, bomb-making materials, money. He wrote it all down.

"Half a million pounds sterling," he said. By his tone he could have been talking about the cost of a tin of sardines. "Anything else?"

"A transmitter."

"I thought they had one."

"It was captured and confiscated by the Irish police."

While he was adding the transmitter to his list, I said, "I wanted to ask you again about my father's death."

He looked directly at me. "A stray bullet." He licked his thin lips.

He placed the pen and paper on the table top. He stood up. I stood up. He approached and stood uncomfortably close. He said, "Never lose sight of what is important, Kurt.

"Family."

"Family is important, yes, but the Fatherland comes first."

The Fatherland. I thought of the devastation that this man, his friends and his death squads had caused to my beloved Fatherland — and to my family. The Party was a gross cancer in the body of the country, and I was quite prepared to give my life to see it excised. It took a supreme effort of will to keep a straight face.

"Honour and duty, Kurt. These are what really count, and they must come before all personal considerations."

"Honour and duty." I repeated the words with tears in my eyes.

"I see you understand something of what I'm saying, Kurt, but some day, when the plans of our Führer are realized – when the Thousand-year Reich is born – on that day you will fully understand."

"You will free my friends?" It was barely a question.

"I shall see what I can do," he said again.

59

May 1942

That weekend, I accompanied Gudrun to Elmshorn. Gudrun's father and mother were expecting us, and made me welcome. Almost the first moment that we met, Herr von Sommerfeld began a long and heated political discussion. Actually, it was more like a dissertation, as he left few gaps in the conversation for me. The depth of von Sommerfeld's hatred of the Nazis surprised me. He seemed unaware of the treasonable nature of his views and untroubled by the potential dangers of speaking his mind so freely to a member of the Wehrmacht. My spirits were lifted by the thought that there must be courageous people like him all over Germany. Perhaps there was hope for the future, after all.

Gudrun refused to be drawn into the discussion, retiring to the kitchen with her mother, who seemed to disapprove of her husband's political indiscretion.

After supper I found Gudrun standing in front of the dressing table mirror in our bedroom. She was wearing her crescent moon earrings, and nothing else. I locked the door.

Standing behind her I wrapped her in my arms. "Isn't it a bit early for love making?"

She guided my hand down below her navel. My fingers headed south. She held my hand and positioned it on her lower stomach. There, I felt marks, and I could see them in the mirror; red lines radiating downward from her navel. I said, "What are those lines?"

"Stretch marks."

Foolishly I said, "You've never had a child."

She turned to face me, a faint smile on her lips, her eyes twinkling. "Just my daughter, Anna."

We lay together then like children, both of us naked in the daylight. For the first time, all of Gudrun's body was open to my eyes and she looked like a hundred million Marks.

#

Anna was a delight. She had freckles on her nose her hair was a tangle of blonde curls. Like any eight-year-old, she had gaps in her teeth. She was elated to see a new face in the house, and she did her best to charm me at every opportunity. It was obvious how deeply Gudrun loved her daughter, and I was amazed – and a little uneasy – that she had managed to keep the secret hidden from me for so long. I asked her why she thought it necessary to conceal her true relationship with Anna.

"I wasn't sure how you'd react," she said, and when I pressed her, she refused to elaborate.

Gudrun's father took group photographs of us all. At my request, he also took several small head-and-shoulders shots of Gudrun, me and Anna.

On Sunday evening we retired early. Our bedroom was generously proportioned, overlooking a sluggish stream that emerged from a wooded area and meandered through the fields toward the sea. We stood together at the window, admiring the view.

"Your childhood here must have been pleasant," I said. I could imagine the trees and the stream as an idyllic playground.

"It was fun. My father never took me rabbit hunting, though." She laughed.

I thought how like a mountain stream was Gudrun. She seemed to live her life with careless abandon, and yet there were depths as yet unknown to me. I said, "The stream reminds me of you."

She looked at me questioningly. "Slow and lazy?"

"No." I laughed. "I'm not sure what I mean. The stream seems bright and carefree."

She smiled and gave me a kiss. "Now, tell me why we need passport photographs."

This was a moment I had been dreading. I knew that I would have to explain at least some of the perils that I – we – were facing.

"We may have to leave the country. If a certain event occurs, our lives will be in extreme danger, and we will have to leave. Uncle Reinhard and his Gestapo have been hounding me for information that I cannot give them. The pressure is mounting. There are secrets that I must never divulge."

She seemed content with this explanation. "Where would we go?"

"To Ireland. My mother's dying to meet you."

"And Anna?"

"She must come with us, of course."

She considered my words for a few moments. Then she asked, "What event?"

I shook my head. "It's better that you don't know. But you will recognise it when it happens."

Later that evening as Gudrun lay in my arms, she said, "What's Ireland like?"

"It's a beautiful country. Very rural. Lots of farms. Lots of rain."

"Anna would find it difficult. She speaks only German."

"She's young. She'll adapt quickly."

"How would we survive?"

"I'm sure we will find work in Ireland. Translation work, perhaps. Contacts with German companies will be important after the war. Or I could teach in a university. I have contacts there."

#

Gudrun's father developed the photographs in his darkroom, and handed them to me as we were leaving, the passport photographs in a separate envelope.

On Monday morning, I rang Heinz. We met at midday outside the office. I handed him the envelope.

"Me and some friends of mine, in need of passports."

"You're leaving?"

"Maybe. It's an option I'd like to have."

"Private work," he said, with a shake of his head. His black hair looked freshly dyed – either that or it was a wig. "I'll have to use unofficial sources. You'll pay?"

"Just make sure no one finds out."

"What names? What nationalities?"

"German. We'll be travelling as a family. You choose the names."

"What about travel permits?"

"Diplomatic staff?"

"That'll be expensive." He scratched his flat nose.

"Whatever it costs."

"Leave it with me," he said.

#

Gunther Speddig was waiting for me in my office.

"I know who you are and I know what you've done," he said without preamble, his magnified eyes glinting behind their lenses.

My heart skipped a beat. "What are you talking about?"

"I know about your uncle."

Could he have discovered my secret already? I held my breath.

"I could never understand why you were promoted so quickly. It made no sense. I was the obvious candidate. But now I understand. It's nothing but fucking nepotism."

"That's hardly fair. I am a hard worker," I said, breathing normally again.

#

The following day, I sought a private meeting with Oberst von Neumann.

"I tried to locate Agent Nightingale when I was in Dublin. I could find no trace of him."

The Oberst raised an eyebrow. "Against my express orders?"

"The photograph in his file at Brandenburg is false. It's a photograph of Gunther Prien, the U-boat commander."

"I see. And you have concluded what?"

"I'm not sure."

"It's quite simple. Henry John Lightfoot is a myth, a pure invention."

This was what I suspected, and yet the Oberst's admission took my breath away. I felt a slight tightening sensation in my chest. My next two questions were delivered with force. "So where were Nightingale's signals coming from? Who transmitted them?"

"You met him in Ireland," he said, unperturbed by my reaction.

"The professor?"

"Of course."

That made at least three roles that the mysterious Professor Hirsch was playing: He was Bullfrog, the defunct agent, Nightingale the silenced one, and a double agent posing as Reinhard Heydrich's personal contact and IRA go-between. As well as these, he was a key member of the Black Orchestra, a full time professor of Mathematics, and a naiad of the swamp.

#

On May 27, word came through that the Deputy Reich Protector for Bohemia and Moravia, Reinhard Heydrich, had been ambushed in a street in Prague. He had been wounded and taken to hospital. Early reports were of a gun battle; later reports mentioned a bomb. At first it was thought that his injuries were minor, but as the day wore on, it became clear that this was not the case, and Heydrich's life was in danger.

The news sent a delicious shiver through my body. I knew it was only a small victory, but it felt good to have played my small part. There was no sorrow for my uncle's fate, just a deep loathing of the man and regret that he hadn't died in the attack. My only sorrow was that Heydrich had not had time to have Alex, Johann and Tania released — if he ever intended to do so. At the same time I was aware of how my own position had changed; the ground had started to shift from under me.

When I came home from work that evening, Gudrun was in the kitchen. I threw myself wearily onto the settee. The radio was on, the assassination attempt on Reinhard Heydrich the main story of the evening news. The report said that the Czech underground movement was responsible, using equipment and money supplied by the British Secret Intelligence Service. The two perpetrators had taken refuge in the crypt of an Orthodox church in Prague, which was under siege. The authorities were confident that the criminals would be apprehended and brought to justice. As for the Reichsprotektor, he was in hospital and expected to make a full recovery.

I ambled into the kitchen in search of Gudrun, and found her sitting behind the door in tears; the food on the cooker forgotten. I lifted her to her feet and wrapped my arms around her. She rested her head on my shoulder and her tears flowed.

I waited until she could speak, before asking, "What are you crying about? Has something happened to Anna?" She shook her head. "Your parents?" She shook her head again. "Then what is it?"

"Reinhard…"

"Heydrich?"

She nodded.

I laughed, and said, "Apart from his family, you must be the only person in Germany crying over Reinhard Heydrich's misfortune."

I was a little puzzled by her reaction, which I put down to her sensitive nature and because she was well acquainted with the man.

60

May 29, 1942

The next day, May 29, I received a telephone call in the office.

It was Alex. "They released me."

Hearing his voice, my heart leapt in my chest with joy.

We agreed to meet for lunch at one of our regular meeting places on Unter den Linden. I arrived early and took a table in the open. I ordered a beer.

When Alex arrived, I barely recognised him. He had aged ten years. I had never seen him wearing a beard before. His hair was streaked with grey; and his hairline had receded at the front, nearly meeting the bald patch on the crown of his head. His face was grey, his cheeks flabby with loose folds of skin; his eyes red-rimmed. He seemed to have shrunk, and he walked with an unfamiliar gait. Despite my concern, I was elated to see him.

Alex's story unfolded as we ate. He had been seized by the Gestapo.

"I put up a bit of a struggle," he said. "They broke my leg in two places, the kitchen and the bathroom." He grinned at his own joke.

Alex had been detained and interrogated in the underground cells at the notorious Gestapo Headquarters, 8 Prinz-Albrecht-Strasse. It seemed the Gestapo knew that Alex and Helmut Becker were friends. Concentrating on Alex's injured leg, they beat him savagely and repeatedly, demanding information on Becker's recall. When they were satisfied that Alex had no more information to give them, they moved him to the hospital wing of the labour camp at Marzahn.

"I assume you did something to get me out," he said in a conversational tone.

I waved my hand in a dismissive gesture. "Where's Johann?"

"Gone." A shadow passed over his face. "It was Johann that sold me out to the police. They had information that could only have come from him."

I considered this revelation in silence. I knew that Johann was a committed Party member with strong political convictions, but to sell out his lover?

I bit my tongue. I had warned him about Johann.

Alex said, "What can I say? I love him. I abhor his politics. I despise everything he stands for. I know that some day his beliefs will be judged insane, but still, I love him. I love what he is, warts and all. I love him even though I could never again embrace his hateful creed—perhaps I love him because of it."

"You love him because he is a Nazi?"

"It's part of what makes him what he is."

Alex's experiences in the labour camp were horrific. He had been put to work in the kitchens before his leg had a chance to heal. The work was not heavy, but the food was inadequate. The guards were all SS, hand-picked for their cruelty.

He lit a cigarette, his hands trembling.

"I'm sorry I didn't act sooner," I said. "I could have saved you some pain."

"There is one good thing about the camps." Alex cocked his head to one side, comically. "They're a great cure for drunkenness."

I laughed.

"How do you know Becker?" I asked.

"We were at school together."

"When did he last contact you?"

Alex glanced around before answering. Fedora was sitting at a table nearby, out of earshot, reading a newspaper. "He wrote to me in September or October of last year. He said that he had infiltrated a secret British deciphering operation, with… that codename."

"Boniface?"

"Keep your voice down!"

"You told the Gestapo this?"

"Yes, of course I told them," with emphasis.

"And did you tell them about his girlfriend?"

"No."

"I think you should forget about it now, Alex. Forget about Becker. I paid Marianne a visit. Becker has been posted to Poland."

"Leaving no records behind?"

The Black Orchestra

"He left nothing with Marianne, but she said he had his own apartment in Neukölln."

"I checked there," Alex said. "There was nothing. And I'm sure the Gestapo would have gone over the place, too."

I told Alex about my telephone conversation with his mother. "She seemed confused."

"I know," Alex said. "I plan to visit her as soon as I can."

#

Berlin was wearing its bright May look, but it felt like a city in the throes of a fatal illness. Steel tram wheels screeched; the tired axles of a passing dray groaned; even passing bicycles creaked like arthritic geriatrics; and everywhere the jaws of the people were set as if facing a grim, uncertain future. Even my beloved Unter den Linden seemed to lose its attraction.

Thomas Kleister rang to say that his daughter had come home.

"That's fantastic news," I said. "Tell her not to ask any more questions. Leave the investigation to me."

When I arrived home, Gudrun had a large turnip on the kitchen table. She was hammering it with her rolling-pin.

I told her that Tania Schaefer had been freed.

"That *is* good news."

"And guess who else is free." I returned her broad smile.

"Alex? You've spoken to him?" Her eyes lit up with joy.

"Yes, we had lunch."

"And Johann?"

"Johann's gone. Their friendship is over."

"Good riddance to bad meat," she said, with a grimace.

We embraced. It felt to me as if a member of our family had been returned to us. I'm sure Gudrun felt the same way. Alex *was* family.

We went to bed early, and made love in the dark. Afterwards, we lay side by side on our backs. Gudrun lit a cigarette. My eyelids began to droop.

"What was that book?" Gudrun said suddenly.

I awoke with a start. "What book?"

"The one that you read while I was away in Elmshorn in September."

I looked toward her. All I could see was her cigarette end, glowing in the dark. "What makes you think I read a book?"

"That's what you said."

"It must have been the life of Richard Strauss."

"Alex gave you that book, on the railway platform when you were leaving for Ireland."

"Oh right."

"So what was the book that you read before that, in September?"

"I can't remember."

She was silent for a long time. My ears were burning, and there was a familiar sinking feeling in my stomach. Once, when I was a boy – maybe ten years old – I stole some money from my father's jacket pocket. Ten marks, I think. I spent a few pfennig on sweets, and hid the change in some bushes. There was so much of it! I had the same feeling then when I realised my crime was about to be discovered. I listened to Gudrun's breathing as she sucked in the smoke and blew it toward the ceiling.

She turned on her side, facing me. Now, I could feel the heat from the cigarette tip, close to my chest.

"Careful with that cigarette."

She moved the cigarette away from my chest. "Tell me about the woman from the Propaganda Ministry."

I considered my reply for a moment or two. Then I said, "Small, with a turned up nose."

"Was she pretty?"

"Yes, in a way. She was petite, fragile."

"You wanted to protect her?"

"Me? No."

"Men in general."

"I suppose so."

"Thin?" She drew on her cigarette, the glow from its tip reflected in her eyes.

"Yes, but she had wide hips. Good childbearing hips – you know."

"Sounds to me like you fancied her."

"No. Not really."

"Eyes?" she said.

"Two," I replied.

The Black Orchestra

Gudrun drifted off to sleep, leaving me sweating. Obviously, she knew about my night with Liesel, but she hadn't gone so far as to actually accuse me of being unfaithful. How did she know? She was in Elmshorn at the time, and I was pretty sure I hadn't left any evidence lying around. I puzzled over this for a while, and as I did my self-disgust rose like bile inside me.

#

Heinz appeared the next day. His hairline looked lower than usual – a wig for certain.

He handed me an envelope containing three false passports and papers providing diplomatic credentials. I was identified as Frederick von Shönholtz, Cultural Attaché. Gudrun and Anna as my wife and child.

"You owe me fifteen hundred Reichsmarks," he said.

Half my annual salary.

Placing the papers in an envelope, I addressed it to Herr van Sommerfeld in Elmshorn. As soon as von Pfaffel had gone to lunch, I slipped the envelope in amongst the outgoing external post on his desk.

Marianne Dreyfuss rang me at the office.

"Helmut is back." Her voice strong and joyful.

I told her to hang up and rang her back from a public telephone.

"Helmut's In Berlin?"

"No. He's been wounded. He sent word. He's in a field hospital in Poland. He's lost some fingers. But he's alive." She sounded excited and remarkably cheerful, considering the probable extent of Helmut's injuries.

"I hope he comes home soon."

"Oh, and I found some of Helmut's papers. I found them in an old suitcase."

She said her English was not good enough to understand them. I gave her my home address, and she agreed to post the papers to me.

61

May 30, 1942

"How much?" Alex gasped, choking on his food.

"A thousand. I'll pay you back as soon as I can."

"You can get travel papers for nothing from the Abwehr," he said.

"It's for Gudrun and me. We have to get out. If Heydrich dies, my life won't be worth a chanterelle."

"You'll miss Germany."

"I don't think so, but I'll miss you."

"What about the beer?"

"Ah, yes, I'll miss the beer," I said. "And the pumpernickel."

I returned to the office to find Drobol Junior waiting for me, his enormous bulk making the room seem even smaller than usual.

"This came in the morning post." He handed me a heavy brown paper parcel tied with twine. It was addressed to me personally and postmarked Prague. I recognised Heydrich's spidery handwriting.

"Thanks," I said.

Drobol made no move to leave. I dropped the parcel on the desk and picked up the telephone.

"Thank you, Drobol," I said again.

"Aren't you going to open it?"

"No. I know what's in it."

"What?"

"Fuck off, Drobol."

His shoulders slumped, he shuffled out of the office. When I was sure he was gone I closed and locked the door. Then I untied the twine and opened the parcel. It was full of sterling in neat piles. There was a note from Heydrich.

Dear nephew,

Further to our recent conversation, here is some money to get the Irish campaign started. The rest will follow in a week or so. Tell Mr. Short when you contact him that I would like to arrange a face-to-face meeting with him, here or in Prague at his convenience. You may tell him also, that I shall make arrangements for a first shipment of small arms for the campaign. Details of the shipment will follow later.

RH

I picked out one stack and counted it. It contained fifty one hundred pound notes. There were fifty stacks. A total of £250,000. I sat and stared at the money in disbelief. My heart was pounding. I re-read Heydrich's note. I counted the money again. There was no mistake. God in heaven! A quarter of a million pounds sterling!

The parcel fitted perfectly in my briefcase. I locked the briefcase in my filing cabinet.

#

That night the British RAF paid another flying visit to our city. On previous occasions, the bombing had been limited to the industrial areas on the outskirts of the town, but this time the city centre was the target.

We covered the windows with thick curtains and blankets. We switched off the lights and sat close together on the settee in the dark, listening to the bombs whistling down and clutching each other at each explosion.

Gudrun cried silently. I could feel her body trembling beside me. I tried to find comforting words, but she shook her head and touched a finger to my lips.

The raid lasted no more than forty minutes. When we were sure it was over, we went to the window and peered out into the darkness. At least two buildings in Horst Wessel Platz were ablaze; people were rushing about the square with buckets of water, calling out to each other. Further away, the overcast sky was red from the glow of fires all over the city.

Gudrun went into the bedroom.

I made tea and brought it to her, then I put on my coat and my Luftschutz Civil Defence section leader's cap.

As I stood at the door I heard her sobbing. I went back to her. "The raid's over, Gudrun. We won't see them again tonight."

She shook her head, tears rolling down her cheeks. Her reaction to the bombing seemed excessive.

I put an arm around her shoulders. "Come on, love, it's over. There's no need to distress yourself like this."

"Remember when you were in Brandenburg with that woman?" she sobbed.

"Liesel. Yes, I remember. And when I got back you'd left me."

She nodded. "I left to protect you."

I stared at her, bemused. "To protect me? From what?"

She wiped her eyes before answering, "From the Gestapo."

"What do you mean, Gudrun?"

"You remember accusing me of informing to the Gestapo?"

Did I? I don't remember.

"Well, it's true," she said. "I had no choice."

The effect was like an artillery shell exploding in my head.

I stood up. "You betrayed me...?"

She held on to my sleeve, pulling at it desperately. "I had no choice. They know about Anna. They threatened to take her away from me if I didn't co-operate. I left you because my presence was placing you in danger, don't you see?"

"So why did you come back?"

"They forced me to."

I took a moment to absorb this information.

"The Gestapo arranged for us to meet that day in Tiergarten?"

"Yes," she whispered.

"And earlier, when we met at Heydrich's garden party?"

She gave a tiny nod of the head.

I roared at her, "So, you never loved me."

"No, no, Kurt. I do. I do love you. That's why I'm telling you this. Can't you see?"

I stormed into the living room. I switched on the radio and stood by the mantel, hearing nothing, feeling my blood pressure rise. After fifteen minutes there was a woodpecker inside my skull, trying to peck his way out.

Gudrun came out of the bedroom in her dressing gown. Her eyes and nose were red from crying. She sat on the settee.

"It's true that I was following orders to start with," she said between sobs. "But I fell in love with you very quickly."

"How can you expect me to believe that?"

"It's the truth."

I turned on her. "Our life together has been nothing but a monstrous lie, right from the start."

After a few seconds of silence she said, "You betrayed me too!" I opened my mouth to object, but she continued, "Don't deny it. I know you slept with that... that Liesel!"

"That was a mistake," I waved my arms about. "She had me under a spell. Anyway, you can't compare my one-night-stand with a betrayal to the Gestapo."

"Betrayal is betrayal. And I had an excuse. What excuse did you have?"

I let myself out to join my Civil Defence team.

I wanted to believe her. I wanted to believe that she loved me; that our relationship had meaning; that the whole thing was not just one of Uncle Reinhard's monstrous lies.

When I returned, several hours later, Gudrun was in the living room on the settee, exactly where I'd left her. After a night of digging bodies from the rubble of their houses, I was drained. The woodpecker in my head had been replaced by a blacksmith and anvil.

I had a quick wash and sat beside her on the settee. She was silent, eyes cast down, waiting for me to make the next move.

"Who's your Gestapo contact?" I said.

"His name's von Kemp."

She turned her head and gave me a quick glance. "I haven't seen him for months. It was last year sometime."

"And what did you tell him?"

"Nothing, really. I told him that you thought some signals had been tampered with. Nothing more."

"Nothing more? Are you sure?"

"I found a beer mat in your jacket pocket. It had a diagram on it."

"You gave him that?"

"I was desperate. He said he'd run out of patience."

That sounded like the von Kemp I knew.

I shouted, "Christ, Gudrun, don't you know what you did?"

"I'm sorry, Kurt. I had to give him something."

"They could have hanged me for that."

"It was just a beer mat."

"It was much more than a beer mat. Von Kemp decided that diagram was treasonous, and that would be enough to put me on the gallows."

"I had no idea!" Her face crumpled again, but she seemed to have run out of tears. "I want to be honest with you. I want us to build a life together – the three of us…"

She looked up at me then, and I searched her eyes for the truth.

"And yet you prostituted yourself for the Gestapo," I said, my tone sharp.

"I *told* you. I had no choice. They threatened Anna."

I asked her how she felt about the progress of the war. She replied that she thought the war was lost, since the campaign in the east had failed.

"And how do you feel about that?"

"Happy. Relieved."

"What if it had succeeded?"

"Then I probably would have killed myself." She suppressing a sob. "I couldn't bear to see Hitler and his thugs continue in power."

I thought she couldn't mean it, but then I saw the look in her eyes and I knew she was serious.

My mind flashed back to the labour camp at Ravensbrück, the Brownshirts in the street and the draper hanging from that lamppost in Leopold Platz.

We both fell silent for a few moments.

"What would have become of your daughter if you had killed yourself."

"I suppose I would have taken her with me," she said, her eyes filling with fresh tears.

On Sunday, May 31, Reinhard Heydrich was transferred from intensive care into a private room. His recovery was progressing well.

I walked into the office.

Siegfried was on duty at the door.

"Sign in," he said.

"No need," I responded with a smile. "I just came in to collect some papers. I won't be more than fifteen minutes." Before he could object, I asked, "Is anybody else in?"

"Just four signalmen," he said.

"What about Drobol the cripple?"

"He's gone home. Sign in."

I signed his log book and took the stairs to the fourth floor two at a time. I had no difficulty picking the lock of Drobol's office and letting myself in. His filing cabinet was not locked, and I found the book of call signs. Turning to the page for English speaking agents, I found a short list of agent call signs in use, and a longer list of call signs for use by future agents. I transcribed both lists to my notebook.

62

June 1, 1942

Helmut's papers arrived the following day in the post. I tore open the envelope. There were four sheets of paper inside. The first two contained signals in raw, encoded form together with the decoded version. The text was in German. I recognised both of them as Kriegsmarine signals from the OKW to the U-boat fleet.

The final two sheets contained a number of diary entries from 1941. They were written in English.

June 13: First contact. Meet tomorrow. Cinema.
June 14: Charlie Chaplin – Modern Times. V. funny. Mary liked it.
Her name is Mary Spencer. Filing clerk.
Works under Major Colin Henderson (a Scot)
June 17: Walk after work. First kiss.
June 20: Bus ride to Kew Gardens. Necklace £3
June 28: Spent the night.
July 5: Moved in.
July 6: Bracelet £5
Aug 10: Asked for schematic of B house. Refused.
Aug 12: Suggested she help me get inside. Fight. Tantrum.
Aug 13: Drinks. Agreed to look for work for me in the house. I think she's fallen for me.
She says I look like Joel McCrea!
I said she looks like Bette Davis.
Aug 19: Interview for job of maintenance man
Sept 3: I'm in! I start Monday. Reporting to Bob Mackenzie
Sept 8: First day in B house. Some areas off limits.
Sept 16: Mackenzie off sick. Access to new areas.

The Black Orchestra

Close to 5,000 staff. Highly secret.
Top people are maths professors!
Definitely code breakers !!
Sept 19: Mackenzie still sick. Access to Hut 4 – roof leak.
Closely supervised.
RN people in Hut 4
Sept 23: Leak in Hut 4 again.
Definite translation activities.
Inner sanctum is in Hut 8
Sept 26: Codename: BONIFACE confirmed
Oct 15: Call for maintenance work in Hut 6
Mackenzie went in on his own.
Oct 23: Access to Hut 3.
Hundreds of women at work here.
Translators. Filing.
Similar to Hut 4.
Saw complete messages decoded (Lorenz?)
Spencer works in Hut 3.
Oct 28: Hut 6 – Hut 3 link
Hut 8 – Hut 4 link
Asked for sample material from files. Refused.
Nov 14: Call for maintenance work in Hut 7
Mackenzie away.
Nov 17: Access to Hut 7.
Machinery. Unknown function
They have an ENIGMA (4 Rotors!)

I took the papers into the office. At about 4 pm I filled out an F17 form and presented it to the Oberfeldwebel.

He peered at the form through his eyeglass. "This is an unusual request."

"I need to double-check the decoding of some old messages," I said.

"The form has not been countersigned."

"Yes, I'm sorry. Oberst von Neumann was not available to sign it. Would you prefer if I came back later?"

He grunted. "You need the codebooks for January to March 1941?"

"Yes, please."

"Lorenz or Enigma?"

"Both."

"This is a most unusual request." He frowned at the form again.

"You do have these code keys?"

"Yes, yes, of course," he said. "Follow me."

The Oberfeldwebel led me to a small table and a chair. I sat down and he shuffled off to his shelves. He returned and placed three volumes on the table.

I found the Lorenz SZ38 code key that was in operation for the date of the first signal. Using that code key to decode the original raw signal produced gibberish. I repeated the exercise, using the Lorenz SZ40 code key for the same date, with the same result. Neither of the Lorenz code keys had been used to encode the signals. I noted down the Enigma settings for the two dates, and went in search of an Enigma machine.

It was close to 5:30 pm when I entered Section I. Gunther Speddig was still at his desk.

"Working late?" I said.

"Just leaving now," he replied. "What about you?"

"I have a little more work to finish."

"In Section I?" He trained his binocular spectacles on my face.

"Just stretching my legs. It's been a long day."

When Speddig had gone I took a four-rotor Enigma machine from the closet and set it up for the date of the first Kriegsmarine signal. Sitting at Speddig's desk, I decoded the first signal. It read:

UBOOT ONEHU NDRED RENDE ZVOUS TWENT YSEVE NTHWO LFPAC KNORT HATLA NTICM APREF ERENC EMZTW OSEVE N

With growing excitement, I reset the Enigma for the date of the second signal, and began to decode it. Again, it decoded perfectly. The second signal read:

FIVEB RMERC HANTV ESSEL SANDT WODES TROYE RESCO RTSIG HTEDM APREF ERENC ENGON ENINE UBOOT ONEON ESIX

I sat back in my chair, and gazed at the results of my work. I now knew that the British had broken the Kriegsmarine Enigma encryption system, and they had done it the hard way – using mathematics. It seemed impossible, Enigma was known to be unbreakable, and yet the evidence in front of me was irrefutable. I considered the significance of my discovery. What it meant was that every signal between the U-Bootwaffe command and the U-boat fleet could be read by the enemy. Daily signals containing location coordinates for each U-boat, and those carrying operational instructions to the fleet from central command, were all available to the British. This explained how so many U-boats had been discovered and destroyed by the British.

The Kriegsmarine version of the Enigma machine was the most sophisticated and the most difficult to break, having four rotors. It seemed more than likely that the British had also broken the three rotor version used by the Luftwaffe and the Army. The implications of this information were staggering; nothing less than the outcome of the war was in the hands of the British.

I remained seated at Speddig's desk, deep in thought, for another 30 minutes.

Before leaving the office, I restored the settings on the Kriegsmarine Enigma and burned the two signals together with my own rough work and the two sheets of Helmut Becker's diary entries.

PART 5

63

June 1, 1942

Drobol the cripple was waiting for me on the staircase. "What are you doing in the office this late?"

"Just on my way out," I replied.

"Before you go, I'd like to show you something. In the archive."

I looked at my watch. "I'd love to stop and talk, but it's late." It was close to 6:50 pm.

"You can spare a few minutes." It was only then that I noticed the small pistol in his hand.

I followed him into the corridor and across to the door of the archive. He seemed more bowed than usual, more like one of Wagner's dwarves. He turned the handle on the archive door and it opened.

I went inside. The cripple followed. The lights were on. Drobol Junior was sitting at the Oberfeldwebel's desk, dressed in his shorts and grubby Hawaiian shirt.

"Now show us how you falsified that signal," Drobol Senior said.

"I don't know what you mean."

Drobol Senior sidled over to the shelves and took down the 1942 English Language Signal Index. He slapped the book down on the desk. "Open it."

I opened the book.

"Turn to April. Find entry 1911 and read it to me."

The game was up.

I read, "Ref.: GM H. Oster."

Drobol Senior squinted at me. "Very inventive. But not such a convincing forgery." He looked like he'd sucked a lemon and enjoyed it.

"Forgery?" I kept my voice calm and even. "It looks perfectly fine to me." My mind was racing. So this was how it was going to end for me – butchered by a family of Wagnerian monsters!

"Ask him about the parcel," Drobol Junior said.

"What parcel?" Drobol Senior snapped.

"The one from Prague. The heavy brown parcel."

"I told you," I said. "It was full of family papers."

"Show us," said Drobol Junior.

"It's at home in my apartment."

Drobol Senior raised his gun, so that it was pointing at my chest. He sneered. "You must think we are complete fools."

"Idiots, both of us." Drobol Junior said.

"No, not at all," I replied calmly. "And I know you suspect that Kleister was murdered."

"Kleister committed suicide," Drobol Senior said. "The KRIPO said so."

"You and I both know that's not what happened. No one could shoot themselves in the head, back there." I pointed behind my right ear.

"What makes you such an expert?" Drobol Junior said.

I ignored that. "I don't know who pulled the trigger, but someone shot Kleister. I just don't know why."

Drobol Senior's gun was looking more menacing now. He said, "The KRIPO were satisfied that it was suicide. You'll never persuade anyone to reopen the case."

I kept my conversational tone. "I wondered why the KRIPO dropped the case so quickly."

"Open and shut," Drobol Senior murmured. "The pressure of the work, the long hours."

"I don't think so. I think they were following orders."

"Orders from whom?" said Drobol Senior.

"From Senior Management in the RSHA. They wouldn't want a thorough investigation of a killing carried out by a valued informant."

"Now what are you saying?" Drobol Senior demanded.

"I believe that someone in the Abwehr is working for the RSHA."

Drobol Junior laughed, exposing his rotten teeth. "You mean us? You think we are SS?" The idea was preposterous; only perfect physical specimens were admitted to the SS.

"Not SS, but I believe you are Gestapo informers."

Drobol Senior scratched the side of his nose with the barrel of his gun. "You're mad."

"Is that why Kleister had to die?"

"I told you," Drobol Senior said. "It was suicide."

"We are good Germans," said Drobol Junior.

And that was when it came to me. Quite suddenly, I had a plan. I checked my watch.

"Yes, I know that." I sat down on the edge of the Oberfeldwebel's desk and continued, in a low, conspiratorial tone. "That's why I was looking for you earlier."

"You were?" Drobol Junior squinted at me.

"Yes," I lowered my voice further. "I have uncovered some information of critical importance to the Reich."

"What information?"

I went over to the door, and closed it with exaggerated care. Then I resumed my position on the edge of the Oberfeldwebel's desk.

"I have uncovered a plot to overthrow the Third Reich by stealth."

"By stealth?" Drobol Junior echoed my words.

"Yes," I whispered. "I happen to know that someone in a senior position in the Party is plotting to undermine the democratically elected government of the Fatherland."

Both Drobols leaned forward, the better to pick up my words.

"And this someone is?" Drobol Senior whispered.

"None other than Reinhard Heydrich himself."

Drobol Senior snorted. "Don't be ridiculous!"

I looked at my watch again. It was four minutes to seven, four minutes to six in Dublin. "Come with me to the fourth floor and I'll prove it to you."

Drobol Senior tucked his gun away, and we climbed the stairs to the communications unit on the fourth floor. There were three signalmen on duty. They looked up as we entered. When they saw Drobol Senior, they turned back to their work. I sat down at one of the spare transmission stations, switched on the transmitter and tuned it to 3137.5 kilohertz.

"That's not one of our frequencies," Drobol Senior said.

I unplugged the headphones so that the signal would be routed through the loudspeakers of the set, and held up my hand for silence. I said a silent prayer. At precisely 7 pm, the transmitter began to receive a signal in Morse code. I wrote the characters down on a yellow pad as they came in.

When the signal was complete, I tore it from the signal pad and handed it to Drobol Senior. He was speechless.

"What does it say? What does it say?" Drobol Junior said, bouncing up and down like a huge child.

"It will have to be decoded," Drobol Senior explained to his son. He turned to me and said, "The information about Reichsprotektor Heydrich was in the missing signal, 1911?"

"Yes. It was of supreme importance that I kept it secret until I had a chance to alert the authorities."

"You mean us?" Drobol Junior said, wide-eyed.

"Who else?" I said.

Waving the signal at me, Drobol Senior said, "If this is what you say it is, Müller, the Third Reich will be eternally indebted to you."

Siegfried was on duty at the main door. "Sign out," he said.

64

June 2, 1942

On the morning of June 2, the radio announced that SS-Reichsführer Heinrich Himmler had visited Reichsprotektor Reinhard Heydrich in his hospital bed. The two men had had a long and productive conversation.

By the afternoon bulletin, Heydrich's condition had deteriorated; the newsreader declared that the Reichsprotektor was now gravely ill. He was still semiconscious, but the doctors had declared that there was nothing more they could do for him. His family was at his bedside.

I had a visit from Drobol Senior. He shuffled into my office and closed the door.

"That signal," he said, frowning, "what code was used to encrypt it?"

"There is a problem?"

"Yes, there's a problem. No one has been able to decode the signal. We've tried every code."

"Lorenz SZ40 and 38?"

"Both."

"And Enigma?"

"Schiller tried them all." He scratched the side of his nose with a podgy finger.

"Have you tried the British ciphers?"

He seemed to nod and shake his head at the same time. "Nothing works."

"Well there you are, then. What more proof do you need?"

"But it might not be a signal at all. It could be simply a jumble of letters, designed to deceive us."

"Why on Earth? And transmitted from where, and by whom?" I said, my eyebrows raised.

"By the enemy."

That made no sense.

"You don't really believe that."

"No." He bowed his head, like a miscreant child.

"So what do you expect me to do about it?" I said.

"If we can't decode the signal," he whined, "we have no proof of anything."

I feigned deep consideration of the problem, my face a study of concern and concentration, like the eagle on my desk, puzzled by the tragic and inexplicable loss of her eggs. "I take it you are listening out for more signals from the same source."

His face brightened. "No. I hadn't thought of that."

"Am I expected to think of everything? I have given you the key. All you have to do is open the door."

"And the code?" he said, backing toward the door.

"I'll give it some serious thought," I said.

As soon as Drobol left, I requested an urgent meeting with Generalmajor Oster. My request was granted, and I climbed the stairs to the fourth floor. As I entered his office the Generalmajor was watering an aspidistra with a miniature watering can.

"Please sit," he said, without turning around. "I'll be with you in a moment." He completed his task with the plant, returned to his desk, and sat down.

"I hate it," he said.

"The plant?"

"It was here before I arrived and I'm sure it'll still be here long after I'm gone. It does nothing, fulfils no useful purpose, and yet I feed and water it as if my life depended on it."

"You could have it removed."

"Nonsense. We all need some greenery in our lives, just to remind us that we are nothing special, just whims of nature – curiosities thrown together by natural selection. Have you read Charles Darwin?"

"No, Herr Oster."

"You should read him. Everybody should read him. It would give us all a sense of proportion, and show us why we're not as important as we believe ourselves to be."

"We Germans?"

"Humanity. Now, what can I do for you?"

I was a little taken aback by this. I had expected some reference to our last meeting, some indication that he remembered it, at least.

"At our last meeting, you said you would investigate Kleister's signal in the Leipzig office."

Oster shook his head. "That was a dead end. No record remains."

This was a disappointment, but I pressed on. "I believe I have identified at least one Gestapo informer working inside the Abwehr."

The Generalmajor leaned forward in his chair. "The cripple?"

"Yes, Drobol the cripple is one – definitely – and his son may be another. I accused Drobol of killing Kleister."

"And did he admit it?"

"No, but he didn't deny it."

"You survived to tell the tale." He raised an eyebrow.

"I told him a cock-and-bull story about a conspiracy by Heydrich and Himmler to overthrow the Reich and take power for themselves."

"And he believed it – your cock-and-bull story?"

"Yes. I let him listen to a transmission from Professor Hirsch to Heydrich. He was convinced when he saw the strange frequency and when his efforts to decode the signal failed. When the Gestapo interrogate me again, I will have my final proof – if they ask about the conspiracy."

Oster leaned forward. "Why haven't they picked you up already?"

"Drobol is waiting until he has a deciphered signal to give them. That way his kudos will be vastly increased."

"You're playing a dangerous game, Kurt," he said.

"I realise there are risks, but as long as Uncle Reinhard is alive, my life is not in any real danger."

"And when he dies?"

"Then I am a dead man."

Again, Oster took a moment to consider my words.

"And what of Oberst Schiller?" I said. "I know he altered that signal."

"If, as you say, Oberst Schiller altered a signal, you may be sure that he had good reason."

"But how did he manage it? The pads are all pre-numbered."

Oster remained expressionless, made no reply.

"What are you saying? Schiller has a duplicate set of pre-numbered pads? That doesn't seem possible!"

"It's entirely possible. Actually, it's essential."

I absorbed this revelation in silence for a few moments. How had it seemed so improbable to me before and yet so simple, so straightforward and so obvious now?

65

June 3, 1942

The evening after that, June 3, Gudrun seemed distant; her manner altogether strange. I pressed her to tell me what was wrong.

It was some moments before she responded.

"You never asked," she said, "but I must tell you who Anna's father is."

"So tell me," I said, a lump in my throat.

"It's not her fault. She's just a little girl, and she didn't choose her father." She started to cry.

"Does he know?"

She shook her head. "I never told him."

"How could this have happened?" I roared. "Didn't you take precautions?"

"You can't ask me that," she shouted back at me.

I left the apartment, slamming the door. I started walking. There were no signs of any Gestapo followers. After a half-hour or so, I arrived at the northern limits of Tiergarten. I walked on. When I came to Adolf Hitler Platz, I turned south and then east and walked some more. I stopped at a small tavern and drank several beers. I turned north and set out across Tiergarten, hesitating near Liesel's apartment building in Viktoria Strasse, before turning for home. On the last leg of my round trip, I considered Gudrun's words. Anna was a little angel, and what Gudrun said about her was undoubtedly true: Which of us can choose our parents – or our uncles? Gudrun filled my mind; I knew that I couldn't live without her.

#

When I returned to the apartment, there was a familiar black car parked outside. The front door was wide open. The undertaker's apprentice was standing in the centre of the living room, demolishing my furniture. I was struck by the absurd thought that he should have removed his flat cap.

He turned toward me, and gave me a jolly smile. "We have a warrant to search your apartment." He had a flat Berlin accent. He had been following me for 12 months and that was the first time I'd heard him speak.

Others were at work in the kitchen. I could hear crockery smashing and wood splintering.

Panic seized my heart. I called out, "Gudrun?"

"She's gone," Flat Cap said. "She's taken all her clothes. There's a note for you on the mantelpiece."

I stepped over the shattered remains of my father's gramophone and read Gudrun's note.

Kurt, Forgive me, I never meant to hurt you. If I have to choose between Anna and you, then I must choose my daughter. I will love you always, Gudrun. PS Your supper is in the oven.

"What are you looking for?" I said to the Gestapo man.

Flat Cap smiled again. "Who knows?" he said, running the serrated blade of his knife across the back of my settee. "I expect we'll recognise it when we see it."

He started on my books. One by one he took them from the shelves, rifling through the pages and discarding them on the floor. Gudrun's books were missing. Flat Cap went over to the radio, picked it up and dropped it on the floor. It survived the fall; it was a Telefunken. He snorted, then lifted a foot and brought his boot crashing down on the radio. The casing buckled, the front panel popped out. A second kick and it spilled its contents across the carpet. Crouching down, he went through the debris with care.

The older man with the fedora emerged from the kitchen. He looked me in the eye as he passed by. "—Evening," he said, and he disappeared into the bathroom.

I looked in the bedroom. It was clear that the room had not yet been searched.

"Stay out of there," Flat Cap snapped, as if it were his apartment, and not mine. "I must ask you not to interfere with our work. Stand over there." He indicated the far corner of the living room.

I closed the bedroom door and took up a position by the fireplace. Flat Cap followed Fedora into the bathroom. I watched, fascinated, as he placed both hands on top of the wash-hand basin and pressed down, using all his strength. An image of Gudrun, half-naked, washing her face in the basin invaded my mind.

Close your mouth, Kurt. Anyone would think—

With a rending crash, the basin parted from the wall. Water gushed from a fractured pipe.

"I'll turn off the water," I said.

"That would be helpful," he grunted, turning his attention to the toilet cistern.

I picked my way through the food and smashed crockery in the kitchen, and turned off the water stopcock under the sink. When I returned to the living room, the two men appeared from the bathroom, carrying the bath between them. They dumped it on the remains of the settee. The wash basin was placed in the bath, followed by the toilet bowl and cistern. Then they disappeared into the bedroom. Water was pouring out of the bathroom across the living room floor.

The hot tank, I thought.

A few minutes later, both men reappeared from the bedroom.

"Thank you for your cooperation," Fedora said.

I looked all around me at the devastation. The place was unrecognizable; four rooms full of rubbish, it no longer resembled my apartment. I picked up a book, *The 39 Steps,* by John Buchan, its pages swollen with water; I checked my father's gramophone records; all three had been broken. I don't live here any more, I thought. Nobody lives here. How could anyone live in this mess? The apartment had been dismantled. The place was awash with water, uninhabitable.

Somewhere deep inside me, I was laughing. Here I was, standing in the wreckage of my past life, and I didn't care. There was nothing here that I grieved over, nothing of my old life that I needed. Everything I needed was in the future, waiting for me in Elsmhorn. My heart soared.

The Black Orchestra

Fedora gripped my upper arm. "Outside," he said.

I dropped the book, grabbed my dark blue overcoat from behind the door, and left the apartment for the last time.

66

June 3, 1942

Flat Cap was waiting outside, holding the car door open like a chauffeur.

"In the car," Fedora said.

I rode in the back seat of the car with Flat Cap. Fedora drove. We took a familiar route south, through the city to the suburb of Lichtenrade, and drew up outside the same house as before. It was a pleasant street, thronged with playing children.

They led me to the room at the back. The three chairs stood in a huddle under the lone light bulb, just as they had when I first saw them. The bricked-up fireplace, the dado rail, the barred window, the bare floorboards, all were as before. The stain on the floorboards had been renewed with fresh blood.

"Coffee?" Fedora asked.

"Tea, if you have it," I responded without thinking. It had been several hours since my last meal and my stomach was grumbling.

Tea from the Gestapo?

The men left and I was alone. The view from the window was of a small suburban garden, beautifully maintained; a neat lawn in the centre, surrounded by colourful flowerbeds. I had visions of stocky men in black leather coats, weeding the flowerbeds and mowing the lawn. I could hear the children playing in the street at the front of the house.

Flat Cap entered and handed me tea in a cup, a biscuit in the saucer.

I took the tea from him. "Don't you ever remove your cap?"

He stared at me blankly, then turned on his heel and hurried from the room.

I ate the biscuit, but it failed to silence my rumbling stomach. I had barely tasted the tea when Fedora re-entered. He sat down on one of the chairs, his back to the door. "Please sit," he said.

I took the chair to his right, avoiding the one facing the door.

He blinked. "If you cooperate and answer my questions, there will be no need for unpleasantness," he said.

"Does Uncle Reinhard know I'm here?" I sipped the tea.

"No," he replied, "and I don't think we should disturb him, do you? The last I heard, the Reichsprotektor was in a coma, and not expected to survive the night."

My heart skipped a beat. I wondered if *I* was going to survive the night. "What do you want from me?"

"Tell me about the Black Orchestra."

"A university chess club, set up in 1909. It's defunct now." My stomach groaned comically. He ignored the sound.

"Who were the original members?" he leaned forward, his face uncomfortably close to mine. Clusters of tiny hairs protruded from his nostrils; I could smell onion on his breath and a faint whiff of Eau de Cologne. He held a bunch of keys in his right hand.

I shrugged. "My father was a member."

"Who else?"

"My mathematics professor from Trinity College, Professor Hirsch."

"The American? Who else?"

"I believe Fritz Todt was a member," I said.

"The Minister for Armaments?" he sat back in his chair.

"And Munitions. Yes."

"Who else?"

"Adolf Hitler."

The movement of his hand was so swift that I didn't see the blow coming. The back of his open left hand struck my face.

There was a dull pain in my head and the metallic taste of blood in my mouth. I checked my teeth with my tongue. They were all there.

My stomach groaned again, louder this time. He went to the door and knocked with his keys on the wood – three taps, then two – and the door opened. He spoke to Flat Cap. Flat Cap hurried into the next room and returned with the remains of a packet of biscuits.

"The sooner you answer my questions, the sooner you may go home and eat," Fedora said. "In the meantime, you're welcome to these biscuits. This is all the food we have in the house."

I took the packet from him. There were six biscuits in the packet. Two minutes later, I had eaten them all.

He said, "I interrupted you. You were telling me who the original members of the Black Orchestra were."

I shook my head. "I really don't know. It was a long time ago, and I've only heard vague stories."

"How many members were there?"

"No idea."

His eyes searched my face, his clenched fists resting on his thighs. "We know that Hans Oster is a member."

"*Generalmajor* Oster?" I said, feigning surprise.

"Can you confirm that he is a member?"

"Since I joined the Abwehr, the Generalmajor has barely spoken to me."

"But he has spoken to you."

"Once or twice, yes. He said that he knew my father at university."

"So it is possible that he was a member of this Black Orchestra."

"It's possible, but that was over thirty years ago."

"Can you confirm that he was a member at that time?"

"All I can say is that he was at the University of Munich at the same time as my father."

"Tell me about Boniface."

My heart jumped in my chest. "I'm sorry, I don't know anyone of that name."

His left fist struck my face with such force that I fell to the ground. The teacup flew across the room, spilling its contents; the saucer clattered after it. I felt a sharp pain in my right cheek.

He helped me to my feet and I returned to my chair.

"It's a British operation," he said. "I know you have knowledge of it."

"You've been misinformed. I can't help you."

He hit me a third time.

"I can't tell you what I don't know," I said, my mouth full of blood.

"You will do better to cooperate."

He stood up and went to the door. He knocked with his keys on the wood – three taps, then two – and the door opened. He left, and the door closed behind him.

67

June 3, 1942

An hour went by – the worst hour of my entire life. Outside, darkness fell; the sounds of the children at play faded and then died. My stomach began to complain again. I thought the questions about Boniface were probably a fishing exercise; but what if they persisted with this line of questioning? The truth was something I could never reveal. The cyanide capsule in the box in my trouser pocket was the only sure way I had of keeping the secret. Would I have the courage to use it if I had to?

When the door opened again, Flat Cap came in holding Liesel by the upper arm. She was dressed in a yellow summer dress, a cotton apron, and flat shoes. She had no make-up on, there was flour on her hands and clothes, and her hair looked like a bird's nest.

"You have three minutes." He pushed her forward and left.

"Liesel? Why are you here?"

"You tell me. I was in my apartment cooking bread, when two men burst in. They brought me here."

"Obviously, there's been a misunderstanding. I'll see what I can do to sort it out."

"You're bleeding." She pulled a handkerchief from her sleeve and held it to my lips. When I took the cloth from my face it was stained with blood.

"I was hoping to run into you again, Kurt," she said.

"I understand. And I apologise for… for… you know."

"No apology necessary," she said. "I was drunk. I think, if anything, it was I that took advantage of the situation, not you."

She reached across and held my free hand. "What's this all about? Can I help in any way?"

"I don't know. I don't think so."

There were voices at the door, a key turning in the lock. Fedora came into the room and escorted Liesel out. Then both men came back. They tied my hands to the back of the chair. I protested, but neither man responded.

Once I was securely tied, Fedora left the room, leaving the door open. Flat Cap took Fedora's chair. "Pretty girl, your girlfriend," he said.

"She's not my girlfriend."

"So she means nothing to you. Now tell me what happened to von Kemp."

"Who?"

He placed his right hand on the third chair, and tapped on the wood with his keys: two taps. In the next room, Liesel screamed.

"This has nothing to do with Liesel," I shouted. "Let her go."

"Answer my question," Flat Cap said. "Where is von Kemp?"

"He's been arrested and interned by the Irish police."

"I don't believe that." He tapped on the chair again: two taps. Liesel screamed again, a terrible sound. I felt sweat pouring down my face.

"It's true. I have the paperwork in my office."

He blinked again. "You would be well advised not to play games with me."

"I'm not playing games. I'm telling you the truth."

He watched me with cold eyes. "Tell me what became of Hans Wenther."

"Who?"

"The Irish police pulled his body from the river."

"I know nothing about that."

Flat Cap tapped with his keys on the chair: three quick taps. From the other room, came Liesel's scream, louder than before, followed by an indignant howl.

"I believe you may have murdered these two men," he said. "Perhaps with the professor's help."

I shook my head.

He changed tack. "We know that a coup is being planned."

The Drobols.

"It's true. There is a plot to overthrow the government. I intercepted a signal. I know only that Uncle Reinhard was involved."

"Reinhard Heydrich." His tone was flat, suggesting total disbelief. "How did you decipher this signal?"

Panic. There was the flaw in my argument. To gain a little thinking time I said, "What signal?"

"The signal you gave to our informers could not be deciphered, and yet you claimed to have discovered the plot by reading a signal. How did you decipher the first signal?"

"It was in a standard Lorenz code. The later signal was in some other code."

"Why would they switch codes?" His eyes narrowed.

I shrugged. "I assume they knew or suspected someone was listening. The Lorenz codes are not really secure."

He considered my words for a few moments. He seemed satisfied with my explanation.

"How do you know that the Reichsprotektor is involved?"

"The codename for the plot is Gruenwald, and the codename for the leader of the plot is Merlin."

"And you took this to mean that Heydrich was involved."

"Merlin is his codename, and Gruenwald—"

"I know what Gruenwald is. That proves nothing. What makes you so sure that Heydrich is involved?"

"He told me he was. He attempted to recruit me to the conspiracy."

"And you refused?"

"Of course," I was indignant.

"When was this?"

My head was splitting. I was finding it hard to concentrate. I said, "I'm not sure. It was late last year. November or December, I think."

"Where did you meet him?"

"In his house, in Blankenfelde."

"That's impossible. He was in Prague from October." He lifted the keys.

"You're right, he was in Prague but he made a special trip to meet me."

"And told you what about the plot?"

"Yes. He told me that many prominent society people were involved."

"Names."

I shook my head. He used his right foot to send me and my chair crashing to the floor. I lay there panting, spitting blood. One of my front teeth was loose. I poked it with my tongue. It fell into my cheek, and I spat it out.

Flat Cap got up and strolled over. He stood looking down at me. I felt like one of the animals in the zoo.

"Get up."

"I can't."

He hauled the chair up and resumed his own seat, his hand with the keys on the third chair, as before. "I think you have something more to tell me."

I said nothing. I was too busy swallowing blood and checking the rest of my teeth.

"The names," he said.

"Reinhard gave me no names."

Flat Cap raised his arm in readiness to give me another blow. I continued quickly, "He did say that the military would respond to his call when the time came."

"What branch of the military?"

I shook my head.

Two taps of the keys, followed by a scream and a profanity from Liesel.

"You bastard!" I said. "Leave Liesel out of this. I've told you, it has nothing to do with her."

"Go on."

"That's all there is. Heinrich Himmler was to be the new Führer. Uncle Reinhard was to be his deputy."

A short explosive sound escaped his lips. It might have been a laugh, but it was not accompanied by a smile. "Tell me about your trip to Frankfurt."

"Frankfurt?" My mind was in turmoil; I couldn't think.

"You took a flight to Frankfurt from Tempelhof."

"That was a personal matter."

"Not the correct answer." He tapped his keys on the chair: three taps. Liesel screamed again, long and loud, a broken sound.

"All right," I shouted. "I was looking for further proof. Frankfurt is a hotbed of revolutionaries."

"The KPD?"

"Yes, the Communists."

He got up and left the room, leaving me with my throbbing headache.

68

June 3, 1942

Fedora came in, pushing Liesel in front of him. Her hair was scattered about her head. Loose strands hung down over her face. Her eyes were red and swollen from crying, as was her nose.

Fedora left, closing the door behind him, and Liesel began to untie my hands.

"What did they do to you?" I said.

"It was nothing." She sniffed, putting a hand to her throat. "It could have been much worse."

"I'm sorry you got mixed up in this, Liesel. If I knew – if I even suspected – that this would happen to you because of me, I would never have—"

She put her fingers to my lips. "Don't say it. It wasn't your fault. You can't take the blame for what those thugs did."

The room was warm. We sat in silence for a while. My eyelids began to droop. I dozed.

Liesel broke the silence. "Kleister was murdered."

Suddenly, I was wide awake. "How do you know that?"

"I obtained a copy of the Medical Examiner's report. As a journalist I can get hold of most things. As a member of the ministry there's nothing I can't see. The cause of death was extreme trauma to the chest, caused by crushing. The condition of his brain matter – described by the Medical Examiner as black with occult blood – proved that the bullet entered his head at least thirty minutes after death."

So Drobol the cripple couldn't have been the killer; he didn't have the strength to kill by crushing. Drobol the giant in the post room sprang to mind as the most likely candidate, but I reckoned any one of the three Obersts could have done it.

She examined my wounds. "It's not serious," she said, "but that missing tooth has spoiled your looks a bit."

"I thought you didn't fancy me."

"I don't, but that's not to say that you're not good looking."

"What are you saying?"

"I'm saying there's probably a girl out there somewhere – even for an ugly stick insect like you."

"Thanks a lot."

The men came back into the room.

"Come with me, Fräulein," Fedora said.

"Where are you taking me? I have the protection of Herr Goebbels—"

Fedora responded, "We're taking you home. You can finish your baking."

"What about Kurt?" She got to her feet.

"Herr Müller will be released in good time. He has a few more questions to answer."

"I'm sorry, Kurt. I'll make some telephone calls, get some help. Is there anyone I can contact on your behalf?"

"I'll be fine, Liesel."

"Come! Come now!" Fedora grabbed Liesel by the upper arm and propelled her through the door.

The door closed and I was alone again.

69

June 4, 1942

I heard the car engine start. The car drove away.

I knocked on the door and shouted, "I need to use the bathroom!" No response. I pounded on the door until the key turned in the lock and Flat Cap entered, carrying a handgun.

"I need to go to the bathroom."

Flat Cap said, "Top of the stairs."

The bathroom was as I remembered it. A bath, a toilet, a washhand basin. Over the basin, a water heater powered by gas. I used the toilet and washed my hands and face. Locating the gas feed, I tore the pipe from the wall. Immediately, the pilot light went out, and gas began to escape into the room with a soft hissing sound. I switched off the electric light and left the room, closing the door firmly behind me.

The next time the electric light switch is used...

Flat Cap was waiting for me at the bottom of the stairs.

"How long do you intend to keep me here?"

He shrugged. "As long as it takes." He pushed me into the room, closed and locked the door.

Ten minutes went by. Then I heard heavy footsteps ascending the stairs. Two seconds of silence. Three. And then a massive explosion. The door to the room flew open.

Flat Cap lay at the bottom of the stairs, his clothes in tatters, his hair and eyebrows singed. His neck was broken. At the top of the stairs, the bathroom was ablaze.

I grabbed my overcoat and left the house. Flames were pouring from the bathroom window. All along the road, lights came on, people ran out, shouting and waving their arms.

Someone grabbed my arm and shouted, "What happened?"

"Call the fire brigade." Shaking free, I moved away.

I took a taxi to the city centre. Alighting near the Potsdamer Bahnhof, I walked the short distance to the office in Tirpitzufer. There was no one following me.

Siegfried was at his desk, his radio blaring. I signed in, took the stairs two at a time, collected the briefcase from my filing cabinet, and checked my train timetable.

As I signed out, Siegfried said, "You've lost a tooth, sir."

"Brownshirts, a bit over exuberant."

"Well, goodnight, sir."

"Goodbye, Siegfried."

I found a small hotel close to the Lichtenberg railway station. The clerk at the desk wore a filthy vest. "It's ten marks per hour," he said, noting my lack of luggage. "Twenty-five for the whole night."

I signed in using the name Ernst Huber.

"Passport," the clerk said, holding out his hand.

"I don't have it." I handed him fifty Marks.

He took the money and handed me a key. "Room fifteen, first floor."

I spent some time in the bathroom attending to my wounds before calling Alex to set up a meeting for the following day. An all-night stall near the hotel provided a meal of pea and sausage soup. I was ravenous. There was plenty of soup and I ate my fill.

#

I awoke early, washed and cleaned myself up as best I could.

It was June 4.

Police sirens wailed all over the city.

I waited until 11 am, then I pulled on my dark blue overcoat, donned my blue Luftschutz civil defence section leader's cap, and left the hotel.

Passing by a Telefunken radio shop, I heard an announcement: A police officer had been murdered in the south of the city. The police were on the lookout for the killer. His name: Kurt Müller, age: about thirty, dressed in civilian clothes. The description that followed was quite accurate, I thought, although it would have suited many men my age. The problem was that there weren't many men of my age in the city dressed in civilian clothes.

A whistle sounded. Two ORPO men advanced toward me. I turned and ran, rounding a corner, only to find more police moving toward me from that direction. I ducked down a laneway behind a row of shops. A cul-de-sac. Fedora appeared behind me. He shouted and he and several ORPO men entered the laneway. I stepped through an open door and hurried through the busy kitchen of a restaurant, attracting some glances from startled cooks, then through the dining room, weaving my way between the tables. Back on the street at the front of the restaurant, I plunged on through the throng. A police car came toward me slowly, its blue light flashing. I managed to slip past by adjusting my speed and positioning myself close behind a woman with a two children for a few metres, appearing as a young married man with a family.

At the entrance to the massive KaDeWe department store, I joined the surge of shoppers entering the store. KaDeWe was packed with customers enjoying a mid-summer sale.

First I bought a suitcase and placed the briefcase inside. Then I bought a tweed Tyrolean coat in a bright green and red check with a hat to match. I put on the new coat and hat. My blue overcoat and Luftschutz hat I placed with the briefcase in the suitcase.

Alex was waiting for me at the in-store café on the top floor.

He laughed when he saw my disguise. "You look like an Austrian tourist." Then, "What happened to you? You've lost a tooth."

I shook my head. "I've been spotted. No time to talk." I handed him an envelope. "Here's the money I owe you."

"You heard that Johann's been arrested?" he said, quickly.

"What for?"

"He was caught holding hands with a boy in public." The pain on Alex's face was plain to see.

"So you're living alone again?"

"No." His face brightened. "I have a new friend. His name's Sebastian."

Alex stood up and we embraced.

"Have a good life," he said, patting my arm.
"You too. Try to stay out of trouble."

I left the store and headed north. Picking up speed, I entered a maze of small streets. After ten minutes, changing direction frequently, I ducked into a doorway. There was no sign of pursuit.

A taxi took me to Lichtenberg Bahnhof, where I bought a third class ticket and boarded a train bound for Hamburg. Belching black smoke, it rumbled and puffed its way out of the station like an old, weary dragon. It was 2 pm. The third class carriages were crowded, and it took a few minutes to find an empty seat. I lowered myself into the space between a large woman and an elderly man.

The engine built up speed slowly, slowly, only to lose it all again at each station that we came to. Shuddering to a halt in a plume of steam, it disgorged passengers and took on new ones. The delights of the passing countryside were lost on me. I was anxious to get as far from Berlin as possible.

Weariness overcame me. My eyelids closed and I dozed, waking at every stop.

The train began to fill up. At 2:50 pm I surrendered my seat to an elderly man and joined the crowd standing in the corridor.

At 3:14 the train stopped at Wittenberge, and news of Heydrich's death was carried on board. He had died from his wounds at 2:55. Quick as a bolt of lightning, it passed in whispers up and down the length of the train.

Fifteen minutes after leaving Wittenberge, we drew into Ludwigslust, the last stop before Hamburg. I watched from the door as passengers alighted and new ones joined the train. The guard blew his whistle and waved his green flag. It was only then that I saw the giant, Drobol Junior, dressed in a full-length green coat, boarding one of the first class carriages close to the engine.

70

June 4, 1942

I knew that I couldn't keep hiding from the evil that was Drobol, just as Germany couldn't keep hiding from the evil that he represented. I pulled my suitcase from the overhead rack and set off toward the front of the train.

At the end of the carriage I was confronted by a railway official in a peaked cap. He inspected my ticket, and handed it back. I moved toward the door, but he held out an arm, barring my way.

"The front portion of the train is First Class. There's no access beyond this point for Third Class passengers."

"How long to Hamburg?" I said.

He looked at his watch. "Forty-three minutes."

"I'll wait here."

I didn't have long to wait. Within two minutes Drobol appeared at the glass panel of the door. He pushed through.

"Herr Müller, why don't you come through and talk with me?"

"I'm sorry, sir," said the official. "This gentleman has a Third Class ticket. He's not allowed into the First Class carriages."

Drobol turned to the railway official. He towered over the man. "I'm sure you can make an exception on this occasion," he growled.

"Of course," the official stepped aside.

Carrying the suitcase, I followed Drobol into the First Class carriage. He led me to an empty compartment and opened the door. When I was inside, he closed the door and drew the blind.

"Please sit," he said.

I sat by the window, the suitcase on the seat beside me. He sat opposite.

"Where are you going?" he said.

"Hamburg."

"You've heard the news? Your uncle is dead."

I detected the trace of a smirk. "I heard."

He regarded me for a few moments. "You're a strange man. You've told us nothing but lies since we first met. And yet I find it hard to believe that you would place such a poor value on your own life. Do you value your life, Müller?"

"As much as the next man."

"If I ask you a few simple questions, will you tell me the truth?"

"Ask your questions."

"I want you to understand that your life depends on whether or not I believe the answers."

"Nothing unusual there," I said.

"That story you told my father and me – the plot to overthrow the Reich – that was a lie, was it not?"

"Yes. A complete fabrication."

"Why invent such a fantastic story?"

"It served its purpose. I needed a distraction. I thought your father might use his gun."

"Tell me why you were interfering with the records."

"I had removed a signal. I needed to cover it up."

"And what was in the signal that you removed?"

"Information about the assassination of my uncle."

"You had advance knowledge that Reinhard Heydrich was to be assassinated and you did nothing to alert anyone? You didn't warn him?"

"No."

"But he was your uncle." His surprise was obvious. To suppress information about an attack on a senior Party official was high treason, but that the target was a member of my own family, made it incomprehensible.

"Heydrich had my father killed."

There was a short pause while he placed this new information on his moral scales. The expression of distaste on his face told me that my explanation had come up short. "What really happened to Wenther in Dublin?"

"I killed him."

Drobol's mouth fell open, exposing his black, rotting teeth. "You killed him?"

"Yes. I tipped him into the flooded river. He drowned."

"And von Kemp?"

"I smashed his skull."

"You're saying you killed them both?" His tone was scornful. "I don't believe you."

His eyes narrowed. I felt like a fly trapped by a child. I had seconds left to live – seconds before he started pulling my limbs from my body. "What of this IRA plan?"

"What IRA plan?"

"Their plan to bomb the British."

That threw me into confusion. Where had his information come from?

"I don't have those details," I said, and immediately regretted my answer. I could have won myself a few more seconds of life.

To gain time, I said, "Tell me about Kleister."

He smiled. "He was just unfortunate. He picked up a signal from Leipzig. He would have exposed us to the Generalmajor."

"So you killed him."

"What's in the suitcase?"

"A quarter of a million pounds sterling."

Suddenly, his enormous right hand was on my chest, his fingers at my throat. I was pinned against the seat. I grabbed his arm and tried to dislodge it. Running through my unarmed combat training in my mind, I searched for a move that would fit this situation. Nothing came to mind. Then I pulled the picklocks from my pocket and, using them like a dagger, stabbed him twice in the lower ribs. They were no more than pinpricks, but it was enough to make him yelp and let go. I launched myself at him, and we fell to the floor between the seats.

I grabbed his neck with both hands and squeezed. The muscles on either side of his neck were as hard wood; his neck thick as a tree trunk. Reaching up, he placed the fingers of his left hand around my neck and squeezed. The pain was severe. Desperately, I dug my thumbs into his windpipe. His mouth opened; his face reddened; his grip weakened. He released my neck. Then his right fist caught me square on the nose, driving me backwards and breaking my grip. A wave of dizziness and nausea hit me. He got up slowly. I struggled to my feet, and we stood face to face, my back to the window, his to the door.

He pulled the picklock from his ribs and threw it onto the seat.

"Your training has not been a complete waste." His face broke into a grimace that was probably a grin.

His hand shot forward, reaching for my windpipe again. I moved my upper body to my left, and, as his arm brushed across my shoulder, I drove a fist into his stomach as hard as I could.

He took a step backward, and produced a long thin knife from his pocket. "You'll have to do better than that." He lunged forward with the knife. This time I dropped to one knee while simultaneously moving my body to the right. Again he overshot, and I buried both fists in his crotch. My unarmed combat instructor would have been proud of me.

He gasped, dropped the knife, and staggered backward. Surprised at my success I stood up. I scanned the floor for the knife, but it was nowhere in sight. He rushed forward again, throwing himself at me. Restrained by the seats on either side and by the window behind, there was nowhere I could go to avoid him. I ducked, and then straightened again quickly, accidentally catching his chin with the top of my head. He reeled back. I reached up to rub my head. And he attacked again. This time I was unprepared. He wrapped his arms around me in a bear hug and began to squeeze.

My left arm was by my side, caught in the bear's grip; my right arm was free, above my head. His face was centimetres from mine, our noses almost touching. I could smell his foul breath.

"Let me show you how Kleister died," he said, grinning.

His grip tightened, and black spots danced before my eyes. I began to gasp for breath. I knew I had only seconds to act before I lost consciousness. With my free hand I reached down into my trouser pocket, and found the cardboard box. Opening it with my fingers, I extracted the capsule inside.

"Sieg Heil," I gasped.

"What?" he said, moving his head back a few centimetres.

"Heil Hitler," I croaked.

He opened his mouth, threw back his head, and laughed.

71

June 4, 1942

The cyanide worked in seconds. He crumpled to the floor, foaming at the mouth. His eyes glazed over. He was dead. It took all my strength to force his body under one of the seats. Taking several deep breaths, I brushed the dust from my clothes, straightened my hat, picked up my suitcase and left the compartment.

The train juddered to a halt; the doors opened, and the passengers flooded out onto the platform. I stepped down and joined the throng. Two men in full length black leather coats stood to one side, scanning the crowd. At the gate, the passengers passed through, one by one, handing their tickets to the ticket collector. An ORPO man in uniform stood to one side, just beyond the barrier, watching the passengers, checking the papers of every adult male that passed through. Behind the ORPO man stood a soldier in Waffen-SS uniform, armed with a Schmeisser machine pistol. The impatient crowd jostled and surged, moving forward slowly.

To my right, there was an open door marked *Hausmeister*. I ducked inside. The room was empty. Two blue overalls, with matching peaked caps, hung on wall hooks. I removed my Tyrolean coat and hat and slipped on an overall. I removed the briefcase from the suitcase before discarding it. In a cupboard I found a galvanised bucket on wheels and a dirty mop. I filled the bucket with water from a tap. Then I made my hair look as untidy as I could, smeared my face with some grease and jammed a peaked cap on top.

I threw a pile of old cleaning rags into a sack, followed by my briefcase, some more rags and several bottles of antiseptic cleaning fluids. I was at the door before I thought to do something about my shoes, which were strong, black and highly polished. Dipping the mop into the bucket, I splashed dirty water on them before scuffing them against some rusty pipes.

Standing at the open door, I saw the two leathercoats jump aboard the train. Taking another deep breath, I swung the sack over my shoulder, stepped back onto the platform, and headed for the barrier, using the mop to propel the bucket forward.

The bucket rattled loudly on the platform.

"Gangway," I shouted. "Coming through." My accent was crude, like a Polish worker's.

The passengers turned their heads, but no one moved aside to let me through. The ORPO man stepped forward and shouted to the crowd. "Make way. Make way there for the hausmeister."

The crowd parted, and I rolled my noisy bucket as far as the barrier. The ORPO man put a hand on my chest to stop me. In my ribcage my heart was beating like a rabbit in a snare. I thought he must be able to feel it.

"Papers."

I shook my head, wiping my nose on my sleeve.

"Where are your papers, *Untermensch*?"

"I have to clean the toilets." I groaned, pushing against his hand and pointing over his shoulder. This hausmeister was a pfennig short of a schilling, his devotion to his duties beyond all reason.

He grimaced in disgust, then snatched his hand away and wiped it on his hip.

"What's in there?" he said, pointing to the sack on my shoulder. "Open it."

Rolling my eyes, I lowered the sack to the ground at his feet. He opened it and peered inside.

"Have to clean the toilets again," I whined, squinting at him, my head to one side like Alex's Quasimodo. "It's time for their clean."

He stood aside. I closed the neck of the sack, lifted it wearily onto my back and passed through the barrier.

"You should carry your papers with you at all times," he called after me, as if to a child.

I rolled my mop and bucket to the right as if I knew where I was going. It was a lucky guess. I found the men's toilets and rolled my mop and bucket inside. There were two more soldiers in Waffen-SS uniform at the urinals, their Schmeissers propped up against the wall.

The Black Orchestra

"I have to clean the toilets," I said in my thick Polish whine.

The two men turned their heads and looked at me. I crossed my arms high on my chest, and frowned.

A third man – a civilian – entered. I stood in his path. "I have to clean the toilets. Come back in five minutes." He sneered and pushed past me to the urinals.

The two soldiers washed their hands and left together, laughing and talking, followed a short time later by the third man. As soon as he had gone, I closed and locked the outer door. I used some toilet paper to clean my shoes, took off the overalls and cap, wiped the grease from my face and tidied my hair. I retrieved the briefcase from the sack. Then I stepped out of the toilet and walked across the concourse toward the station's main entrance.

"Halt." A loud voice from behind me.

I stopped and turned. The ORPO man from the barrier came forward, his hand outstretched. The two Waffen-SS men from the toilet had joined their comrade. All three turned their heads to watch. It was only then that I realised this was part of a Special Operations Unit, one of Heydrich's murderous Einsatzgruppen.

"Your papers," the ORPO man said.

I gave him my Irish passport. He inspected it carefully.

"Your name?"

"Kevin O'Reilly," I replied, with a slightly distorted accent.

"Date of birth?"

"The thirtieth of June, nineteen thirteen."

"You are an Irish national?"

"As you can see. I am diplomatic corps." I looked at my watch. "And I have a flight to catch."

"What's in the briefcase?"

"Diplomatic papers."

"You travelled from Berlin to Hamburg?"

"Yes."

"And you are catching a flight from Hamburg? Are there no flight from Berlin?"

"I'm meeting my wife and daughter at Hamburg. We will travel together."

"You have no luggage, I see."

"My wife has the bags."

"Your flight ticket." He held out his hand.

"My wife has the tickets."

He stared into my eyes. I tried not to blink.

"Open the briefcase."

At that moment there was a loud cry from the platform. The two leathercoats had emerged from the train and were running down the platform toward the passengers. They had found Drobol's body.

The ORPO man handed me my papers.

"Have a good journey," he said, in English.

"Thank you," I replied in English, and he hurried back to the barrier, gesticulating and shouting at the crowd.

"Make way. Give way there. Police coming through"

I walked slowly out of the station without looking back.

72

June 4, 1942

I took a taxi to the airport. Gudrun and Anna were waiting for me in the departures area.

"I was worried," Gudrun said, kissing my cheek. "Have you been in a fight?" She touched my face. Then, "You've lost a tooth!"

Anna was excited to see me. "Uncle Kurt," she said. "Look what mama bought me." She held up a rag doll.

"Remember what I told you, Anna," Gudrun said. "You must call him Papa just for today."

Anna was crestfallen. "I forgot."

I squatted down to her level. She handed me the rag doll. "She's beautiful. What's her name?"

"Anna. Her name's Anna."

"But that's your name. Shouldn't you call her something else?"

"I could call her Heidi," she said. "That's my friend's name."

"Right, Heidi it is. And what's my name?"

"Papa."

We had an hour to wait for the flight. We made our way into the departures lounge. Gudrun and Anna went shopping again.

I rang Generalmajor Oster's private number. The Generalmajor answered on the second ring.

I said, "Drobol junior killed Tristan Kleister."

"You're sure?"

"He confessed before I killed him. He asked me about the planned IRA bombing campaign invented by the professor. I have no idea where he obtained that information."

The Generalmajor was silent for a moment. "One more mystery to solve. Thank you, Kurt and Bon Voyage."

Next, I rang Thomas Kleister and told him who had killed his son and why.

"I suppose there's no prospect of justice for the death of my son," he said.

"I've taken care of it," I replied.

Tania came on the telephone and she thanked me. She was crying.

After that call, I sat down and closed my eyes for a few minutes. When I opened them again, I found a leaflet lying on the seat beside me. The first few lines read as follows:

THE - WHITE - ROSE

Nothing is so unworthy of a civilized nation as to allow itself to be governed without any opposition by an irresponsible clique that has yielded to basest instincts. It is certainly the case today that every honest German is ashamed of his government. Who amongst us has any conception of the enormous shame that we and our children will feel when eventually the veil drops from our eyes and the most horrible of crimes – crimes that eclipse all atrocities throughout history – are exposed to the full light of day?

I read through the whole leaflet and my heart took flight. This was the true voice of Germany, the voice of reason. There were brave Germans willing to stand against the tyranny of the Reich.

I knew then for certain that I would return. I couldn't abandon my country in its hour of greatest need.

The flight to Lisbon was called. Gudrun and Anna returned.

Anna said, "Look what Mama bought me," and then, "Papa, why are you crying?"

I lifted her into my arms and we walked across the tarmac to the aeroplane.

Another man in black leather stood at the bottom of the steps. When it was our turn, Gudrun smiled and handed him our papers.

"Frau von Schönholtz."

Gudrun nodded.

"Papa," Anna said.

"And Frederick von Schönholtz, diplomat."

I nodded.

"And this must be the lovely Fräulein Anna von Schönholtz."

"Papa," said Anna. "Papa, Papa, Papa."

He smiled at Anna.

I looked at the little girl, and suddenly I was looking at Uncle Reinhard's face. I could see his forehead, his small eyes, his long thin nose, the turn of his mouth; the likeness was uncanny. I panicked. For a couple of seconds I thought that the Gestapo man must recognise that face, and our cover would be broken.

"You look upset, Herr von Schönholtz," the Gestapo man said.

"It's nothing. I'm sad at leaving the Fatherland."

"Have a pleasant flight." He gave me a knowing smile, handing Gudrun back the papers.

THE END